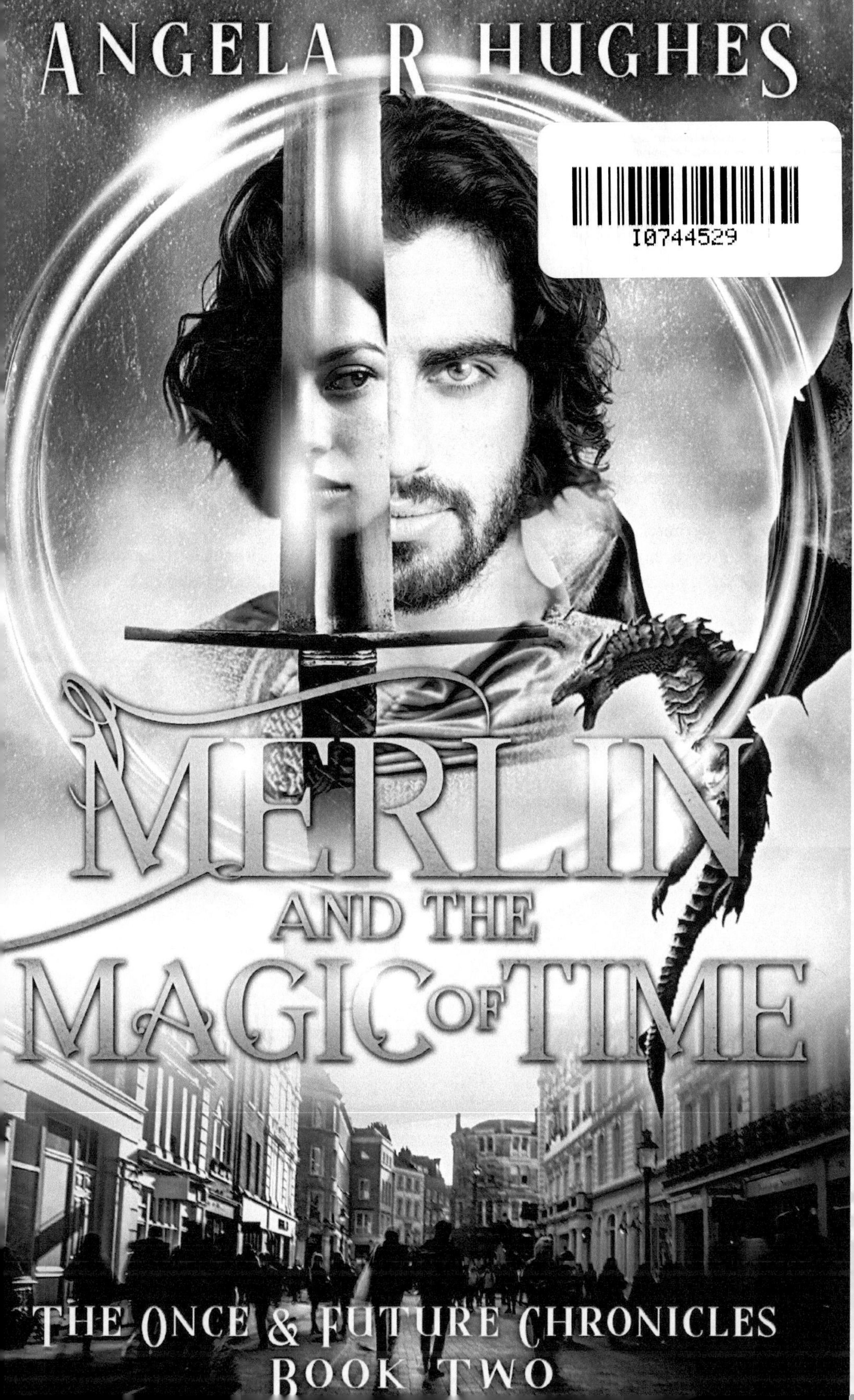

ANGELA R HUGHES
MERLIN
AND THE
MAGIC OF TIME
THE ONCE & FUTURE CHRONICLES
BOOK TWO

SQUARE TREE PUBLISHING
www.SquareTreePublishing.com
IMAGINE NOW PUBLISHING
www.angelarhughes.com

Illustrations by Sindi Fatkoja, Instagram @sindifatkoja
Cover design by 100Covers, www.100covers.com

ISBN 978-1-957293-23-3 (Paperback - Square Tree Publishing)
ISBN 978-1-7362443-1-9 (Hardback - Imagine Now Publishing)
Library of Congress Control Number: 2023900442

Angela Hughes expands her epic reimagining of the *Arthurian legend* by taking readers into the modern age! The magic, wonder, and rich lore continue in *Merlin and the Magic of Time,* book two in *The Once and Future Chronicles.* Themes of identity, hope, finding courage within, and believing in one's destiny lie at the heart of this story, inspiring each of us to embrace the gifts and calling in our own lives. Each of these universal themes Hughes weaves through her main characters' arcs as they scour present day Wales to find the sepulcher where Arthur—the Once and Future King—lies buried, asleep, awaiting his long-foretold awakening. Your heart will race alongside these characters as the moment of promise unfolds, breathing new life into this timeless legend.

Hughes is a storyteller who has recaptured the essence of the Arthurian legend and given it a chance to touch our hearts in new and imaginative ways. Magic stirs on every page, inviting you into this fantastical adventure steeped in Welsh history. Hughes's command of language and knowledge of this ancient legend is a treat for fans of *Merlin and Arthur's* incredible story and will enthrall those not as familiar with it. As you read, prepare to enter a realm of enchantment, encountering legends from folklore, ballads, and poems, where time holds mystery and awaits the ones chosen to unlock it.

-Stephanie Cotta, *Fantasy writer and award-winning author of The Conjurer's Curse*

Dedicated to my children, Ezra and Brielle…
Thank you for seeing the magic and the wonder. You gave me a reason to
tell stories. May you swing on the branches of these stories and someday be
inspired to tell your own. You made me brave and remind me that every gift I
hold is yours to go further than I ever could.

And to MERLIN, Druid of the Old Age of Albion…
Your magic wasn't in enchantment. No…Your magic was in service of
something higher and in the dream of something new. You inspired me to
renew your story and tell it with redemption. Your story will no longer be
without hope but filled with the faith of something more.

CONTENTS

Land of Britain
Scotland
Hadrian's Wall
Carlisle
Cumbria
Bassenthwaite
Isle of Man
Aberystwyth
England
Wales
Cardiff
London
N
W
E
S

PROLOGUE

THE SHADE

"Merlin! You must pay attention," the balding old man scolded. "Come here! Now is not the time for chasing every *flitting fly* that passes by. Put down your stick and come sit. I turn my back for *one* second and you are off." His thin bearded lips formed a chiding grin. "You're getting too old for this, and I am far too old to chase you down."

The spry adolescent twisted around. His floppy raven hair flung out of his bright eyes, exposing his fresh ruddy cheeks. "I am sorry, Ollamh. You had fallen asleep while talking of the ashes of acorns. I did not want to disturb you."

"Bah!" he puffed with irritation. "*Asleep?* I was not asleep."

"Then I suppose you snore when you breathe."

The old Ollamh shot a stern gaze underneath his wooly weathered brows, but then softened. "Bwah!" He swished his hand with a shrug of surrender, admitting that he had fallen asleep. He patted Merlin on the shoulder and settled down next to him on the ground.

"I am sorry, Ollamh Dai. You know I take my lessons very seriously." Merlin did take his Ollamh teachings to heart, but it was hard to pay attention when Ollamh's monotone lessons even lulled *him* to sleep.

"Yes, you are a quick learning filidh; however, very distracted. I know your mother is proud of your progress. Now, settle yourself. Today is an important lesson." Dai hesitated, then said, "Today I will teach you of the shade."

"Shade!" Merlin's bright eyes widened. "I thought shades were of the darker ways."

"Ah, yes, it is a dangerous power. It is a power of illusion that is forbidden by the order because it can be used to deceive and manipulate. Great evil has been done with shades, and most that desire this power have a corrupted heart buried within their chests. Those who are patient will develop the power of the shade with wisdom.

But the corrupted ones murder and use blood to gain power in haste." The ollamh leaned forward and winked. "Are you trustworthy, young Merlin? Can you understand a power without being twisted by it?"

Merlin scratched the back of his head, giving his ollamh a puzzled look. "I think so. But isn't the very nature of this power to twist someone's perception?"

"Sometimes the power twists many minds at once."

"Why would I need such a power?" Merlin asked, wrinkling his nose in thoughtful concern.

"It is not always wrong to conceal oneself or to be cunning enough to give yourself the advantage over an enemy. It only becomes dangerous when one's motives are nefarious."

Merlin sat back onto his heels. The gentle wind tousled his curls as he gazed at the surrounding trees in thought. The verdant leaves jostled together on the branches, creating a tranquil ambience. The breeze whistled through the leaves, and they sang with a hush. Pockets of light burst between them, warming his face.

"Merlin," the old man said in a soothing voice. "Your destiny is unlike others. Your magic is something that the order has never known. We believe it is important that you know some of the old magic that other young filidh are prohibited from learning. Direct your heart to the Great God. Only He is a trustworthy guide. He created these abilities for us to use to do good in His world, though many corrupt them. Tell me, is it wrong to know the times and seasons and prophecy them?"

Merlin shook his head. "No, Ollamh."

"Ah, but it does become erroneous when prophecy is used to gain an upper hand instead of to guide. We are given these things to hold with our hands open in humility. But many will use them to gain *power*, which is contrary to druidic laws." Dai's face grew somber. "I know you have seen with your own eyes how many have rebelled, and allowed themselves to become corrupted by their lust for power."

"So, why teach us such giftings at all?"

Ollamh Dai lifted his brows. "Because there is always an opportunity to do good and to wield power in service of others instead of one's own self. Now, enough of these questions. Are you ready?"

Merlin twisted his mouth, then nodded.

"Good. Let us begin." Dai placed his hand on Merlin's shoulders and drew a line with two fingers to his eyes. "Now, focus your eyes on mine. Engage the awen and think of yourself as a mirror or reflective pond."

Merlin sighed, scrunching his face as he focused his eyes. Then, he imagined a crystal pool of water.

"Instead of seeing your own reflection in the pond, you will see mine. See my wrinkled, aged eyes and the thin, white hair on my head. Focus on the edges of my mouth and the lines on my lips."

Merlin's vision locked onto Dai's reflection. His high cheekbones and graying skin.

"You are my mirror. See my clothes—my hands." Quietly, the ollamh watched as Merlin activated his sense of magic. His young yellow eyes flashed, dancing over Dai's form. The golden light of the boy's eyes was unique and unusual. Gradually, a faint but colorful shadow appeared, lining Merlin's frame.

"Now, stop." Dai waved his hands and snapped his fingers to break the trance.

Merlin gasped. He shook his head and blinked his eyes.

"You must understand. The ancients have used the power of the shade and animal shifting for generations. It has been our way. But times are changing, and things are not as they used to be. The Great God will use you, young Emrys, to transform this world. The old ways must become new."

Merlin furrowed his brow at Dai's words, not ready to understand the fullness of it all. *What did Dai mean, 'Old ways must become new'?* He'd heard his mother say it too. She reminded him every day that he was different. His magic set him apart.

Some felt threatened by his magic. He was unsure if he wanted this great destiny that his mother and Dai always talked about. He wanted to be a warrior and grow up to fight on the Roman battlements. All the young boys trained at his age to become warriors. All of them prepared to one day ride to the Great Wall and protect the borders of Prydain from the wild blue Picti of the north. Merlin wanted to be among them, but because of his unique powers, he was here with the druids instead.

At least Merlin's grandfather taught him how to fight. He would race to smack blades with him before the sun set.

Merlin smirked. *If only these lessons would end. Then I could really get to it.*

Dai clapped his hands, jolting Merlin out of his musing. "Merlin. Pay attention. This is important."

"Sorry, Ollamh," Merlin said, snapping to attention.

"We must go slow in teaching you how to shade. You are already connecting to it quickly, and I want you to have proper understanding as we go."

Merlin nodded and jumped to his feet.

"Ready to be done, are we?"

"Oh…" Merlin tried to conceal his disappointment and swiftly returned to his seat.

Dai threw his head back and laughed, placing his hand on Merlin's head. "We are done, young one. So distracted and ready to run. Go pick up your stick and hit something. I will see you tomorrow."

Merlin smiled and leapt to his feet, eagerly dashing off toward the trees.

"Merlin!"

"Yes, Ollamh!" He halted and faced Dai. A solemn luster hung in the ollamh's gaze.

"Do not practice the shade on your own. Not yet. There is much to understand. *Yes?*"

"Yes, Ollamh. I will not," Merlin said, waving his hand over his head in goodbye. He ran home. He couldn't wait to cross swords with his grandfather, and his silhouetted frame disappeared into the light between the trees.

PART ONE

THE BOOKSHOP

Merlin walked through the doors of the bookshop, his heart thumping and his fingers tingling. The shop was disorienting, its shelves loaded with strange looking, multi-colored books. The bell at the door kept ringing as people entered behind him. Each chime made Merlin anxiously peer over his shoulder. So many foreign sights and sounds invaded his senses.

Distracted, he bumped a table display and several books toppled to the floor. A man standing behind a counter shot him a jarring glare.

Merlin's face reddened and his adrenaline rushed through his bloodstream. He gave an uncomfortable nod to the man behind the counter, then plucked the books from the floor and replaced them on the table. Many strange eyes bore into him like he was a man possessed.

Taking a breath, he narrowed his eyes, bringing his senses back into focus. He knew what he needed to do. The memory of Elanor and the old man was still fresh. Forcing aside his uneasiness, he squeezed around a line of shelves, frantically looking for the familiar corner where he had seen her.

I must be there before she arrives, and I must… His mind tried to think as he rounded another shelf. *I must use a shade.* For he now understood that *he* was the old man in the memory.

He had not used a shade in many years. As a practice of the old religion, it was not a magic he reached for. His ollamh Dai had only just begun to teach him when he died. Merlin was so young in those days, just a boy. Others of the order tried to teach him, but those were the days when everything changed. The monks of Eire had come, heralding news of the Triple God and of Esu, fracturing the construct of the druids forever.

After all that had happened, it seemed unimportant to learn to shade. But the words of Dai remained within him—that his destiny would require certain skills. So, he pressed into the power and eventually attained the art of mirroring, transforming his appearance. Though rarely did he use it. The shade always felt to him a forbidden magic.

But this moment required it. He needed to transform if all was to happen as he had seen it in the memory.

Flustered, Merlin's heart pounded in his ears. *If only I could calm myself down and discover that blasted spot where I will find her.*

He turned a corner and entered an open space with green, overstuffed chairs. An old man sat, resting his chin on his palm as he read in the center chair.

Merlin gasped. *It's him! The very same old man from the memory—with his small blue eyes, green wool cardigan, and sideways curling lips.*

Feeling strangely caught, Merlin ventured over to a line of bookshelves on the other side.

The old man glanced up from his book and gave a sardonic laugh. "Young man, what *are* you wearing? Heh." He smirked condescendingly. "Really, the toggery you lads wear."

Merlin halted and turned to the old man, patting his leather vest. "Toggery?"

The old man grunted down at his book. "You appear lost in more ways than just your attire."

"I… I…" Foreign words tumbled out of Merlin's mouth, and he worried they might not come out right.

"Well? Spit it out." The old man rolled his eyes and lifted his expectant brows. "Can a gent get any peace? I just left home because my wife wouldn't stop chittering on, and now"—he flailed his hand at Merlin—"I am interrupted by a lad dressed as though it's time to retake the highlands."

Retake the highlands?

Merlin stared blankly at the old man, who made it abundantly clear Merlin was disturbing his peace. "S-sorry. I am searching for"—he thought of what he could say —"books about King Arthur. Do you know where I could find them?"

The man thumped his book closed. "You are looking for the Knights of the Round Table, eh?" He snickered. "Thought you would get dressed up all fancy to set the proper mood? Oh, I cannot wait to tell my Suzy. She will have quite the laugh."

Shaking his head, he continued to chortle with disdain as he rose from his seat. He shuffled feebly toward Merlin and pointed his finger to the left of Merlin. "Over there," he said, sniffing, and with a wave ushered Merlin forward. "Follow me."

Merlin trailed behind the frail man's sauntering steps. The triumph that he would find the right place excited his spirit. He stared at the old man, taking in his every detail.

"Here." They rounded the corner, and the man motioned for Merlin to follow in-between two aisles of bookshelves, dead-ending into a wall with a realistic picture of a fierce dragon painted on it. The old man ran his fingers across a line of books, pursing his lips as he read the titles. "Ah-hah!" He grinned with a twinkle in his eye and pulled a red book from the shelf. An illustration of a warrior wielding a sword and the words *King Arthur and His Knights* donned the cover. The old man slapped it into Merlin's chest. "Now you can be one of Arthur's men. Your delusions can come true." The man shook his head as he scooted away.

"Wait," Merlin said, hoping to see the details of the man's face one more time.

The man turned with a loud sigh.

Merlin memorized the man's eyes, his white hair combed over to the side, and the silver stubble on his chin.

"I do not have all day. Is there something else you want, or can I go back to my reading?" The old man hesitated and scrunched his wrinkled face, waiting for a reply, then swished his hand. "Pish-posh—probably just go back to my Suzy. It is better than this lunacy." He waited one last second, but Merlin offered no final words.

Before the agitated man even turned the corner, Merlin stood in the full shade of the old man, holding a book about Arthur in his hands.

The bell at the front door jingled.

Could it be her?

He waited near the end of the row, glancing through the slit between the bookshelves, hoping he could spy her silken dark hair turning the corner.

Footsteps.

Merlin quickly opened the book in his hands and pretended to scan its pages. His heart beat faster. He held his breath, and then… a young man traipsed past.

Oh, Great God… Merlin sighed in relief. He wanted to see Elanor so badly, yet his restless nerves prickled at the thought of her appearing.

What if she never even comes? He gulped, trying to calm himself. *I must stay focused or else I will lose the shade.*

His thoughts tumbled with all he needed to say if she did appear. His palms moistened as he squeezed the pages of the book in his fingers.

The bell jingled again. He whipped his head into the book, as if the fiction would cover him. Sweat formed on his lip with anticipation. He paced his breath, setting his fingertips in the middle of his forehead. The thumping of approaching footsteps distracted him—he must concentrate. His eyes focused on the pages, and he read the heading, *Chapter 5: Arthur Meets Guinevere*, when a figure entered the aisle.

He could smell her, the scent that solely belonged to her, like lavender and honey. He dared not lift his eyes but remained settled on the page, fearing what he might see when he lifted his head. She came closer, and his heart leapt into his throat.

He couldn't resist. He raised his eyes over the lip of the book, and there she was. The brightness of her gaze pulled his heartstrings. He wanted to drop the book and embrace her, but he couldn't. Everything inside him ached to touch her—to feel her. But this was not *his* Elanor—not yet. If he was to get through this moment, he would have to contain his emotions and not slip out of the shade. He clenched his jaw and gently exhaled.

"Hello," Merlin said. His hands trembled, and he lowered them to his sides.

"Hi…" was Elanor's hesitant reply. Her blue eyes beckoned to him, and he wished to weave his hands through her hair.

The melody of her voice washed over him. But then the memory of her dying in his arms shot through his mind. Would he ever see his wife again? The one whom he had walked with and loved. This girl's innocence and light had not been touched by the pain of dark evil. No poison, shadows, or gwyllgi. Did he want that for her?

"King Arthur, huh?"

Her voice shook Merlin out of his thoughts. "King Arthur? Oh, uh… yes." He lifted the book, giving it a quick glance. He rubbed his lips together and gathered his words. "Is that the sort of book you are looking for? Maybe something with magic?"

Elanor nodded with a mild giggle. "I suppose, yes." She turned from him and scanned the bookshelves. "The thing is, I had a dream and I am doing a bit of research."

The dream—of course.

She had been dreaming of him, and he of her.

"Not that a book with magic should help me discover anything. Not even really sure I am looking in the right place." She shrugged. "Though books with a bit of magic are always the best kind."

Merlin could not feel her magic. It seemed far away. He forced himself to sound casual as he coaxed, "Do you have magic, I wonder?"

"What? Me have magic?" She laughed, rolling her eyes. "That is a very strange question."

He could tell his question had made her uncomfortable, but it was important. She must remember. The moment was coming soon when she would need to remember her magic. "Is it?" he said, watching her closely. He knew by the look in her eye she was reeling.

"When a strange man in a bookshop asks me if I have magic, I should think he's crazy and find a new section of books to browse." Skepticism flitted through her eyes as she pondered, drawing her finger across her tightened bottom lip. Conceding with a tsk, she said, "Okay, as a child, I used to believe I had magic." She paused, appearing unsettled by the memory.

Yes. This is what she needs to remember.

"My father told me it wasn't good to keep pretending I had magic. Only I didn't know I had been pretending. I remember…"

"What do you remember?" he pressed gently.

"Feeling sad," Elanor almost whispered. "I haven't thought about any of this for a long time. Maybe my father was right. I mean, it probably was just my imagination anyway."

"What was the magic you were supposed to have imagined?" He saw her spark, his wife emerging in the corner of her eye.

"I… I knew things. I thought I could look at someone and see them. *Really* see them. I could know their mind and feelings—sometimes even know who they would be. It was only my imagination, as my father had said." Her brows laced together. "I even think I imagined healing a bird once. It had flown into the window, unaware of the glass." She gnawed at her cheek. "Once revived, my father said it had probably just been knocked out. There was more, I think, but I don't remember."

"I think," Merlin said, daring to pull on what lay hidden in her, "that you still must have magic, or else why are you still talking to me? I am just a strange old man that you happened upon in this bookshop. But you felt something. You felt a pull, a sense, a feeling, and so you talked with me." He stopped, noticing her confounded, yet intrigued stare. In the memory, he remembered her learning to engage her magic. He sensed the connection building between them. She likely felt it too. "Listen, would you do this old mad man a favor? Would you look into my eyes and tell me what you see? Just like you did when you were a child."

Elanor stiffened. Her eyes darted around uneasily before centering on his. "I don't know why I am doing this…" She seemed resistant, but curiosity had gripped her. "No guarantees."

She stepped closer. Merlin's heart quickened. His temples pulsed as she reached for him. He hoped with all his soul that this was all leading him to her. The Elanor who knew him.

Elanor took an abrupt step back, shaking her head. "What am I doing? I'm sorry, I am not sure where all of this is leading, and this is getting a little strange. I almost convinced myself for a second that something was going to happen." She sighed, rubbing her forehead, and turned to leave.

No!

He could not let her go. "Elanor!"

She halted.

"Do not run away. Come back," he beckoned.

She steadily turned around; her mouth parted with awe. "How do you know my—"

"Try again," Merlin said, holding his hand out to her. "You will remember. It will come to you. The magic—it's there."

She let out a deep, hesitant sigh and stood before him once again. Grabbing hold of his hand, she lifted her eyes to meet his.

"Peer into my eyes and see beyond them. It's there. In the thoughts and memories within your heart and mind."

As Merlin locked eyes with her, he searched, desperate to find some semblance of the Elanor he knew. *His* Elanor.

Her eyes flared. *There it is.* Merlin's thoughts ran wild as he watched Elanor unlock the magic deep within her, the magic that made them uniquely tied.

Please, Merlin begged silently, *return to me. My soul. Come back.*

The image of the dove fleeing from his hands passed through his mind, and his heart wrenched. The pain of grief churned in his gut.

"Do I know you?" she asked, shaking Merlin to his core.

"I—" He halted. "I cannot say." He forced himself to speak with a slight smile. "What did you see?"

Empathy brimmed in her eyes. "You are grieved."

Her words stole his breath as she revealed his thoughts.

"You have lost someone you loved. Perhaps many, I think. You have seen many things in your life."

Tears welled in Merlin's eyes, but he forced himself to maintain his grasp on the shade. Hot emotions radiated on his face.

"But I feel the loss is almost over. Somehow things are changing for you now. You will not be alone much longer."

A long-suffering sigh exuded from his chest. *Does this mean I will find her? Please… please… I pray it will be true.* He could not stifle the tears. One rolled down his cheek. Within her eyes, he saw the fire of his beloved.

If only I could take her up in my arms!

He covered his eyes, wiping his tears free. "So, you see? You do have magic. Thank you for that. You cannot know what this has meant." Gathering himself, he remembered the blue book. "I have something I would like to give you. To say thank you for humoring an old man." He riffled through his satchel and revealed the little blue book.

"It is faery stories," he said, pointing at the cover. "It is very old, and you will not be able to read the writings. They are in an older language. But you will find beautiful pictures within it. This book is very special. It belonged to someone important to me."

Elanor's eyes widened. "I cannot take your book."

"Please," Merlin insisted, his heart groaning within him.

Elanor took the book from his hands, her fingers reaching to open the cover.

"Oh, no, no, no! Do not open it here. It is very old. Take it home and open it there. There you will be able to look at it better." He rested his hand on the book as a warning. "Not now."

She nodded, placing the blue book into her bag. "I do not know what to say. Thank you?"

His heart brimmed with empathy. "Your father should not have told you that you did not have magic."

Merlin watched as his words almost knocked her backwards. The wind of them shaking off the dross of all the things he knew she had forgotten. She placed her hand over her heart, her eyes glistening with tears.

Then, he added, "And, King Arthur was not a fiction." He handed her the other book he held. "You ought to be careful believing what they have written down in these books about him. They are mistaken."

Her quizzical eyes narrowed. "Mistaken?"

"Yes, mistaken," he said firmly, knowing all she would soon come to know about him and the whole world she belonged to.

She slid the book from his fingers. "Well, I am not reading the book to learn about Arthur."

"No?"

Elanor nodded. "I am reading it to learn about Merlin."

Merlin couldn't breathe. The mention of his name from her lips was almost more than he could bear. *Elanor…*

She hesitated a moment, then turned to go.

"It was nice to meet you," she said, waving over her shoulder.

Don't go! His heart screamed as his grip on the shade relented. All at once, he was himself again, watching Elanor's hair swing as she glided away.

Get a hold of yourself, he scolded, forcing his mind to sober. He leaned against the bookshelf, knocking several books down. He breathed heavily from the effort it took to maintain the shade.

Jingle, jingle. The bell on the door rang, and Merlin sucked in sharply.

She's leaving! Quick! Follow her!

2

ELANOR OF ANOTHER TIME

Merlin rounded the bookshelves and rushed toward the entrance. He stopped short before reaching the glass paned door. Through the window, he saw her. She lingered just outside, staring strangely at the book he had given her. Her brows were knit with bewilderment, but she soon plodded forward. Merlin hardly waited a second before flinging open the door.

The foreign world around him was a blur as his eyes remained fixed upon Elanor. He had to keep pace; a sea of people flooded the gray path on all sides. People bumped him, but he couldn't lose sight of her. He zeroed in on the two bags she carried, one on each shoulder, as she meandered through the crowds. The bright green designs of the one, the other, a solid blue, helped him single her out from the crowd as people bustled across his view.

Blasted. Why are there so many people? So many of them scurrying around like rats?

"Reminds me of Lindonium," he murmured with distaste.

He tried to keep a distance from her without allowing too much space. He did not want her discovering him or, worse, recognizing him from her dreams. He followed her a short way when she took a sharp turn down a side alley. He dashed over to the opening, carefully peering around the corner. The narrow, cobbled alley dead-ended into a wall of bricks. Then Elanor disappeared into another dark opening of an adjacent building.

He darted down the alley, running to the passage. Quickly, he spied around the ledge and saw her walking up a stairwell. He jumped back so he would not be seen while she stopped to unlock a door.

Click.

Peeking around the corner, he watched her open the door and walk inside. She shut the door behind her.

Merlin caught his breath, leaning his head against the cold stone building. What to do next? He was unsure. The sun was setting. All he knew was that he needed to stay close to her. In this strange future time, he had no other clues. He had come for

Elanor, but not this one. He grimaced and considered his options. Where else could he go? This seemed the only path to take.

I must stay near to this Elanor who does not know me, he reasoned, *if I hope to find the one that does.*

He climbed up the stairs to a dingy brown door with the number 1A in dirty gold letters. As he touched the silver knob, he wondered whether to open it. Should he knock? What would he say? Surely, he couldn't just nonchalantly greet her and march on in.

He considered for a long time but came to the firm decision—he must enter. Maybe he could use the shade once again. Though the power of the shade remained a tricky one. Its illusion cloaked him with the face of another, but what it truly did was affect the minds of those that gazed upon the enchantment. A shade could also deceive a mind to see nothing, but this was hard to pull off without first making eye contact. He would not want to alarm her. He was certain he could use his powers to put her to sleep if necessary, but how would this help him?

What am I doing? he thought, eyeing the door. He felt lost. *What kind of predicament is this? Do I just wait here until she emerges again, and hide from her continually? I have no way of knowing how to navigate this world.* He squeezed the space between his brows. Nervousness agitated his stomach.

I cannot wait out here all night. I must move forward down the only path that is present.

He fidgeted with the knob but discovered it was locked. He hovered his hand above the handle and whispered, "Agor." The door clicked lightly and creaked open. He leaned back against the wall, not wishing to be seen, and held his breath.

Hearing nothing, he stepped forward quietly and leaned inside. The chamber was vacant—Elanor, nowhere to be seen. He passed the threshold, scanning the room. It was not a big chamber, so he could easily see its entirety.

Where has she gone?

A melody reverberated from behind a closed door, coupled with the trickling of water pouring and splashing onto the floor. She was just on the other side. His eyes darted around the room for somewhere to conceal himself. There was a bed, a long fluffy bench—*Where? Where can I hide?*

The sound of running water ceased abruptly. Merlin's wide eyes settled on a floral dressing screen at the side of the room. Without thought, he stepped behind it, hoping its sheer cover would hide him. Panic overwhelmed his senses as he pressed his back against the wall and sank to the floor.

Still the soft, muffled humming echoed from behind the door. The timber of Elanor's voice brought Merlin calm, and he caught his breath. She opened the door, and now her humming resonated clearly. Through the tiny holes in the screen, he saw her. Her wet hair laid heavy on her back. She wore the very same strange clothing he remembered from when he first saw her. He could never forget. The odd knit red and gray cover.

She crossed the room to fill a kettle with water, and Merlin considered whether he hadn't made a terrible mistake. Setting the water to boil, Elanor placed her elbows down on the countertop, resting her chin in her delicate palms. Soon the kettle sang, and she popped open a peculiar green and red box. She retrieved a small square from the box and tossed it into a white handled cup that read, "Hot Mess." Then she poured the steaming water into her cup and smiled as she lifted it to her nose, inhaling in the swirling vapors.

Merlin's heart fluttered. It was curious to see Elanor in this world, living as she did before she came to Prydain. Though she smiled, loneliness shadowed her face. She seemed so far away from knowing who she truly was—resigned to the life she had been dealt—without a spark.

Cup in hand, Elanor walked over to her bedside and set her cup down on a small white table. Merlin froze, her body within inches of the screen, as she bent forward to fling her hair above her head and wrap it up tight.

"Right!" She beamed. "Now for the book." She grabbed the book she'd left sitting on the counter. "Oh, yes! I nearly forgot." She rummaged through a nearby bag and pulled out the blue book. She smiled, running her fingers across it. She gave a satisfied nod, and with both books in hand, returned to her bed. She fluffed her pillows and wrapped herself into a cozy bundle.

"Now then…" She took a sip from her cup, wincing at the hot steam before lifting the blue book closer, exploring its cover.

As Merlin marveled at her every movement, magic ignited within the pit of his stomach. The foreign, prickling sensation gave him no doubt—the dragon's magic of time kindled within him. It beckoned to him and guided his thoughts. The revelation it revealed flooded his mind. His mouth dropped open as, just as he had recalled the memory of the bookshop, a new memory formed.

He had been here, in this very room, and now he knew what he needed to do. He lifted his hand toward Elanor and whispered, "Sleep."

She had just opened the book when she started to fumble. She crumpled back into her pillows, and the blue book fell from her hands onto the floor.

Now that she was asleep, Merlin rose. Walking over, he grabbed the little book and set it onto the table beside her. He gently took her hand that had fallen over the bedside, caressed it, and laid it carefully onto her chest.

"M-Mer-lin," she stuttered out in her sleep. She was in the dream, and Merlin understood. The magic of time was upon him, and for the first time since he had met Elanor, he now knew it had been him all along. It hadn't been the dream, or the Great God that had torn her through time. No. Maybe that was why he'd felt so guilty when the event had almost killed her. Somehow, deep down, he knew *he'd* done it.

Whenever the dragon's magic came, it unlocked its purpose. One could not have known they had already been there, until the moment was upon them, and that moment had now come.

The white flames ignited in Merlin's palms; his golden eyes blazed. He almost didn't want to do it, knowing what it would do to her. In this unique moment, he could choose to leave Elanor here. If he didn't use the magic of time, she would never be abused by Osian's wicked disciples. If he held his hands back, she would never be the target of evil. He would never meet her, and never regret.

Merlin rolled his hands into fists as he considered. The flames rolled up his arms. Either the magic would send him back, or it would send her. What would be his choice? Though hadn't he already chosen? Could the history be re-built or erased?

"Do not fear time!" a voice, loud and strong, echoed inside his mind. Again, it thundered, heavy with rebuke. *"Do not fear time! Do not fear what has been, or what could be. I AM LORD OF IT ALL."*

The final words rang in his head like a gong, setting a fear within him to obey. Without hesitation, Merlin set his hands upon Elanor. White flames seared down his arms and out through his hands, consuming her.

Elanor's back arched, and she screamed as the flames rolled around her. The white fire howled like the wind. Her voice gradually slipped away, like an echo, quieting at each reply. The flames turned whiter, hotter, then… she was gone. There was nothing left but silence and the thrum of Merlin's stuttering breath.

He stared down at his hands, eyes wide. Then he fell to his knees, touching the bed where she had laid. Still warm. Merlin squeezed the sheets in his fists. He stumbled over, falling onto his side, and watched the steam still emanating from her cup. Her absence created a vacuum of fear within him. *What had he done?*

Hope slipped away from him as shock coursed through his bloodstream. In grief, he shouted, "Is this why I came here? Is this why you sent me? To send her away?" Incensed, he exhaled deep into his chest, tears streaming from his eyes. "WHERE IS MY WIFE?"

Merlin pressed his face into the bed, trying to believe that Elanor still existed somewhere and that he could have her again.

She used the magic of time, he reasoned. But as his anger flared, reminders of the arrow piercing her chest gripped him. He remembered the blood dripping from her mouth, and he felt a fool. *Could she really be alive?*

He rolled to the floor, onto his back. Hot tears dripped into his ears. "It was you," he accused, pointing at the ceiling. "Man in Blue. You told me not to fear time. What has time given me?" He placed his hands onto his forehead. He thought of his Gwendolyn and her little cherub hands. She had said he would bring her mama home. Marcus, too, had offered him hope.

After a long while, Merlin sat up and glanced around the room. He wiped his face dry with his palms. His heart refused to settle; he could not keep his tears within his eyes, and soon his cheeks shimmered again. Tears blurred his vision, but his eyes captured something in the corner of the room. Tilting his head, his red eyes squinted into focus, and he stood to get a closer look.

A painting stared back at him. A blurry depiction of his own face. He remembered Elanor saying she had painted him. The gold in his eyes had layers of yellow, and the lines of his face were precisely drawn. He extended his fingers, touching it. The paint was still wet, and when he withdrew his hand, it left white and amber on his fingertips.

"Am I to believe," Merlin said, staring up at the ceiling, "that I have sent her back, only to be run through with an arrow?"

His anguish threatened to rise again when something deep within his heart stirred. A warmth filled him with tranquility, bringing calm to his storm. The awen ignited within him. He saw two stars in the sky, and Arthur sitting upon his black horse—his finger pointing up toward the stars.

Seeing the vision, his mind recalled the prophecy. "The two stars awaken the sleeping king. Gwenddydd, the young Pendragon, would do it. Could she be dead, and all still come to pass? And Arthur... a thousand years..."

Hope tapped at the door of Merlin's soul, beckoning for space in his heart. He wanted to believe.

He glanced at the empty bed. "Come back to me, my love, or else... how will I find you?"

He wandered back over to the bedside and crumbled to the floor, leaning his torso over the low mattress. He closed his eyes, feeling heavy. The day had been upside down from the start. Elanor was there before him, but he could not touch her. This was all too much for his mind to hold onto, and he drifted off into sleep.

CRACK!

The loud noise snapped Merlin out of his sleep. At once, he jumped to his feet. Something had changed. He rubbed his eyes and took in the hazy form in front of him.

Am I dreaming?

Maybe he had not sent Elanor back to the past like he had thought.

There, laying on the other side of the bed, was a woman. The dross of sleep still hung heavy on him, and clear thought evaded him.

"Elanor?" he murmured. Her hair was tousled and her face dirty. Blood covered her mouth and neck, soaking the front of her dress—still torn from the arrow. She lay ashen and still.

What kind of evil trick is this? This has to be a nightmare.

Merlin's heart dropped into his feet. She appeared dead. He quickly stumbled over to touch her, kneeling beside her. "E-Elanor," he whispered. He placed his hand underneath her neck and touched her cheeks, hoping to rouse her. "Elanor?"

She had come. She lay right in front of him, but held no life—her skin, cold to the touch. What was he to think? Nothing had prepared him for this. He raked his fingers through his hair as that familiar, sickening pain rose within him..

Is there something I am meant to do? You must do it NOW! He commanded himself.

He reached out his hands, willing his healing magic to surge, but before he even touched her Elanor shot up, heaving as if she had been trapped underwater.

Startled, Merlin fell back onto the floor.

She writhed, struggling to return air into her chest. She wrenched at her throat, her eyes wild and strained. Coughing and sputtering, she at last inhaled a full breath. Awareness settled on her face; her cheeks reddened with color. Her frantic hands grasped at her chest and back—where the arrow had pierced her.

Nothing. There was nothing. No wound.

"*Merlin!*" Elanor screamed, her lips trembling with emotion. "Oh my God… Merlin!" She leaned forward, lifting onto her knees, still struggling to catch her breath. She sobbed a moment, her hands covering her mouth.

Merlin couldn't move from the floor. He was frozen, overloaded with the intense shock of finding her.

Speak… Call out for her, he told himself. But he couldn't make his lips or his hands move.

DEATH TO LIFE

Elanor rose, her legs shaky as she gasped for air. She rested an unsteady hand on her chest. Her fingers trembled. She peered around her flat; the small countertop and kitchen before her. She glanced to her left, at the painting of Merlin. "Merlin?" she called gingerly, tears misting in her eyes. "Please… Gwendolen." Her mind raced with panic.

I left her? Will I ever see my little Gwendolen again?

She remembered staring into Merlin's eyes as suffocating pain radiated through her chest, and life left her body. It had all happened just as she dreamt. The horror had been inescapable, but then, like a piercing heat—she felt it. The magic the dragon had given her. The memory connecting her to a time and place. Merlin would find her here; she knew he would. He had the magic too. But as she stood, alone in her flat, she doubted. In one quick instant, she feared she had been sent back to her future time, away from all she loved, without hope of return.

Reaching out with faith, she whispered again, "Merlin?"

She looked down at her hands, still dirty, and a single tear dropped from her cheek into her palm.

"I am here…" a quiet voice said behind her.

Elanor gasped, and her hand shot up to cover her lips. She turned around, and there was Merlin, standing not far from her. Tears flooded from his golden eyes. He dashed over to her, enfolding her into his arms, and they both collapsed to the floor. She wept into the folds of his tunic, clinging to the fabric. The revelation that he had found her came pouring out in grateful sobs. Merlin enveloped her into his strong arms; his chest quavered against her ear.

Before she could even calm her breath, Merlin dipped his head and kissed her. Elanor's lips responded, moving instinctively against his as though neither time nor death had separated them. Euphoria flowed through her like a song, and she sank into his chest with the urge to press closer and let the moment stretch on forever.

"I found you," Merlin whispered with relief. "I found you." He cradled Elanor's cheeks with his palms and stared longingly into her glassy eyes. He lowered his hand, searching her chest where the arrow had pierced her. His fingers gently touched it. Only peach skin was revealed on the other side. "How can this be?"

Elanor clutched his hand to her chest. "I don't know."

"I do not care how it is that I have you back in my arms. All I know is I have you once again." He lifted her face until their noses touched. Closing his eyes, his brows curved tenderly, and he released a longsuffering breath.

Her heart aching with longing, Elanor nudged closer to Merlin's eager lips, and he lunged in with a passionate kiss. His warmth intermingled with her own. His reassuring embrace tightened, and Elanor flung her arms around his neck. His hands searched through the tendrils of her hair. Death had tried to tear them apart. The fear she would never have him again abated with each touch.

Merlin sank his head into the crook of her neck. "I missed you," he whispered. "I thought I might never find my way back to you." He pulled back to look into her eyes. "I will never let you go again, my dove. I cannot breathe without you." He closed his eyes and dropped his forehead against hers. "My hope waned as I searched for an entire season. I even searched for the dragon."

Elanor gaped at him. "An entire season?"

"Yes. You were lost to us in the depths of Samhain, then through Imbolc I searched. Beltaine was upon us when I discovered the memory."

Her confused brows laced together. "What memory?" she asked, gripping his wrists tightly. Only moments had passed since she lay dying amidst Osian's trap.

"I remembered you—in the bookshop. That's when the fires of time ignited."

Elanor released him, her mind racing to remember. Her eyes grew wide. "The bookshop?"

Merlin nodded and walked to the small bedside table. He grabbed the blue book and came back, setting it into her hands.

She opened its pages, mouth wide, as the meaning of it unlocked. "You were there?" She quickly searched her memory. "But I do not remember you."

"I used the ancient shade magic. You have seen it before, when the witch Aberva tried to disguise herself at the festival of Beltaine."

Elanor nodded in awe. Chills ran down her spine as she remembered the witch's attempt on her life.

"I used a shade and covered myself with the mask of an old man so that you would not recognize my face."

Elanor's jaw dropped even further.

"The Elanor I met there did not know me, but she had dreamt of me. I did as I recalled in the memory, and I delivered the book to her. And I followed her," Merlin said awkwardly, shifting his shoulders. "I did not know how else to find you. I followed her to this place. And while I waited, hidden behind the screen over there"—he pointed—"the magic of time came. Elanor, it was I who placed a deep sleep over you and sent you through time."

He lifted his palms and stared at them. "This magic of time is mysterious. I realize that when the dragon gave us this gift, we traveled all the places we would go in a heartbeat. It seems these memories… moments in time, are places we have already been. They must come to us at set times. It is not something we control or have governance of."

Elanor sat dumbstruck. The bookshop—the memories. All of it aligning in her mind. "All this time, I thought this book had somehow sent me to Prydain." She faced him, bewildered. "I thought magic like the shade was of the old religion; fallen magic." Her brows scrunched. "I did not know you used that kind of magic."

Merlin nodded. "Not all of the old ways are fallen; just fallen men. Though most times, I do not meddle with it." He lifted his chin and sighed. "I had an ollamh once, who taught me that some of the old magic could be used if a heart is properly surrendered." He paused, "Still, it is not wise to use the magic. My years have taught me that wisdom. Scarcely have I ever reached for such powers."

Elanor nodded, searching her thoughts. "How will we get home to Gwendolyn?"

"That I do not know." He placed his arms around her waist. "Though as I sat here—hoping that I would see you again—I had an awen."

Elanor leaned into him. "Tell me."

"I saw Arthur pointing at the two stars in the heavens. I remembered the prophecy, and how the king's curse could be broken after a thousand years." Merlin's eyes seemed distant, as if lost in thought. Elanor could almost see the stars appearing in his eyes as he shifted into a bard. A magical feeling emanated from his unshifting gaze.

"I think Arthur is here," he said at last. "We must find him."

Elanor gaped at him. "Of course."

"Our purpose in this time must be for this one thing. We will have no hope of returning without him."

"How will we find him?"

Merlin shook his head. "The prophecy said he would be awakened." He pressed his lips together in thought. "Which gives me rise to believe he is still sleeping within the Hill of the Kings."

"Would that place even still exist? Merlin, we are more than a thousand years in the future. Landscapes, places—they have all changed. There is no Hill of the Kings anymore." Elanor rubbed her forehead, thinking. "It may yet exist if it has not been unearthed or built over. Somewhere grown over with earth."

"He is meant to be found. A curse has kept him at rest, which makes me believe that the hill he sleeps in could also be enchanted—protected in some way. He is waiting for us," Merlin said with confidence.

The thought of meeting Arthur, of finding and waking him, made Elanor's heart pound. She had dreamed of seeing his face— wondered what he looked like. Would she connect to something she had lost? He was her father…

With an abrupt gasp, Elanor said, "My father!"

"Arthur?"

"No, my father. David. He's a map maker." She snapped her fingers, focusing her thoughts. "A cartographer. He teaches geography and cartography at the university. He may know how to help us find the Hill of the Kings. Maybe." Elanor bit her lip. The idea of reaching out to her father, who she had not seen for many years, put her on edge. She had missed him so much, but with him came Helen—her mother. The whole Evans family. The thought of them intimidated her.

"If I could see a map, then I might know the location."

Elanor nodded, her mind racing with how this might all work.

Merlin rubbed his red-rimmed eyes. "I need to rest."

His words broke Elanor out of her strained thoughts. Her own weariness washed over her. She noticed the exhaustion that lined her husband's face and nodded. "Yes, we both do." She brightened as she glanced toward the bathroom. "A shower!" She grinned widely. "Oh, my Great God!"

Suddenly energized, she hopped to her feet. "How I have missed the shower. Warm water. Shampoo. Merlin, this, this is…the best!" She scrambled over to the door and opened it. It was still damp and smelled of fresh soap. She beamed while taking it all in. "There is not much I miss about being away from this world, but this…wait till you give it a try."

Merlin smiled, enjoying her enthusiasm.

"I'm going first. You can go after." She hastily unlaced the back of her dress. "Oh, and my robe!" she squealed, grabbing up a red fluffy garment. She turned and smiled at Merlin, then shut the door.

Her demeanor lifted Merlin with a happy curiosity as the flow of running water kicked on. The same echoing humming he'd heard earlier leaked through the door. He leaned back on the bed with a mirthful grin.

But then, the door creaked back open and Elanor peeked her head out. Steam rolled out in plumes around her bare shoulders, enticing Merlin to see more. He jolted up, allured by the gleam in her eyes. Sweet herbal smells emanated from behind her.

"Would you like to join me?" She extended her hand, curling her finger. Her pink lips called to him, as did the rest of her.

In an instant, he was on his feet, shaking off his vest. He yanked his tunic over his head, tossed it to the ground, and raced toward the sound of the splashing water. He couldn't pull his boots off fast enough and stumbled through the door. He almost tripped over her discarded red robe. Excited, he snapped his eyes up, discovering her delicate shoulder blades. She dangled her hand under the falling water. The silver spout distracted Merlin's hungry eyes. He lifted his hand under the water. The bracing heat astounded him, and his mouth parted with awe.

"Does it come out hot? How?" His lips curved into a delighted smile.

"It's the magic of the modern age." Elanor stepped into the tub and dunked her head under the stream, pulling the curtain. "Come on?" She laughed.

Merlin threw off the rest of his clothes and jumped into the tub. The warm, flowing water rushed down his skin. A welcome sensation to ease the mounted tension.

"This is a miracle?" He grabbed one of the odd, green bottles from a shelf.

Elanor snatched the bottle from his hand, wagged her finger, and set it down. Water streamed over her eyes and hair, drawing Merlin's gaze down her ivory frame. He peered back at her radiant blue eyes. All the evidence of the trauma—washed away. Caressing her shoulders, he pulled her to his lips.

Merlin had searched for her—longed for her—and now she was back within his grasp. Whatever they needed to do to find Arthur in this strange world was possible, now that he had her.

Buzz… buzz. Buzz… buzz.

Elanor sat up, blinking sleep from her eyes. Disoriented, she forced herself to remember what that *blasted* noise was.

"What is that?" Merlin asked, rubbing his eyes open. The bright sun shone through the uncovered flat windows.

Buzz… buzz. Buzz… buzz.

Merlin pointed. "It's coming from over there."

"Oh!" Elanor jumped up, scampering into the kitchen, and grabbed an object lighting up on the counter. "It's… it's my mobile," she said with a chuckle. "I had forgotten all about these things."

"Mobile?"

"Yes." Elanor beamed. "Here, I'll show you." She enjoyed the puzzled grimace on Merlin's face as she yanked the charging wire from her mobile then hopped back over to his side. "I nearly forgot," she said, tapping on it. She moved her fingers across the device, and Merlin stared in confusion as lights flashed and pictures changed.

"Oh… I remember. It was my birthday, or at least it would have been yesterday, but that was so many years ago."

Merlin's eyes were wide. "Is this *'mobile'* magic? How extraordinary."

"Hah! No. Not at all," she said, giggling. "It is science." She twisted her mouth, considering. "Though, I suppose it is a type of natural magic, but people of this day would not consider it so."

"I remember seeing such machinery in the memory you showed me when I first met you."

"There is hardly a person that doesn't have one of these in their hand, all day, every day. It is information. Connection. All the maps ever needed are in the palm of my hand, right here. My father, however, would *still* be the expert on how the landscapes may have changed. You see," she said, smiling and drawing the strange contraption closer, "it buzzes when I get a message. I have a few here—people wishing me a happy birthday." She faltered, glancing down at her mobile. Her face dropped, forlorn.

"What is it?"

"My father… he sent me a birthday message." She tapped to open the message.

Merlin glanced at the screen.

David Evans—Have an amazing birthday, Sweetie. Please come see me soon.

Merlin reached for her hand. "He wants to see you."

Elanor grinned, astonished. "You can read this?"

"Yes. Strangely, I have been able to understand and speak to everyone I have encountered."

"Curious. Well, at least that will make things easier. Do you think it is the dragon's magic?"

He shrugged. "I can think of no other explanation. When I first arrived, I was baffled that I comprehended the written language on the busy street corners, and the loud words spoken as people passed outside the bookshop."

"How horrifying it must have been, arriving in such an active square."

"Your memories prepared me some, but truly, I would have been lost if I had not discovered the shop behind me."

"My entrance into Prydain was so confusing, fortunately I had you and Cilaen to guide me through. I cannot imagine coming into a place the way you did. And you braved it so well. You truly are a wonder, Merlin. I am sure most others would not have fared as well as you did. Elanor smiled. "Now, we need to get you into some modern clothes. You cannot go around wearing this," she said, kicking away his tunic that lay on the floor.

"I was definitely getting some strange stares yesterday. I even got yelled at by one odd looking fellow. I suppose I was the odd looking one."

"Yes, definitely, you were the odd one. Nobody wears clothes like these unless they are going to Glastonbury for Festival or some sort of Medieval themed party." Elanor smirked, looking him over. "The problem is, I do not have anything that would fit you. We will need to remedy that if we are to go anywhere. I'll have to go to the shops, and after that, we can make a plan."

"Ah. And we will need to start with your father."

Troubled, Elanor lowered her eyes.

Merlin lifted her chin. "Wouldn't you like to see your father?"

"Of course, it's just…" She sighed, peering at the door, and imagining the long winding road to her family's home. "I have not had to face *her* for a very long time."

"Could he not meet us?"

She shook her head. "It wouldn't work that way. Besides, the Evans' home is not *that* long of a drive from here. I know well enough that Helen won't likely prevent me from coming, but she *would* prevent my father from coming to see me. It is the right choice to go to them."

"Evans?"

"It is the family's surname. It is like the title Pendragon. In this time, everyone has a surname. My full name is Elanor June Evans. My family are the Evans—David, Helen, Jack, and Nancy Evans."

"You have the names June and Evans?" Merlin smiled. "You never told me you had these names."

"In truth, I never felt very connected to them. Especially because I was hardly accepted as a member of the Evans family. Once I was in Prydain, it didn't seem necessary to keep up the charade that those other names belonged to me. I liked being known simply as Elanor. But then, I was given more names. Names like Gwenddydd, and…"

"Pendragon."

"I am not really sure I have earned that title either," Elanor said, touching the torc on her neck.

Merlin skirted his fingers down her cheek. "You are Pendragon."

Elanor looked away uneasily. "We have a lot to do," she said, changing the subject, "and in this world, you cannot do anything without a little bit of tea or coffee." She strolled into the kitchen and grabbed a container from the cupboard. Opening it, she inhaled the aroma with pleasure. Her mouth curled into a slow grin.

Speaking to the container of coffee in her hands, she said, "I have been without you for far too long."

THE PLAN

Elanor came swinging back through the door with several white bags hanging from her arms. "I hope these will all fit," she said, dropping the bags like bricks onto the floor, placing her hands onto her hips with an exasperated sigh. "I hope I measured correctly before I left and found the right sizes. It was so strange going to shops like I never left." She shook her head with a quirky grin, then turned to rifle through the bags. "The busyness and chaos is so stifling."

Merlin sat at the counter with a wry smile, his curls damp, a towel wrapping his waist, and a mug in his hands. "I don't know how you drink this," he said with a grimace. He stared into the cup, and his nose wrinkled before slurping down another sip. His lips puckered at the bitter taste.

"And yet, you keep drinking it. That's how it gets you. It grows on you, and all of a sudden, you can't live without it."

"Hm?" Merlin stared into the mug, lifting a smug brow at the coffee before setting it down. He gripped his towel to keep it from falling and meandered over to look at the bounty Elanor brought in with her.

"I think I got everything you will need."

"What are these?" He picked up a plastic pack of pants.

"Well…" She giggled. "Those go underneath everything." She snatched the pack from his hands and tore it open, lifting up a pair to show him. "I got you some jeans, trousers, shirts, and a jumper. Here." She pulled an orange box out of a bag. "Try on these shoes."

Merlin opened the lid and lifted out white runners with blue stripes on the sides. "These are strange."

"Heh, yes, they are strange. But they are very comfortable. Here." She grabbed up several pieces of clothing and shoved them into his arms. "Put these on, then try on the shoes." She folded her arms with an amused smirk. "Let me know if you need any help."

Merlin scooted away, scrutinizing all the strange wears. "Toggery," he mumbled as he picked up the gray jeans, scratching the material.

"It's so nice to be on the other side of all the awkwardness. I remember when Samara first struggled to put me in a dress. I had no idea what was going on." Elanor leaned back against the counter, picked up Merlin's cold coffee, and stole a sip. "How did you enjoy your second shower?"

"It is *truly wonderful* to have warm water to bathe whenever you want it… and the toilet," Merlin remarked, tossing his towel over the changing screen next to him. "Aack! How is this done?"

Merlin squirmed and grunted, trying to figure out how each of the garments went on. Elanor sputtered in laughter as she watched Merlin's particular struggle with the button fly on his jeans.

With a frustrated glare, Merlin held up a white garment.

"Oh… uh, that goes underneath," Elanor explained with a light-hearted grin, roaming her eyes across his fine physique. His muscular torso against the jeans was a new delight. "The jumper goes over the top."

"Is this the jumper?" he asked, whipping out a black garment, staring at it with disdain.

"Ha-ha-ha!" She doubled over, wrapping her arms around her belly to hold it all in. She snickered as she composed herself, sighing and wiping a happy tear from her eye. "Who thought getting dressed could be so entertaining."

"Amusing for you?" Merlin growled, then asked again, "Is this the jumper?"

"Yes, yes," Elanor replied, going back through the shopping bags. "I also bought some sausage rolls. You'll like them. It will help you gulp down the rest of your coffee."

With a huff, Merlin shot his hands out, presenting himself fully dressed in his new gray jeans and black jumper, with the hem of the white t-shirt hanging loose. The runners were awkwardly tied but appeared to fit.

Taken aback, Elanor gazed at him with a wide smile. His long, damp curls rested beside his face. He looked every inch the modern man. It was strange to see Merlin dressed so casually. He appeared less mysterious—a sight she was unaccustomed to. He always carried himself with an air of austerity, but that had been suddenly diminished by the clothing. Now, he looked like a normal young man, apart from his golden eyes.

"Perfect," Elanor chimed as she approached him. She pushed one of his curls behind his ear. "Strange to see you appearing so modernized. Now people won't gawk at you. They will have no idea that the very legend of their stories stands in their midst. Hmm?" She beamed happily, kissing him. "Seems I have done a good enough job finding clothes that fit. How do the shoes feel?"

"Odd," he said with a shrug, rolling his hands over the sleeves of his new jumper. "But I think they are good."

"I still cannot believe we are here."

"I still cannot believe I have you back in my arms," he said, throwing his hands around her waist, and squeezing Elanor tightly. "Every time I look at you, I am grateful, and I hope I am not only dreaming. As the sun rose, I woke with the urgency to find you. The insistence has been my companion for many long days. But then, I found you nestled beside me."

"Well, at least here—in this time—we do not have to fear hooded demons in the forest or dark shadows."

Elanor noticed Merlin's uncertain gaze. His dark brows tautened with warning. "I hope that is true. I fear because our aim is to awaken the king—if we can find him—that this may be a different sort of world than the one you knew."

"Truly?" Her forehead creased with worry.

"We assumed too much before, that only the druids of the new way had seen the signs of the two stars and divined the prophecy. We were wrong to underestimate the awareness of the dark ones. Though this world may appear different from our own world, it would be foolish to assume they would not be prepared for us here and now."

Elanor considered his words for a moment and smiled. "Our world," she repeated softly. She liked that what he said had become true. Even during her short time back in the future, she felt Prydain slipping away and wanted to pull it back. Her daughter. Mothers. Friends. "I want to go home."

"I know. I do also." Merlin sucked in a sharp breath. "Are you ready then?"

Giving a reluctant nod, she picked up her mobile.

"You can call him," he assured her. "It will be alright."

Elanor sighed. She looked into Merlin's steady eyes, feeling unprepared. Calling her father would open a Pandora's box of pain and hardship. In Prydain, she never had to face Helen's scathing glare or rejection. Now, she had no choice. Unlocking her phone, she scrolled to find the number; a picture of her father's smiling face appeared. His beautiful, dark round eyes, short black hair, and brown skin. She missed his smile, the glint of white from his teeth and the happy wrinkles that appeared under his eyes.

With a quick breath, she pressed the number.

Beep, beep. Beep, beep.

She tapped the speaker button so Merlin could hear.

"Elanor!" came the deep voice, muffled by the poor connection.

"He-e-ey, Dad." Elanor's voice trembled. A tear welled but remained held within her eye.

"Sweetie, how was your birthday? Please don't tell me you spent the whole day by yourself again. I am sorry I couldn't come meet you in the city. You know I would have come if I could."

"Um? Well, actually..." she stammered. "Dad, I have so much to tell you. I..."

"Is there something wrong, sweetie? Are you okay? You sound upset."

"No… I—" Elanor sighed. "I just… really miss you, and I have somebody I would like you to meet." Her insecure eyes flickered up at Merlin.

Her father chuckled. "Elanor… have you actually gone out and met someone? Those baby blues of yours finally distracted the right bloke, eh? Never thought I'd see the day."

Elanor blushed. "*Dad.*"

Merlin's eyes gleamed at his wife. Her interaction with her father intrigued him. It revealed a vulnerability and softness in her he had never seen before.

"It might be some time before I can make it to the city to meet him. I am assuming this is a boyfriend."

"Yes… well, in a way."

Merlin squinted his eyes, confused.

"O-o-h my—my little girl has crawled out of her cave and gotten a life."

Elanor grunted. "Dad, I had a life—I mean…*have* a life." She hesitated. "Listen… I want to bring him to the house to meet you."

"What? You'd come here? Well, this must be serious. You know how Helen is."

"It is serious. Dad. We were hoping—"

"We? Oh, sweetie, how long have you known this guy? Have you been keeping him a secret from me?"

"Well… it's complicated. Anyway, we were hoping you could help us with some of your cartography skills."

"Oh, I see. So, you have an agenda pushing you to come see your ol' man."

"Y-e-e-e-sss," Elanor drawled.

"Hah!" Her father chuckled. "No matter, no matter. You know I am glad to see you however you come. And you know, I love to talk about my mapping. It would be a pleasure to help."

"When could we come?" She peered at Merlin, biting her lip.

"Now let's see. It's the weekend, and it is already properly loaded. Could you come Monday evening? I could twist Helen's arm to make a roast. She will be so cross, but it will be like old times. Though she might rightly behave herself with the company. Jack and Nancy will be home as well."

"Ah," Elanor said, with an obvious struggle to mask her disappointment.

"I know they can be difficult, Elanor, but it has been a long time. Maybe it will be better."

The enthusiasm in her eyes deflated a little more. "Maybe."

"Prepare your man—they may try to ruffle him. Elanor… are you sure you want to come here? I could meet you in the city in a few weeks."

"No, it's alright, Dad. We will come on Monday."

"Alright then…" David waited for a moment. "Sweetie, are you sure everything is okay?"

"Yes, more than fine. I promise. I cannot wait for you to meet Mer—"

"Oh, hang on, sweetie." He shuffled with the phone, and his voice sounded distant. *"I'll be off the phone in a minute… No… it's Elanor… just wait… I'll be there in a moment… What? Fine…"*

The phone's speaker creaked and clacked, and…

"I am sorry, love. I have to go. We will see you on Monday. Come at half five, okay?"

"Okay."

"Love you, sweets."

"Love you too, Dad."

The phone disconnected. Elanor delicately set the mobile on the counter, slumped her head into the crook of her arm, and groaned.

"When is Monday?" Merlin gently prodded.

"Day after tomorrow," she mumbled from her arm.

"Your voice sounded different when you spoke to your father."

Elanor didn't lift her head from her elbow.

"Am I a boyfriend?" Merlin asked, confused. "Could you not have told him I am your husband?"

At Elanor's surprised glance, Merlin shifted his eyes away to hide the hurt and insecurity the word *'boyfriend'* stirred in him.

She squeezed his arm. "Well, this is where it all gets a little complicated, doesn't it? As far as all the people in my life are aware, I have not even been gone a day. In truth, I have been gone for more than four years. It would be completely strange that I am now suddenly married. I think it would be better for people to think of you as a new boyfriend."

"Ah…" Merlin said, slightly offended. "And what exactly does it mean that I am your boyfriend? I am a man, and surely not just your friend."

Elanor laughed. "Well, I suppose it *is* a strange word. You are my friend. But it is true that you are much, much more than that." She winked. "The term 'boyfriend' is not to call you a boy. It means that we are… um… seeing each other with romantic intentions."

"Romantic?"

She smiled. "It means that we would be perceived like when we first fell in love, before we were married."

Relief passed over Merlin's face. "I understand," he said, nodding. "Now we wait?"

"Now we need a car, and for that, I will need to make another call." Elanor groaned. "Ugh! I will need to call Jess."

COFFEE WITH A MADMAN

"Okay, so you're telling me you're not coming to work today."

"No, Jess, and I need you to cover for me," Elanor said, phone cocked between her chin and shoulder while she pulled on a yellow cardigan and wrapped a gray scarf around her neck. "I am only coming to collect your car keys. Thanks again, by the way."

"No probs. What are you going to tell the boss?"

"I don't know yet. That is the least of my problems right now."

"Right. Going to see that monster of a mother of yours is a dodgy choice. Why are you going there again? I thought you had sworn off the Evans."

"It's a long story. Maybe if you could meet me in the stairwell, I could avoid having to chat with Case and you know who."

"Yah! Send me a text when you get here."

"Okay, will do. I'll see you in a few."

Elanor grabbed her green bag sitting by the door and turned to Merlin. "Are you ready?"

Merlin saw, trapped within her eyes, the anxiety of what lay ahead for her. "Come here," he said, wrapping her in his arms. Tension also tightened in his gut. He wasn't so much worried about meeting the Evans, but entering back into the unknown world outside Elanor's flat left him a bit unnerved.

He had gotten to hide away for a few days, with Elanor safe by his side—helping him forget about the insanity of this crazy, fast-paced world. At least now he looked the part; his new clothing helped him blend in. Though the lightweight clothes made him feel strange and exposed. He was out of his depths in this new environment. How should he react if faced with danger in a world so unfamiliar?

"We will come back here and gather our extra things once we have the car," Elanor told him.

The car.

Merlin's stomach churned at the thought of traveling at such fast speeds in those… those iron chariots. He'd observed them from the window over the past few days as they sped past. Elanor explained that there were also other traveling machines that carried people from one place to another, but it all just made him wish he could saddle a horse instead.

It will be fine… It will be fine.

They walked out the door, and strange smells and loud noises permeated Merlin's senses. He kept his eyes on Elanor, who waved her hand, encouraging him forward as they descended the stairs. Even *she* seemed unfamiliar and new. The rhythm of her language changed, and she carried an obscure heaviness. He appreciated how free she appeared in other ways, though. She moved with a confidence she did not have in Prydain. She knew this world. He would have to lean on her, like she had leaned on him all those years ago.

Her unusual clothing put a lightness into her step, and her hair curled and wisped in a strange, loose, flowing style. She wore black half-boots with a lifted heel, which accentuated her shapely legs beneath the tight black trousers she wore along with her long white blouse and thin cardigan. A rousing, sweet floral scent emanated from her, lingering from her shower.

They rounded a corner into the throng of marching people. Elanor gripped Merlin's hand, pulling him along with a smile. When they reached their destination, she stopped and pointed at the signage above a shop door. *The Cuppa Café*, the sign read.

"Let's go in. I loved this place. I used to stop here every morning for coffee. You might like the coffee here even less," Elanor teased, wrinkling her nose. "Maybe I should get you something sweet. You might like that better. Come on." She smiled brightly, dragging Merlin into the café by his arm.

The aromatic smell of coffee and sweet pastries smacked Merlin in the face. The lovely and rich atmosphere, surprisingly, riled a desire to try one of the promised perfect beverages. The café echoed with chatter, and loud screeches pitched from the large silver machine brewing the brown liquid.

"Elanor!" yelled a man from behind the counter. A balding, red-headed man smiled around the large coffee machine. "I've got your coffee, love. Give me jus' a minute."

"Make that two, Bill. But one with mocha."

Bill turned back to lean over the counter. Seeing Merlin, he chimed, "Who is this now?"

"This is Merlin. He is—"

"Merlin? Hah!" Bill chortled, glancing at Merlin. "Your mother a fan of wizards?"

Elanor smirked at the jest.

Bill winked. "New boyfriend?"

Elanor grinned. "Yes, something like that."

"Ah. You must be a good fella to capture her eye."

Merlin gave the friendly man an awkward nod.

Bill happily smacked the counter and went about his business.

"Look." Elanor pointed, directing Merlin to the paintings on the wall. "Those are mine." She tilted her head, squinting her eyes. "Funny… the paintings look so different to me now. Those horse's legs look like Brynn's—look, it even has her spots."

"They are wonderful!"

Elanor gave him a dismissive shrug. "Some might think so."

"Do not be like that. What would make you doubt?" Merlin eyed her earnestly, waiting for an answer, but she ignored his question. "And that one—that dragon has gold and green scales like…"

Elanor's eyes brightened as she reengaged. "Like Gwyliwr! Wow. You know? I think I had been seeing Prydain all along."

Merlin's thoughts whirred as he took in the paintings. Where had Elanor's magic come from? The origin of her ability was still a mystery. Was it true that she had been born with magic as he had? Merlin always surmised that his magic had been passed down through his lineage as a fair folk and through his father, who also had a mysterious bardic power. But Elanor? She was a Pendragon. Where did her magic come from? Was it the Great God who had graced her with such abilities? Surely, it was possible. After all, his magic had been more extraordinary than his parents'—with no explanation as to why.

"Your colors and details are beautiful."

"I never really tried to make them so. I think I had been reaching for Prydain my whole life. Always so lost…" she murmured. "It was always before me, and I could never quite get to it. At least, not until I met you."

"The calling was always there." Merlin nodded, scanning the paintings, and reflecting on the one of himself in her flat. "It all meant something. Like your dreams."

Elanor flinched at the mention of her dreams.

Bill shouted, "Here ye are!" He placed two cups on the counter. "Happy ta meet ya, Merlin. Take care of our little miss."

Merlin nodded, lifting his cup to thank the man. He fixed an apprehensive stare at his drink, which came in an odd container.

Elanor tapped the lid. "You drink out of that hole."

"Right." Merlin smiled at her, but his willingness to try the peculiar beverage had waned.

They sauntered out of the café. Merlin hardly had a moment to attempt a first sip when a suspicious man appeared in his view. Amid the passersby surrounding them, the man loomed in his grimy, torn clothes, and he shouted at the air.

Merlin slowed, giving him a cautious stare.

"It's alright. He is just a vagrant. A street person." Elanor wrapped her hand through the crook of his arm. "Unfortunately, there are many needy people within the city."

Merlin considered her words. Elanor was more familiar with this world, but still, he could not shake the growing sense of disquiet pressing against his thoughts. Demons of the otherworld had a particular steely appearance. He glared forward with discernment.

The man groaned and bit at the wind, shouting wild obscenities. He snapped violently right, then left, as if being repeatedly bitten by an unseen insect. His disturbed behavior grew more erratic the closer he came, making Merlin unsettled. He had seen madmen before, but this man was no ordinary *vagrant*.

As the man neared, Merlin took a guarded step back, clearing a space for him to pass. The man heaved closer, writhing like a rabid dog, but froze before crossing their path.

Merlin pulled Elanor tight to his side. The man was silent, his aura eerie with intent. Merlin stepped to walk past, and the madman's head whipped toward them. He fixed a menacing glare at them, his fierce eyes barely visible underneath the tilt of his head.

In a low growl, he said, "What are you doing here, EMRYS?!" The pitch of his voice rose as he said the name, causing others to turn their heads as they rushed past.

Elanor inhaled sharply, gripping Merlin's arm.

Alarmed, Merlin raised his hands, staying vigilant and ready to defend themselves.

The man twisted his hand upside down, pointing at Elanor. "HE'S GOING TO DIE! DIE! DIE! That man… He knows it, but you don't know it. YOU DON'T KNOW!" The madness escalated. Coughing, the man leaned closer, his pale lips foamy and wet from the spit dripping over his dry, chapped mouth.

"Go! Leave us!" Merlin commanded under his breath.

"She's afraid of the pain—you're afraid of the pain," the madman accused. "We know. WE KNOW! You'll see… You'll see."

Enough, Merlin thought.

He lifted his palm and whispered, "Gefnau," and a gust of wind steadily blew. Magic pushed the man backward, his feet scuffing the ground. The madman's eyes were wild, and he covered his face with his arms to shield against the wind.

Merlin's wind continued to push back the madman until meters separated them. When the power ceased, the man paused, looking baffled. Then he roared wickedly, "HA-HA-HA-HA-HAAAA-HAAAA!" His head rolled with his eyes. Fortunately, he turned and ambled away, hollering drunkenly as he turned the corner and disappeared.

Merlin gritted his teeth, fuming, and looked at the cup in his hands. He no longer wanted it. The putrid encounter evaporated his thirst. "Was this not out of the ordinary? Why do people walk by as though they do not see?"

Elanor stared forward with her mouth agape. Her coffee spilt on the ground by her feet. She faced Merlin, her eyes consumed by fear. "*No*—no. No, no, no, no."

"Shhh, shhh. It was false, Elanor. *False.*" He grabbed her arms, steadying her.

"Truth does not come from mouths like this. It was a darkness within him that spoke. Do not be disturbed by it."

She weakly mumbled, "The shadow finds us already."

Merlin glanced at the corner the man had disappeared around, then back at the sadness that stole the bright luster of Elanor's countenance. "The realms of the otherworld can always see. It does not mean that the darkness has found us. That foul thing was prodding to find weakness."

"I dreamed I would be pierced by an arrow, and it came to pass, just as I dreamt it."

"Elanor." Merlin jostled her to snap her out of the trance of despair. "Look at me. Look. That dream came from you, not a demon. And though it did come to pass, it was not as we had thought. Look at me. Both of us are standing here alive. We could not see all ends, but the truth is you did not die. The dream did not become the omen we had feared. The dragon gave us a gift that protected us. The Man in Blue guided us."

Elanor gave a slow, methodical nod, allowing Merlin's reason to sink in.

He sighed. "Come on. We must go." His suspicious eyes darted right, then left. He did not believe the foul demon's words spoken through the poor lost man to be prophecy. Nor did he think that the shadow of Osian had found them. However, he did believe that their presence had flared like a signal fire—confirming his previous suspicions that this world was not without dangers. Already darkness crawled out from the corners of the busy streets. The more darkness saw them, the more exposed they would be. They needed to keep moving.

Elanor laced her fingers with Merlin's, and with determination, led him forward. They moved down a few blocks and turned up one street, then down another when at last, she stopped.

"This is it." She glanced up at the towering building, then pulled her mobile from her bag and tapped away on the screen. "Jess will bring us the keys in a moment." She scowled, kicking at the ground.

Buzz. Buzz.

Elanor looked down at her phone and sighed with displeasure. "We have to go up. She says she can't come down." She rubbed her forehead. "That means I will have to talk to Case and explain why I will not be coming to work today."

"Who is Case?"

"He is my boss. He's the guy that runs the design department. God!" She huffed. "What am I going to say?" She contemplated for a moment. "I could say I have a family emergency, and I have to go visit my father. It is a little true. I mean, I could tell him nothing and risk losing my job."

"Do you want to keep it?"

Her brows scrunched together. "Well, I suppose I'm not planning to return to work." She tittered oddly at the thought. "Though, if we somehow cannot get back to Prydain right away, we might still need it… so strange to think. Feels odd to just quit. Anyway, Case will allow my excuse this time, but now we'll have to deal with Demetri. He's relentless."

"Demetri?"

"You'll see. Be prepared. Ack! This is so inconvenient. I just wanted to get the key to the car and go. Well, there's nothing for it. I suppose we have to go up there. Jess isn't coming down, and we need those keys."

6

JESS & DEMETRI

They stepped through the door into a brightly lit white and gray room. They were met with a barrage of beeping and buzzing as people bustled from place to place. Papers rattled behind what appeared to be strange square boxes people sat inside.

"Those are cubicles," Elanor explained, not missing Merlin's baffled expression.

A woman sped past them. "Hey, Elanor," she muttered, a paper cup in hand, as several more people rushed by them without acknowledgement.

"Busy," Merlin noted.

"I hardly noticed it before, but now… it seems a brash slap in the face."

Off to the right sat more desks gathered in bunches, with large windows making up the wall behind them. A girl at a desk waved Elanor over. She had an afro of dark-golden hair and brown skin.

"That's Jess," Elanor said. "I'll go see her, if you want to wait there." She pointed to a row of red chairs off to the side.

"I'll stand."

Elanor set her shoulders, then walked over to Jess, who waved her hands, chittering away into a small wire set at her mouth. Black circles capped her ears. She covered the wire with her hands as she hugged Elanor, then flicked her head in Merlin's direction and mouthed, "Is that him?"

Merlin peered over, rolling his shoulder to feign confidence, pretending to be ignorant of Jess's disapproving stares. He turned away, then jolted, finding a pair of green eyes glaring at him. The green-eyed man had a head of blonde hair, combed into a perfect wave on top of his head.

"Who are you?" the presumptuous man asked.

Merlin squared his shoulders and stood a little taller. "Merlin."

"Ppfftt," the man snickered, rolling his eyes. "Merlin, eh? Why are you here with Elanor?"

Merlin eyed the man as realization struck. *Ah. I wonder if this pompous young man is Demetri?* "I'm with Elanor."

"When you say 'with Elanor,' you mean…" The man leaned forward, lifting his chin.

Unafraid to meet the affronting challenge, Merlin simply offered, "I am her boyfriend." He used the foreign word, hoping to communicate what the young fool needed to comprehend.

"Ah." He curled his lip and narrowed his eyes. "So, when did this happen? Over Elanor's supposed *alone time* this weekend?" He glowered at Merlin. "Enjoy it while it lasts, mate, she just—"

"Demetri," Elanor burst into the conversation. She shot Merlin an apologetic glance.

"El, this bloke says he's your boyfriend. I was about to put him straight." Demetri, folded his arms with a smug look.

"Demetri—shut it!" came the command from Jess as she sauntered over to them. "You really are an arrogant piece of work, you know?"

Demetri rocked back onto his heels with a prideful tilt. He shot his hand out to Merlin. "Demetri Palmer."

Flat-faced and unimpressed, Merlin shook his hand.

"What in the world…?" Jess shoved Demetri in the arm.

Elanor turned to Merlin. "I have to talk to Case. I will be right back." She glanced warily over at Demetri.

"I'll keep an eye on things," Jess offered, glaring at Demetri with pursed lips.

Elanor nodded hesitantly, then moved down the aisle toward a closed door. Demetri followed her with his eyes, his hands lining the silhouette of her curves as she walked away. "Now, *that* is a woman, am I right?" He elbowed Merlin.

"What is wrong with you?" Jess interjected with disgust. "Why don't you go back to your corner and do something useful?" She turned her harsh stare toward Merlin, eyeing him up and down. "I'm Jess, by the way. El has told me a lot about you."

Merlin shifted uncomfortably under Jess's stare. He could tell she wasn't keen on his presence.

Demetri shrugged. "Just pointing out the obvious, eh, Merlin? I mean, all us blokes are already looking. I'm just not afraid to make it plain."

Merlin's gut roiled with disgust. Who did this rake think he was? Elanor had warned him that Demetri was a bother, but he rarely met the like. Sleazes like this existed in the back corners of Lindonium and Rome and around the backs of dark taverns.

Demetri rattled on. "Where did you meet El?"

Merlin hated how he said her name.

"That is none of your business," Jess said, with a scathing glare.

"Well, I had asked her to go for a…"

Merlin scowled as Demetri prattled on.

I shouldn't have to answer to this weasel.

Merlin placed his fingers on the side of his mouth and rattled a combination of noises. "*Whistle...* Twrch, Sth."

Jess and Demetri stopped, giving Merlin a strange stare.

"Oh my God..." Jess said. "I hope you're not crazy."

Merlin just grinned.

Demetri started to speak again. "Thrupt... bin... mumm-mmm." He stopped with an uneasy laugh and tried again. "Boobah... shrug glummum." His eyes widened. "Gaffol lablup?" He smacked his hand over his mouth, horror flooding his face. He huffed and tried to speak once more. "Looma dum flurpadap." Demetri's eyes rounded with panic, and he rushed away, shutting himself into the adjacent bathroom.

Jess looked at Merlin, her eyes wide. "Did you just do that?"

Merlin smiled, relieved to see Elanor approaching. He turned to Jess and winked. "Don't worry, he'll be fine in a day or two."

Elanor grabbed Merlin and Jess by the arms, pulling them out of the office and into the hall that led to the exit.

Jess stared at Merlin in alarm, pointing at him shakily. "Elanor... he..."

Elanor tightened her grip around Jess's flailing arm, dragging them along.

"Wait, Elanor!" Jess yelled, yanking her hand free. "Hold on a minute. What is going on? Who is he?"

"Jess, I know this all seems crazy. I wish I had more time to explain. To be honest, you probably wouldn't believe me if I told you anyway. Listen." Elanor sighed at her friend's confusion and distress. "I know it appears that I have just met this man, but, Jess, I have known him for a long time."

"Is *he* the man from your dream?"

"I know it sounds crazy." Elanor reached to calm her.

"Yes, it does, El... This is mad. I'm worried about you." Jess grabbed Elanor's wrist, pulling her away from Merlin.

Elanor exhaled loudly. "Alright. Alright. Let me show you." She held her hands out to Jess. "Come on, give me your hands."

Jess shot a dubious stare at Merlin.

"It's going to be okay—trust me." Again, Elanor offered Jess her hands.

Jess hesitantly rested her hands in Elanor's.

"Close your eyes."

Jess shot her an apprehensive glare. "You want me to what...?"

Elanor encouraged her with a nod.

"This is bonkers." Jess sighed and closed her eyes. A second later, Jess lifted her chin and rose onto her toes. Her eyes raced back and forth underneath her eyelids, making the anticipation mount in Merlin's stomach.

Elanor let go of her friend's hands, and Jess opened her eyes. The tension slowly fell from her face as she gawked at Elanor, then over at Merlin. He lifted his hand and blew gently. His eyes sparked with golden light, and a gentle breeze whirled through the small space, blowing their hair and clothes before settling.

"Whoa! I think I'm going mad," Jess murmured. Astonished, she tilted her head at Elanor and folded her arms. "I don't really understand what I just saw, but I felt it… It was real. An apple orchard, and a building of stone. I saw you–somewhere else—with him?"

Elanor nodded coyly. "Sort of."

"Ah… I'm not sure I can believe any of this. You are Merlin… *the* Merlin?"

Merlin nodded, stepping closer to them.

"Well, before you showed me what you did, and this guy"—she flipped her hand at Merlin—"started doing magic tricks, I knew something had happened." Jess leaned closer to Elanor. "I could see it the moment you walked into the office. Your face, your eyes… El, you are completely changed. Remember that when you see Helen today." She shook her head, baffled, and pulled her keys from her pocket. "Don't wreck it."

Elanor took the keys from her hand.

"It's on the third level of the car park, just a block down. You know the one. Space 3-20 or 21."

Elanor exhaled and embraced Jess, kissing her on the cheek. "Thank you."

Jess's eyes grew misty. "I won't see you again, will I?"

"I don't know."

Jess nodded and smirked. "Just be sure you let me know how I can find my car, okay?"

"I will," Elanor promised.

Jess walked back to the office door, but before going inside, she turned. "Really, El? Merlin?" She cocked her head, looking bemused as she pushed through the door.

"There it is," Elanor said, pointing to a small yellow car in space 3-20. "Jess's Vauxhall."

Merlin eyed the dented yellow thing and his stomach swirled.

"It's really a hunk of trash, but Jess's father fixes cars for a living and has kept this one running for her. That's why she never really has a problem lending it to me. She's not too worried about what happens to it."

"Well, that does not build my confidence in this… *car.*"

"It will be fine. Truly, Merlin, you've gone charging into battle with swords and spear, and this car is what's got you bothered? Here," she said, unlocking the side door and opening it. It creaked as it swung open. "Get in."

Merlin grumbled as he ducked inside and situated himself on the black, slippery seat.

"Here, take this," Elanor said. *Vrip.* She pulled a thick strap over his shoulder.

"You'll have to strap yourself in. Take this silver part and click it into the piece on your right."

Merlin glanced around, a little lost.

She laughed. "No, down by your hip."

"This?" he asked, pointing at the latch and scowling at her amusement.

Click.

Merlin finally fastened the seatbelt.

"There. You'll be safe, I promise."

"Do people never crash in these *things?*"

"Eh, well, of course they do, but it's fine, Merlin, really." Elanor shut the door and crawled into the car through the driver's side door. She put the keys in the ignition, shooting Merlin a mischievous grin. Turning the key, the car rattled with a *vroom.* Instantly, a loud, angry racket boomed throughout the car. Merlin's hands flew up to cover his ears.

"Oh, sorry." Elanor rushed to turn knobs and press buttons, giggling. "Jess likes her music loud."

"That was music?"

"Ha-ha-ha! Oh, Merlin, this is all very strange, isn't it? Here," she said, continuing to giggle as she poked a few more buttons on the black dash in front of her. "You might like this."

A gentler trill thrummed throughout the car. The delicate humming was much more appealing than the brash blast of noise.

"What is this?" Merlin asked, removing his hands from his ears.

"Vivaldi, I think. The instrument is called a violin."

Merlin gave a pleasant smile.

Elanor pulled down on a stick that was set between them, then jerked it over and down again, and they started moving backwards. "I have not driven a car in so long," she said un-assuredly as the car made a cranking whirr.

Merlin gripped the side of his seat with white knuckles.

"There's a handle, just there, if you really need to grab hold of something," Elanor teased, pointing to the small handle above the window.

She fidgeted with the stick again, and they lurched forward with a few stutters. They drove down, around, and through the gray roofed car park until they buzzed out into the sunshine and out onto the street, pulling alongside other moving cars as they puttered down the road. Merlin began to relax as the pace did not feel as frightening as he'd anticipated. A slight smile curled up the side of his mouth.

"See?" Elanor encouraged. "It's not so bad. Kind of nice, really. Just wait until we are on the open motorway. That's when we will really get going."

Merlin grimaced with a chuckle, relieved that the worst was over.

They pulled up along the curbside in front of her flat. Quickly, they gathered all the things they needed from inside and returned to the car. Ready to leave, Elanor gripped the wheel and sighed.

"You do not have to fear her. I will be beside you."

"I'm fine. It's fine," she said with an edgy tone, tapping the wheel. She exhaled, long and hard, then turned the key and forced a smile. "Now to hit the M4. That will really give you some perspective of the landscape. It has changed so much. None of it is as wild as it used to be."

They crawled through the city and launched out onto the motorway. Merlin resisted pressing his hands against the dash as they sped faster, and cars and lorries careened past them. The gray of the tall, bustling city disappeared behind them, and features of the land shifted. Merlin saw strange buildings that looked like homes, but as they turned to go down a more country road, he spotted some stone and old thatch that almost resembled aspects of Prydain.

"We need to put together our story," Elanor said.

"Right. We cannot be telling the Evans that I am a traveler from a time past."

Elanor simpered. "We will need to have a pretty solid one since they will all be asking questions. Especially Dad and Jack. For one thing, how did we meet? What do you do? Where are you from? The best lies always have a strand of truth."

"What do you know of lies?" Merlin winked with a wry smile.

"I don't. That's just the problem. Never been very practiced at lying to my father, at least."

"Fortunately for both of us, I do have more of a knack for deception than you might think. My cunning has been the very wit that navigated Arthur and his men through many evils. No need to place an aura of integrity on me. And you are right— clever deception stems from truth. I can navigate the field of the Evans, but you will need to trust me. If I am… as you said… a new boyfriend, you can assume you do not know a lot about me either."

"Huh. I never thought of that. But where would you be from?"

"Dyved. You showed me on the map that the region still exists. My mother is still Adhan. No need to make up stories when we don't have to."

"Well, this might be easier than I thought. But the area is not *really* called Dyved anymore. Maybe we could say St. David's or Carmarthen?"

"I think the more we have it planned out, the more broken and out of rhythm it will become. Just let me speak when asked a question. Do not try to fill in any of the gaps. That is where we will get trapped. Let whoever is lying navigate any misunderstanding. We are not trying to lie to them anyway. They are not prepared for the truth, so we will give them only the pieces they can swallow."

"Where did we first meet? This one I might need to know. I definitely cannot tell them I was pulled across time and landed in your bedchamber," Elanor huffed derisively. "What edge of truth could be told if asked that question? And I know they will ask. That's the first thing everyone asks when meeting a new couple."

"Well," Merlin said, smiling, "this one should be easy. We met in a bookshop."

She returned his smile. "Hm… clever. Maybe we could say we met some months ago," she said. "Can't have them thinking we only met two days ago, and I'm already bringing you to meet them. Seems a little too soon." Elanor's head turned, and her eyes tracked a sign as they sped past. "Not long now. Less than an hour away."

Merlin watched Elanor's countenance darken. Her desperate eyes searched the road ahead as if looking for a way of escape. Her fingers fidgeted over the top of the steering wheel, while her nervous knee bounced, jostling the keys. He raced to put her mind at ease.

"Perhaps I should tell them I was raised by faeries of the otherworld." He gave her a sarcastic wink and nudged her arm with his elbow. "Upon discovering they were evil, I escaped to live with the humans in the world above."

Elanor sputtered through her lips, "Yes…" Her shoulders loosened, and she grinned, leaning into Merlin's game. "I think you really should. I'd love to see the look on their faces when they realize I have brought home a total loon. Maybe you should add that you have a pet unicorn while you are at it." She giggled, seeming pleased with herself.

Merlin mused, admiring the twinkle in her eye, satisfied his distraction had worked. They continued sharing their best, most shocking scenarios as they sped up the motorway closer to the Evans.

THE EVANS

They drove up the coast a ways, then turned inland. The road narrowed, and tall hedges grew up on either side. Quick glimpses of the countryside flickered between breaks in the hedges. Sheep appeared, scattered over the rolling fields of green, and fences of stone separated the pastures.

Merlin kept quiet, absorbing the foreign landscapes.

Elanor broke the silence. "My father and Helen teach at Aberystwyth, a university in the nearby town. The house is just up through these roads. My mo—Helen teaches literature." Elanor sighed; her eyes fixed on the road.

Merlin felt anxiety emanating from her. "Elanor?"

She stared forward, and her breathing quickened.

"Think of your father. He will be glad to see you. I know how much you have missed him. Helen has no power over you—no authority over your heart."

"Easily enough said. I wish I could turn it off and not care—but I can't. I just can't. It always angered me that I couldn't have my father without her attached to him. She could never just let him love me. And then…" Her chin quivered. "Maybe she was right to hate me. I—" She sniffed. "I took him away from them."

"That is not the truth. It was your father's choice—not yours. You had no power over the circumstances you were raised in."

"That is rational… it is, but I have been made to believe something different for so long. I know it was not my fault, but because Helen blames me, it is my fault." She sighed. "No matter what the truth was or how faultless I could've been, I am to blame. She hates me so much… Her eyes when she looks at me—it's so painful. All I ever wanted was for her to love me… and she never will. Damn it!" Elanor smacked the steering wheel as a tear escaped her eye. "I didn't want to cry. Why do I care so much about what she thinks? Why can't I just turn off my feelings?"

Elanor's emotions boiled over, manifesting not only as tears but also as distressed lines reddening her neck and cheeks.

"I can't do this!" she yelled. Her foot stomped the brake, causing Merlin to jolt forward. Elanor jerked the car over to the side of the road and turned it off.

The sudden stop shocked Merlin, and he placed his hand on his chest, inhaling in and out. Recovering, he looked over at Elanor. Her head drooped and her shoulders sagged. He reached for her, resting a hand upon her back. He now grasped the profound impact this *one* woman had had on Elanor, wounding her so completely.

"Maybe this is good," Elanor began, rubbing her forehead. "Get all my emotions out before I see her. Then I will be fully prepared." She lifted her eyes and pointed. "We are almost there. Only two more gates to their drive."

Merlin gently stroked her back. "I cannot imagine what it is like. I have faced many who have hated me, but none of them were my mother or father. I have had to face the shaming stares from people whom I loved and loved me." He paused, remembering Guinevere and Cilaen's disappointment. "I hid from those stares for as long as I could. But Jess was right. You *must* know you have changed," he encouraged softly. "You are *not* the same as the last time you saw Helen. You faced down a serpent, and even *death*. Helen is small." He glanced out the window with a smirk of disdain. "She could never match any one of these. And *you* are not motherless. Not anymore. You do not need her to love you."

"Hm." Elanor bit into her bottom lip. "I don't need her," she repeated under her breath. She faced Merlin, and her fears seemed lightened. "How could I forget?" Timidly, she smiled. "I don't know why I let her get me so bent out of shape. So many things bigger in the world than Helen."

"Sometimes it is the small things that hurt the most." Merlin searched Elanor's eyes to see if she had been consoled. "Though I don't think things like this can be measured big or small."

"Right." She nodded, taking a deep breath, and turned the keys. The engine revved. Putting the car into gear, they edged forward and pulled up to the drive— turned right, through the gate—and approached the house.

The house was white brick, with a blue door and a garden that appeared to wrap around the back. The drive was wide, and the gravel crackled under the rolling tires.

"It's an old country house," Elanor explained. "Old. Hah! I guess that is all relative now. The house itself is more than a couple hundred years old but wouldn't have even existed in our time. Does that make us both very old, or just you?" She giggled; her laughter jingled like chimes.

Merlin indulged her jest with a sarcastic gasp, enjoying her spark of humor.

Pulling in beside another car, Elanor turned off the engine and rubbed her shaking hands together. "Well, they would have seen us pull up. There is nowhere to hide now." She pressed her lips together, lifted the handle to open the door, and hesitated. She looked at Merlin with a timid gulp and pushed the door open.

Merlin did the same, watching her apprehension as she got out of the car. She leered at the house as though it would eat her. Her lips pressed into a thin, tight line.

The blue door opened. Out emerged Elanor's father with a happy, wide smile on his face. He stretched his arms out as he bounded toward Elanor, his dark eyes sparkling.

"Oh, sweetie. I am so happy to see you." David's short, black hair was speckled with white. "It has been a few months since I have seen your bright eyes. How was your drive?" He reached for Elanor and gave her a generous squeeze. His eyes lifted to Merlin. "Ah, and this young man is?" He held out his hand to shake Merlin's hand.

"This is Merlin."

Her father's thick dark brows crimped in surprise. "Mer-Merlin?" he repeated, staring at Merlin with a stunned look, as though he had seen a ghost. His head tilted back, observing Merlin's height, but his eyes remained stark. "Y-yes. Sorry. Merlin." David grabbed hold of Merlin's hand and shook it vigorously. He glanced at Elanor, appearing a tad rattled. As he pulled back his hand, he fumbled his fingers over the front of his striped shirt and lifted his uneasy gaze back at Merlin.

"I-I am David," he stuttered. "It's wonderful to have you to our home."

"Are you alright, Dad?"

"Yes… uh, yes. Right, just right. He's, uh, a tall bloke, isn't he?" David said, patting Merlin on the shoulder. He grinned, nodding his head, and scrunching his dark brown eyes.

"Dad, I—" Elanor stopped speaking as Helen stepped out from the house, her daughter following close behind.

Merlin was surprised to see a short woman with flaming red hair. He wasn't quite sure what he expected Helen would look like—perhaps someone looming taller with an intimidating stance. But instead, she had squinty green eyes and glasses that rested on the brim of a small nose. Her face was dwarfed by her voluminous frizzy hair. She wore an apron and sauntered over with a cocked smile and a towel in her hand.

Her daughter resembled a snooty copy of her with slight variations: her red hair was curled, her skin was olive toned, and her eyes were large and brown. She didn't wear glasses, but a perturbed glare threatened them from above her freckled nose and pursed lips.

"Come to show off your boyfriend?" Helen bit coldly.

"This is Merlin," David said, presenting him with an open hand.

"Pfftt! Merlin," Nancy sneered, rolling her eyes. "Is that his name?"

Helen swiped at Nancy with her towel and gave a chiding smirk. "Nancy. Don't be rude. This lad doesn't seem like a complete muppet."

A muppet? Merlin wondered if he was being insulted. Though not eager to give them any sort of satisfaction with a reaction, he simply nodded. Gazing at Elanor, he took hold of her hand.

Elanor forced a grin. "Merlin, this is Helen and Nancy."

Helen squinted her eyes, making them even smaller. "Well, I hope you aren't one of those daft artist types that only eat vegetables. I've cooked a roast and a pudding. Come on in when you are ready." She turned and walked back into the house with her daughter shuffling behind her.

David put up his hands. "Don't mind them. Hopefully, Elanor has warned you.

Be prepared for battle." He chuffed. "The kids have dropped in for a visit as well, so we've got a full house. Should make for an interesting evening. Nothing you can't handle though, eh?"

"Look who's come visiting!" came a shout from behind them. A tall, thin but broad shouldered young man came hurtling a ball around from the back of the house. "Oi! Look out!" he shouted, kicking the ball in Merlin's direction.

Merlin threw up his arms to block the ball as it bounced past him.

"You've got to think fast, my man."

"This is Jack." Elanor gestured toward the young man.

"Good to see yah, little sis. For real, it's been ages."

Jack looked like his father, only much taller and leaner. He wore a red and white colored shirt with *Liverpool FC* written across it.

"Jus' been kickin' the ball around in the back. You a footballer?" He nodded to Merlin. "What's your team?"

Merlin hesitated a moment, unsure how to respond, but then held out his hand. "I'm Merlin."

Jack shook it, smiling at Elanor. "Is this guy for real? Bloke walking around with a name like that. That's brilliant. Wish my name was Merlin. Hey, Dad, why didn't you name me Merlin? Or better yet, Dumbledore."

"Knock it off, Jack," David said, shoving his son with a threatening smile. "Stop teasing our guest. Jack's just come in today as well."

"Yah, probably passed you on the motorway. Had to get out of the city, yah know? Crazy times," he said, elbowing Merlin and giving him a wink as though he should understand.

Elanor said to Merlin, "Jack lives in the city too."

"We see each other every now and again, don't we, El? Never see you out much, though. Surprised you went and found yourself a bloke. Always sittin' around in your flat like a hermit, just like you did here. Hidin' in your room and climbing up tha' tree." A sudden mean stare crossed Jack's brow. "Ah, you know you're better off away from people, don't yah?" He winked as he jabbed. "Wouldn't want to go ruinin' anyone's good time. It's better when you keep to yourself."

Jack's upbeat demeanor had taken a swift turn. It was apparent to all that he had aimed to wound Elanor with his last comment. And she caught it. Merlin watched her crumple into herself. She winced like she had been punched in the gut.

Merlin's insides burned. They had no idea who it was they had living in their house all those years. A princess. Arthur's daughter. The child Pendragon of their own beloved legend. The way they dismissed her was shocking. She had hardly said anything, and already they all had plenty to say.

Merlin glared at David. Why wasn't he defending her? He stood there as though disarmed, while the rest tore her down without one word of defense from his lips.

No wonder she doesn't believe in herself.

Bitterly, Merlin clenched his jaw, suppressing the desire to dash them all to pieces. He pulled Elanor closer into his side, squeezing her shoulders, affirming his place between her and them.

"Now, come on, Jack," David said, clearly aiming to ease the tension. "Let's all go inside and have some supper."

That was it? That was his measly attempt to rein in Jack?

Merlin now had a new level of empathy for Elanor. What would it be like once they got inside? He hoped that at least they would be civil.

The evening light was fading, and the soft yellow glow within the house gleamed as they drew closer to the door. Once inside, the smell of the roast permeated the air, with a hint of cinnamon. Merlin was baffled to find the home warm and inviting. The walls were heavily decorated with multiple colors. The hall was lined with smiling pictures of the Evans family, but Elanor was strangely absent from all of them.

How awful to have spent the entirety of her childhood as an invisible member of a family! Elanor had told him of her family, but now he knew how difficult it had been for her. Even since he had known her, Merlin had watched her struggle with the pain of abandonment, but to see it with his own eyes was revealing.

A stairwell sat at the entrance, with several doors lining the hall. The final door opened into a large kitchen, with a long family table set to dine. Ornaments and portraits of chickens cluttered every open space. Above two glass doors leading out into the back garden were the words, *Family is Everything*. The very idea of the sentiment offended Merlin. So swift had been the introduction. He was firmly aware that the façade was untrue. It couldn't have been that they excluded Elanor and also treated each other with respect. Merlin had lived long enough to see the patterns of human nature.

"Supper will be ready soon," Helen piped. "Go ahead and have a seat. David!" She barked his name like an angry command. "What are you doing? Don't sit. Get out the wine."

"Right, right," David muttered, moving with reluctance to a back cabinet.

Merlin and Elanor took their seats at the table.

"David… no… not that one," Helen chided. "What's wrong with you? The Malbec." She snapped with an audible sigh, placing her hands on her hips. "Nancy, could you please go help your father? Elanor… *darling*"—she flashed an unloving stare—"are you expecting me to serve you? Come and help. You might not have eaten here for some time, but you know what you should be doing."

Elanor's head lowered and her cheeks reddened. She rose from her chair, her eyes darting to Merlin before obediently walking into the kitchen. Merlin's eyes narrowed, watching Elanor pull glasses from a cupboard and fill them in the sink.

Helen scolded, "No, not *that* water—we have filtered in the fridge."

Elanor rushed to obey, changing directions like a small child about to be punished.

Merlin was baffled. What in the world was she doing? He turned and caught Jack smirking across the table at him.

He shrugged. "Welcome to the Evans'. Never a dull moment."

Merlin had a sudden urge to wipe the grin off Jack's face, but he reined in the impulse swelling in his fists. Instead, he gave a stiff nod.

David and Elanor placed the glasses and the wine around the table, as if they were partners in the dinner routine.

"So, you and El, huh?" Jack asked, taking a sip of his wine.

Merlin pressed his lips together, and again, he returned a silent nod.

"How did you meet?"

Everyone paused, eager to hear Merlin's response.

There it was. The question he and Elanor had prepared for.

"We met in a bookshop. Elanor had come in search of a book, and I was there. We talked, and it was like… magic." Merlin winked sideways at Elanor.

She returned a knowing smile as she moved back to the kitchen to collect more things for the table.

"A bookshop," Jack noted with mild interest. "Of course, that's where you met. How fantastically *boring* of you, Elanor."

Elanor shrugged.

"So, you're a loner too, then?" Jack voiced with growing amusement.

David scolded, "Jack!"

"Well, I have definitely had my seasons of hiding away," Merlin said. "Elanor has helped me reconnect to the world."

"Really? Elanor? Huh." Jack glanced at Elanor with skepticism.

Helen and Nancy started bringing platters of food to the table. A fabulous looking roast with carrots, peas, and potatoes. A boat of gravy and a basket of bread on the side. Elanor settled back next to Merlin while David gazed at them with pleasure.

"You seem like a solid young man," David remarked, grabbing some bread. "Any new paintings, Elanor?"

"Heh," Helen scoffed with rancor. "Stop encouraging her, David. Really? The lack of talent. She needs to redirect her focus." She glanced at Elanor matter-of-factly and wagged her finger. "Though I suppose that is all we should expect from her."

"Don't start, Helen." David pointed to her after scooping a forkful into his mouth. "Why do you always have to pick on her? Her art is beautiful."

Helen, Jack, and Nancy snickered under their breath.

What is going on here?

Merlin was dumbfounded as he watched Elanor sit there, picking at her food in silence. He had never seen her this way. He supposed she had gotten used to the mockery, feeling powerless to stop it, but she did not have to take it anymore. She could stand up for herself.

"Her art is beautiful," Merlin chimed in, capturing the attention of the table. "Have any of you really ever looked at it? I find that critical people can always find something to criticize. Keeps people from pointing a finger at them."

Nancy's mouth fell open, and everyone looked to Helen, waiting for her response with bated breath.

Helen picked up her wine and focused her eyes on Merlin. She took a sip. A vile smile stretched across one corner of her mouth. "You've picked one with a backbone," she said to Elanor without shifting her stare. "Tell me, Merlin, what is it that you do? What does someone with such a smart mouth do for a living?"

If only she knew, he mused.

Elanor shook her head and interjected, "You don't have to—"

Merlin gave her arm a reassuring squeeze. He leaned and whispered in her ear, "Trust me." The Evans' eyes lingered upon them; Elanor peered wide-eyed, twisting her napkin over her finger on her lap.

On the drive, Merlin had thought of all the things he could say. He could tout himself up— make them aware of his authority. Really, all he had to do was wave his hand, and the atmosphere would shift. They would all see him for what he was. However, it was better to remain veiled. If they wanted to think he was some sort of foolish child—so be it. He did not need their understanding or respect, but surely, he would give them something to open their eyes a little. Maybe it would shift things for Elanor. Make her brave, or even remind her of who she was.

Merlin cleared his throat and turned to Helen. "I am a storyteller. A singer of sorts."

Nancy sputtered and crossed her arms.

Jack scoffed and shook his head. "A musician? Brilliant! *Well done,* El."

Helen huffed with a smug scowl, as though she had known all along. *Of course, he is a fool,* she spoke with her eyes.

A shadow fell across Elanor's face; her eyes veered down at her plate. Merlin gripped her hand under the table and stroked her knuckles with his thumb. He knew it would be alright. He knew what question would come next.

"So, you are one of those young artistic types who thinks he knows the ways of the world better than anyone else," Helen said, her eyes judgmental. "I know your type. Boys like you make up more than half of my students. I am fortunate enough to help sober them from all their naive arrogance."

David dropped his head in surrender and glanced at his food.

Jack appeared amused, leaning back in his chair, as though ready to stir up the action. "Why don't you give us a song then? *Singer* of sorts."

That was it. The question Merlin hoped would come. He rose from his chair and cleared his throat.

8

THE WARRIOR & THE HAG

"You're really going to stand up and start singing, then?" Jack said, taken aback by Merlin's easy acceptance of his challenge.

Merlin breathed in, then out, intentionally releasing a magical atmosphere. The ambience of his enchantment shifted the room with the grandeur of his authority. The Evans shuffled uncomfortably in their seats and stared at one another, dumbstruck.

"You see, my father gave me a talent to tell stories with song, Jack."

Jack cowered and jostled in his seat, intimidated by the way Merlin spoke.

David, however, leaned forward with a hopeful glint in his eyes.

Merlin waved his hand with a pleased look, observing the effect his magic had on them. Then, he continued softly, "There once were two warriors who both set out on a mission to uncover a relic of great power."

If the Evans wanted to mock him, this would have been their moment. But with Merlin's bardic magic ignited, they were left disarmed and unable to engage. His voice flowed and wove a hypnotic power. The music lifted as his voice rang out and the story commenced.

None of Merlin's songs were ever just a simple melody. Its purpose would be captured, even if a heart was too hard to fully understand.

"The relic, a silver bowl, that sat aloft on a tree branch—hidden atop a mountain. It was said that within the bowl was a magical liquid that replenished each day with morning dew. If found, the elixir healed any ailment, from a broken heart to sickness or even a diseased mind.

"The king of the land longed for it, for he had lost his queen and felt he would never recover from the grief that overwhelmed his heart. He yearned for his own death, but also, he knew that his people needed him.

"'I will search to find the bowl,' a bold warrior declared to the king. The warrior's mind was set on the glory he would receive for such a mighty deed; his name renowned forever.

"Another declared, 'I will also seek it.' However, this warrior thought honorably of the king and kingdom, desiring to restore hope, and the heart of his king. 'What have I to gain,' he said, 'if the king remains broken?'

"The king sent them both into the wilds, and they searched far over lands and mountains—refusing to give up. However, the heart of the first warrior darkened. He brooded about killing the second warrior, so all the glory of finding the relic would be his. But for now, he needed him, as the second was shrewd.

"He also surmised keeping the bowl altogether and never delivering it to the king. Should he find the vessel, he would become powerful—never having to serve another and building his own kingdom.

"One day, the warriors came upon a fortress within the forest, with green towers and people who appeared otherworldly. They offered them food, rest, and guidance.

"'These are scoundrels,' the first warrior said to the second. 'They want to discover our mission and take the bowl for themselves.'

"The second warrior disagreed. 'Hasn't our path led us to them? Maybe it is they that will point us to the proper path. Until now, we have searched in vain and have discovered nothing.'

"'Perhaps,' the first warrior said with a nod, though treachery twisted in his mind. As they dined with the green folk, he reveled maliciously, 'This may be to my advantage.' He set his dark plans into action. While they ate, he leaned into the king's ear. 'This warrior beside me plans to kill you as you sleep.' The king's eyes flared with alarm as he turned to observe the second warrior. 'I will depart during the night and leave him for you to deal with—but only if you can tell me where the silver bowl lies hidden.'

"The green king nodded. 'I do know of this silver bowl, but the path is perilous with dangers along the way. A dangerous giant is lord upon the hill, and there is also a black guardian who challenges those that seek to take the relic.'

"'Tell me the way.'

"'You have not far to go. Only leave the green kingdom and follow the trail set before you up the mountainside.'

"Certain he had cleverly taken the advantage, the devious warrior smiled within his heart. As the moon rose high and all the green folk lay upon the floor asleep, he snuck away, leaving the second warrior to his fate.

"He rode out into the night, up the mountain path. The next morning, he came upon a meadow, alive with fox, deer, and pheasant. Seeing his opportunity, he grabbed up his bow and aimed it at a stag that lay sleeping at the base of a rock in the center of the glen. Out of thin air, a giant uncloaked upon the rock. He rose like a mighty oak, angry and fierce, with a club the size of a tree clutched within his fist.

"'Leave my meadow!' he roared down at the warrior.

"'I must cross your meadow to reach the silver bowl at the top of this mountain.'

"'You are not worthy,' the giant growled. 'Your heart is impure.'

"'Who are you to make such judgements of me, *giant*?'

"'I am the lord of this forest. Cross me, and I will *not* bless you on your path.'

"'I do not need your blessing,' the warrior proclaimed pompously, drawing his bow, and aiming at the giant. 'My path is set before me, and I will take the silver bowl for my own.'

"The giant lifted his club above his head to bring down upon the warrior, but the warrior let loose his arrow. The arrow sailed through the air as the giant faded into a ghostly vapor, and it launched into the heart of the sleeping stag. The deed forced the animals within the meadow to scamper away in panic, and the green light of the forest faded and darkened. Even the ground trembled. The warrior sprinted through the meadow, escaping from the curse as it fell.

"Unhindered, he pressed up the trail to a high, rocky bluff. He climbed with determination, aiming to reach the top before any ramifications from what he had done caught him. As his hand reached the final rock, he pulled himself onto the landing and breathed out with exhaustion. There before him was a twisted, silver, leafless tree, with a bowl cradled in the fingers of its branches.

"A mist descended, surrounding the warrior and the tree within its white, whirling cloud. A dark figure hobbled out toward him and called out, 'Help me! Have you come to help me?'

"He watched as the shadow transformed into an old, ragged hag. She extended her crooked hand to him. The warrior recoiled in disgust. 'Help me' she groaned. 'Save me from the black rider that haunts this place by marrying me; then the bowl will be yours.'

"'Leave me, woman,' the warrior sneered. 'I will fight the black guardian of this hill, but I will *never* marry you. You are old and are worthless to me.'

"The old woman winced at his words and covered her ugly face with her shriveled arm. She cried in anguish as she fumbled away in shame—back through the mist.

"A loud blast, like a chorus of horns, echoed in the distance, and the mist cleared away, revealing a black rider. He sat atop his horse with a sword in his hands. His black clothes, tattered and ripped, tossed in the wind—appearing like a demon and not a man. His helm covered his face, with four spikes rising from the top.

"A seething whisper rose from the dark hole in his helm, 'You are not worthy to face me. You dishonored the green king and lied to him, throwing your companion away into death. You had no respect for the giant and his meadow. You refused to help the woman who cried out for your help. What sort of a man would do this?' A fierce green light lit underneath his helm as he pointed his sword at the warrior. 'A man that will never touch the elixir within the bowl.'

"The words of the black guard seared through the warrior, shaking him with fear. He shouted in his defense, 'I did not know I was being tested.'

"'And so, you should not have known. For only then could your heart have been truly revealed.' The black rider launched toward him, and before the warrior could even lift his sword, his head thudded to the ground, severed from his body.

"The next morning, the second warrior awoke. He found himself lying in a bed of soft linens; a tray of milk and sweet bread rested by his side. Lost, he scanned the unfamiliar chamber, when the king of the green kingdom entered the room.

"'Worry not, fair warrior. You have been blessed with rest for three days. Your journey has been protected, and we have taken your weariness from you.'

"The warrior rose in urgency. 'But my friend—we are on a mission to find the silver bowl. Our king is in dire need of its mercies.'

"'Your friend went on without you, and it is as it should be, for he wanted us to kill you. He had a wicked desire for the relic. But we discerned his lies. Men of impurity cannot pass through to the bowl without the consequences of death. We placed you into a deep sleep so that you would not be compromised by your friend's unrighteousness. You, however, hold others in your heart and desire peace and honor. So, we have chosen to help you. Remember as you follow the path up the mountain: *A man of honor will sacrifice for others and bring healing to all who ask for his help. And always consider that things may not be as they appear.*'

"The second warrior thanked the king and then left to journey up the mountain. When he reached the meadow, it was brown and withered. The trees had lost their leaves, and a deserted, cold wind blew across it. In the center lay a stag with an arrow through its heart.

"Without warning, the giant appeared, already lifting his club to crush the warrior. 'GET OUT!' he roared, shaking the air with his voice. 'Get out of my forest, you destroyer. You destructor.' The warrior rolled to the side as the club came down, nearly smashing him to dust.

"The warrior reached for his sword but noticed tears flowing from the giant's eye. He glanced once more at the stag, its nose resting on the earth. He lifted his hands. 'I do not want to fight you, giant. Nor do I want to cause any more pain.' Cautiously, he moved back and nodded to the stag. 'What has happened here?'

"The giant, disarmed by the question, let his club slide to the ground. The warrior kept his eyes steady on the giant and edged closer to the stag, touching its antlers.

"The giant sighed. 'This stag is the spirit of my meadow, and I am its lord. A warrior like you came and killed him. Before this, my forest was green and full of life. Now it is dead.'

"'I seek the healing liquid within the silver bowl at the top of the mountain. Surely, there would be enough to heal your meadow.'

"The giant wept. 'If you seek to do this, I will bless you on your path.''

"'I will swear to do as much, or my life is forfeit.'

"The great giant nodded and disappeared. The dead leaves blew across the carcass, leaving the warrior to feel the sad emptiness left behind by the first warrior. Resolved, he moved forward up the path. He now had even more purpose in retrieving the bowl.

"As he reached the precipice, he too saw the twisted tree—a silver treasure set alone on the hill. As before, the mist rolled in, and the old hag began to call, 'Help me… Please, have you come to help me?' She neared him, revealing the ugly gray lines on her face and yellow rotten teeth. 'Please,' she cried, 'you must marry me, so that I can be free of the black rider.'

"The warrior gazed beyond, into her eyes, and saw the cursed sorrow. How long had she been there, desperate and crying out, wanting to be free? Maybe she had once been young and beautiful but was now trapped and alone—without hope of rescue. How could he think about himself? He was there to sacrifice for the king who needed his heart healed. He was there to restore the meadow, whose spirit had been destroyed. And now, he could not turn his back on a woman who had been captive by a dark devil.

"'Of course—I will marry you,' he said, 'that you may be set free from this curse.'

"At his words, a loud chorus of trumpets blasted. The black rider who guarded the bowl appeared next to the tree, and a wind blew away the mist. The rider climbed down from his horse and stood before the warrior, who nervously gripped the hilt of his sword.

"'Have you kept this woman a prisoner?' the warrior demanded. 'I will do what I must to set her free.'

"The dark guard removed his black helm and beneath were the kind eyes of the king of the green kingdom.

"The warrior let go of his hilt, his mouth agape.

"The king said, 'You would marry this old, disgusting hag to set her free?'

"The warrior looked compassionately upon the hag. 'I would do so. No innocent, no matter their appearance, should remain cursed.'

"'Then you will marry her now. Come.' The king beckoned the hag to stand beside the warrior.

"The warrior smiled and nodded, holding his hand to help her stand with dignity. The king commenced to marry them on the spot. 'Embrace your bride and kiss her. Then she will be free, and the bowl will be yours.'

"The warrior did not wince but aimed to give her honor and gave her a gentle kiss on the lips. When he opened his eyes, before him stood a beautiful fair maid of the green kingdom.

"The king grew teary-eyed. 'We have been waiting many long seasons for one so worthy as you. We knew you would come to heal these broken lands.' He wiped his eyes. 'This young maid is my daughter, and now she is your wife. She has never been a prisoner, nor has she ever been haggard. It was all an illusion to test the heart, to find a champion whose selflessness could set us all free.'

"The king lifted the bowl from the tree and set it within the warrior's hands. 'You have done all that is required to heal. Drink.'

"'It is not for me to drink. I go to heal the meadow and the king of my lands.'

"'If you only pour the contents upon those with need, it will run dry, but if you drink it, you will carry the power to heal for as long as you live.'

"The princess cupped her hands beneath the warrior's and lifted the contents to his mouth, and he drank until the last drop of dew had been consumed.

"'Now,' said the king, 'my kingdom is yours, and my daughter is your wife. Heal the meadow, and your king, but you must return to take my place. Guard the bowl and protect it from those that would use it for their own gain.'

"So, the warrior returned to the meadow, his wife by his side, and pulled the arrow from the stag. The spirit was restored, the meadow became green, and the giant gladly sat upon his rock to lord over his abundant garden, once again. The king let his grief be lifted and the warrior returned to reign over the green kingdom and guard the life of the silver bowl."

Merlin's song ended, but his magic remained, having fully captured the Evans. When he spoke again, his voice vibrated like an echo that rattled their insides.

"What you have been offered is a chance. Your choice should have been easier, for you were not given a hag but a gift of light. What should be considered are the choices you have made in regard to her. What quality have you shown to be true?"

Their faces were stunned and perplexed. They couldn't understand. What did he mean? His magical words could not be perceived, but the rebuke was full, surpassing their ability to reason. Already the story and the words faded away—they wouldn't remember them, but the effect would remain deeply seeded within their minds.

Merlin took his seat.

Nancy and Helen stared at their plates. David's mouth hung open, his face pale and befuddled.

"What the hell, mate?" Jack said. "That was cracked. My face is numb." He blinked, confused, as if coming out of a trance. He rubbed his cheeks, then started eating again. "Nice voice, though." Between chews, he peered up at Elanor with conviction in his eyes.

The legs of Nancy's chair screeched against the wood floor as she pushed away from the table. She stood, her arms crossed as she glared at Merlin and Elanor before storming out of the room. Her footsteps pounded up the stairs.

"Oh, there she goes. What's her problem anyway?" Jack muttered. "Always throwing fits, that one. She apparently didn't like your song, Merlin. Really, when is she going to grow out of that, Mum? She's almost thirty."

"Leave her be, Jack!" Helen commanded. She cleared her throat. "Well, that was unusual, Merlin. I'm not sure what language that was, but I suppose…" She pressed her brows together. "You've got some talent." She glanced at Elanor through the corner of her eye but seemed afraid to make eye contact.

Merlin knew what he had done: curtailed his beloved's harassment from her own family. He hardly recognized Elanor in her defeated cower, but the song had illuminated her eyes— hopefully reminding her of her strength.

David stared intensely at Merlin with a gleam in his eyes.

He knows something.

9

DAVID'S LETTER

Elanor sat a little taller and reached over to squeeze Merlin's hand. The glimmer in her eyes conveyed she understood what he had done. However, a heaviness still lingered on her face. Merlin hated seeing her placed so far underneath Helen's thumb.

He leaned over and kissed her cheek. "Remember who you are," he whispered.

Helen rolled her eyes at his kiss as if they were both fools.

"Well… I need the loo," David said, wiping his hand on his napkin and standing up from the table.

Helen groaned. "David! Really? Can't you excuse yourself without announcing to us where you'll be going?"

David just shrugged and ambled off through the door.

They all sat in the uncomfortable silence. The sound of their knives and forks scraping their plates magnified tenfold. Elanor glanced around, as though working hard to appear composed, but her hand trembled as she lifted her glass of wine to take a sip.

Finally, David returned, bringing an inaudible but largely felt sigh of relief. Within the fold of his arm, he carried a yellow folder.

"What is that?" Helen asked, with a raised brow.

"Never you mind. What about the pud? Didn't you make an apple tart?" He winked, patting his stomach as he nestled back down in his seat.

"Hm?" Helen said with a dissatisfied look.

"Yah, Mum! Let's have it. More wine too," Jack said, tapping the top of his wine glass.

"How about some tea, Jack," Helen rebuked coolly. "You can drink at the pub with the lads. I'm not pouring more of my nice wine down your wasteful trap."

Jack grumbled, "Fine, tea, then."

Fixing her eyes on Elanor, Helen said, "Well?" Perturbed, she put her hands on her hips. "Father and Jack want pudding and tea."

"Right!" Elanor shot up from her seat. "Do you want me to make the custard or the tea?"

Helen squinted her eyes and pursed her lips at Elanor. Merlin could tell she was pondering whether to strike or concede.

David chimed in. "Elanor, you do not have to do anything. I would be happy to make everyone their tea. Helen, *you* can make the custard. Merlin? Would you like some tea?"

Merlin turned to Elanor. *What is tea?*

Elanor nodded at her father. "Yes, he'll have some."

"How do you take it?"

"Milk and sugar. He likes it with milk and sugar."

Helen glared at David as he ambled into the kitchen and set the kettle to boil. She tsked, then wandered to the kitchen to pull the tart from the warm oven and mix the custard.

"I'll help, Dad," Elanor said, walking to his side. She grabbed the tea from the cupboard. They grinned at each other, shoulder to shoulder, while Helen fumed.

Elanor's exchange with her father pleased Merlin.

"Thick as thieves, those two," Jack indicated with a nod. "Always been that way." He took a sip of his water through his teeth. "How long have you and El known each other? This"—he pointed back and forth between them—"does not seem new."

Jack was perceptive, and Merlin needed to be careful. "It is not."

Jack nodded, pressing his lips. "Huh? How long have you—"

"Stop drilling him with questions," David said, carrying several mugs to the table. Elanor followed close behind with the rest.

Helen brought the tart and a small, white pitcher of custard. Venturing back into the kitchen, she returned with spoons and bowls.

"It looks wonderful," David said, licking his lips with eager eyes.

Jack scooted out from the table. "I'll take mine upstairs. I'm going to watch the match." He glared down at Merlin. "See you later, mate," he growled as if accusing Merlin of something.

"Elanor, Merlin, let's take ours to the back garden. It's a nice night. We have a table and chairs set out there now. Helen has done a beautiful job with the gazebo. It's all lit up and everything."

"Escaping to your garden, David?" Helen sneered from the kitchen.

"You're welcome to join, love."

She waved her hand, grabbed her cup of tea, and wandered out of the kitchen.

David winked. "Right, now we can really have a proper chat."

They shuffled out through the glass doors into the cool air of the garden. Crickets chirped as they settled around a white table with ornate garden chairs, set with red pillows. Over their head, a wooden lattice ceiling hung with a mix of fairy lights and wisteria vines, releasing a pleasant, sweet scent into the night air.

"It just started blooming," David said, pointing to the vines as he plopped into his chair. Grunting, he leaned forward, nodding up at the stars and smiling. "Look, Elanor."

Elanor stared up at the night sky. "I see them." She grinned lightly. "It has been far too long since I peered up at them. Our stars."

"Maybe Merlin could sing us a new story about them, eh? Ah…" David swished his hand. "You're probably too grown up for my silly little tales. There's no need to comfort you from the fear of the dark now." He leaned back, taking a sip of his tea.

Merlin took his first drink of the light brown liquid. It was much nicer than the coffee Elanor had been giving him. "*Now, this* I can drink." He beamed at her.

"Never had tea before, eh?" David asked knowingly. "Don't think there is a single person from Britain that has not had tea." He took another sip from his mug, then smacked his lips and tilted his head. "I know there is more to this story. Come now. I know my daughter. She comes to see me, and her face appears entirely changed. Her eyes—they have been far away all evening." He set his cup down and leaned onto the table, entwining his fingers together. "My family is foolish and did not see it, but I saw what you did in there. I felt the magic in my bones." He lifted his hand into a tense fist. "I used to experience this sort of magic when El was a child. All the time, there was this lil' spark in her blue eyes—golden like flames."

Elanor's eyes widened. She shot a staggered look to Merlin, who was equally astounded.

"You knew I had magic?" Elanor asked, bewildered.

"Eh?" he huffed, waving his hand. "Of course I did. Don't you remember?"

"Remember? You told me that I didn't have magic," she gently accused, an angry spark in her eye.

David winced. "Yes, I did that."

Elanor grew agitated at his confession. "Do you have any idea what that did to me? How it confused me? How much of myself I had to kill to believe that to be true? And… and… I did believe it." Her voice steadily rose. "I… How could you…?"

"I am so sorry, Elanor. But you must understand." David reached out to touch her hand.

Elanor twitched, almost yanking her hand away, but it remained.

"Please forgive me… I did not know what else to do. You know that the people of this world do not believe in those sorts of things. If Helen *ever* caught a glimpse of your magic, she would have had all the grounds to make sure I could not keep you. You were so little. I could find no way of teaching you to hide the magic. I didn't understand it myself. I thought it best if I convinced you it wasn't real. Maybe that wasn't the right choice. All I know is that I did the best I could to protect you. To be your guardian and keep you safe. I was afraid." His head dropped with shame. "It was even hard for *me* to believe any of it was real."

Elanor shook her head, squeezing her eyes shut, as if forcing herself to understand. "Wait, what are you saying?"

David leaned on his elbow and pointed at Merlin. "I have been waiting for him for a very long time."

Merlin furrowed his brow. "For me?"

"But, Dad…" Elanor stammered. "You don't understand."

"No, El… I *do* understand. Or at least I understand a little. I should say, I have been waiting for understanding since the moment I saw you wrapped in a blanket on that stump." He grabbed the yellow folder, looking at it for a moment, and handed it to them. "Look inside."

Merlin nabbed the folder. He opened it, his eyes raced over the parchment, and his jaw dropped.

"What is it?" Elanor asked, leaning over his arm to see.

"This is what I found rolled up and set inside the blanket Elanor was found in." David nodded to Merlin, scooping a bite full of tart with a satisfied air. "I thought it was some ridiculous prank when I first read it. Though the odd style of paper, and even the material of the blanket, was unusual… almost ancient." He pointed with his spoon. "Read it."

Merlin examined the parchment and the familiar style of handwriting. Mystified, he lifted his gaze to meet David's, then lowered to the document. It was a letter—and one written in his own hand.

Squinting with intrigue, Merlin leaned closer to read:

David,

The moment has come that I must leave this small infant in your care. She is called Elanor. She is of high importance, and her life is in danger. She is a princess that must be lost in order that she may never be found. Someday I will come for her, and I will explain all of this. But until that day, you must protect her with your life. This is your destiny.

You do not know me now, but one day you will, and you will tell me of a little boy who dreamed of being a knight. You will tell me of the small wooden knight the boy played with and hoped to one day give to his son. The boy imagined he vanquished dragons—brave enough to give his life to save a princess. This little boy's dream has become real, and this child is the princess he must protect.

She is not from this world and will not be like others. Though one day, it will be the right time for her to return, and she will help me push back the darkness that threatens her. But for now, she is too fragile to abide the evil.

I love her. She is my entire world. I leave her here with you because I know you can be trusted. I have already borne witness to the sacrifices you will make for her.

You will love her, too. Though Helen will not accept her—you must. She was not brought to you by me only—for there is a force much higher than myself that placed her within your arms. All had already been decided long before I wrote this letter, and long before I laid her on this dead tree.

I dreaded taking her away from her broken-hearted mother, but if I do not, she will never return to me. She will never know me. So, it is with great pain that I leave her here for you to find, knowing she will be greatly loved by the white knight who defended her.

Merlin Ambrosias

Merlin fingered the crispy, aged parchment. He stared at the lines within the ink he knew he had written.

I am the one that leaves her?

This *magic of time* stretched Merlin's comprehension and what he imagined was possible. He now understood why most could not handle the dragon's immense magic. His emotions pushed into his chest like needles.

Elanor gasped and curled back into her chair. "Why have you never shown this to me?" Elanor peered at Merlin, shock widening her eyes. "Why didn't you tell me?"

Aghast, Merlin said, "I have yet to even write this letter. I…I wouldn't even know—"

"I have been eager to show you," David interjected, "but I waited. I hoped the day would come that I would meet the Merlin who wrote this letter, face-to-face. I figured it had all been a crazy joke. It had to be. Through all these years, I wondered how the writer could have known of my childhood dream. I had told no one."

David pulled a small wooden knight, painted white, from his pocket. "I did not dare believe so many things about the letter, but there was a part of me—the child part—that hoped it would somehow be true.

"It was the child in me, as I lifted that baby girl into my arms, that drove me to decide I would keep her safe no matter what. I held her… and her blue eyes looked into mine. I wanted to protect her. I thought I had gone mad to stubbornly insist on adopting her. Even though I struggled to believe the words of that letter—I could not refuse them either.

"Elanor, when your magic began to spark, something inside me started to believe. We… we tried to find your parents," he said. "We tried to find any evidence of where you had come from, because it wasn't rational to believe you had come from another world."

His next words were tentative and apprehensive. "Are you? Are you from another world?" His eyes danced back and forth between them. "I have rehearsed what I would say at this moment for so many years. I had the letter set with the white knight, just so, in my top drawer, ready to grab should Merlin come knocking at my door. I"—he laughed—"I expected an old man."

Elanor stared at her father, her mouth agape. "Of course you did." She shook her head incredulously. "Father? I can't believe this. This… this is extraordinary."

"Please, I have been waiting all these years." David looked to Merlin, his eyes beseeching. "Tell me. I want to know where my little girl came from."

Elanor reached over and took the letter from Merlin. She read it again, her eyes scanning every line. Merlin sat back, combing his hands through his hair as it all sank in.

Merlin would bring me here? Elanor wondered.

She felt she could no longer deny her birthright. David's revelation seemed to piece together the puzzle of her existence. Her doubt surrounding her Pendragon lineage melted away. This was the secret that had kept her identity-less, and in an instant, her whole life began unlocking.

Pulling herself back down to earth, she said, "Everyone thinks Merlin is supposed to be old. I remember thinking that." She glanced up from the letter and looked at her father.

"So…" David started. "Are you *the* Merlin? King Arthur? The roundtable?"

"I don't know of a round table," Merlin said, "but, yes. Elanor has told me there are legends of us here. Though the truth may be nothing like you have heard."

"Wait…" David leaned forward, shaking his head. "So, what does this mean? How are you here? How is Elanor here? How did you write that letter, yet you sit before me so young?"

"Dad," Elanor interjected, "this is far more complicated than you know."

"I am sure it is. I have waited years for someone to tell me I have not been crazy. That I haven't waited in vain with this stupid little knight." He got up, letting the figure roll from his fingers onto the table.

Elanor picked it up. "This was yours when you were a little boy?"

David nodded with pleasure. "I was going to be that knight. I was going to grow up and go on a quest to save the princess. Slay the dragon and sit with the king."

Elanor observed the details on the small knight. He looked like a medieval chess piece. He had a round helm and white armor, with a tiny sword that had been chipped. He held a shield with a traditional coat of arms etched into it—a crest of three stars on one side and stripes on the other.

"These kind of knights do not exist where I am from," she said after a moment. "Or at least they won't exist for another few hundred, or more years." It felt right to say it that way. Always, she had been the forgotten girl, and then she was the girl from a future time. But now, her heart soared—she now knew where she had come from.

David's eyes grew wide.

"I am from the past," Elanor continued. "Not another world, just an older one. Probably fifteen hundred years in the past." She knit her brows together as she considered what to say, pulling her mouth to the side. "Dad…" Elanor sighed. "I have only just come back. I have been back in my world, with Merlin, for over four years."

David stared at her, awestruck. After a long, speechless moment, he muttered, "I knew you had changed. This… This is unbelievable."

"Merlin is not my boyfriend either. He is my husband… and we have a daughter. She is—" Elanor gasped, gulping down the rising tide of emotions. Desperation fluttered in her heart to resolve the separation of time so she could hold her daughter again.

Merlin placed an affirming hand on her shoulder. "We will get back to her, I promise."

She gave a hesitant nod, composing herself. "She is getting so big. Soon she will be three."

"What?" David tossed his head back. "I am gob-smacked! I cannot believe this. I mean…"

Elanor watched as her father wrestled with the logic, his eyes darting between them.

"I know this is a lot to take in. If I had not experienced it myself, I would think it all mad. But I think"—Elanor turned to Merlin for approval, and he nodded—"that this would all be much easier if I showed you."

"What do you mean?"

"Give me your hands—I have a gift. This will help a lot of it sink in, but there is much to show you."

David was both apprehensive and excited as he took hold of Elanor's hands. Within an instant, Elanor showed him the dreams and how she had arrived in Prydain. The sights and sounds of Caer Lial, the Palisade, and the Great Hall. Elanor's heart ached, yearning for Gwendolen, Adhan, and Gwynevere as she revealed their faces. She couldn't separate who they were as she showed him their blessed faces. Oh, how she longed to be back with them. Cilaen and Bedwyr—her friends. Her memories jumped to when she and Merlin stood beside Brynn, waiting to ride out to the village where the young girls had been plagued with dark magic.

She began to lose herself in the memory, taking David along with her.

Merlin caressed her hand. She was hesitant to leave Gwendolen and Caer Lial. She didn't know that when she kissed her daughter's round cheeks in the dark hours of that morning, she would be separated from her through time—separated from them all. As Merlin kissed her, it did not alleviate the foreboding that invaded her spirit. Still, she pulled herself up onto the saddle and prepared to leave.

Had she known that what they were about to walk into was a trap, she may never have gone. The constant dream of the arrow piercing through her back had been a warning all along, but she did not see it coming until the trap had actually been set.

Merlin yelled, "Run!" Panic rushed through her as she dashed toward the forest on her horse—Bedwyr right behind her. She saw him charging for her, just before Merlin sent her running. She glimpsed over her shoulder to see the terror in Merlin's wide eyes. She didn't even have a chance to turn around before she was struck by what felt like a hammer slamming through her chest—hurtling her through the air and onto the ground.

The impact knocked the wind from her, and she laid on the ground in utter shock. The world spun as the stamping horses whinnied and warriors' voices faded into the background.

Bedwyr charged past her. She wanted to reach for him—yell for him, but she had no voice.

Merlin's strong arms scooped her up, sending searing pain from her chest down into her toes.

His eyes—his eyes were so sad. She was trying to hang on—to stay connected to him. His desperate cries muffled in her ears. She didn't want to be taken from him. She wanted to stay, but it was hard to fight as her blood drained and her body numbed. Merlin's face went in and out of focus. She reached to touch him and pull him close.

Cilaen was there. Why didn't he come closer? Why didn't he touch her? Then everything went quiet. She could only hear her heart beating as everything slowed. She focused on Merlin's eyes and traced his mouth. It was just the two of them, and she knew she was dying.

Then a spark! She felt it rise out of her spirit. A memory of her flat in the city, and Merlin there to meet her. That's when she knew. The magic of time moved through her, and she didn't resist. The desperation of the moment melted away. Everything was going to be alright. Flames. White flames flared around her, and everything faded into darkness.

Ripping her fingers from David's grasp, Elanor grabbed her chest, heaving. The memory was so vivid, she lost her breath. Her power to share memory was potent this time. The mixture of the dragon's obscure magic with her own made it hard to differentiate.

Merlin reached for Elanor, knocking her cup of tea from the table. The mug smashed into pieces on the cement. "Are you alright?"

Elanor's head spun, but she forced herself to say, "Y-yes!"

David slumped forward, his face in his hands.

"David?" Merlin asked.

Taking a deep, labored breath, David began to weep.

MIDNIGHT ESCAPE FOR ARTHUR

"Dad?"

David held up his hands.

"I am sorry if I showed you too much. I have a hard time controlling how deep the memories go sometimes, and this time it was… unusually intense." Still breathing heavily, Elanor turned to Merlin. "The dragon's magic."

David murmured, "I am just forcing myself to take it all in. I… I just…" His red eyes glistened. "I just saw you die. My own breath was stolen from my chest." He winced as more tears streamed down his face. "I saw your daughter… She's beautiful."

He covered his face in his palm, muffling his voice. "How have you come back here? How is Merlin here?" He dropped his hand from his face, and his sorrowful eyes rested on his daughter. "We must get you back to them… and…" David scrunched his face. "What is dragon's magic?"

Elanor touched David's hands. "That white fire you saw, that was the magic of time. It was given to Merlin and me… by a dragon."

"Dragons? Really?" David's eyes rounded in disbelief.

Elanor nodded. "It's a lot to understand—I know. Let's just stick to the fact that we are here because of that magic. When that magic came, I was dying, and somehow it sent me through time—and Merlin also. When I arrived, I was no longer wounded. I was well." She placed her hand on her chest and glanced down, still in wonder.

"Can you not go back?"

Merlin leaned in. "We do not fully understand how the magic works. We cannot just *will it* to send us home, and… we believe there is still purpose in us being here. We hope once we have completed our task, the magic will lead us back home."

"What purpose?" David asked as he wiped his face and composed himself.

"Dad… I am sorry if we have shown you too much. This has distressed you."

David burst from his seat and pulled Elanor up into his arms. "My little girl," he cried.

Elanor tucked her head into his shoulder. Tears formed. David cradled Elanor into his chest. "I knew you were special. I knew it. I cannot imagine what it must have been like for you, all these years with us idiotic people. How Helen has abused you!"

"I am happy I was with you," she mumbled into his arms.

"I saw her…" David said, pressing his chin into the top of her head, and kissing it. "Your mother. At least I think that is who she was. I could feel it as you showed me her face. Who is she? Do you know your father?"

His question stung Elanor. Her heart leapt into her throat, and she turned away. She didn't want to tell him. She didn't want him to know. David was her father. He had been the one who raised her.

"Did I say something wrong?"

Merlin shook his head. "No, you did not."

"Elanor? What is it?"

"My mother," Elanor said, still facing away—her chin trembling, "is the queen. She is Gwynevere."

David's jaw dropped. "Gwynevere? As in Arthur's Gwynevere? Does that mean…?"

Elanor spun around. "YES!" she yelled. "Arthur is my father." She clenched her fists to her side and gritted her teeth. A tear rolled down her cheek. She didn't know why the admission angered her. Maybe it was all the built-up anxiety from anticipating her visit with the Evans.

Before she'd read Merlin's letter, she was still doubtful she had any true claim to the past, but now she was thrust into that reality. The paradigm shifted so fiercely; her emotions triggered. It had always been her with the Evans, and then her with Merlin in Prydain. Now, it felt like those worlds were colliding.

Merlin gripped Elanor's hand, and her tension crumbled. She fell back into her chair.

With a somber stare, David's gaze returned to the stars.

"She has not met him—Arthur, I mean," Merlin said. "He is here. That is our purpose. That is why we are still here. He was cursed to sleep for a thousand years, and now we are here to wake him and take him back home. If Arthur does not return to the Prydain of our time, Elanor will never be born."

David sputtered and turned to them. "So, this is why you need my mapping skills?" With a deep exhale, he knelt before Elanor, putting his hand on her knee. "Sweetie," he soothed, "none of this is computing in my old brain, but…" He sniffed, grabbing up the wooden knight and setting it into Elanor's hands. "I have been your guardian since the moment I saw that sweet little bundle. I haven't always been a perfect father, but I have loved you and always sought to do exactly what Merlin had written down in that letter. This is my destiny… right, Merlin?"

Merlin smiled and gave an affirming nod.

"Now," David said, pulling himself up to stand, "I will need to get my maps."

David returned with books and a pile of maps and laid them out on the table. He took one map off the top, unfolding it.

"There," he said, rubbing his hands across the map to smooth it out. "Let's start with a map of Britain."

Elanor scanned the map, leaning against her folded arms.

"Ah. There," she said, tapping her finger on the map near Carlisle. "This is where I think Caer Lial would have been. The Hill of the Kings would be near Caer Lial, right?"

"Yes—just south toward the mountains."

David said, "In Cumbria?"

Elanor nodded.

"South of Carlisle would be the lake districts of the Cumbrian Mountains—within the Whinlatter Forest. Is this where you think it might be?"

Merlin pursed his lips at the map, uncertain. The shape of the area seemed correct. He pointed to an island off the coast and dragged his finger along the map, tracing to where the location of the Caer would have been.

"That is the Isle of Man," David said.

"Avalon," Merlin mumbled, his eyes focused on the map.

"Right!" David jumped with excitement. "Many have said that Isle might have been Avalon in the times of legend."

Elanor's eyes sparkled at her father's enthusiasm.

"The Hill of the Kings was not far from the Caer. It was slightly south, and then west. There is a range of mountains that leads to the base of a lake… then another mountain here." Merlin drew his hand west. "And it was nestled within this area of land. In our time, there would have been a well-traveled road that led to it."

"Well," David said, pulling out more of his maps and opening one of his books. He put on a pair of glasses to analyze the area and bit his bottom lip as he followed the gridlines. "Fifteen hundred years ago? Phhhfff!" He rummaged through his maps once more, then picked up his mobile with a flustered brow. "This might not be as difficult as I thought. The landscape has changed, but this particular northern region has remained more wild. Though it will be quite the drive to Cumbria—we will need to leave early."

"No—Dad, you're not coming."

"Heh." David chuckled, raising his brows. "It's foolish to think you could navigate these plains without my help. We will likely be searching off trail. That's really where my expertise kicks in."

Elanor shot a worried gaze at Merlin.

"David, we appreciate your willingness to come, but if you could just give us your knowledge, we will find it."

"No, my directions will not be enough. I know how to navigate the forest."

Merlin leaned back, folding his arms. "I have lived on wildlands my entire life. I am not out of my depth."

"Oh, but you are. Think soberly for *one* moment. These lands have changed, and this is not the world you know. I have a history of maps that will help guide us—a little." His confidence revealed a hint of doubt. "This will not be an easy task."

"Dad, you don't understand."

"What don't I understand?" David snapped. "Since we started this conversation, you have told me, time and again, how little I understand. But apparently, I have tracked this far."

Merlin gave David a grim stare. "There is no way to know what our enemy might look like in this world. In our time, we have been vehemently opposed. You saw. In Elanor's memory, they aimed to kill her—kill us. I cannot believe that there would not be dangers here also. Our enemy would know for many generations that the day would come when we would awaken Arthur. I hoped that maybe we could sneak through this world without the enemy's awareness, but already we have encountered a disturbing warning."

"What warning?" David asked worriedly.

"Dad," Elanor pleaded gently, "I could not risk something happening to you. Please, let us do this alone."

David grunted, looking down at his maps. "This"—he winced with a heavy sigh—"this is what I have been waiting for my whole life. When I found you in that stump, it was as though the stars had aligned. My whole reason for existing has been to find you and protect you. How can I sit back and just wave 'good luck'—sending you on your way? No! I won't do it."

He smacked the table with his palm and shot a finger at Merlin. "Merlin is living and breathing in front of me. I have a chance to be a knight." He stopped, considering his next words. "This is my quest. My destiny." His final words, they all knew, he was desperate to believe were true.

"But... Dad—"

David slammed his hand against the table again. "Damn it all, Elanor!" He sighed, unable to contain his emotions. "I can help you, and I *will* help you. Maybe you could find this place. This Hill of the Kings—if it even still exists—without my help. Maybe you could... But let me do what I can. Give me a chance. I could truly be a king's man." He laughed softly, as if lost in his own thoughts. "Seeing Arthur, the king of all British kings. What a thing that would be."

He thrust his thumb toward the house. "I am just a joke to them. Always have been, and that has mostly been my own fault. But to you, I have always been more." He pushed the maps to the side and grabbed up the letter. "Merlin trusted me. The Merlin who wrote this letter knows me better than the Merlin that sits in front of me now. He called me out to protect you, and I want to follow through to the fullest extent. Please."

"Elanor?" Merlin asked gently.

"Alright," she said, rolling her eyes. "After that speech, I doubt I could stop you even if I wanted to."

David leaned forward and placed his hands on Elanor's shoulders. "As a father, I have failed you in many ways. But this..." He shook his head. "Not this. Here I will not fail. It is not your job to keep me safe, but it is mine to protect you. I chose that years ago."

Merlin searched David's earnest face and had a newfound respect for him. "You are a man of quality, David."

"Well, then, we must prepare to leave."

Elanor leaned forward, perplexed. "Now?"

"I can pack us some food. Helen will not be bothered with us for the rest of the evening, so now is the time to slip away unnoticed. If we leave soon, we will arrive in the early morning. That should give us loads of time." David turned to Elanor. "You go pull the car closer to the garden shed. I have lanterns and some camping equipment in there. But do it quietly. I don't want the family to start asking questions about our activities. What have you brought with you?"

Elanor shrugged. "Not much. Mostly clothing and a little bit of food."

David sighed. "See, already you are going to be better off with my help. I will grab up some mats and sleeping bags. Now, quietly."

"Dad, this might take a few days. Won't Helen be worried for you?"

"Nah. I'll leave her a note. She'll think you left to go back to the city. I would be getting up early to go back to the uni in the morning anyway. Sometimes I stay in the town all week for my classes. She won't expect me."

In the upstairs sitting room, the football match blared. Jack tried to focus his eyes on the TV screen. Anger festered in his thoughts. Merlin had stuck his fingers where they didn't belong. His eyes threatened Jack. His very presence wrecked things, shifting them out of their proper place. He wasn't sure why this was even a problem for him, but he didn't like it—and couldn't settle because of it.

Seeing how much Elanor had changed also bothered him. She still cowered like a little imp, but he could tell she was different. Confidence sparked in her eyes, and her face had strength in it.

Jack liked to harass her. It was what the family did, but he didn't hate her. In fact, sometimes he liked having her around. Sometimes he even loathed how his mom and sister treated her, but he couldn't seem to change, or stop. This was how it had always been.

It's because she doesn't belong, he brooded, switching the channel. The match had been crap, so he searched for something else to occupy his mind. *She needs to be reminded that she is not an Evans. She isn't. She came to live with us, and all Dad cared about was her. I could be the best footballer in Britain and still he wouldn't look at me like he looks at her. It's not fair. I should not have to compete with someone who isn't really my sister.*

Jack pressed the off button on the remote and threw it down onto the sofa. "There is nothing but rubbish on the tele, anyway." He got up, letting out an exasperated sigh before grabbing his cup and heading for the kitchen for more tea. The slam of car doors outside the window stopped him in his tracks.

Probably just El and her crap boyfriend leaving. Good riddance, Jack thought as he moved to the window.

Red lights beamed as Elanor's car backed up to the shed. He grimaced, spying closer into the yard.

"What the…?" Jack's curiosity piqued as he watched his dad exit the house with two packs loaded over his shoulder and a sleeping bag hanging by strings from his fingers. He began loading the car, and Jack's brows deepened into a scowl.

What's Dad doing? Borrowing them some things?

Jack could hear the faint jingle of keys as his dad opened the shed. The three hauled more supplies out of the shed.

What in the world are they doing?

Their haste alarmed Jack. Clearly, they were on a mission.

What the hell is going on?

His dad walked back into the house, and Jack had the mind to go down and ask him what exactly was going on. He hesitated, watching Elanor and Merlin, who at that very moment were locked in an embrace. Then they kissed.

"Bloody hell," he cursed with disgust.

He scowled into his empty cup and started toward the kitchen, but hasty movement outside the window caught his eye. His father had returned with mats and more sleeping bags underneath his arms.

Jack dashed back to the window's ledge. His mouth dropped. His father had climbed into the car with Elanor and Merlin.

Where the hell is he going? Why is he—

Putting his hand on the window as they pulled away, Jack's lips curled against his clenched teeth. He stared out the window as their rear lights disappeared from the drive.

"This will *not* do," he growled. He stepped back, incensed. He didn't want tea anymore. His mum would have to deal with a bottle of her *fine wine* going missing. He needed a stiffer drink than tea. Unbeknownst to him, his thoughts opened a door, and a dark, familiar spirit seethed into Jack's heart.

11

NO TRESPASSING IN CAMBRIA

Elanor slept in the back of the car, leaving David at the wheel. Merlin's restless eyes watched the white lines on the road until he noticed David's sudden gaze. With a tight swallow, Merlin relaxed his shoulders and breathed out a long sigh.

"We'll find it," David said, biting into his lower lip. "The Hill of the Kings."

"We must. If we cannot find where Arthur has been laid to rest, I wouldn't know how else to find him. I am certain that this is why we are here." The past weighed heavily on Merlin. How would they get back home? Even if they found the spot where Arthur had been buried, how would they get to him? Layers of earth likely covered the hill. "At least in Prydain I knew how to navigate the unknown. Here I am without wisdom on our path."

"That's why you have me." David thumbed to himself and sported a grin.

Merlin gave a light laugh. "Yes, I suppose you are right." He glanced out the window. "It looks like colored stars."

"Oh, the city lights?" David nodded. "It must be odd for you, all this."

"I am trying to take it all in stride. My one relief is seeing how unstrained Elanor seems in all this strange… 'science,' as she calls it. In Prydain, she was so resilient, but even after four years, it still has been hard for her to feel natural. Here she whisks from one thing to another without stress. Though I have never seen her more unlike herself than I did in your home. Each word spoken against her made her dwindle. In Prydain, she is brave and she holds her head high." Merlin turned back to the window with a harsh stare. "Why do you let them tear her down like that?"

David's shoulders slumped.

Merlin knew that look of shame floating in David's stare.

David shot Merlin a quick glance from the corner of his eye, then focused back at the road. "I didn't intend to bring her up in such hostility. I have no excuse. I feel horrible how hard I worked to squelch her magic. I was so hard on her. I could see it crushing her spirit." He sighed, lifting his gaze to the rear-view mirror. "Helen…

refused to adopt her. In order to keep my marriage, I became a coward. Though I remained adamant that Elanor not be turned away. I tried to comfort myself with knowing that she at least had a home. However, I often questioned whether she wouldn't have been better off with a family that wanted her."

He broke off, squeezing the steering wheel in his hands. "But I wanted her. Maybe I was selfish; keeping her when I knew that my family had rejected her. Maybe I am selfish to help her now. Maybe it was just my own need to feel important." Guilt lined David's forehead.

Merlin's own guilt pricked as David spoke. He remembered the moments when he chose to keep her close when he could have let her go.

"I am not sure I could have made another choice," David continued. "I am not sad to have loved her and to have gotten to see the spark in those blue eyes every day as she grew. She and Brando delighted my heart as they pranced around the back garden. Her laughter, so bright. My other children could have chosen to love her, but my wife poisoned them against her. Was that my mistake, or should Helen be blamed? I don't know…

"That song you sang…of the two warriors." David exhaled sadly. "Maybe what I am doing now is seeking the healing silver bowl above all else. Not for selfish gain, but for love. Though I know within myself it is all mixed up. But sometimes you must take the ugly to be worthy." He looked at Merlin. "Why couldn't my family understand the words you sang, but I could?"

Merlin considered David's question. "The Cymry people of my world have learned to position their hearts to receive the words of a bard. When a bard's magic is refused, however, it becomes indecipherable. It is confusing and unclear to unreceptive ears. They can feel the magic, the intended effect is still released, but they do not comprehend. A bard's aim is to prophecy, teach, convict, and even inspire. To an open heart, the bard's words enliven, but a closed heart is often offended. Your family felt accusation instead of conviction. They may not have been able to understand my words, but it still shut their mouths." He faced David. "Your heart received me, so it strengthened you, helping you reason in earnest."

"Hm? It reminds me of the parables I was taught in Catholic school as a boy—about seeds falling on hard ground."

Elanor roused in the back seat. She rubbed the sleep from her eyes and sat up. Looking out the window, she stretched her tired muscles. "Where are we? Is there a leisure station coming up soon? I think I might need the toilet."

"I could definitely use some tea," David said with a smile. "It's almost five. The sun will be rising soon, and I think the car will need some petrol, anyway."

Elanor yawned. "After we stop, I could take over for a while if you need to sleep."

"Maybe a few winks would do me good." David arched his back, stretching.

They found a station some twenty minutes later, just as the sky gradually turned blue. The early morning still made the lights of the leisure station harsh and intrusive. Elanor ran into the building, leaving Merlin to follow along after David. Inside the station's quiet atmosphere, Merlin saw a few people scattered along the benches and tables. All of them listless; awaiting the sun to rise. The air inside was odd with a lingering stale smell. A dully lit café flickered, with a man drooping behind the counter.

"I'll get us some tea," David said, then ambled over to the café.

Elanor came out from a bright hallway, shaking her hands dry. "This has to be so strange." She smiled, curling her arms around Merlin's waist as he leaned against the scummy wall. "Honestly, it has become strange to me too. I used to be so familiar with these places, but it's been so long since I've been amongst all this… this"—she waved her hand at a loss for words—"convenience." Elanor chuckled. "I am glad that Dad is here, though. I still can't believe all these years, he… sort of… knew. Still having a hard time believing that he is with us, ready to go on a quest to find Arthur. It's bonkers."

Merlin smiled. "Bonkers?"

"Heh—crazy. Mad. Insane." Elanor glanced up at Merlin, and a serious look passed over her face. "So, you really think we will find the Hill of the Kings—that we aren't wasting our time on a wild goose chase? I mean…" She inhaled sharply. "It seems an impossible task."

"We must have some level of faith that destiny is leading us. I mean, just think," Merlin said, nodding over at David at the café, "how your father waited all those years with a letter. And now we are here. I'd rather be a fool and discover there is nothing to be found than have turned my back on the possibility that Arthur is waiting for us. If the Hill of the Kings cannot be found—maybe it will lead us to other clues."

David returned, precariously balancing three cups of tea and a few bags of crisps in his arms. "Ready?" he asked, offering the tea. "They didn't have much, so I got some of these. We can eat when we get closer to the town. I am sure we'll be able to find breakfast. Probably only an hour or two more to Carlisle. From there we will be able to get a view of the mountains. The mountains themselves would not have changed as dramatically as the landscape below them."

They drove on as the sun rose, brightening the sky and the view. Mountains peaked up, purple and bold around them.

"Stop!" Merlin shouted.

Elanor pulled the car over to the side, and he jumped out of the car. Elanor was quick to follow after him.

"We are not quite to Carlisle," David said, tripping over himself as he scuttled out of the car.

Merlin pointed. "Those mountains." He drew Elanor over to his vantage point. "Those two peaks. The one sharp peak. Look at it."

Elanor squinted at the jagged top. Recognition rushed over her. "Of course. Caer Lial would have been on the other side to the east."

David pulled one of his maps from the car and unfolded it onto the hood. Then he grabbed his mobile and inputted their coordinates. "Those are the Blencathra

Mountains." Excitedly, he waved them over to look where he was pointing. "So, you think Caer Lial would have been located…"

Merlin focused his eyes on the map before returning his gaze to the mountains.

"We are on this side of the mountain." David tapped on the map.

"Caer Lial would have been here." Merlin drew his finger west. "And… this is the direction that the Hill would have been. Within these mountains. There would have been a lake."

"There still is. If this is correct, we would be heading in this direction." David gestured to the other side of the road. "More toward the Keswick and Skiddaw Mountains. How close to the lake would the Hill have been?"

"It would have been off from the lake and deeper in, between some hills. There would have been a road leading between them into an open landscape."

"Look at this." David opened some images on his mobile, tilting his screen for Merlin to see. "This is Bassenthwaite Lake." He swiped to display another picture. "Here is the lake from different angles. Does any of this look familiar?"

Hope rose in Merlin as he stared at the pictures. The hills and mountains did appear marginally familiar. Though the land used to be more heavily wooded, with fewer open plains. If this was the same lake he had known, its shape had also shifted. It was at this lake where Arthur had received Excalibur. Merlin's heart warmed as he remembered.

The lake's shore was lined by trees and surrounded by forest along the perimeter. Merlin and Arthur had stopped, exhausted, to water the horses and lay underneath the shade of the pine. The sword that Arthur had wielded, Aurelius's sword of kingship, had been shattered. Arthur was despondent—unable to believe it was truly his birthright to take the throne without the sword.

He and his Cymbrogi had won the battle, vanquishing the Saecsan hoard that terrorized the western shores. He had done it. He had overcome, conquering the unconquerable. But his final strike broke the sword that named him king. Now here he was, on a pilgrimage with Merlin, with only a jagged stub attached to a hilt in his sheath. It was at that moment when the beautiful, gentle song of a maid came ringing through the trees. Gliding closer in a small boat upon the lake was the king of the fair folk. He was a king of a lost kingdom—his people dispersed and faded. Wounded, the Fisher King approached them.

Merlin was shaken out of the memory when Elanor asked, "Is this where we should search for the Hill?"

David pointed down at the map again. "This angle of the lake would be on the west side of the Skiddaw Mountains."

"It is not the same," Merlin remarked, "but these hills look like they could be the right ones."

"Right," David said. "Then there is no need to go all the way to Carlisle. Let's go toward Keswick."

Piling back into the car, they drove until they arrived at the long, wide lake appearing on their right.

"This seems a good spot," David said to Elanor. "Let's see if we can tuck the car back around this railway a bit. That way, hopefully, we won't get ticketed. This is definitely not a proper place to park."

They got out of the car, and crossed the road; a rail blocking their entrance onto the green read, *No Trespassing.*

David shrugged. "Well, let's load up the packs. I have a feeling by Merlin's description, we will have some ways to go. Probably need to bring our equipment."

With packs hoisted, they climbed over the rail, ignoring the sign. They went on through the field of green toward the two mountainous hills looming before them. From where they started off, it looked as though the hills were squeezed tightly together, but as they trekked forward through the pasture, the way opened wider. Large, gray boulders lay scattered across the hills like sleeping guardians. As they entered the valley, a darkened evergreen forest slumbered between the two hills.

The deeper they hiked, the more Merlin questioned their path. Nothing was the same, though the smells of the wild forest did spur nostalgic memories of home. He scanned the ground for anything that reminded him of the places he used to know, but with little evidence of familiarity, discouragement pressed in.

As David traipsed forward, undeterred, Elanor shot a worried glance over her shoulder at Merlin, who had stopped his march. He faced where the road had been. They spent a couple hours on a constant trek deep in the woods, and the sun now crossed the middle of the sky. If they were going to turn back, this was the moment.

"Thinking of heading back?" David shouted. "Look." He dropped his pack to the ground and rifled through it. "I have a tool that will help us know where we are."

Merlin sighed, glancing around with uncertainty. "These hills were the most familiar. Even as I recall the landscape you showed me, there was not another place around the lake that would have been right. Perhaps this is not even the right lake. Can we keep walking without a sign? It seems like we should have spotted some clues by now."

"What if we give up just as we are about to find it?" Elanor pressed.

"I say we keep searching this area," David said firmly. "We have food and supplies to camp. We are far enough in that no one will bother us for being here." He studied his map and his device. "We have not gone off track from where you thought the Hill might be found." Sighing, he slumped to the forest floor, returned his supplies back into his pack, then pulled out some food.

"Here." He tossed a sandwich at Merlin, and another to Elanor. "We'll think more clearly with some food. Sorry, they're a little smashed."

"I am not getting a sense of anything," Merlin growled, frustrated. He hunkered down and unwrapped his sandwich.

"Dad, how far do you think we have gone?"

"Well, according to my GPS, we are a good eight kilometers from the road."

"Gosh!" Elanor said, taking a bite of her sandwich as she examined the forest around her. Massive hills rose with pointed trees on their right and left. She turned a quizzical look to Merlin. "Have I been to the Hill before? Why have you not gone to see it? In all the years I have been in Prydain, I have never known you to visit it. I haven't even known Gwynevere to seek it out."

As she asked the question, the scent of disappointment and grief floated into Merlin's soul. He had avoided visiting the Hill. His eyes had not graced the cairn since Aurelius. Not even when Uther was laid to rest there. Stones had been lifted for each of them. Beside the Hill, a second hill had been constructed after the Battle of Camlan for all of Arthur's men. King Ector—Cai, Gwain, Bors, and Gwalahad would have all been buried there. Merlin had not seen any of them buried. Instead, he ran away, honoring none with his presence. The memory of his grief still haunted him; he wished he could reverse time and see their faces again.

He still was unable to face the guilt of his absence at their burial. He longed to see the circling stones that honored each of them, but he also wanted to forget it—in hopes time would somehow relieve him from ever having to look.

"It has been eight years," Merlin breathed, "since Arthur left us. And yet, the thought of the loss never eases. The hope that we might have Arthur back with us lessens that pain, but not the agony of all the others lost at Camlan. They will not be returning. I will never see the luster of Cai's wild smile again, nor the strength and god-like perfection in the swing of Gwain's arm." Merlin's eyes fell to his lap as his chin tightened. "It is still more than I can bear." His face reddened, and he swallowed down the rising emotion.

"To hear such legendary names," David uttered, "spoken from your lips is a privilege. To think they all existed. Such mighty men."

David's statement brought a smile to Merlin's face. "That they were."

"Well." David rose to his feet. "Let's keep going. We should go as far as we can before the sun starts setting."

Elanor stood, taking a final gulp of water before jamming it back inside her pack. And once again, they were off, through the pointed pines that seemed endless.

All at once, the space between the hills widened, and the trees became sparse. Soon, a large plateau rose before them. The mountains and hills surrounded the opening like giants bowing down in a circle, with the smaller plateau settled in the center. It was much larger than the hill would've been in Merlin's time, rising high, with evergreens covering it. The mound sloped and rose to a plateau, and then up again to a second elevated plain.

Merlin's heart leapt. It appeared completely changed, but it was right where the Hill of the Kings would have been. His pack rattled as he picked up his pace. David and Elanor followed directly behind him. The closer they got, the more his head tossed, fretfully searching for anything that remained of the stone cairns. Their path was inlaid with gray rock, but the stones of a cairn would have a distinctive look. Might they have lasted through time?

Sure enough, as they got closer, Elanor shouted, "Look!" She ran over to three long stones. Two laid on the ground, while one remained standing. She placed her hand on the upright one and rubbed her fingers across the ogham lines that were barely visible—worn down through time.

Merlin sighed, and a smile spread across his cheeks. "This is it. It must be." Not far from the long stones was a pile of rocks, shaped in a cylinder that domed at the top. "The cairn!" With a swift turn, his eyes glanced up the hill. "It would not have been such a large hill back in our time. The ages have covered it and raised it higher. There would have been a second hill. They have likely become one." Putting down his pack, he started climbing the hill.

Elanor quickly followed, and soon all three of them had left their packs behind and climbed to the top of the hill with a newfound strength. Halfway up, they discovered more remains of what used to be cairns. Some half standing, others toppled onto the ground. They reached the top, and there, as they caught their breath, was a circle of thin stones. Eight of them, standing strong.

"Eight." Merlin's face grew somber. "The Hero's Mound—all of them would be buried here."

"They're not all gone yet," Elanor said, laying her hand upon his back. "Time is telling us they have all passed, but Bedwyr and Peredur still remain. They are still with us. Gwynevere and Cilaen, also. Gwendolen. Your mother."

Merlin placed his hand upon the first of the stones. "But there are seven of Arthur's men. Who is the eighth stone? These would have been erected for Arthur's men alone."

"Maybe there is another. Time will tell."

Merlin stared at the mysterious stone and whispered, "Yes." A surge of pain shot through his heart as he thought of the loss. He rested his head against the stone. His emotions were a jumble of relief and sudden penitence. He dropped his head with a quiet sigh. "We have found it."

"Now the trouble is," David said, stamping the ground with his foot, "how to find Arthur?"

12

THE HILL OF THE KINGS

"We'll set up camp," David said as they climbed down the hill. The sun inched closer to the horizon. Come morning, they would need to figure out how to find Arthur. They set up camp on some flat turf amongst the trees, fifty meters or so from the hill.

"What is this?" Merlin inquired, holding up a flashlight he pulled from his pack. Elanor laughed. "It's a torch."

"This is not a torch." Merlin waved the foreign item in confusion.

"No?" Elanor teased. "Here, let me show you."

Their long trek had brightened Merlin's ruddy cheeks, making Elanor want to kiss them. She grabbed the torch from him, flipped the switch on the side, and it lit up.

"Hah!" Merlin curious eyes flared, gazing at the glowing beam of light extending from the device. "A torch! More effective than ones made with fire, I would say."

Elanor gladly handed it to him. Merlin was like a child with a new toy, shining its beams into the forest.

David shouted, "Here!" He tossed them a red, oblong pack. "This one should fit the two of you—barely. It is only a small pop-up tent. Should be easy enough to set up. I have one here for myself. I'll start the fire and get some soup warming."

"Are you sure about the fire, Dad?"

"Well, there is nothing worse than cold soup."

Elanor tsked. "You know what I mean."

"I don't think anyone will see us clear out here. Anyway, it will be worth the risk to have some warmth. It's going to get chilly once the sun goes down."

Merlin raised an eyebrow. "Are we not allowed to set a fire?"

David shook his head. "No. And we are not allowed to be camping out here either. But there is no reason to believe that we would be spotted. We are far from any disapproving eyes. The trails don't come through here, and we left all the homes behind us when we entered that treed valley. We'll be fine."

Merlin's eyes panned the surrounding trees. "Strange not to be allowed to lay your head down within the wilds."

"Yah, too many rabble-rousers wrecked things. They spoiled it for the rest of us," David said, unzipping a bundle that held his tent.

"What an unusual place the world becomes."

Elanor pulled the tent out of the bag, and as she unfolded it, it popped into place, making Merlin jump. She chuckled. "Well, that was simple."

Merlin blinked at the tent. "How does such a small object burst into this red domed–thing?"

"You'll still want to peg it down," David hollered.

Elanor put her hands on her hips. "It will be a tight squeeze for the two of us in there."

Merlin smiled, tilting his head at the little red tent. He hunched down, edging his head through the flap, and then clambered inside. "Curious."

Elanor giggled, shaking her head at his wonder. Grabbing a sleeping bag, she tossed it into the tent and crawled in behind him. "What do you think?"

Merlin grimaced. "I think I might be more comfortable outside."

Elanor laughed, not surprised by his response.

"You seem to be enjoying my discomfort."

"Yes—a little. It's delightful watching you completely puzzled at every turn."

Merlin placed his hand upon her cheek. Elanor relished the secluded moment, and leaned into his palm, connected with his stare. The light of her eyes gleamed as her seeing gift peered inside his mind.

"You are worried."

Merlin smirked, laying back on the crackly floor of the tent. "I want to be unconcerned and simply rest. But come morning, I am unsure what we may face. Our enemy's eyes are surely watching this place—that is if we *truly* found Arthur." He shuffled uncomfortably. "The sight of those eight stones was painful. It reminded me of the death evil brings. As we descended the Hill, I wanted to forget it all. All day, I have been worried—hoping we had not entirely wasted our time going in the wrong direction. And now that we are here…" He squeezed his eyes shut for a moment, then turned his gaze to Elanor. "Once we open that door, it cannot be as easily shut. Whatever we unleash—"

He stopped himself, shaking his head. Leaning up on his elbow, he slid his finger down Elanor's cheek. "We found the Hill in one day, but I am not sure it will continue to be so easy."

Elanor's brows laced together as she nestled into Merlin's chest. His warning disturbed her. What were they about to walk into? How could they have any way to prepare? What about her dad? Through her weariness it made it hard to think. Her legs still throbbed from the long day of walking.

After a moment, they heard the hollow clunk of sticks fall in a clatter.

"I better go help," Merlin said, sitting up. "David won't have to stress over starting a fire once he knows how easily I can light one." He scrunched his way back out of the tent.

Elanor lay there contemplating, staring at the rippling ceiling. The red color highlighted everything in orange hues. She exhaled, listening to the two men she loved the most ramble about the proper techniques to start a good fire.

Exhausted and her body spent, she drifted off. The sun was setting, the light faded, but the tent was still warm—making it even harder for her to resist sleep. The second her eyes closed, she fell into a dream.

"You don't belong here, Elanor."

Helen's aggressive voice echoed through Elanor's ears, triggering old wounds. Elanor stiffened. She couldn't see Helen's face clearly—just a blurry figure emerging from the darkness. But her voice rang clear.

"You took him away from us. You ruined our family. But that is what you do… You destroy things."

In a flash, Jack towered over her. Terror seized Elanor. His teeth were gritted, and his jaw clenched with anger. A storm raged in his eyes. "You are not my sister," he spat, the accusation dripping from his words like poison.

Elanor wanted to run from him but remained stock-still, unable to move even her arms. She had never feared Jack before—at least, not like this. As he drew closer, demonic threats pulsed in his eyes.

"You destroyed our family. You ruined everything!" He launched at her with a roar, his hands lunging for her throat.

With a gasp, Elanor shot up out of her dream, clutching her chest. Her heart pounded with adrenaline. She knew this feeling. How the distress of nightmares surged through her, shaking her into a cold sweat. It had been a long time since she had one like this. Jack's words still rolled through her head.

Soft light came through the tent, and Elanor realized it was still dusk. She had not been asleep long. She placed her hand on her forehead and sighed with relief.

It was just a dream.

She exited the tent to join the men, forcing herself to forget it as she settled down next to Merlin.

He glanced at her and frowned. "What's wrong?"

"Just tired," Elanor said dismissively. She avoided Merlin's lingering gaze, knowing her answer had not satisfied him. "I am ready for sleep, that's all. I think I'll eat and go to bed." Her eyes fixed on David, who quietly stirred the soup on the other side of the fire. His face rippled in the flickering orange light, and guilt struck her heart.

"Are you sure?" Merlin pressed, running his fingers through her hair.

Elanor nodded, bringing her knees to her chest and wrapping her arms around them. She nestled her chin onto her arms.

Safe.

The moon loomed high overhead, casting its ghostly white light upon the ground. A mournful old owl hooted from the boughs above, and a chilly wind blew through the camp. The fire had burnt to its coals, and Merlin sat alone, ruminating while the others slept.

He wanted to rest, but the fear on Elanor's face earlier—something in her eyes—had snapped him out of his momentary peace. He had learned to recognize when she was *seeing*, but she appeared unready to tell him about it. He wasn't going to force her, but her silence left him wondering what clues he might be missing. What shadows might be lurking that he was unaware of? Demons in this time hid behind people's faces and the words they said. They didn't stand in the clear light.

For Merlin, these secrets needed to be revealed. So, he closed his eyes, searching for the awen. He wanted to reach out to the otherworld in the way he always had, but he stopped himself. The words of the old prophet Balek, and Marcus, spoke into his thoughts:

"Who leads you, Merlin? We are druids of the new way, and we have learned that it is not in magic where we find our answers."

But what was the new way, truly? Merlin was still unsure. He knew that it shifted things and changed the way things had been done. The understanding remained unclear to him. Then there was the Man in Blue who seemed to be a guide. Maybe he was the path in this strange new world.

"What do I do?" Merlin whispered into the air. "How do I see into the hidden things on our path?"

As if in response to his question, the wind stopped blowing, and the noises of the night silenced. Merlin opened his eyes and noticed the branches hanging above him. A tiny light appeared upon one of the tree's limbs. He jumped to his feet, getting a closer look. Another light appeared, then another, and another. Soon, the tree was teeming with the little golden lights.

What is this?

A loud sigh undulated through the breeze, pushing the lights from the branches—out to hover in the air before Merlin. The curious lights floated forward, and Merlin followed. Hundreds of them swirled around in the darkness, dancing along an invisible path, leading him ahead. Then they flickered and went out.

"Don't go," Merlin uttered, wondering if the phenomena had ceased. His cold, excited breath curled in the air, lit by the lonely white of the moon. Then he heard a sudden sputtering of igniting fire, and a small flame burst alight ahead of him. It was a white, golden color and hovered just above the ground. He inched closer, almost reaching it, before it snuffed out. Another one lit before him, and he leapt to follow. Again it went out.

Merlin smiled in wonder as the flames lit, one after the other. The faster he walked after them, the quicker the flames ignited along the way. He started to run, exhilarated by the anomaly. He couldn't see in the darkness, but he knew the flames were leading him to the Hill. In all his furor, his foot smacked against a stone. He careened to the ground, and his chin scuffed the grassy earth.

"Blast!" he grumbled, spitting dirt. He rubbed his face clean and looked up, hoping to catch sight of the flame. It was still there, burning brightly. "Could you have at least taken me around the rock?"

Merlin glanced down at what tripped him, and the flame lit on one of the fallen stone markers. He sprang to his feet, and as he did, the flame rose high into the air, then burst back into tiny golden lights. They zipped around like flies, flitting sporadically through the air. Then they levitated to the side of the hill and halted as if waiting for Merlin. He got his feet beneath him and advanced.

As he rounded the dark corner after them, the light suddenly vanished. His eyes darted back and forth until they caught the sparkling lights just behind a tree, up the side of the hill—half covered with shrubs and brush. He wasted no time reaching the spot and rounded the tree. There, lighting up the embankment, glittered the lights in the shape of a door.

"Here it is!" Merlin said, breathing heavily, glancing at the heavens. Relief showered over him. He chuckled lightly. "Thank the Great God!"

He touched the ground and the lights flickered and went out. A sudden, violent pulse shot him back, catapulting him down the hill. He tumbled and thrashed against the ground.

At the bottom of the hill, Merlin's eyes fluttered open. Pain lanced down his side and arm. He knew that burning sting only cuts could give, so, carefully, he brushed the gouge on his shoulder and cheek. "Aah!" He winced.

Upon the hill—where the lights had been—towered a white, gleaming entity holding a drawn sword. Ominous and quiet, he stared down at Merlin, leaning as if ready to charge. His chest heaved against his breastplate, and his free hand clenched into a fist. He wore a white helm with antlers sprawling from the sides, the back strung with horse's hair tousled by the wind. His shoulders rolled into an intimidating stance, and his labored breath echoed down the hill.

Merlin held up his hand in surrender. "I do not mean this place harm. There is no need to threaten me."

In eerie silence, the white warrior remained unmoved, ready to attack.

"Who are you?" Merlin whispered. The solid muscle in the warrior's arms and legs made Merlin wary.

Merlin slowly rose to his feet, trying not to provoke the warrior. "I do not desire to challenge you. We have come here…" He hesitated, surmising his next move. "I have come here with the lady Elanor. It is our destiny. We are here to awaken the king."

At his words, the warrior marched down the hill, aggressively poised as he brandished his sword.

"I am MERLIN!" he shouted; his golden eyes ablaze. His hands shot from his sides with force, releasing a powerful wind that pushed the warrior back. "Emrys Wyllt and Gwenddydd have come to awaken the sleeper. Do *not* hinder us."

At Merlin's warning, the warrior halted his charge. He steadily lowered his sword, though his stance remained tense.

Merlin licked blood leaking from the corner of his mouth. He was ready to strike, his hands outstretched toward the warrior as the wind whistled between them.

Then the warrior relaxed his stance and turned, walking back up the hill.

What is he doing?

Adrenaline surged through Merlin's veins as the warrior fiercely arched his sword over his head. It rang as it sliced through the air. With both hands wrapped around the hilt, the warrior jammed the sword into the sloped ground where the door had been lit.

The air pulsed in waves down the hill. Merlin quickly shielded his head with his arms. He pressed his hands against the magical waves as he peeked between his arms. The warrior remained steadfast, gripping his sword. A rumbling and grinding of stone emanated from the ground, almost as if he were turning a gigantic key. Then suddenly there was silence. The sword and the warrior faded and disappeared.

Merlin buckled forward, staring into the darkness where the anomaly had just occurred. Taking measured breaths, he climbed back up the hill in the stark blackness of the night. Blind without the little lights to guide him, Merlin searched with his hands, being careful to stay on the path leading toward the faint, silhouetted tree in the distance.

At last, his hands brushed against the bark. Shifting around the trunk, he wedged himself between the door and the tree. Merlin patted the ground to feel if anything had changed. Maybe there had been a door uncovered. He wished he had one of those torches he'd discovered earlier.

"Nothing," he said, swiping his hands over the ground. Nothing but hard dirt and brush. He rolled over onto his back—exhausted and bruised, he didn't know what to do without light to guide his eyes. He couldn't leave the spot, as he feared he would not be able to find it again come morning light, which left only one option. He would have to remain where he was throughout the night.

He gripped his throbbing shoulder and found his jumper's sleeve had torn from his fall. He closed his mouth and inhaled sharply from his nose, squeezing his eyes shut. The torn flesh of his shoulder stung.

Who was that white guardian? He had no dark feeling or evil foreboding. He seemed to be guarding the door, and I—I passed the test.

Merlin replayed the moment in his mind. If someone commanded this supernatural warrior to guard the door, surely Arthur would still be inside. Hope kindled in his heart, and the scent of magic lofted into the air.

KNIGHT DAVID

"Merlin! Merlin!"

Merlin woke with a start and a severe ache in his head and shoulder. His eyes opened to sunlight shining through the leaves in the tree above. Sitting up, he assessed his injuries through his torn shirt.

I must have fallen against a hard root or rock.

He placed his hand on his cheek and felt the crusty dried blood and a scrape running across his cheekbone. His fingers gingerly rubbed a tender, throbbing bump on the side of his head.

"Merlin!" Elanor's voice grew frantic as she called out from a distance.

Through his groggy throat, Merlin coughed out, "I'm…I'm here!" Speaking made his head pound. He held his forehead. *"Over here."*

"I heard him," David called to Elanor. "Merlin? One more time. Where are you?"

The crunch of pine needles carried, and Merlin directed his gaze to the base of the hill. David emerged around the bend. "Up here," Merlin called.

David's gaze traveled up the length of the hill and leveled at the tree. "What are you doing up there?" he asked, racing up the hill. "Lord, look at you. What happened?"

Elanor quickly followed around the bend.

David hollered down to her, "He's up here."

"Merlin, what happened?" Elanor yelled as she hurried to his side. "Oh, my Great God." She caressed his face, scowling at the dried blood, and tenderly pulled open the ripped shirt at his shoulder. Her face paled at the sight of his wound. "What…"

Merlin slipped his arms around her waist and pulled her close, taking in her sweet aroma. "I found it."

Elanor melted into him, her eyes wide. "What?"

"The door." Merlin glanced between the two of them.

David and Elanor stared at each other, puzzled.

Merlin laughed with a broken, weak smile. "The door to Arthur."

"Last night?" Elanor asked incredulously.

"Yes." Merlin smiled and gave a mild chuckle. His head twinged at the vibration of his own voice, and he cradled his head in his palm.

Elanor lifted her fingers, touching his cheek with a worried look.

"I'm alright. I fell. I stayed here throughout the night because I didn't want to lose the location in the darkness. I was led here. Lights lit the path, and then I was almost attacked by a tall warrior in white. He was an enaid, Elanor. He stuck his sword into the ground right here, and I could hear it unlocking something below the dirt."

David pointed at the earth. "Right here?"

Merlin turned and patted the ground. "Right here. A door illuminated." He brushed his hands over the spot. "I hoped by the light of morning I would see something more."

David asked, "How do we get to the door? Dig?"

Merlin shook his head uncertain, wincing at the movement.

"Well, we're not doing anything until we take care of your injuries," Elanor interjected. "Did we bring a med kit?"

"Yes." David nodded. "In the left side pocket of my pack. All this from falling down that hill?"

Merlin shrugged. "Well, it was less of a fall and more of an explosive push. The white warrior was unusually strong. He threatened to cut me down with his sword. I am glad I was able to convince him I was not a menace, or else I might have ended up with more injuries."

"How strange," Elanor mused, baffled. "To think of such a powerful enaid appearing here." She stood up eagerly. "Arthur really must be here."

Merlin squeezed her shoulder. "Yes. I think we've found him… or at least the way to him."

Elanor tutted. "Look at you." She stood, placed one hand on her hip and brushed his forehead with the other. Her gaze deepened with concern.

Merlin tenderly grabbed her wrist. "What is it?"

"I could heal you, but I cannot seem to kindle the magic."

"Remember," Merlin said, kissing the palm of her hand, "the magic to heal will call to you when it is meant to come. You know this."

"I just thought…" Elanor tightened her lips, and dropped her head.

"You and I have magic that flows from who and what we are. But there is another kind of magic that requires the hand of something greater to call it forth. It calls to us, and we respond. Your healing magic is not a trick you can just pull from your pocket. It is a deeper, older magic that is coupled with timing and wisdom." Merlin dipped his head to capture her eyes. "I am alright. Just a little bashed up. I do not need healing magic."

Elanor exhaled. "Well, I can at least patch you up. I'll be back. Stay here."

David settled down next to Merlin, and Elanor worked her way back down the hill and over to the camp. "Here." He handed Merlin his water flask. "That must have been some fall. It's a rather steep incline."

"It happened so fast. I didn't have a chance to brace myself." Merlin hissed, gingerly touching his cheek. "I don't even know what I hit. It was too dark."

"You're lucky you don't have any broken bones." David grinned, patting Merlin's back. He huffed with relief as he stared off beyond the trees. "Glad you're alright. Can't have *Merlin the Magnificent* breaking his neck before we figure out how to crack into this hill."

Merlin pressed his palm into his shoulder and rolled his stiff joint.

"Wish I could've seen it," David said, lifting his chin, wonderment besetting his eyes. "A warrior spirit. That must have been brilliant."

Merlin smiled, admiring David's fascination.

"Reminiscent of all those epic quests I used to imagine as a boy. Me and my little white knight adventuring together."

"Where did you come by your wooden knight?"

"My grandfather. Heh…" David wavered with a grin. "He had three of them. A red, black, and a white one. My grandfather was an officer in the British Army during World War II.

"He and his regiment passed through a destroyed section of Berlin. He wandered through a part of the city where people had lived. All that was left was rubble and the debris of what had been before the bombs.

"My grandfather was scavenging through some remains when he found a small wooden box, half crushed underneath some bricks. Inside were three little knights. They had likely belonged to a small child who had either fled or been killed in the attack. Anyway, he kept them, and when I was only six, he gave one to each of his grandchildren. My two older brothers and me.

"The minute he placed that little knight in my hand, I glanced at his sword and armor, and I knew…" David lifted his chest with a mixture of pride and sorrow. "I knew I wanted to be just like him. Brave and strong like my knight… just like my grandfather."

David beamed. "I read the *Code of Chivalry* until I had it committed to memory." He lifted his hand as he recited, "A knight protects the weak. He is to serve the king with fealty, and always be truthful, brave, and honorable above all." He winked and nudged Merlin with his elbow. "He must of course also gallantly defend the ladies."

Merlin chuckled.

"I dreamed of saving the princess and slaying dragons with my little knight by my side. But…" David shrugged. "I grew up and discovered that those ideas were just fairy tales. Though I still hoped I'd get caught up in my own heroic fantasy somehow—just in some sort of real-world way. I wrote stories that almost made the dream tangible. It was a way I could still be brave and maybe someday take others with me."

David nodded, lowering his head. The creases on his forehead deepened, as if acknowledging his own foolishness.

"Aah, but then I had to grow up. Magic and fantastic adventures were for children. Not grown men. At least not in this world." David, on the edge of grief, firmed his lips. "I went to university. That's how I met Helen. She and I took literature courses together. She was so beautiful in those days. I liked how she took control, and I could lean on her." He sighed. "She was a ginger through and through." David paused and looked down at his open palms. He squeezed them shut and faced Merlin. "Helen was always the aggressive type, but… she used to be happy. More kind and congenial. I still see that spark of kindness in her—it's not all bitterness, ya' know?"

Merlin gave a compassionate nod of understanding.

"I don't know if it was the mundaneness of life, or if it was my own failings as a husband that pulled out her coarser side. I am certain, taking in Elanor against Helen's wishes didn't help.

"Anyway… as I pursued Helen, I knew it had come time to choose a more practical profession, and so for me, the stories of knights and their glory disappeared. Funny thing is"—David pointed at the air— "the day I discovered Elanor in that tree stump and that letter found its way into my hands, it rekindled hope. I thought maybe there was a way in this bitter, ordinary world I could still be brave. Maybe my life could count for something, or someone."

David turned and faced Merlin. A sad glimmer was in his eyes. "But, as it was, I was not brave when it came to defending Elanor." He clenched his hands, considering whether there was strength within them. "When tested, I was still only a child with a dream. Not a man that could defend and protect." He sniffed with a serious air. "The warrior in the story you told had been given a chance to be a man of honor who would sacrifice for others and bring healing to all who asked for help. I guess I have always wished to have that exceptional quality."

"Stories," Merlin began delicately, "sometimes have a way of making short the trials and challenges it takes to really be men of quality. It is *never* without failure. Here people have legends of Arthur and his wise wizard Merlin. Those stories tell of all sorts of brave feats, but the truth is, I have failed. Arthur failed. And I…" He swallowed, almost unable to vocalize his next words. "I abandoned a kingdom that needed me. Gave up on them while I wallowed in my grief." Merlin gestured to their camp. "She gave me a reason to choose better."

He placed his hand on David's shoulder and squared him in the eye. "We do not have knights in my time. It is an older time than your stories tell of us. So, I do not fully understand what one is, or what one should be, but I do know of warriors who are honorable and brave. Every one of them has the regret of blood on their hands. Blood that I hope you can be glad you have never spilt. There is no glory in it. No romance. And many a fair maid has been ravaged without the opportunity of rescue."

David lowered his sullen eyes to the ground, and he kicked at the loose dirt. "I guess my romantic ideas are foolish then."

"No, the desire to be honorable is *not* romantic. That, in itself, is a star I wish more men would reach for," Merlin affirmed.

David sighed, and his gentle eyes misted. "I am dying," he breathed with a stutter, his lips and chin trembling. "Cancer. I'm riddled with it."

Merlin's eyes widened. "What is cancer?"

"It is an illness that consumes you. Some can recover with medicines, but…" David shrugged. "Not me. No one knows. Not even Helen. So… this is my chance."

"Elanor could heal you. She could at least try to—"

"No…no…no." David swished his hands, then gave Merlin a serious stare. "Please. I do not want you to tell Elanor."

"She has a healing magic. She is not always able to heal, but she could…"

"Please," David said firmly. "Do me this favor."

Merlin narrowed his eyes, confounded, but relented with a nod. He hoped he could convince him later. "Are you in pain?"

"Sometimes. But not now. Now I am at my happiest," David said, a faint smile spreading across his face. "I am with Merlin—awakening the king and rescuing the princess."

Merlin cocked his head, flashing a sober grin. "Right. Epic quest."

"Exactly."

Elanor appeared at the bottom of the hill, her arms loaded. A blue and white box hung from her fingers, and she carried a fresh shirt for Merlin.

"Here," she said, tossing a small, wrapped parcel of food at Merlin. Noticing their somber expressions, she asked, "Why the sad faces? What's wrong?"

David gleamed. "Just a little brotherly heart to heart—that's all."

Merlin stared at the ground. He couldn't look Elanor in the eye. David's revelation would be difficult to keep from her. He struggled to swallow the heartache and move on as though he had not just heard jarring news. He unwrapped the food and took a bite. The chalky, mushy bar was odd, and he grimaced. "What is this? This cannot be food."

Elanor giggled. "Terrible, isn't it? It's a protein bar. I hate them, but in a situation like this, they will give you all the nutrients you need."

"Vile," Merlin spat, taking another bite.

"Now, let's get you fixed up." She took some gauze from the med kit and started dabbing it with clean water. After delicately cleaning Merlin's cheek, she pulled out some small square packets, and tore one open. "This will sting," she said, lifting a brown-red swab to the gash on his face. "It's iodine. It will keep your cut clean."

"Ah," Merlin winced.

Elanor laughed. "It only stings for a second." Finishing, she butterflied his cheek. "Now for the shoulder," she said, with a wink.

Merlin grunted, pulling off his jumper so she could finish the job.

"Mostly scrapes and bruises," she noted, sticking the final piece of white gauze to his shoulder and handing him a new shirt. "Here." She took a larger, white, square pack from the kit, and popped it before handing it to him. "For your head."

"What is this?" Merlin asked, pulling his shirt over his head. Then, grabbing the pack from her hand, his mind burst with curiosity. "It is cold."

"Exactly. Put it on your head; it will alleviate the pain."

"Modern magic?" he asked, with a smirk, placing it on his head.

"Science," Elanor confirmed, loading all the pieces and scraps back into the kit.

Holding the strange cold pack to his head, Merlin stood and said, "Now, what to do about this door?"

David scrunched his face. "It seems strange that it would be so high up. I would imagine an old tomb like this would be found much lower, maybe even deeper beneath the ground."

"It is odd," Merlin agreed. "But this is where I have been led. Even so, there is no door or tunnel. Just hard earth. We could try digging as you suggested."

David quirked his mouth to the side. "It would take a very long time to excavate. All I brought is a small spade and a knife. Those tools won't get us very far."

Elanor examined the flat incline, gazing at the empty ground. "Is there a form of magic that could be used? Maybe if the white guardian has unlocked it, there is also a way for it to be revealed. Like you did at the Crystal Cave," she said to Merlin.

"True," Merlin said, rubbing his chin. "Though that door was not buried under the ground, and the ancient words were written upon the stones to open it. There may be something to what you say, however. Enacting the right words in the *time between times* could raise our chances."

David frowned. "What is the time between times?"

"It is the time when the sun rises or sets. This is the time where the line between our world and the otherworld grows thin. During this time, it is easiest to access that world, cross over, or even see the unseen. On high days, like Beltaine or Samhain when the solstices align, it is even thinner. It is but a spiritual reality of the days, seasons, and times. Those dimensions can be opened wider when the timing of sunwise circles is matched with the time between times." Merlin bit his lip, deep in thought. Leaning forward, he pressed his hands onto the incline. He closed his eyes and, releasing a concentrated sigh, listened intently.

"Elanor," he said, his eyes still closed, "read the land with your magic like you do when you look into a man's eye. Remember: There are things that can be seen that may seem like shadow."

Elanor nodded, her gaze panning the landscape.

"Agor," Merlin spoke with quiet authority. They waited silently, but nothing shifted. "Amlygu… dadorchuddio."

Nothing.

"Wait—" Elanor broke the silence, her voice rising. "Say that last word again."

"Dadorchuddio," Merlin said, pressing deeper with his magic.

"I saw a faint shadow when you spoke that word, almost like a door interlaid over the ground. It is there." Elanor pointed, excitement building in her voice.

Merlin sat back on his heels. "It is there, but how to get to it. The word I spoke commanded the door to unveil itself. The authority behind the word is making it visible to you. Unfortunately, it appears to be doing nothing more. It remains shut."

"Perhaps if we spoke the words at the time between times," Elanor suggested.

Merlin nodded. "But that would take some planning. I would need to know how long it would take to circle this hill sunwise three times, finishing as the setting sun sinks into the horizon. That is if the unveiling word is all that needs to be spoken."

"What's written on the stone marker for Arthur?" Elanor asked. "You know, the one of the three down below—maybe that could be a key. Or at least words to try."

Merlin tipped his head back, fixing his eyes on the sky. "It says, 'Artus rhi, pennaeth brwydr o'r Briton.' Arthur King, and Battle Chief of the Britons.*"

"Wow!" David exclaimed. "Good thinking, Elanor. That's my clever girl."

"Yes, well, I do not think those words will have the power to open the door, but it is a step in the right direction." Merlin chuffed. "Certainly does seem that terrible protein bar is working for you, dear Elanor. Not sure I can say it is working for the rest of us."

"Well," she teased, "you did hit your head pretty hard."

Merlin smirked and dashed after her, trying to catch her in his arms.

Elanor shrieked, jumping away with a giggle.

Merlin laughed, giving up. "I think those words will be well worth a *gallant* try." He winked at David. "It's something to go on unless something else presents itself. Until then, I have nothing. I could speak in the old tongue of the druids all day, but I have a hunch it won't get us any closer to opening that door."

"Right, then," David said, smacking his hands together. "Let's get to work."

14

THE CALL OF THE GUARDIAN

Elanor approached the domed cairn at the base of the hill. Setting a timer on her mobile, she launched into a steady stride. To get a more accurate idea of how long it would take to circle the hill, she would need to time it at least twice.

While Elanor traipsed, David and Merlin dug near the tree, using whatever tools at their disposal to uncover anything just beneath the surface.

The hill was rather large, and after she rounded it the first time, Elanor clocked it at twenty-six minutes. The jaunt hadn't been difficult, aside from the stream and ridge at the back of the hill that she'd had to climb around.

Taking a moment to rest, Elanor leaned on the cairn and closed her eyes, inhaling deeply. A flash of white blinded her, and loud voices crashed into her mind. Her hands flew up, clutching her head just as the sensation ceased.

Opening her eyes, she looked around, but there was no one there. Only the three kings' memorial stones were clustered beside her.

What was that?

She rubbed her head and, with a suspicious turn, eyed the cairn behind her. Then, she looked back at the three looming stones, two of which lay fallen on the earth like sleeping giants. One was for Aurelius, one for Uther, and one—one was for Arthur. She placed her hand on the single standing stone, running her fingers down the ogham lines. She wished she could read them. She desired to know which stone was Arthur's. Merlin could tell her, but he was on the hill with her father.

The thought occurred without warning: soon she might be standing face-to-face with Arthur—*her real father.*

What would I say? Would he be happy to have a daughter?

"I'm your daughter, Elanor," she said to the stone. The words felt like a lie as they tumbled from her mouth. She tsked and let her hand drop back to her side. "You feel like you are far away. Unreal. You have only ever been a legend to me." She thought about the stone face of Arthur in the Hall of the Kings, atop the Palisade in Prydain.

Elanor shrugged. Lifting her mobile, she started the timer to go around the hill a second time. Her heart weighed heavily with thoughts of Arthur—King of the Britons. Now that it had come to it, she felt apprehensive and afraid. The feeling amplified as she briskly walked around the looming hill, passing trees and the stones that laid upon the earthen mound encasing his body.

Finally, coming back around to the other side, she approached the cairn once again. "Twenty minutes this time." She smacked the cairn with her hand. Rays of white light obscured her vision, and angry voices rang. Someone was shouting—shouting at her.

Elanor fell to the ground as Helen's voice resonated through her.

"Who do you think you are? Here you go again, trying to make yourself special." Helen accused with condescending laughter. *"You are nothing but a stupid… stupid little girl. You can't save him. You can't even save yourself."*

Elanor tried to plug her ears, but Helen's voice was inside her head. "Save who?"

Helen's image was replaced with that of young children. They were crying, holding hands as they stood before Elanor. It was Jack and Nancy.

"You took our daddy away from us. You ruined us. Ruined our family. You are a wrecker!"

Elanor couldn't wake up. She couldn't pull herself from this nightmare. "Make it stop!" she yelled, covering her head with her arms as she writhed on the ground. The voices and relentless accusations echoed. She didn't want to believe them, but the more they spoke, the truer they felt. Who *did* she think she was? Maybe she had stolen their father and ruined everything. Where was Merlin's voice of reason to help her? Where were his soothing words?

I don't deserve to be comforted. I am nothing. I am a wrecker.

Anguish filled her heart, and tears cascaded down her cheeks as she lay on her back, jamming her fingers into her ears.

"Help me," Elanor cried with a timid sob. "Help me."

The bright, raging light dimmed. She opened her eyes, her back against the cool earth. The malicious laughter and shouting dwindled and faded away. Beams of light radiated in front of the cairn, reflecting rainbow prisms. Elanor blinked, seeing the silhouette of a tall man. He knelt beside her and brushed his gloved hand across her forehead and through her hair.

As he stared down at her, her eyes focused. A white helm donned his head. His shoulders were broad, and he appeared to be strapped in white leather, prepared for battle. A white pulsing light seeped out from the helm shielding his face. The helm was majestic, adorned with the ivory antlers of a stag. She could hear his breath as he hovered above her.

Elanor reached for his hand as it caressed her head. She was baffled to find that it was warm. They hung still for a long moment, then the white guardian rose to his feet and walked away. A white cape draped from his shoulders and flowed behind him. He twisted back to face her, and in silence, unsheathed his sword. The guardian flickered, his silhouette fading. Then he disappeared, blown away by a wind that whispered, "Gwenddydd."

She blinked again and found Merlin gripping her shoulders. Her eyes were teary, and her breath still stuttered with sobs.

Merlin leaned in, his face radiating concern. "Elanor… Elanor."

Elanor wiped her eyes, forcing back her tears as Merlin helped her sit up. She peered at the cairn in front of her, and there stood her father, in the very same spot the white guardian had been. "Dad?"

"I'm here, sweetie. What happened?"

"We heard you screaming and found you here struggling on the ground," Merlin said.

Elanor rose to her feet and placed her hands over her cheeks, approaching the cairn. She lifted a hand to reach for it but hesitated. "There is magic here. Something does not want us to discover it. I… I saw the white guardian. He was here." She lowered her hands and faced Merlin. "I touched this cairn, and I was attacked by dark voices, and… he… he came and helped me."

Merlin embraced her, pressing her head to his chest. "There is definitely magic about this place. Light and dark. Are you sure you are alright?"

Elanor nodded, though she still felt disturbed.

Letting go of her, Merlin placed his hand upon the cairn and closed his eyes. Elanor watched his eyes race beneath his lids. His brows pressed together, straining as he kindled his magic.

Merlin's eyes shot open, and he leapt back, heaving from the effort. He turned to Elanor with foreboding in his eyes. "We must be prepared. There is dark magic here. This guardian is holding the place of light and is battling the dark curse." He glared at the cairn. "But we have discovered our key. I can feel it. Maybe it should have been obvious to me, but I did not consider this cairn."

David touched the stones, mystified. "How will it work as our key?"

"We will do as we planned, only instead of marching around the hill, we will encircle this cairn during the time between times. Now that I can feel the force of magic in these elements, I can more easily navigate. But we must be careful. The dark sorcery has been set here on purpose to oppose us. It is very old and has been waiting for us." Merlin looked gravely toward Elanor's father with serious warning. "David, this is where you must decide if you want to continue on with us. It may be better for you to remain within the camp where you will be safe."

"Pffft! Nah." David stood taller—his eyes set. "This is why I've come, mate. I'm not going to retreat just as it is starting to get exciting."

"You have no idea the danger," Elanor insisted, fearing for his safety. "The violence I have witnessed. This is serious, Dad."

"Oh, Elanor… You think I'm going to hide away while *my daughter* goes to face the danger? Don't be daft." David shook his head. "I saw you…" He pointed at her. "I felt that arrow go through your chest. I felt the life drain out of you. The terror of death that seized you." He scowled. "Please don't patronize me, Elanor. I know I have not been with you in the time of Cymry warlords and demons, but don't belittle me as a man. I am your father."

His face reddened with emotion as his truth struck Elanor in the heart.

"I am strong, and I will not stand here and let you go in there alone. It is my calling to protect you. I will *not* fail."

Elanor turned to Merlin helplessly.

Merlin agreed tenderly. "Do not keep your father from what is in his heart to do."

She sighed, dropping her head. Her thoughts still pounded with the words that had assailed her.

You took our daddy from us.

You are not special.

You are a wrecker.

Elanor pulled on the hem of her sleeves. Confused by the lies and the fear, she felt doomed by her father's persistence. "What of Jack and Nancy? Helen? What if something were to happen to you?"

"They have not needed me for a long time." He shook his head with a somber grimace.

"That's not true." She hesitated, biting her lip. "You have only ever fought for me. What if you were to fight for them?"

David sighed. "It is complicated, isn't it? One thing I know for sure, it is not your responsibility to govern my choices, right or wrong. Nor to bring peace to the Evans family who have never chosen to fight for you." He lifted Elanor's chin with his knuckle. "I am here with you. I made that choice when I got into the car to come this long way. No looking back, hm?"

A tear leaked down her cheek and hung on her chin.

David wiped it with his thumb. "Let's wake the king so you can meet your father."

His words pricked her heart. All these years wondering who her father was, and what he would look like, disappeared into David's eyes. Her desire to keep him safe overruled everything else. David *was* her father.

"Is there nothing I can do to stop you?" Elanor pleaded.

"No. I am decided."

Refreshed after having eaten, they returned to the cairn. The sun was drawing close to the horizon. It was hard to tell the exact moment of the *time between times* with the mountains and hills surrounding them, but David kept them on track with the information he had retrieved on his mobile.

Merlin kept his eyes glued on the sky and prepared himself for what was to come: creating a portal to the otherworld, and unleashing the spirit world to overlap the natural.

"It's time," Merlin said with readiness. His eyes darted with warning to David, who nodded back.

"Right." Merlin took his first step, then continued around the cairn. He murmured words underneath his breath, circling once… twice… then on the third time around, he crossed the front of the cairn and halted. He stepped back, and they all breathed in anticipation.

A moment passed.

"Did anything happen?" David asked.

At his words, there was a loud CRACK, like lightning. The hill rumbled and rocks scraped against each other in a thunderous growl. Trees shook, their leaves rustling, creating a resounding thrum.

Elanor gripped Merlin's arm as the ground quaked beneath them, then suddenly stopped.

"Now that was something," David said, his eyes as wide as saucers.

The trio took off running to the hill, stumbling up the side until they arrived at the door.

"What? Nothing has changed," David huffed with unmasked disappointment.

Merlin beamed, eagerly eyeing the ground. "It has changed. What we felt was the shifting of the otherworld breaking way to open our path. Stand back." Merlin put his hands upon the sloped ground. "Agor!"

15

THROUGH THE OPEN DOOR

As Merlin spoke, the dirt shrouding the promised door quaked. The ground vibrated, shaking the compacted dirt free. Then, as though the soil had become sand, it sifted through fractures fissuring across the surface. The crevices grew wider and the dirt poured through, until a domed door took shape, revealing large rocks that had been piled and compressed to block the opening.

Merlin didn't hesitate. The moment the rocks were revealed, he jammed his fingers between the crevices and pulled. The rocks effortlessly rolled free, toppling several others with them. Excitement buzzed, and all three of them set to work removing the rocks, tossing each, one by one, down the hill. The filtering sand hissed as it fell over their feet.

Lines of old, rotted wood were exposed, covering a black chasm that yawned at them between the fissures. Merlin kicked the damp, decaying wood and it gave way, crumpling under his weight. He jerked back before he could fall through the gaping, bottomless chasm.

David pushed down the rest of the wood, breaking it away with ease. A cold, stale air wafted out, and the redolence of musty earth and mold infiltrated their noses.

Elanor snapped up a torch from her pack and shined the beam into the hole. Dirt and roots formed the roof, but the way ahead did not capture the light.

"Shine it down below," Merlin instructed.

Elanor tilted the light down, revealing a steep, declining path. Loose, damp earth made the slope appear difficult.

Merlin asked, "David, do you have any cord?"

"Rope?" David shook his head. "Sorry, I didn't think to bring any."

Elanor leaned toward the brim. "There isn't even a ledge."

Merlin sighed. "I will lead the way." He took an awkward step through, positioning himself on the edge of the doorway. "Be sure to lean back—Elanor, go next. David, you bring up the rear."

The earth loosened under Merlin's grip as he lowered himself onto the slope. He navigated forward, struggling to hold his torch, as he searched for a foothold before letting go. His foot padded the surface and found there were small rocks that jutted through the slope. He put his weight on the first rock, but it shifted and rolled out from underneath him. His foot slipped but quickly caught onto another stone. Taking a steadying breath, he shined the light before him, illuminating the perilous path.

"Let me go a little further in before you come," Merlin hollered, glancing up at Elanor and David. "You'll likely fall, knocking me—"

The rock beneath Merlin's foot gave out, and he slid with cascading dirt.

"Merlin!" Elanor shouted.

Merlin leaned back, clawing at the dirt, but found nothing to secure his hold and tumbled down the slope. His light crashed to the ground, rolling away from him, lighting up the new leveled space. He had not fallen far. Aside from a few scrapes, he was uninjured. Getting to his feet, he dusted his hands and scanned the dully lit excavated tunnel.

"I am well. There is a tunnel not far from the top. It will be hard to reach without a fall—be careful."

Elanor kicked her legs over the edge. Merlin positioned himself to catch her; the glowing light behind outlined her silhouette.

"I'm coming," Elanor hollered down. Carefully, she slid down with a light agility. Merlin thrust his arms out just as she burst from the slope and into his chest.

"Phew!" she exhaled sharply.

"Alright?" Merlin pulled back so he could look at her.

Elanor nodded, extending her light down the tunnel. "That went on further than I expected."

"Now you," Merlin called to David, then chuffed. "Be careful old man."

"Who's calling who old?" David returned.

His shoes scraped the dirt before he haphazardly plunged down the slope. Elanor jolted after him as he careened in a bumbling roll toward the ground.

"Ah!" he hollered, twisting up from his side.

"Dad!"

David grasped Elanor's hand and smiled. "I am fine, sweetie." He pulled his elbow up to inspect it. "Scraped my elbow." He lightly patted it, then whistled through his teeth. "That is going to be a hard one to crawl back up now, isn't it?" He wiped the damp dirt from his jeans and picked his light up from the ground. "Where are we?"

"This tunnel was dug by hand," Merlin said, pointing in the darkness to the tool-etched lines that had been preserved. "It would appear this place has been visited over the years. Let's move on. We cannot be far from Arthur's tomb, but"—he shined his light at them— "be cautious."

The air was thick as they journeyed deeper into the abyss.

They went along the tunnel for a ways, with no event, until it dead-ended. A tall, circular stone protruded from the earthen wall. As they drew closer, fine lines revealed a whorl carved into the stone, twisting into three round circles.

Merlin leaned his body onto the stone and shoved. "Of course, it's too heavy," he said, breathing deeply, "but it was worth a try. Not to worry." He pushed his index finger into the center of the whorl. "This is druidic magic." He tenderly grabbed Elanor's hand and pressed her palm onto the whorl. "Concentrate… Connect with the magic."

Elanor glanced at Merlin, appearing doubtful, but gave an agreeing nod.

"Your father rests on the other side."

At his words, Elanor's hand dropped from the whorl. A sinking sadness pressed into her chest. Loss taunted her, as though a treasure she held most precious was about to be consumed by fire.

"You were meant to be here," Merlin encouraged. "Do not be afraid."

Elanor timidly placed her hand back onto the whorl and closed her eyes. The lines beneath her hand pulsed, and she ripped her hand away.

"It's alright." Merlin put a reassuring palm upon her back, and the tension in her body lessened.

Elanor exhaled and returned her palm to the stone. Again, it pulsed in a rhythm that matched her heartbeat. Her fingertips tickled as if small, warm ants crawled beneath them. She breathed into the magic, and the pulses increased and brightened. Blue colors burst inside her mind. The din connected to the light, and she began to quietly hum.

Oh, how she had missed it! Even as it rose, the song enlivened her, reminding her of its luminous and powerful comfort. It was part of her. It was who she was in the depths of her soul. She opened her mouth and sang. Her song flowed, light and subtle, bouncing off the walls of the underground passageway. Blue light sparked, starting in the center of the whorl, and moving out through each of the lines until it was completely illuminated in a sapphire hue.

A rupture reverberated, and Elanor's eyes opened, glowing with effulgent light. The stone split from the center of the whorl into three pieces, tumbling open and revealing a crevice at the top of the doorway. The magic dissipated into silence.

"That was beautiful," David uttered from behind her. "To think I kept you from this magic all those years."

Elanor turned. Her father's face was spellbound and somber. She embraced him, burying her face into his shoulder. "No… Dad. You weren't wrong."

David wrapped his arms around her and held her, squeezing her tightly. "Now," he said, pulling her back to look at her, "let's go wake your father."

Elanor went rigid at his words. "But you're my father."

David lifted loose hair from her face. "I know. I know." He kissed her forehead and squeezed her arms. "I am grateful for that. But it is right that you should know your true father, and he should know you. That will never take away from what we have. Never."

Elanor exhaled. That same sinking feeling still clamped its cold fingers around her gut. But she knew her dad was right. She nodded and plastered a smile onto her face to appease him, though the dark foreboding swelled within her.

Merlin shined a light through the gap in the doorway. "There is a chamber on the other side." He pulled Elanor's hand gently and tilted his head toward the opening. "Come."

Merlin climbed over the broken chunks of stone and shimmied through the small opening at the top of the doorway. Worming his way to the other side, his feet stepped down into a hollow chamber. He lifted his flashlight while the other two crawled through after him. Their beams crossed one another, scanning the round tomb. On the surrounding walls were platforms where small clay lanterns rested, most of them crumbled shells of what they had been. In the center was a stone coffin, sculpted into the likeness of a naked king. His rounded head was surrounded by a circling halo, and within his hands, laced between his fingers, he held the hilt of a stone sword. Whorls etched throughout the stone told a story only the Cymry would understand.

"This is the same depiction as his memorial stone in the Palisade," Elanor remarked.

With a tentative nod, Merlin approached the coffin and patted the figure's hands. "It's time to awaken, my friend," he whispered, his emotions bubbling to the surface. In a few short moments, he might be resurrecting Arthur. He had grieved many years over his loss.

To see him again, Merlin thought, breathing into the nervous hope rising in his chest.

"Help me," Merlin said, putting his hands against the side of the stone pall. Elanor and David stationed themselves beside him.

Merlin commanded, "Push!"

They pushed upon the coffin's lid, grunting as their faces reddened from the exertion. Their feet slid against the earth as they thrust with vigor to shift the weighty lid.

Merlin hefted, yelling, "Aahhh!" and a supernatural force released out of his palms. The stone lid scraped and shifted. The black crevice opened wider as they shoved. The lid finally careened over the side, crashing to the ground and splitting in half on impact. A cloud of dust billowed before them, obscuring the opening.

Merlin waved his hands to clear the air.

Mystified and anxious, Elanor shone her light inside. The light beam highlighted the circling dust until it shined into the yawning cavity.

It was empty. No one laid beneath the dust. The blackness of the shell glared back at them.

"Where is he?" David asked, baffled.

Merlin puffed out heavy breaths. He wiped his face with his arm and leaned against the coffin. His mouth fell agape as he swiped his hand through the empty container.

How can this be?

"If... if he is not here," Elanor stuttered, "where would he be?"

Merlin held up his torch, squinting around the chamber. "If he is not here, then why all the magic to keep us at bay? Why create a tunnel and seal the tomb with druidic runes? No—there is something more we are not seeing. Both darkness and light have worked to conceal him, or else it is all a trick. Or worse—"

"A trap," Elanor said grimly, gripping her arm.

Merlin nodded, scanning every detail of the chamber. The only remnants in the room besides the stone coffin were the decaying clay lanterns.

"Maybe there are markings I have missed," Merlin said. As soon as he spoke, his light settled beside the one lantern that remained unbroken. Faint marks, like scratches left by an animal, appeared above it. Dread filled him as he neared and brushed his hand over the marks.

Merlin's eyes widened with recognition. His mind flashed back to the dark marks discovered in the yellow hood Thul had recovered, and the stone he had found in the burnt village. These were the runes that followed Osian's dark devilry.

"Here," Merlin pointed, clearing more of the dirt away. "Osian's witchery marks the wall."

Hate swelled inside him. The taint of these marks was like poison, making him want to spit in revulsion. Death had always been attached to the discovery of these dark runes. He loathed that what appeared before him was the only clue he could find. But, of course, it was the work of the dark druids that had cursed Arthur to sleep, so the marks of darkness should not have been a surprise. He felt naïve to think Arthur would just be found sleeping.

Something sinister was at work. Merlin felt it in his bones.

Anything could happen.

He fixed his solemn gaze upon Elanor, and then David. "We may have to undo this curse. If I do what I think I must, there is no telling what we might face. No one is to make a move without me. Do not assume you can understand darkness. It has no rationale that aligns with hope or truth. It deceives and tricks. It always lies." His lips curled against his teeth. "Do you understand?"

In his heart, Merlin regretted that either of them were in the chamber beside him. "There is no mercy within these cursed devils. If you are offered it, do not accept it. DO YOU UNDERSTAND?" he demanded.

Elanor lifted her chest, and fear flickered across her face. Her fingers clung onto Merlin's shirt.

"David," Merlin said, remorse clawing up his throat. "I am sorry we have brought you down here. I should have insisted you stayed."

David straightened his shoulders and set his jaw. "I made my choice."

Merlin lifted his chin and sucked in sharply. He hovered his hand above the lantern, then snapped his fingers. A flame flickered to life and danced upon the small, lifted spout.

16

THE CYHYRAETH

The flame flickered, and the three of them tensed. The stillness stole the whisper of their breath. In silent anticipation, they awaited what would come.

A freezing wind blew through the chamber and snuffed out the light. Their torches flashed, then blinked off, leaving them in a heavy, tangible darkness.

David smacked his flashlight to try reigniting the light, but it was of no use.

An anguishing, deathly moan howled through the room, sending tingles of fear straight through them. The moaning creature's respirations pulsed heavily while the blackness swallowed them, amplifying their vulnerability. The unknown entity crept through the chamber, its movements scratching and rattling in the dark. The sound conjured images of bones and chattering teeth.

Their lights fluttered back on.

Merlin cautiously lifted his torch toward the grim chattering. His light skipped across the empty, cold floor and alighted against the edge of the stone coffin. The light peaked higher still, finally revealing a nightmarish figure hunched within the bowl of the cist. The demon faced away from them but swiveled its eerie head over its black shoulder.

Its fingers, long and pointed spindles like a spider's legs, scraped against stone as it gripped the cist's edge. Two white, ghostly eyes appeared. Their hollowness created a vacuum of terror. Sparse hair hung from its head in black tendrils. The clicking wavered as its body twisted around and faced them, revealing a skeletal frame. Gray flesh covered muscle and tendons appearing like tree roots. Its nose-less face was pendulous, and its mouth hung open like a black abyss as it moaned.

The sound made them recoil, clamoring into their ears like the painful cries of someone dying in agony.

Elanor dug her fingers into Merlin's arm, her face pallid as the creature crawled out of the coffin and rose before them.

David's flashlight clacked as it jostled in his hands.

The beast loomed taller, yet its head still hung low. A cloak, like a shadow with floating wisps, surrounded it, and the skull of a dead horned beast rested upon its head. Its very presence embodied death. Its deep, breathy voice purled like a growling whisper. "I am the Cyhyraeth. Death is all I seek. Death..." the creature groaned, "is... all I know. I have slept for centuries... awakened to curse this place. I... was given the task to keep all who seek the Pendragon at bay. But I grow weary... the Pendragon's curse keeps me from what I seek—from what I crave."

Merlin glanced at Elanor, then up at the demon. His breath trembled on his tongue as he dared to speak. "W-We have come for the Pendragon."

The Cyhyraeth moaned, its mouth hanging unhinged as it cried, harkening the promise of death. Its white eyes focused on Merlin, revealing an unnerving void.

Merlin was struck with his own ineptness. He gritted his teeth, struggling to resist the hopelessness.

"I know why you are here, Emrys-s-s and Gwenddydd," the demon moaned. "We all know you in the otherworld. But him..." The wraeth uncurled its demonic finger at David. "I do not know his name." It edged nearer to David, hissing as it shifted like a rippling shadow.

"Stop!" Merlin commanded.

The entity winced back, whipping its head like a viper toward Merlin. A continual sputtering moan oozed from its mouth, like vomit splashing onto the floor.

"What must we do to find Arthur?" Merlin beseeched the demon.

"Death is all I want... I am hungry. A life for a life."

This demon itched to kill, and Merlin did not know what to do. This wraeth could not be slain. It was spirit. That left only two options: figure out how to cast it away and break its power. Or give it what it wanted.

Merlin clenched his fists, wrestling with his decision. If he could ask the right question, maybe he could stay the creature's lust for death, giving him a chance to unravel the riddle. The creature was key to finding where Arthur lay hidden.

Warily, Merlin asked, "Where is Arthur? If we could see him, we might be more prepared to make a deal."

David shifted behind them. Merlin lifted his hand, warning David to be still, but did not dare take his eyes from the demon.

The demon chattered and moaned. "The Pendragon is within your mids-s-s-t. He is shielded from your sight... It is not his curse that covers him, but mine. Os-s-sian delved deep to call me forth and set me to this place. I am owed," it growled. "I care nothing for Osian and his craft or desires. He set me here... starving me." It hesitated, staring at them with a ravenous hunger. "Neither do I care for you, Emrys-s-s and Gwenddydd. Death is all I want. I am hungry. A life for a life."

"Osian," Elanor whispered. The fear was thick in her voice, but Merlin couldn't let it infect his marrow.

"Osian is long dead to this world, Cyhyraeth," Merlin persisted cautiously. "You are free to spend your lust for death. This place no longer claims you."

"The otherworld does not have the limits of time... like you mortals do. Os-s-sian is alive to me, and he is dead to me. This you should know more than any mortal. I," it proclaimed with the screeching of tortured voices crying out, "I am an ancient creature. *You* cannot best me with your mind. You have *no* power or authority over what I am…" The demon hissed. "I will have death if you are to claim the Pendragon. Death is all I want. I am hungry. A life for a life."

Merlin gritted his teeth; uncertainty tugged at him. He reached for whatever light lay within him but the pitch dark was like a suppressing shroud, keeping his spirit imprisoned. He began calling from within his spirit to the Man in Blue to help them. This creature was formidable, but Merlin refused to bargain with it or surrender their lives into its hands.

I will never give evil its desires, he solidified in his mind. Resolute, he positioned himself, ready to pull on the magic within him. He gripped Elanor closer, pulling her behind his back.

"I am growing impatient," the creature seethed darkly. "You cannot dispel me and discover Arthur. You have no other choice." Its empty eyes shifted, glaring at David. "He has-s-s already chosen for you."

David left Merlin's side, stepping toward the creature.

"N-no!" Merlin's breath escaped him. His heart plummeted into his stomach. He reached to stop David but it was already too late.

Elanor shrieked, "Dad, what are you doing?" Her face went sheet-white, eyes locked in horror at her father.

With love in his eyes, David glanced over his shoulder at her. "Doing what I must."

"No—there is another way!"

"I am already dying, Elanor."

"What?"

David glanced up at Merlin. "A knight does what is right, even when faced with death." He faced the creature with the boldest stare. "A life for a life." He raised his hands. "Take mine."

The voracious creature groaned, sending the shreds of its nebulous cloak closer to David.

Elanor dove for him, but Merlin yanked her back into his arms. "You cannot, Elanor! It is too late."

She wrestled to get free, but Merlin squeezed, locking her in tight. She couldn't do anything to save him, and neither could Merlin. If she got in the way now, she would lose her life as well.

"Dad! No! Let go of me!" Elanor pushed against Merlin, flailing out her arms. "Merlin—*No!*" Sobs crippled her voice as she thrashed, trying in vain to reach for her father.

The shadowy tendrils stretched closer to David, and the creature moaned. Deep guttural groaning and clicking emanated throughout the room.

David looked at Elanor once more as a tear fell from his eye. "I love you."

Screams of death poured out of the creature. Its white fingers covered David's face. The horrifying cries of David's agony invaded their ears.

"NO!" Elanor screamed.

Merlin squeezed her harder. He could not let her get free. He could not lose her. This was not supposed to happen. He could have found another way.

The wraeth fully encompassed David within its cloak of shadow, then faded into a black mist. Its heaving groans and crackling bones ricocheted off the stone walls, dissipating until the wraeth was gone.

David was left standing, his face drained of color, though his chest still rose and fell.

"Let go of me," Elanor commanded harshly, pushing Merlin's hands off her.

In all the trauma, Merlin hadn't realized he still had a tight grasp on her.

Elanor dashed for her father. "Dad?" she cried, her eyes bouncing over his stunned face. Her gentle hands gripped his shoulders. Slowly, his eyes connected with hers.

"Yes—look at me. It's alright," Elanor said, her eyes desperately clinging to his face.

David collapsed to his knees, then crumpled to the ground.

"Dad… Dad?" Elanor tearfully begged for his response. She touched his cheeks. "It's alright. Just look at me. You'll be okay." She closed her eyes, and Merlin sensed she was pulling on her magic to heal her father, but nothing kindled. "Please…" she cried, begging to some invisible force. "Help me save him."

David's breath was labored. "I… I am a man of honor who would sacrifice for others and bring healing to all who ask."

Merlin hung his head in sorrow and knelt, setting his hand on David's chest. "You are a king's man of the highest quality," he whispered.

Locking eyes with Elanor, David struggled to speak. "I protected the… princess?" He raised his hand to brush her cheek.

"You did well," Merlin said, his voice choked with emotion. "Y-you did all I asked of you."

David nodded weakly. His proud eyes settled on Elanor. He opened his mouth but was unable to utter a word before a final breath escaped his lips. A passing sigh poured out from his throat, then his eyes settled, disconnecting from his spirit.

He was gone.

"Dad… no… Dad?" Elanor's grief brimmed in her throat. "Merlin?" She pleaded for his help.

Dread rose in Elanor's eyes, and Merlin shifted his tearful eyes away, knowing his own remorse only confirmed the worst.

Elanor buckled forward into silent convulsions. Her painful sobs rang in Merlin's ears. All he wanted was to turn back time. To go back and do something different. To keep David safe when he'd had the chance.

She leaned over and kissed her father's forehead, then whimpered, "No…no. He can't be dead." Her breath seized as she sat up and screamed with a crescendo of anguish, "NO! NO! Please no…"

Tears leaked out of Merlin's eyes, watching his wife hunch over David's lifeless body, struggling between gasps. He reached out his arms to embrace her, but she pushed him away.

"No!" Elanor's angry eyes flared as she fell back down onto her father's chest, twisting his shirt between her fingers. "Why did you let him come?"

Her words—their cutting edge—raked against Merlin's chest. Sorrow pressed upon his throat. He understood her accusation. He knew what this felt like. The feelings of grief mingled with anger were familiar adversaries. Tears awash in his eyes, he stood, leaving his wife to weep.

The evil, vile wraeth had taken a life for a life, but what of Arthur?

The heavy, depressing void left in the wake of David's death felt like defeat.

Had David's sacrifice been for nothing? Merlin didn't want to believe it, but the silence unfurling in this oppressive darkness offered no glimmer of hope.

It killed Merlin to hear Elanor's keening sobs, but he could give her no answer, no measure of comfort that all of this horror had been worth it. He could not look back at her, not face her anguish. The weight of responsibility sank like a jagged stone in his chest. And regret… regret slithered in his thoughts like a coiling snake, hissing the choice he should have made. The one that would have kept David alive.

Merlin kept his back turned to Elanor and fixed his gaze at the stone pall. He gasped. Hope came flooding back to him in an instant. For what had been an empty, shallow coffin now held a sleeping Arthur.

How is this possible?

Merlin's legs nearly failed him. Overwhelmed, he rushed, half-stumbled, to his friend's side. Relief lifting his despair, he reached his hand toward Arthur only to hesitate. Were his eyes deceiving him? Only one way to know. Merlin lowered his hand.

The king's skin was warm, and his lips were pink with no sign of decay.

The last time Merlin had seen Arthur's face, he was sailing away from Avalon to be entombed. Never again did he believe he would see the familiar lines and features of his truest brother.

"Elanor… Arthur—" Merlin swallowed, finding his voice. "…*He is here.*"

Elanor did not move from her father—still in the throes of travail.

Merlin shook Arthur's shoulders to see if he would wake.

Of course, it wouldn't be that simple.

Merlin placed his hand upon Arthur's head, straining to figure out what to do next. His mind reeled as he considered his options.

The ground quivering beneath his feet shook him from his thoughts. Merlin peered up at the ceiling, and earth rained down through a fissure that quickly stretched across the chamber.

There was no time.

"Elanor!" Merlin shouted. He glanced quickly between his wife and his king.

"Elanor," he called again, reaching for her urgently. "You have to help me pull Arthur from the chamber."

17

THE HOUR HAS COME

Elanor clung to her father, clenching her eyes shut, wishing she could ignore the world crumbling around her, but the force of Merlin's voice commanded her attention. Merlin's face trembled with alarm, expelling her from her mournful daze.

He bent to her level and gripped her arms, forcing her to look at him. "We must go. You must leave him."

What is he saying? Leave my father? How can I leave him?

"Now, Elanor!" Merlin grabbed her hand and yanked her to her feet. He frantically assessed the fissures overhead and jerked her forward.

Elanor resisted, taking a step back. Tears stung her eyes as she stared at Merlin.

"I'm sorry," Merlin said, his eyes rimmed with empathy, "but there is no time… We have to go now, and we need to get the king out."

The king?

A loud crack quaked above her head, and a heavy load of dirt cascaded into the chamber. Elanor stared up in horror at the fissures forming across the earthen ceiling, and she immediately sobered to the dire situation. Any minute they would be buried. Without a second thought, she dashed with Merlin to Arthur's side.

There he was, lying in the concave stone. She could feel his warmth as she wrapped her arms around his legs—Merlin at his shoulders. They lifted him from the stone and staggered hastily to the rock laying in pieces before the doorway.

"Lift him onto the stones," Merlin commanded. "You climb through and pull him from the other side, and I will push."

Elanor repositioned Arthur's legs under her arms, girding them tight. As she moved closer to the exit, she saw her father. Her heart wrenched, rupturing open like a spurting wound. She lost her breath.

This couldn't be real.

Was she really going to just leave him there?

A life for a life. A father for a father. A cruel, sick twist of fate. Elanor's mind—her heart—couldn't abide it.

"Elanor!" Merlin shouted severely. "We must leave him."

She sucked in the pain as one last tear fell down her cheek. She shot a last fleeting glimpse at her father's body before she climbed up over the rocks, numb with shock. The ground rumbled like thunder, and she feared they weren't going to make it out.

"Go… Hurry!" Merlin urged.

She squeezed through the opening and dropped to the other side. Merlin pushed Arthur through next, and Elanor pulled him by his broad shoulders. As she pulled, her foot slipped from the stone she'd used for leverage. She screamed in pain as her shin smacked into a sharp corner of the stone.

Arthur fell, tumbling from the hole in the doorway, and crashed on top of her. His heavy frame crushed her ribs, squelching the air from her lungs.

Within moments Merlin was there, lifting Arthur off her. Blood dribbled down her leg, but there was no time to stop and consider her injury. At once, she was back on her feet.

"Lift him," Merlin commanded.

Elanor heard the quaver in his voice. He didn't think they were going to make it.

She hefted Arthur's legs up and hauled him through the tunnel. Her muscles ached, struggling to hold him. But she had no choice. Panic and desperation urged her forward. Her knuckles screamed with fatigue, and her lungs burned in her chest.

They moved fast, clumsily maneuvering down the tunnel. Elanor caught her foot on rubble, and all three of them crashed to the ground.

"Get up!" Merlin yelled, getting to his feet first.

Elanor's adrenaline pumped as she jumped into action, lifting Arthur again. Every ounce of her strength rebelled against the urgency, but she couldn't relent.

Frazzled and heaving breathlessly, they approached the sloping hill that led to their exit.

Elanor faced Merlin in panic. "How will we get out?"

"Just go!"

There was no time to think. No time to reason or make a plan.

Elanor pulled herself onto the ramp of rock and soil, scrambling as best she could up the slope. She slipped and struggled to get a foothold, yet climbed far enough ahead and was ready to pull Arthur. She pressed her feet against the side walls for leverage, but the dirt threatened to give way. Merlin heaved Arthur over his shoulder and launched him in such a way that Elanor could grab hold of his arms and pull while Merlin pushed from the bottom.

Arthur's weight bore down. Elanor could barely hold him and started to slide. She risked releasing one of her hands and dug it into the earth behind her. Her fingers sank through dirt, shoving mud underneath her nails. She clenched her teeth, fighting to hold on.

"I'm losing my grip!"

Merlin echoed a loud yell, followed by a CRACK. There was a burst, and Arthur flew, crashing into Elanor's chest, forcing her backwards up the slope. She slammed against a wall of dirt and found she was leaning halfway out of the opening, holding Arthur by his torso.

Dust whirled like a cyclone up the tunnel, and she released an urgent scream, struggling to pull Arthur's heavy body up over the ledge. Her strength was ebbing. All she had to do was yank him over the side, but as she heaved, she lacked the power to lift him. Her heart beat wildly.

Where's Merlin?

The domed roof rained down rock and debris. She closed her eyes and held Arthur tightly.

Out of the plummeting rubble Merlin appeared, bucking himself up as the tomb caved in behind him. His eyes shined golden as he reached for her. In a snap, Merlin's arm fastened around Elanor. His strength drove her up and out into the fresh morning air. She held fast to Arthur while all of them rolled away from the sinking doorway.

In the rush of escape, Elanor jumped to her feet. But before she could even get her bearings, the side of the hill caved. She reached for Merlin, but the earth gave way, and they were hurtled down the hill along with chunks of earth and rock.

Her head hit something solid, then she tumbled into a tree.

"Dad! Dad!" Elanor screamed.

Dark, shadowy fingers wrapped around him, pulling him away from her. He reached for her, but as she reached back, Elanor found he was already too far away. Her feet were immobilized, keeping her powerless to save him.

Fingers extended in vain, she screamed, "Fa-a-a-ther!"

A soft, urgent voice returned her plea. "Elanor."

Her heart heaved, grasping for hope, but that voice was not her father's.

Merlin's muffled call echoed above her, beckoning her to wake.

"Elanor," he said, gently shaking her shoulders.

She opened her eyes to his blurry silhouette.

"That's it," he soothed, cradling a hand beneath her chin.

Elanor rubbed her eyes, forcing her vision to clear. Merlin curled his arm painfully into his chest. The gash on his cheek freshly bled.

Sadness draped around her like a heavy cloak. She steadily sat up, and the movement made her head pound. Her leg throbbed when she brought her knee into her chest. Blood stained the jeans above her shin. But none of this matched the searing, disorienting pain running rampant in her heart. They had left her father behind in the rubble. The unfathomable thought wrenched inside her gut.

She glanced at the hill where he lay buried. The left side had indented where the tunnel collapsed, leaving trees toppled along the fault. Dust still floated up into the air.

Merlin must have dragged them away from the hill, for they now lay a short distance away. Dizzily, she turned to her side. Her heart leapt, discovering Arthur lying nearby. She pulled her gaze away.

Merlin asked, "Are you hurt?"

"Not badly, I don't think," Elanor said. With a careful twist, she checked her body and felt the bump on her head. "You?"

Merlin grimaced. "My shoulder is out of joint."

Elanor gasped, seeing how his arm awkwardly dangled from the socket. "That looks painful." She touched it gingerly. "I didn't think we were going to make it." She pulled her hand back, and her body trembled. Her head swam in a dreamlike state, and the ground beneath her seemed to sway.

Merlin pulled her head into his chest with his good arm. "Are you sure you are uninjured?"

"Yes… I'm fine. Nothing serious." Elanor lifted her eyes at him, still dazed.

Merlin touched her cheek. "We made it. We are alive."

His words stung. They hadn't all made it.

Merlin bit his lip, clearly regretting his words. He leaned forward and scooted himself near Arthur, then rested his forehead against Arthur's chest. Relief seeped out as he sighed.

Elanor's heart beat faster as she glanced at Arthur's breastplate. It was hard leather embedded with fiery leaves, pointing up to a whirling Celtic red dragon. Fine shining leather rimmed with gold beads wrapped around the arm that laid beside her on the ground. His strong hand and forearm were brushed with gold-colored hair.

She couldn't believe they had found him. All this time wondering, and here he was. Her eyes lifted toward his chin. She jerked her head away. She didn't want to see his face.

"Is… Is he injured from the fall?"

"I don't think so…" Merlin sat back with a pained look. "We must wake him.".

Elanor responded with a somber nod.

"But first," Merlin said, clenching his jaw, "we need to fix my shoulder." He gripped it from underneath with his palm. "I need your help to pull, if you can." With extreme care, he offered his arm.

Wide eyed, Elanor maneuvered over to him and wrapped her fingers around his wrist.

"Now, when I count to three… pull while I yank away from you. It… will be very quick, and I need you to not let go. It will be very painful, and I do *not* want to have to do it more than once."

She pressed her tense lips together and tilted her head, confirming she was ready.

Merlin shifted into position with a heavy sigh. "Ready?" He waited for Elanor's confirmation, then said, "One… two… three." He yanked, Elanor pulled, and there was a large resounding *pop* as his shoulder set back into the joint.

"Aaah!" Merlin yelped. Saliva dripped from his mouth as he crumpled forward. His eyes watered and his face reddened.

Elanor scooted closer to assist him, but he lifted his hand to stay her. "I…" he panted through his teeth, "I will be alright. J-just give me a moment."

She sat back, giving him space to recover. She inspected the large bump on her head and the cut on her leg. She carefully lifted the cuff of her jeans and found a gash underneath. It pulsed with a dull ache. She discovered scrapes on her chin with the tips of her fingers, but the rest of her aches appeared to only be bruises.

Wind whisked through her hair, and she sat motionless, staring silently at the hill. It could have been minutes, or even an hour she sat there dazed; she didn't know. Numbness crept like a trickling stream through her mind and body. Her emotions were bound. She couldn't find the strength to think, cry, or even be mad. Every last bit of energy had been spent.

After a long time, she turned to Merlin, who still lay on the ground cradling his arm. Maybe she, too, could lie down and rest, just for a minute. There was still a residual sense of urgency clinging to her nerves, but her fatigue overruled it. Sleep took her by the arms and pulled her under, making the choice for her.

It was still daylight when she woke. Merlin's warm hand rested on her back.

She sat up, noticing Merlin's pale and despondent face. He narrowed his eyes. "Do you feel ready to wake him?"

Elanor responded by lifting her quivering hand and hovered it above Arthur's chest.

"We will do it together," Merlin comforted, squeezing her hand.

"How will we do it?"

"This task was prophesied to be done by us. The magic is within us. You have healed a dragon and moved the spirit with your song. You will find it within you." Merlin squeezed her hand affirmingly. "Reach for Arthur within your awen. Pull on your magic to heal. Your gift will guide you."

Elanor rested her hand upon Arthur's chest. Her eyebrows rose as she felt his chest lift beneath her hand. As much as her heart ached, she could no longer deny his existence. Exhaling long and hard, she closed her eyes and willed her magic to kindle.

Merlin placed his hand upon hers, his palm heated as it radiated magic. His words charged the atmosphere. "Byddwch fyw ac nid marw—You will live and not die."

The words ignited Elanor's awen. All at once, she saw Arthur sitting upon his black horse, the same way she had seen him in her long-forgotten dreams. However, his face remained unclear within the vision. She couldn't remember if she had ever seen the distinct lines or details of his face, or if she had just forgotten.

She extended her hand, beckoning him. "Arthur. It's time to awaken. Take my hand." She saw her own immaterial hand reaching out.

Arthur swung his leg over his horse and dismounted. He edged toward her, but appeared hesitant.

"Take my hand," she encouraged.

Merlin appeared beside her and called to him. "Arthur, it's time to awaken."

Arthur pressed nearer as a radiating buzz rose in crescendo. He lifted his hands to take hold; gold and blue light emanated from their outstretched hands. The buzzing swelled with a rising pulse, and the light became blinding.

Elanor strained. She felt a strange resistance but pressed all the more. The buzzing started to burn inside her head. The louder the buzz, the less she could see Arthur.

Dark shadows covered her eyes and gripped her wrists, fighting to force them behind her back. However, the dark shadow only served to enrage her. She thought of her father; stolen by a wicked demon.

Not again!

She pushed against the darkness. The song was forming within her heart. She would decimate this evil curse with the song of light.

But she halted, hearing Helen's voice cry out in anguish, *"You killed him. You did this. His blood is on your hands, Elanor. I told you; you would wreck everything!"*

Within the awen, Elanor's heart was struck with guilt and fear.

"You should have died. The promised death should've been on you. You cheated—you cheated. You do not deserve life."

"No… no!" Elanor cried, struggling to resist. But the lies were too strong. Her arms flung behind her back, and the darkness infiltrated, twisting into her.

It's lying. Surely, it's lying.

But she doubted, and her strength gave out. Coldness enveloped her. The duress left her with nothing else to pull from. Defeated, the darkness bound her, and light drained out from her fingertips.

Merlin struggled to hold fast to his magic as Elanor released an agonizing scream. He gripped her hand and opened his eyes. Her whole body was alight with blue magic.

"DEFFRO!" he shouted over Arthur, his eyes ablaze.

Elanor's light diminished, starting at her feet, moving up through her body, and out her fingertips. Her body tensed with pain. The light transferred from her fingers to Arthur, encompassing his whole body. The blue light pulsed, and was gone.

Elanor crumpled to the ground.

"Elanor!" Merlin reached for her as the white guardian appeared once again. He stood strong—his helmed gaze upon Elanor—while his breath echoed as if contained inside a drum. The guardian knelt and touched her feet.

Merlin gripped his injured shoulder and dragged himself to Elanor's side. Her gray, pallid face frightened him. He glanced uneasily at the guardian before pressing his ear upon Elanor's chest.

A heartbeat and shallow breath. Merlin exhaled shakily, relieved to hear the thud of her heart and the air moving through her lungs.

"What has happened to her?" he asked the guardian.

The guardian-warrior was silent. He remained stoic and still, the horns of his helm gleaming with phosphorescent light.

Alarm gripped Merlin. He lifted his hand and touched Elanor's cheek. She was unusually cold. He gripped her pale, frigid hand and turned to Arthur. He still slept.

An icy feeling sank into Merlin's chest. His chin tensed as he considered the possibility that their efforts to revive Arthur had failed. That David had given his life in vain. That Elanor…

His chin trembled, guilt weighing heavily on his shoulders. He looked down at his wife. She was still unconscious, and though her pulse gave him some relief, her ghostly appearance frightened him.

A deep, gentle breath pulled Merlin back to the present. *What…?*

His eyes drew over to Arthur's resting body. Arthur's chest rose, his eyes fluttered, and as he sucked in another breath, he opened his eyes like he was waking easily from a night's rest.

With rigid anticipation, Merlin leaned forward, grasping Arthur's arm.

Arthur's flaxen brows pressed together. "Did it work? Were the monks able to heal me?"

Merlin gasped at the sound of Arthur's voice, and tears flooded down his cheeks. "No, Arthur… they did not heal you." Lifting his mournful eyes, he stuttered, "It… it has been many years, my friend."

"What?" Arthur scowled, blinking at his surroundings. He rolled to his side, and his eyes settled on Elanor lying beside him… then on the ghostly warrior. Arthur went rigid, his eyes growing wide.

The warrior withdrew his sword and Arthur recoiled, flinging up his hand defensively. But the guardian did not attack. He knelt, extending his sword at Arthur's feet. As the sun set lower behind the hills, his luminescence faded into a translucent vision. He rose and turned to walk away, disappearing to reveal the lonesome side of the collapsed hill.

Arthur searched Merlin's face, his mouth wide. "Where am I?"

PART TWO

18

ARTHUR

Merlin wiped his wet cheeks. "I thought I would never see you again. Brother…" He gripped Arthur's shoulders and embraced him.

Stunned and disoriented, Arthur sat upright. His eyes panned Merlin's strange attire and the wound on his face. "You look terrible…"

Merlin sniffed in his tears, then chuckled. "It was not an easy task bringing you back to life."

"Back to life?" Arthur faltered. "I remembered dying—my wound." He placed his hand on his side—the poisoned sting was gone. As if coming into awareness, he again noticed the woman beside him. "Gwynevere!" He snapped to reach for her.

Merlin put his hand into Arthur's chest, stopping him. He shook his head. "That is not Gwynevere."

"But she looks…" Arthur pressed his brows together, gaining a closer look. "Who is she? She looks unwell."

"She is the one who helped me wake you. She—she is…" Merlin clenched his teeth and dropped his chin. "She has sacrificed more than you know, and right now, I need to help her."

"What has happened to her?"

"I am unsure." Merlin scooted his arms underneath Elanor and tried to lift, but his shoulder strained, protesting the movement. He groaned. "Gah!"

"Are you injured?"

"Yes," Merlin said through gritted teeth. "Injured from pulling your arse from that hill."

"I do not understand."

"Not now," Merlin groaned gruffly, his concerned gaze fixed on the curious woman. "Are you able? Can you help?"

Arthur squinted his eyes at Merlin. There was something in Merlin's face

Arthur had never seen before as his eyes lighted on the woman. It was more than just concern, but a tangible connection. It unnerved him. She was too much like Gwynevere, and Merlin's gaze—his eyes—were those of a seaman called away by a siren's song.

"I know this is confusing for you. I will explain later—I promise. But now… can you help?"

Arthur nodded apprehensively, then lifted Elanor, cradling her up into his arms. He observed her face, and her features transfixed him.

Merlin glowered and pointed. "The camp is this way." He labored to his feet and stumbled forward, leading Arthur on.

Merlin fell to his knees outside a strange red dome. "In here."

Arthur knelt and carefully lowered the woman onto a thick mat inside.

Merlin rushed in. "Thank you… Give me a moment with her." He glanced at Arthur with a weary sadness gleaming in his eyes, then nodded and dismissed him. "I must see what I can do to heal her."

Hesitantly, Arthur exited the tent. His mind reached for understanding as he observed the strange objects scattered about the camp. Another green domed tent sat on the other side where a campfire had been.

Arthur stared into the tent where Merlin lay hovering over the enigmatic woman, and his heart raced. He had seen her hands, her mouth—why did she remind him of Gwynevere? Why was he bothered by Merlin's closeness to her? Everything jostled inside his mind as he struggled to put the puzzle together.

Arthur glanced at his hands—his arms. He was completely covered in dirt. He patted the residual dirt and ran his fingers over his breastplate. Why was he wearing it? He hadn't been headed into battle. He lifted his head and inhaled sharply. Of course, this armor had been placed on him in honor of his burial.

His heart sank, and he cringed thinking of it. He lifted his fingers to his shoulder and unbuckled one side of the leather covering. Grief rose up in his throat. Merlin was here, but where were the rest of the ones he loved?

Loosening his breastplate, he reached to undo the other side. Heaps of dirt wedged in the buckle clasp fell to the ground as it released. He let the plate drop, then lifted the bottom hem of his tunic and looked closer at the wound that had taken everything. A red scar remained. Another lining up to match the other marks he had received in battles past, but this one… this one had knocked the kingdom right out of his hands.

Arthur placed his palm upon it. He remembered the field. He squeezed his eyes shut as memories of Cai and Gwain passed through his mind.

Gwalahad and Bors. He sucked his emotion into a tight breath. *It was all my fault,* he thought, lifting his hand to his chest. He felt heavy as the shock of waking wore off.

He remembered the sickly pain that surged through his wound as he stared upon the devastated remains of battle on Camlan. His men's bodies scattered amongst the red and black gore. The agonizing memory struck him with a fierce sorrow that pierced his heart like a sword.

After that moment on the field, everything faded into a fog—becoming scattered fragments of time. He recalled laying in his chamber in the Palisade when he understood he was dying and would not be saved. It was the stark countenance on Merlin's face that revealed there was nothing left to be done. He remembered his regret being worse than the knowledge that his death was imminent. So many had been lost, leaving marks of grief like the scar on his side. They would never leave. Forever a reminder of what he had allowed to happen.

Why did I leave them?

The importance of his quest for the Holy Cup—now foolishness. He never gave up. He never surrendered his search. This formidable, stubborn strength dominated every evil that rose up against him. But now, he considered his own pride with a deep pang within his gut.

He remembered Gwynevere weeping as Bedwyr and Peredur hovered above him. He watched them longingly while he and Merlin pushed off from the shore toward Avalon. His last salvation would come from the Christian monks of Avalon. The same monks who sent warning, dissuading him from seeking the cup. Merlin had warned him also. It was at that moment that he struggled to remember his justifications.

The memories resurfaced, and he was back in the cold stone healing rooms, where the monks scrambled to save him. In fervent prayer, they administered their medicines. Their mournful voices echoed into the empty chamber, mixed with furls of incense floating into the high, lofty rafters.

Arthur faded in and out as the sweaty fever ached through his body—when ultimately, he knew his time had come. Merlin held him in his arms as he weakly peered at him. He saw Merlin's spirit break inside his dark pupils. Merlin the wise was giving up.

He wanted to help Merlin—to remind him there was still purpose, but even he had lost what remained of hope. Arthur's words had been spent, and he could not lift his brother back to life. His own life was slipping away.

"Please…" Arthur struggled to say. "Brother… do n-not surrender." The coldness of death stole through his limbs, and his world melted into black.

Arthur fell into deep darkness… but it did not last. Light swirled into a repetitive rhapsody of a dream. Arthur saw himself on horseback, leading a charge of Cymbrogi warriors. The enemy remained hidden, but he could see two stars rising high in the heavens. He pointed to them as beacons to the warriors, who were armed for battle. These stars—the reason they could fight. The rush of battle surged through him as he dreamt, and always, they charged on—never reaching the fray.

But now, Arthur stood in an unfeeling, empty forest of pine—more lost than ever. Unsure he was worthy of whatever magic had brought him back. Though, as he stared down at the dragon emblem on his discarded breastplate, determination rose within him. He clenched his fist—*I will not dismiss what fate has brought me back.*

He looked back at Merlin and the woman. *Gwynevere... I desire to feel her comforting embrace and look into the sweetness of her eyes once again. I cannot refuse that chance.*

Arthur breathed out and sank to his knees, holding his head within his hands.

Merlin emerged from the tent, seeing Arthur slouched and cradling his head in his palms. Merlin's emotions were stretched thin. He desired nothing more than to collapse and succumb to listlessness. But he could not leave Arthur to reel alone.

He hastened to him and laid his hand upon his shoulder. Arthur's body relaxed at his touch, but he did not lift his head. "How is she?" he mumbled from his hands.

Merlin bristled at Arthur's question. He had been so hopeful to see Arthur alive again, but now, mixed with his relief, there was also anger. A tear leaked from Merlin's eye. He swallowed. "She will be fine. She used all her strength to raise you and break the curse. I believe it has drained her. She just needs rest." He peered over his shoulder at the tent with concern. "But... I have never seen this happen before."

Arthur looked up at Merlin. He pressed his lips together. "She has magic? Is she druid? Who is she?"

Merlin's shoulders slumped, and he narrowed his eyes at Arthur. He felt unready to dive into it all. He took a moment to gather himself and turned to rummage through some nearby supplies. He returned with a canteen of water and handed it to Arthur.

Arthur frowned at it but accepted it. He lifted the canister to his lips. The first sip was small, then he ravenously gulped it down.

The corner of Merlin's mouth lifted. "It's been more than fifteen hundred years since water last touched your lips. Drink, my friend."

Arthur choked. He sputtered, coughing water onto the ground.

"You are probably hungry as well. I know I could use some refreshment."

Arthur wiped his arm across his mouth, then faced Merlin with widening eyes.

With a sly grin, Merlin yanked the canteen from Arthur's grip and drank down what was left. He smacked his lips and glanced sideways at Arthur's shocked face. "Heh. You must prepare yourself, brother. There is a long-sordid history of what has led us to find you."

"If I have come back to a world that no longer contains my kingdom or the woman I love... Please, place me back into my slumber. Why have you brought me here?" Arthur said, bemused. "How is it you are here?"

Merlin firmed his lips as he considered how to begin. He gestured with the canteen still in his grasp. "That hill... is the Hill of the Kings."

Arthur spun around. The large, treed hill was now lined with fallen pines along its side. "Please... It cannot be."

"It is." Merlin told him. "We had a dark tangle with a witch who told us that

Mordred's poison blade had a magic that cursed you, not to death, but only to sleep for a thousand years." He chuffed. "The news was almost too impossible to believe, but it gave us hope that the promised kingdom might still come, and our Great Pendragon would return."

Merlin placed his hand on Arthur's knee. "Brother… you will see Gwynevere and your kingdom again. It is why we have come. We have discovered a magic that has brought us to this future time to find you, and we hope that the magic will bring us back home again."

"How can any of this be?" Arthur stared at the ground, befuddled. "Why would Mordred curse me, and not kill me?"

"Yes, well…" Merlin paused, nodding hesitantly. "I have thought long and hard over that. The truth is I do not know, and…" He sighed. "I believe the truth is likely more sordid and complicated than a simple answer. And since Morgan and Mordred are now dead, we will likely never know the true answer, but what I do know is that Mordred's treacherousness was easily hidden from us because there was some truth to his honor of you as his Pendragon. Not everything about Mordred was a deception. Torn between his promise to his mother to betray you and the respect you showed him as one of your men—Mordred may have hoped to find a way of not entirely killing you."

"Or," Merlin said, shrugging, "it may have been a way to manipulate the rest of us, had he lived."

Merlin glanced over at Elanor through the tent flap. "There is more. And… this will be difficult for you to understand." He exhaled. "The woman's name is Elanor."

Arthur leaned back at the mention of her name, drilling Merlin with inquiring eyes.

"She… she is important. She…"

Arthur eagerly searched Merlin's countenance, then demanded, "Who is she?"

"She is my wife." Merlin grimaced, nervousness and willful purpose swirling in his stomach.

Arthur threw his head back and burst into a jovial chuckle. "What? Merlin has found himself a woman? That… that is impossible. I have known you the whole of my life and have never seen your head even lift toward a woman. Hah!" He slapped his leg, then pointed at Merlin's chest. "I could see a strangeness in your eye when you looked at her."

Arthur tsked, looking up at the sky. His face shifted to a fiery intensity. "Why does this news make me want to punch you in your face?" He rose and approached the tent. "What else are you not telling me? I know her. *I feel it.*" Then more force-fully, he asked, "Who is she?"

Merlin stood and met Arthur's eyes. He pulled his aching arm against his chest. "She is Pendragon."

"What? I am the only living Pendra…" Arthur's face dropped. He stared at Merlin soberly.

Merlin nodded. "She is your daughter."

19

DAUGHTER OF THE KING

Elanor woke disoriented. She couldn't remember where she was, and she felt sick. The orange light from the tent spun, and her head screamed. She rolled to her side to hold her nausea in, squeezing her arms tighter around her middle. Shivers surged through her, and she wished for a blanket.

She squeezed her eyes shut and tried to remember. *What happened?*

A flash of her father wrapped in the terrifying tendrils of the cyhyraeth struck her mind. Her stomach swirled with immediate regret. Elanor wished she hadn't remembered. The pain of the moment collapsed in on her. With clenched teeth, she started weeping.

Maybe I can just go back to sleep and it will be as though none of it ever happened.

She rocked back and forth, trying to comfort herself within the vacuum of grief. Each thought reminded Elanor her father was gone. It was like reaching for air while spiraling deeper underwater—she hoped for anything… *anything* that could bring her reprieve. Every sob stole her breath a little bit more. Her father had been her world most of her life.

It can't be real, she thought. *Please…please, make it all disappear. Let it all be a bad dream.*

Elanor couldn't control her sobbing wails as she lamented this great loss. She doubled over in anguish, barely feeling Merlin's hand curve over her shoulder. At first, his comfort came as a welcome, his nearness made her feel secure. But then, a surge of anger struck her, and she jerked away.

Merlin gently persisted, placing his hand on the center of her back.

Maybe if I ignore him, he will go away.

She hardened her resolve, curling tighter into her chest, closing herself off from his compassion. But Merlin enfolded her into his arms. She wanted to resist him but found the warmth of his chest comforting.

"Sssh!" Merlin soothed as he placed a damp cloth across her forehead and wiped her face. "You have been unwell. It has been a day and a night. Drink." He tenderly lifted water to her lips.

The taste of the cool water on her tongue made her voracious, and she snatched the bottle from his hand. She sat up and guzzled it down.

He offered her bread, but she stared at it with disgust and pushed it away.

"You must eat. I know this food will not relieve your heart, but it will help your body."

Elanor's chin trembled. "I don't care," she whispered spitefully.

"You must." Merlin sighed. "I know it's difficult, but you must eat. We need to leave this place soon and… Arthur waits to meet you."

She had all but forgotten about Arthur. She leaned forward and pressed her eyes closed, unable to imagine how she could possibly reconcile seeing Arthur face-to-face. "He's here?"

"Yes… We did it. You and I… We broke the curse."

Elanor lifted her woeful gaze to Merlin. Her eyelashes were wet with tears.

"I have told him everything. He knows who you are."

"Oh," she said despondently, dropping her head. She felt her face, moist with tears, and ran her fingers insecurely through her knotted, dirty hair. She glanced at the grimy ripped sleeve of her shirt and rubbed the cuff between her fingers. She couldn't see him like this.

"I will bring you some water and some of your fresh clothes." Merlin brushed her cheek. "How do you feel? You have made me *very* worried. You still lack color in your face. Your skin is so pale."

Her bottom lip lifted sadly. "I don't know." How could she know? All she could feel was the rending, painful loss of her father.

"I am so sorry," Merlin said, grabbing hold of her hand.

Her heart felt empty at his words. She squared her shoulders and yanked her hand away with an icy stare. "You're sorry?" The bottom lids of her eyes became bowls, holding back enraged tears.

Merlin leaned back. The severity of her glare was clear. Gently, he conceded and turned toward the tent flap. But before he left, he glanced over his shoulder. "I will return with the things you need to clean."

How dare he? Elanor bristled. *Sorry? Sorry?*

She wanted to blame him with every ounce of her being, as if that would give her justice and ease her pain. She buckled into herself. The events played out in her head. Over and over, she rehearsed the moment her father stepped forward— surrendering himself to the clutches of the horrible demon. And Merlin had held her back. *How could he…?*

What had her father meant when he said he was dying? What hadn't he told her? She wanted him back.

The memory of the dark creature filled Elanor with hate. The demon's clicking and groaning resonated in her ears. The very harbinger of her father's life being stolen from him.

Please... I just got him back.

The idea of having to see Arthur after losing her father was unbearable. But she couldn't hide in the tent forever.

Elanor carefully peeked underneath the small opening of the tent flap to see if she could catch a glimpse of Arthur.

Maybe I could run away.

But the more these thoughts escaped her mind, the more she felt like a child. In truth, she had never felt more vulnerable and orphaned than in this desperate moment. Trapped between what she knew she must do and the little girl that wanted to hide.

Where is my apple tree now?

She laid there a long time until Merlin returned with a small pan of water and her pack. His discerning eyes scanned her face as he delicately settled the pan and bag next to her.

"I know how hard this must be for you," he said, his voice wavering, "I wish I did not have to force you to do things that you are unready for, but I cannot make it disappear. Not even with all the magic I possess." He stared at her with stern compassion. "Elanor... Gwendolen needs her mother to come home."

Oh... Elanor gasped at her daughter's name.

"We must move forward... with Arthur... if we are to get back home again."

Elanor's tears flooded down her cheeks. His words connected her back to purpose. She peered gratefully up at him and nodded her head. The reminder strengthened her. There were things bigger than her grief. A reason to meet Arthur that could not wait for her understanding.

Merlin turned to leave, but Elanor reached to pull him back. Waves of grief and resentment crashed over her, even as her hands grabbed hold of his shirt, but she wanted him close. She embraced him wordlessly.

Merlin kissed her head with relief and firmly pulled her in. "I know this pain well... I wish I could make it go away. But all I can offer is this." He unfurled his hand between them. In his palm rested the little wooden knight.

Elanor gingerly lifted the knight from his hand. The creases of her forehead deepened.

Merlin touched the blue pendant he had given her, which hung over the top of her shirt. "I have never properly understood grief, though I have spent many years of my life chased by it. I discovered that no matter where I ran, it always found me. It has remained my unwelcome companion—never leaving me. It was you who helped me face it."

He squeezed the pendant in his palm. "Peredur found it. It had fallen from your neck that day in the forest. He placed it into my hands, and I remember feeling so angry. So helpless. So..." He shook his head, and his dark hair fell over his eyes. He folded Elanor's fingers around the white knight and cupped her hands within his. He pressed his lips sadly. "Take your time." He moved out of the tent, leaving the flap to unfurl over the opening.

Alone with her conflicted thoughts, Elanor stared at the small figure and rolled it between her fingers. All that was left of her father—in this tiny knight. She sniffed, considering what David had told them about this treasure. She imagined him, a little boy, running free through his garden, holding his knight within his sunlit fingertips.

Elanor didn't know how to move forward but resolved she would anyway. Through tears, she set the knight down. Grabbing the cloth, she began to clean herself, forcefully meditating on Gwendolen. Maybe there would be space to fall apart another time, but this was not that day. She swallowed hard. Merlin had been right to remind her of their mission.

Trembling, she washed. Her body still felt unwell, but there wasn't time for that either. She sobbed as she ran a brush through her hair. Something about pulling through the tangles inflamed her tears. She gritted her teeth and tore through her hair furiously. The pain and frustration felt good with each pull. The brushing felt like a silent scream releasing her pain. However, once her hair had become smooth, the dissatisfaction returned.

Keep moving, she told herself as she cast off her old clothes and washed herself clean. Her heart wrestled with letting the dirt, grime, and clothes go. They were reminders that her father had been with them.

Keep moving. Tenderly she unwrapped the dressed wound on her leg that Merlin had treated. It was a small gouge that no longer needed a bandage. She pulled on her clean clothes; their fresh smell brought no comfort. Just more emptiness.

Keep moving. She pulled on her boots, the last of her tearful stutters diminishing.

Elanor glared up at the tent opening. On the other side of the flap, gently lifting with the breeze, was Arthur. She wished it could have been only Merlin. What was she going to say to him? Would Arthur see in her what everyone else had?

She wondered what he looked like. Her true father. Was his face like hers as everyone had said? Her curiosity grew, mingling with an apprehensive fear.

I am strong. I can do this.

Her heart thumped, and adrenaline heated her face as she leaned over to the opening. She picked up the white knight and lifted the flap.

The sun was bright as she took her first step out of the tent. She exited with her back turned, looking the opposite direction. That moment, she wanted to dive back inside, but it was too late. She heard them stop behind her. She squeezed the wooden knight, then slipped it into her pocket.

Merlin rushed to her side and settled his hand upon her shoulder.

He smiled encouragingly, tilting his head with a nod. "Elanor..." he began. "This is Arthur, the Great Pendragon. King of all Prydain."

Slowly, she turned with a lump fully lodged in her throat. Her lips quivered.

Her eyes alighted first on the ground, then forward until they settled upon his feet. He wore a pair of Cymry, soft leather boots tied off at the knee, below his brown breeches. A dirty white tunic hung loosely, bound by a red sash. His shoulders were broad, his stature tall, with a golden torc wrapping his neck. She closed her eyes and gulped, afraid to see his face.

She could hear his feet moving closer, crunching in the brush.

She leaned her head into Merlin's chest and opened her eyes. Within the peripheral of her eyes, she saw him. Timidly, she turned to him and was met by a familiar pair of deep blue eyes. His gold, wavy hair flowed into a flaxen-red beard that wrapped his solid jaw. He was… her father.

20

APPOINTMENT WITH DESTINY

Arthur could hardly speak. He was thunderstruck the very moment Elanor stepped out from the tent and he saw her raven hair cascading down her back. She reminded him of Gwynevere. His heart wanted to run to her. He held his breath as she turned, expecting to see his wife.

He struggled to believe all that Merlin had explained to him, and Elanor remained the deepest, most enigmatic part. How could he have a daughter? One that had yet to even be conceived?

But as his eyes alighted upon her face, a force awakened within him he never expected. For not only had he seen his queen in her, but now, staring back at him was an undeniable reality. His eyes widened as he observed her face. He saw himself within the blue of her eyes and the angle of her cheekbones. Her lips, perfectly shaped like her mother's.

"How…" Arthur swallowed. "How can it be that you exist?" He lifted his nervous hand, as if seeing his own reflection in a mirror. "You are the image of…" He stopped short, staring at Merlin in shock.

Merlin nodded in agreement. "She has the face of her father."

Arthur moved toward Elanor but halted, seeing a painful tremble in her eye. "I cannot imagine what this must be like for you after…" He faltered, nervous to continue. "I…I am so sorry for what has happened." He placed his hand on his chest and bowed his head as a sign of respect.

Elanor made no movement. Her face was stoic and emotionless.

Arthur tensed at her lack of response, and his nerves prickled as he gazed at the impossible before him. Her familiar eyes captured him, awakening his affections. How could he feel so much responsibility… maybe even care for someone he had never met? With all his heart, he wanted to know her more, but he remained silent.

Elanor's expression shifted ever so slightly. Her face lifted, and a timid smile threatened the corners of her mouth. Tentatively, she held up her wavering hand and offered it to Arthur.

Gently, he took it.

She stuttered as she choked with tears, "I have… always wanted to know what you looked like."

Her words pulled strangely at his heart, and he pressed her hand within his strong fingers.

Elanor yanked her hand away, thrusting her eyes to the ground.

Arthur squared his shoulders and stepped back. He understood she was in turmoil and gracefully allowed her the space. In many ways, he too was unsettled by the strangeness of the situation.

Merlin stepped between them, glancing up at Arthur. "It is with all haste that we must figure out how to return to our own time. Time is pressing against us. I can feel it. There is a dark druid that has failed to stop us from waking you, and he will be vengeful. The kingdom of Prydain needs us to protect it."

"Ah," Arthur said. He was glad for Merlin to give him something to chew on amidst the awkwardness. "Now there is the Merlin I remember. Always about the business of our enemies."

Merlin reached for Elanor, pulling her close with tenderness in his eyes.

Arthur twisted his mouth. "How is it that *you*"—he pointed to Merlin— "have married my own blood? Of all the maidens that never turned your head, you picked my own. Gwynevere approved of this?"

Merlin laughed. "Well, as I explained to you, brother, we were unaware of her connection until it was already said and done. Though," he added with a wink, "the queen has gladly blessed the match."

"Match," Arthur grunted.

"Well, I have to admit, it was a little awkward for us all when we first discovered she was Pendragon."

"Truly." Arthur smirked. "How is it that you saw her above all others?"

"Beyond her beauty, it was her magic that bonded us. A magic I thought was unique to me… She helped me feel I was no longer alone. She was pulled through time and given to me. And I grieved less when I saw her."

Elanor lifted her head to Merlin, her eyes softening.

Arthur didn't understand. "No one else saw how much she resembles me?"

"We would have all thought ourselves fools to think it. You were dead, and… we felt maybe that was part of her gift. Gwynevere believed she was *you* returned to us in some way."

"Apparently, Merlin has an affinity for Pendragons, that's all." Elanor deadpanned.

"Hah!" Arthur laughed, leaning forward to smack his knees.

Merlin was taken aback by the unpredictable humor and slight from his wife.

"Y-yes." Arthur chuckled. "Now I am really going to twist your arm over this one, Merlin. Hah, my old friend could not live without me."

Merlin managed a weak grin, as though unappreciative of the fun being made at his expense. He threw up his hands in surrender while Arthur continued to jab at him.

All at once, Elanor's expression sank. Merlin wrapped his arm around her shoulders, as though to keep her from falling back into despair.

Arthur sniffed and sobered, noticing it too.

Elanor's face contorted as she tried to put a smile back on her face. She glanced at Arthur. "T-truly, it was the magic. It was my magic that fascinated him first."

With grace, Arthur offered, "How is it that you have magic?"

Elanor shook her head. "I… I was born with it."

"How?" Arthur turned to Merlin.

"It is a mystery I have not yet discovered."

"Completely strange that…" Arthur stopped, watching as Elanor turned away from them to face the Hill of the Kings.

She sighed, her chest heaving as she pointed. "We left *him* in there."

Merlin dropped his head. "I wish we had been given another choice."

Elanor's face fell. Her shoulders bounced with silent tears as she walked away from them toward the hill. They watched as she moved with purpose to the memorial stones. All three stones now lay fallen on the ground, and as she approached, she fell to her knees.

Merlin muttered grimly to Arthur, "We had no choice. We had to leave him to escape before it was too late. He was already dead, but…"

"It is never right for a man to be left behind."

Merlin grimaced. "She left the only father she has ever known to rescue a father that never was."

"This will be hard for her to reconcile."

"It will take time."

They left Elanor to mourn, then later followed her to the hill. The timbre of her weeping rose as they approached.

Elanor lifted her wet cheeks from her palms at the sound of Arthur's solemn voice behind her. With careful solidarity, he said, "We will construct a cairn and remember him. This hill was earthed to honor kings and the men that served them. And now, it will also honor a man that has given his life for the daughter of a king."

Arthur and Merlin set to work constructing a cairn. The determination on Merlin's face— wincing through the pain of his injured shoulder—brought a stillness to Elanor's grief.

The tapping and grinding of each stone was a cadence that soothed Elanor as she wept. Eventually her reddened eyes saw the dome taking shape. The sweat that dripped from Merlin's and Arthur's brows filled her with gratitude. Their steady hands had done so much, and now she wished some of her pain, tears, and sweat could also be part of what was being built.

Just then, a stone tumbled free from Merlin's grasp. He grimaced in pain, grabbing hold of his shoulder. As he reached to pick up the stone, Elanor rushed to halt him.

"Let me," she said, pressing her palm to his chest.

Merlin lifted his brows but stepped aside.

Elanor turned to lift the stone. Her fingers strained, her elbows pulled straight, and the stone slipped from her fingers. Determined, she shut her eyes to try again—she wasn't about to give up. This she could control. This was a battle she didn't have to lose. She grappled to get a better hold, and wrenched it up from the ground. Finally, she stood with it firmly wrapped within her arms and, with gritted teeth, maneuvered to the cairn.

She heaved, pulling it to her chest. Arthur reached to help her, but she bit fiercely, "No! Let me"—she grunted— "do it." She clumsily positioned the stone underneath her palms. With a red face, she pushed and rolled it into place at the top. She released a satisfied gasp. "There."

Her breaths were labored as she stared at the cairn, composing herself before turning to face Arthur. As she studied his face, she was struck by the unwavering strength within his eyes. He appeared as everything a king should be—unrattled and proud. It made her feel strangely secure as her gaze stayed fixed upon him.

The wind blew, rifling through Arthur's blond hair and loosening Elanor's strands stuck in the tears on her cheeks.

Somehow, Arthur's solid stance quickened something old and long forgotten inside her. The loss of identity, home, and family began to unravel the longer she looked at him. Was she like him? Would he be as a father to her?

All her life, she had been in a fog. Her discovery of Merlin and magic had unlocked some of the hidden pieces, but seeing Arthur unearthed a fuller picture. His piercing gaze made her think that maybe she, too, could be strong and proud. His stance reminded her of holding a sword, slicing its cold steel through the air. She had always felt she had no business wielding a sword, but now… now she began to think that maybe she did.

An abrupt flashback of David sobered her. Elanor closed her eyes as her heart cringed. Her fingers rummaged through her pocket—pulling out the little figurine. The white knight with its sword and shield was so small. She pressed it into her palm as another tear fell from her eye.

She turned back to the cairn and discovered a perfect place. She nestled the knight into a gap between two stones and turned it to face outward. Brushing it with her fingers, she sighed sadly and stepped back. And then, as if on cue, Arthur grabbed another rock, and the building of the cairn recommenced.

As the sun moved below the horizon, Arthur placed the final rock, scraping it against the stones below until it perfectly capped the top. They all stood back to look upon it.

With his own cheeks wet with loss, Merlin lifted his voice and recited:

"A knight protects the weak and serves the king. He is always truthful, brave, and full of honor. Gallantly, he defends the weak.

"David, you were a man such as this. A man who chose to make the ultimate sacrifice—bringing help to those who asked. You chose to be one of exceptional quality."

"Stories," Merlin went on tearfully, "sometimes have a way of making short the trials and challenges it takes to really be men of quality. I now understand what a knight is and should be. You could not have been just a romantic fool and do what you did—raising Elanor and giving your life for her. You reached for the stars and you caught one."

"Gorffwys yn dda fy mrawd." At those final words, Merlin's eyes lit like flames, and the gaps between the cairn's stones glowed bright orange and white, cracking with heat as they melded together.

As heat radiated from the cairn onto Elanor's face, her heart ached. How had it come to this?

"His sacrifice," Merlin murmured, "will be felt by those that never knew him. History will know him before he is even born. When we find our way home again, this hill will be marked with his name."

Elanor nodded helplessly at his words. She wanted to be strong, but she couldn't find it within herself—at least not right now. But she would go on. She would get better. David's death would be worth something.

"How are we going to get home?" she asked Merlin, her face ashen and worn.

"That, I wish I knew."

21

TRAVELS BACK TO THE FUTURE

Merlin's concern grew as they wandered back to camp. The spark had diminished from Elanor's eye. Something lingered that stole from her, and it wasn't due to grief or trauma. He could not feel her magic, and he worried that she was growing weaker. The hollowness in her eyes and the gray color of her skin was unnatural.

"We have to leave come morning," Merlin said, leaving Elanor to rest as he approached Arthur, who was placing the kindling for a fire.

Arthur sat back on his haunches and grimaced at his hands, bleeding and calloused from building the cairn. He clenched them and faced Merlin. "Do you think she will recover? She still appears very ill."

"She is resting now, and I hope that come morning she will improve. But even if we must carry her out of here, we are running out of what little food we came here with, and I am not sure lingering here is going to give us the answers we need to get back to Prydain."

"You do not know the way back to Prydain?" Arthur probed with increasing concern.

"No," Merlin confessed, shaking his head. "I came here in faith that I would find Elanor and our path would be presented. This… this magic of time…"

"The magic from the dragon?"

Merlin confirmed with a nod. "It comes only when it wills."

"Could we be stuck here?"

"I cannot believe that." Merlin held his hand before the kindling and spoke, "Ennyn." The flames ignited, and he dolefully stoked the fire with a long stick. "We were meant to find you and bring you back. And there remains the direness of Osian, who *must* be dealt with."

"Bah!" Arthur said, angrily kicking dirt into the fire. He rose furiously. "Tell me again—who is this villain, and why has he been allowed to cause such devastation?"

Frustrated, he rubbed the bridge of his nose. "To wake and find so many things backwards. It was my responsibility to keep the kingdom safe and prevent such evil."

"As it was mine."

Arthur glared at Merlin. "As if I could blame you." Vexed, he settled back down beside the fire.

Merlin clenched his jaw. "Osian was the child that ran off with that cursed relic. The moon-shaped talisman with a white stone that was meant to remain hidden."

"The one causing all this pain is that spineless, little brat?"

"Well, if you remember, there was a reason the talisman had been kept hidden. It wielded a power that twisted minds and manipulated the weak. It was an evil, evil thing and should have been destroyed long ago. If I had *only* gotten my hands on it, it would have been." Merlin leaned closer to Arthur. "Osian's perception *must* be distorted, having had such a relic all these years demonically influencing his thoughts. His power is unlike what we have *ever* seen—even from Morgan.

"His evil minions appear and disappear without a footprint—carrying dark sorcery that hastens death. He cleverly hides because he knows he is no match for me—hindering us from stopping his schemes. He covers himself in shadow and conceals himself behind men, demons, and witchery." Merlin mused darkly. "And worse, he has manipulated King Lugh and has infected much of the southlands. And then"—Merlin raised a finger toward the fire— "his level of depravity has resurrected dark enaid that have not been seen for an age. The likes of the demon wraeth that guarded your cursed sleep."

"But... there is light." Merlin nodded toward Elanor in the tent. "The Great God has awakened his own enaid and has been with us—guiding us. I think we must understand, Arthur... We think too highly of our own power. I am seeing a plan unravel before me that is bigger than us all. We are but vessels that are being used, and if we are willing, something better than we have *ever* imagined could be established.

"All those years, we thought we held the kingdom within our hands, but it fell through our fingers like sand. Now, I am comforted to know I could never have had the authority to hold anything more than my own choices. And now we are being given the chance to choose better."

"Choose better?" Arthur mused at his friend.

"I am greatly sobered. We were fools to think that the kingdom we had before Mordred's deceit was unshakable. It has been proven that in our own strength, we lost it all. But there is something more. The Kingdom of the Sun from the songs of old. I just wish I could grasp it."

The next morning, they rose early. Elanor came out of her tent, a pallid and empty look in her eye. Without so much as a word, she broke down her tent and began loading her pack.

"What are you doing?" Merlin asked worriedly. "You do not look well. Let us do the work."

She peered at him with hollow eyes and turned back to her work as though she hadn't heard him.

"Elanor?"

Icily, she whispered, "Leave me alone, Merlin. I'm fine."

Merlin stepped back, angered by her response. Her words felt hardened. He knew she was grieving, but the inflection of her voice caught him off guard. "Why do you bite at me so? I am only worried for you…"

She twisted away from him and continued to shove her belongings into her pack.

"Elanor… I cannot feel your magic."

At his statement, Elanor froze. She turned back around, holding her hands palm up in front of her. They were pale as she rubbed her fingers together. Glancing up at Merlin, her eyes softened. She started to speak but stopped. Her eyes turned cold once again, and she returned to her work.

"Elanor…"

With her back turned, she said, "You knew he was dying—didn't you?"

Merlin gripped his shirt, feeling caught. His heart sped up at the accusatory edge in her voice. He scrambled to gather his thoughts. "Elanor… I—" He gulped down a hard lump in his throat. "I never sought to keep that from you. You father… D-David… he only told me a short time before we went leaping down into that hill."

"Would you have told me?"

Merlin shook his head with uncertainty, then sighed as he lifted his chest and squared his shoulders. "It was not my truth to tell. Though I may have told you if the time became right for me to do so."

Elanor glanced at him over her shoulder.

"He… he said that he had a cancer. I do not know of the sickness, but he did tell me that he had told no one. Not even Helen. I promised him I would not tell you."

Her lips drew tight. "Should it make me feel better that he was going to die anyway?"

"No… Never." Merlin sucked his lips closed. "I think he came with us in hopes of redeeming himself before he died. He said he wanted to be a man of quality. You believe he already was—but David did not. He should not have died that way. I wish he had not done what he did. I would have found another way. But your father believed that his choice to sacrifice himself was what he needed to do. And, ultimately, he died believing he was the man he always hoped to be. For you, and for himself."

Tears streamed down Elanor's cheeks. "I want to be mad at you—blame you for everything that has happened, but I can't. I want to find someone to hurt. I don't know why."

Merlin knelt next to her. He placed a tender hand on her shoulder. "I understand."

"I feel so tired. Drained and weak. I cannot find myself or think straight. We went into that hill, and I don't feel like I ever came back out."

"I am worried about what has happened to you since you used your magic to awaken Arthur." Merlin lifted Elanor's chin with his finger, his eyes scanning her sallow appearance. "It is as though your spirit was drained. Your bright blue eyes are gray and dull."

Elanor squeezed her eyes shut. "What has happened to me?"

"Grief would have been enough, but unfortunately, something else has eaten away at you. We will discover it. But first we need to leave this place. Are you able to walk the distance? We could leave many of the supplies behind and carry you if need be."

Elanor dropped her head. "Merlin," she began quietly, "I do not think we should leave any evidence that we have been here. My father will now be considered missing. You can't disappear in this world and not have the authorities come looking. That is only if Helen becomes concerned. It may be a few more days before that happens." She took a shaky breath. "I don't know. If they were to find anything connecting us to his disappearance, they may assume we had something to do with his death. Things here are not like Prydain when a man dies. We could be detained. Arrested. There would be an assumption of ill intent. They would seek justice for his… for his possible *murder*."

She looked down at her hands. "This is my fault. This is *all* my fault." She glanced at Merlin with disgust at her revelation.

"I did this. All of it! I am the wrecker. I took him away from them."

Merlin sought to stop her but was halted by an odd buzzing resonance. Elanor's face shifted and darkened. Her body slumped, and she shouted, "I KILLED HIM!" She faltered, desperately clutching her chest as her feet crumpled beneath her. "I killed him. It was me." She bent down between her knees and covered her head.

"You didn't kill him," Merlin protested, grabbing hold of her. He couldn't tell if he was getting through to her—there was something invisible hovering between them.

He lifted Elanor's face and looked her in the eyes, but they appeared disconnected. "Elanor!"

The loud, radiating buzz surged inside Merlin's head, darkening his thoughts. He jumped up, covering his ears in distress. Raising his hands above his head, he clapped, and the sound pounded like a drum. "STOP!" he shouted.

His declaration released a swift wind that blew the darkness from his mind, dissipating the madness.

Merlin tilted his ear to listen. The buzzing had ceased. He swiftly knelt, pulling Elanor up from between her knees. "Are you alright?" He searched her face to see if anything had changed. Her eyes remained empty.

Elanor pushed him away, glaring like a dog ready to bite. "I'm fine," she snapped. "Leave me be, Merlin." She twisted around and went back to tossing things into her pack.

"There is something amiss happening to you. I can feel its insidiousness."

Elanor spun on her heels and spat, "There is nothing dark here, Merlin. Other than the fact that my father is dead." She threw her pack to the ground and stormed away.

Reeling from her venomous attack, Merlin dashed after her. "Elanor," he called, reaching for her arm and grabbing hold of her wrist.

His pull stopped her, and she turned to face him with a glaring ferocity. "MERLIN." She yanked her wrist from his grasp. "NOT EVERYTHING IS A DEMON."

"I KNOW," he shouted. His anger was rapidly rising, and he inhaled sharply to calm himself. "Listen… there was something…"

Through her teeth, she uttered, "Leave me be." Her hair whipped as she turned and tempestuously marched away from him into the trees.

Infuriated, Merlin clenched his teeth and pinched his brow.

Arthur's footsteps crunched the brush behind Merlin. "What's happened?"

Merlin glowered at him from the corner of his eyes. His lips curled as he growled, "Demons."

"Demons?"

"Mmm," he mumbled lividly. "I hate this place." He scowled at the trees Elanor had stormed into. "She is grieving. I know. I am not a fool." He tightened his hands into fists at his sides. "If that alone were the problem, I would be glad to give her space, but I am discerning enough to see the devious rumbling of darkness."

"In Elanor?"

"The demons hide in this world. That waxen darkness covering my wife's face is not the weariness of grief. Something occurred when she was within her awen helping me break that curse from you."

"What do we do?" Arthur growled, bristling his shoulders as if preparing to fight.

Merlin lifted his hand to stay his friend. "I do not know." He looked up at the sky. "First, we need to get out of here. Rain is coming."

22

THE GRAY OF GRIEF

"Hey, Mum?" Jack said, barging into the kitchen with a hell-bent demeanor. Helen was busy at the table, shuffling through papers and preparing her lessons.

"What is it, love?" She sighed, perturbed. "I have quite a lot of work to do. I thought you were headed back to the city."

"Where's Dad?"

"He is working from town this week."

"From town?" Jack's suspicion flared.

"Yes. He left a note saying he'd be staying in Aberystwyth."

"Have you spoken to him?"

Helen tsked. "No! Now, Jack, what's the problem?"

He twisted his mouth. He wasn't sure he wanted to tell his mother that he had seen his dad jumping into the car with Elanor and her stupid boyfriend a few nights back.

"Nothing," he grumbled, pressing his lips together. "I just haven't seen him, that's all. Not since we had supper when Elanor came with… with…"

"That daft boy? Heh. They deserve each other. What a strange, arrogant young man."

"Dad spent the whole night with them. He never came in to watch the match. He said he'd watch with me. Turned out to be a crap match anyway," Jack muttered.

"You know how your father gets when Elanor comes 'round. He spent most of the evening showing them all his maps. In fact, he's left them all out there on the table. I should leave them out there. It's supposed to rain. That would teach him. Honestly," she tutted, "as much as he loves those maps, I'm surprised he didn't take care to put them away. Probably forgot. Had too much wine and was up early the next morning."

"What was he showing them all his maps for?"

Helen shrugged, adjusting her glasses that pinched her nose. "Is there anything else I can help you with? I really need you to bugger off so I can get my work done."

"Gah! Fine," Jack spat, angrily swishing his hand at her. "No sense tryin' to talk to you."

"Heh," she huffed, unconcerned, and started ticking away on her keyboard.

Curious, Jack glanced out the glass doors at the back garden and saw his father's maps sprawled out on the table under the gazebo. One of them flapped in the wind from beneath one of the books. Aggravated, he slid the door open. He wasn't sure what he was hoping to find, but this whole business wasn't setting right with him. Maybe these maps could give him a clue.

One of his father's heavy atlases lay open, displaying a map of England. He rolled his eyes and thumped the book closed. He started shuffling the maps together so he could put them away when his eyes were captured by red marks on the map beneath his hand. There were notes written and portions that were circled.

"Cumbria," Jack mumbled, his interest piqued. He touched the map, his finger gliding across to Carlisle. He leaned closer, squinting to read the scratched notes... *Caer Lial... Hill of the Kings... Arthur.* He lifted his eyes, scrunching his face in confusion. "What in the hell?"

Surely, they hadn't gone there. Or had they?

He thought back to the night they departed. He remembered them loading camping supplies and sleeping bags. He fumed, remembering Elanor and Merlin wrapped in each other's arms. Elanor's contentment offended Jack. He didn't know why, other than he had so rarely seen her that way. He was unaccustomed to it. Maybe if she had been kissing someone he liked more, he wouldn't be bothered.

They probably just dropped Dad in town and went by themselves on some ridiculous road trip, he reasoned. But the more Jack thought, the more his anger flared.

"I'll check it out for myself," he mumbled, pulling his phone out of his pocket, and scrolling to his dad's number.

Beep, beep... Beep, beep... the phone rang.

He sighed, exasperated, waiting for his dad to pick up. "Come on... Pick up!"

Nothing.

Irritated, he canceled the call. He glanced at the phone, then back at the map.

Maybe I'll call El. I hate having to call that little twat.

He sighed, perturbed, and entered her number. Again, the call rang, with no reply.

"Gah! Where is she? Dad better not have gone with them. Why does Elanor get all his attention? If Dad's gone with her all the way to Cumbria"—he ruminated darkly— "they'll have hell to pay."

He shuffled the maps together and scooted them inside the pages of the atlas, tucking the map with the notes into his back pocket. He stormed back around the front of the house—of course his father's car was still parked there.

Jack walked back into the dining room, slamming the book and maps onto the table in front of his mother.

"Really, Jack?"

"You know, I saw Dad leave with Elanor and Merlin in the middle of the night."

"Well, that's strange." Helen shrugged. "Probably taking him to university. Maybe he didn't want to get up extra early to drive there himself."

"Has the thought not occurred to you that it was strange he just *effing* left without his car?"

"You know he often leaves his car. Your father prefers the bus. It allows him time to clear his head. You know how he is."

"Have you even *called* him?"

"Jack! What is the matter?" Helen stared at her son with a troubled expression. "Your father and I have never been very good at phoning one another. Would it make you feel better if I gave him a call now?" She stood up with her hands on her hips. "Is there something you would like me to ask him for you?"

Jack glared, setting his jaw. "I already called him. He didn't answer." He hadn't really taken the time to understand why he was so upset—he just hoped his father wasn't with Elanor. She didn't get to have him. He wasn't *her* father.

"I'll phone him—you're clearly distressed by his absence. Here." She held up her finger, then picked up her mobile to dial David. She held it to her ear, pressing her lips together and raising one eyebrow at her son. She waited. Nothing.

"He's probably busy. It is the middle of the afternoon. You know he doesn't just sit around with his thumbs up his arse like you do."

"What if he's run off with Elanor somewhere?"

"What? Don't be absurd. Is that what has you worried? Why on earth would he do that? No, no, David would not go venturing off with that girl—not without telling me first. Besides, I wouldn't let him. The less of that girl in our lives the better. She is always so needy, and so... sad looking. Bleh." Helen shuddered, shaking her head.

"Mum... what if he has gone with her?"

"Look, I am not sure what has gotten into you, but I do not have time for it. Your father is just busy. I will phone him later—you'll see. You're just bored. Letting your mind create strange conspiracies. I mean, really..." She huffed, "Do you even know my dad? He is the most boring, humdrum sort of man. Sitting around, piddling in his garden all day when he isn't at the university. He wouldn't even know which end was up or down if I wasn't there to help him. Helpless, really. Can't even go to the corner market for eggs without getting confused." She tsked, turning and slumping back down into her chair. "Beyond looking at his maps, he has never had the bones for adventure. He'd fall into the first hole he found."

"Huh." Jack was unconvinced. He knew how little his mother thought of his dad. He was quite capable but happy to keep his mother thinking he depended on her. "Anyway—I'm going to call Michael at the uni. Maybe even swing by there. Dad might like some company for supper."

"Suit yourself."

"Can I take Dad's car?"

"Just be sure to put some petrol in it. Don't want your dad breaking down on the side of the road because he forgot to check the gauge."

Jack walked over and pulled the keys from a hook on the wall. He glanced at his incurious mother, who had dismissively returned to her work. He wouldn't be as easily satisfied as she was. His gut wouldn't let him. He *would* find his dad. If he was right and his dad had gone off with Elanor, Jack was going to set things straight.

The gradual rain fell as they trudged through the path, leading them back to civilization. But the heavy gray clouds swept in and dumped a downpour. Elanor felt even more wearied as the cold dripped down her back.

She refused to let Merlin see her weakening. She, too, was afraid that something more sinister had happened within her. She felt empty. Her empathy and compassion were missing. All she had was sadness and anger. There were moments where she would have sanity, but then she would crumble back into a bleak abyss. She couldn't find the light of her magic. It was as though it had drained out of her, leaving her a lifeless zombie as she pushed forward.

Her hope remained in her denial of it all. She could pretend her father hadn't died and that she wasn't ill or depraved. Maybe if she kept it up long enough, it would become true, and the devastation would all go away.

Merlin struggled to carry his load; his injured shoulder was useless. He was forced to carry his pack on the one side. Arthur carried the largest load after helping Merlin bind his arm to his chest before they left.

Elanor didn't want to speak to Merlin after their fight earlier that morning. She knew better. She knew he'd only wanted to help, but she couldn't push through the anger that buzzed in her ear like a swarm of bees. She fumed at the thought of him.

So, she walked alone and even sat away from them when they rested. She wished she could curl up into a ball and sleep until it was all over. She cringed as she avoided Merlin's stare. His worried look made the weight in her chest more burdensome. She hated feeling like she had failed him by not being stronger.

She was sure she had disappointed Arthur. He had probably hoped to have a daughter more like himself and Gwynevere; fierce and noble. But she couldn't will herself to be any better than she was.

She overheard Merlin preparing Arthur for the strange new world ahead. The people, the iron chariots, the bright lights, and the loudness that invaded one's ears. Elanor swallowed it all down and tried not to think as the valley opened into a field. The road could now be seen far ahead. It was hard enough facing Merlin and Arthur with her drought of self, but now she would have to put on a mask to face the rest of the world.

Would she be so indifferent if Adhan or Gwynevere stood before her? Would she slap down Cilaen like she had Merlin? She felt like a cavern, devoid of even an echo, her spirit chased away.

Cars whizzed by on the road as they neared. Arthur's breath was nearly stolen as each one roared by. A great wooly ram with his coiled horns tore at some grass. The bell beneath his neck jingled as he lifted his head to gawk at them as they labored by. He appeared undisturbed by their presence, and Elanor wished she could feel the same.

The other side of the *No Trespassing* sign dripped with rain as it rattled on its chain in the wind, blocking the field from the road. The time had come to cross over. They had initially arrived with David leading the way, but now they were about to enter back into the world without him.

Elanor stopped at the sign and turned back to face the hills. She could not convince herself to move another inch. Stepping over that line would be like acknowledging all the bad that had happened, and she wasn't ready. Her chest felt like it was caving in as the rain dripped off her nose.

"Maybe..." The sound of her voice caused the men to turn. She hadn't spoken for the entirety of their trek back. "Maybe if we go back, he will be there—waiting for us." Her words split open the grief, and she bit her lip to lock the tears inside her eyes. "I... I don't think I can do it," she implored, her eyes locking on Merlin's.

Merlin came beside her, casting a somber gaze over the valley.

"I don't think I can cross the road." She stood there, wet and frigid, with her hands trembling. "I'm sorry..." Elanor whispered. "I don't know what's wrong with me."

Merlin sighed. "I know."

She squeezed her hands in front of her chest. "It's as though I am not even here. I can barely feel the cold."

"We must move on. It will not change things to be held back."

Elanor lifted her chin with a swift, sad nod. Her voice broke. "I want to go home."

Merlin held out his hand.

Reluctantly, she accepted it and allowed him to assist her over the chain. Needles pricked her heart as she lifted her leg up and over the rail. She pressed onward numbly, crossing the road to where the car had been hidden. The low buzzing in her head amplified at each step. She rubbed her forehead as she walked down the ledge and behind the large shrub, revealing the car's rear bumper. Stumbling, she approached the car door and unstrapped her pack to find the keys.

"You killed him," the voices began. *"You took him away from us."*

"You are nothing but a stupid silly girl, trying to think of yourself as special." The buzzing grew louder. *"You don't even have your magic anymore—Merlin will see what you truly are. Nothing."*

Elanor's hands fluttered more violently as she fumbled with the keys to find the right one.

"It's all your fault."

She dropped the keys, throwing her arms up to cover her ears. A cold hand grabbed hold of her fingers, pulling them away from her ears. Merlin's eyes blazed with yellow light, but she couldn't hear his words over the buzzing.

All at once, the voices stopped, and she exhaled with relief. She ground her teeth and squeezed her eyes shut, angry that it had happened again.

"I can hear the buzz that presses upon you," Merlin remarked. "I am not able to break it."

Elanor didn't know what to say. She was tired… too tired to care. And now the idea that Merlin would cease to value her consumed her thoughts. Maybe all that had made her special had been taken away. Honestly, it was all too much for her to think about. Maybe driving away from this place would make it better. They all had been without food and rest—maybe that would help.

"There is a town, not far up the road," Elanor struggled to say, wincing as her head ached. "I should have enough money to get us lodging and some food. Maybe that is all that I need. Maybe that is what we *all* need."

"Can you drive?"

She nodded. "Uh-huh." She wasn't actually sure, but in truth, they didn't have that far to go.

Merlin lifted his chin over at Arthur. Their eyes locked, both reflecting concern for Elanor's dire situation.

Merlin sighed. "Right. Arthur, let me show you how to get into the car."

Elanor searched for the keys in the high grass, then placed them into the lock, opening the door. She reached across to unlock Merlin's side.

Arthur stepped back, his eyes wide. "So… we are going in there, then?"

Merlin chuckled, breaking the tension. "I know the feeling, brother. This chariot goes fast. Not to worry, Elanor seems to have a good handle on driving it."

Now, even Elanor managed a smile. It was humorous watching Arthur, *a king of legend,* struggle to get into the back seat of such a small, mundane car. His face painted in wonder, he stared at all the strange materials and gadgets as he scooted inside.

Elanor couldn't help but burst into laughter. It was the first moment of relief she had felt from her sadness since the tomb. It bubbled forth with all the emotion and built-up tension. Tears leaked from her eyes as she giggled.

This made Merlin roll into chuckles along with her.

"What?" Arthur demanded at their laughter. "Now we find reason to be amused? At my expense… I cannot…" He slumped with a grumpy glare.

"Ah…" Merlin breathed, squeezing Elanor's hand. "It is good to see you smile, and you, brother"—he turned to Arthur— "you are about to get even more uncomfortable. This world is only about to get stranger."

23

THE VOICE IN THE DARK

Elanor seemed to perk up once they had gotten into the car. The drive itself had been fairly short—and amusing. Arthur's jaw hung open the entire way, especially once they arrived in the town. The buildings and the people baffled his sanity.

Merlin's concern for Elanor still remained, but his unease waned as the heater warmed the car and dried their clothes. Elanor, though still pale, appeared brightened by the distraction of Arthur's uncouth reactions to each sight.

"He belongs here even less than you," she said with a growing smile. And it was true. Arthur would stick out like a sore thumb and likely never blend in the way Merlin had.

Elanor pulled up to a tall, white building set on a lane of what appeared to be a marketplace where people scuttled through the rain—some carrying odd mushroom-shaped covers above their heads. Elanor turned the car in between two buildings and drove on back behind it where there were many other iron chariots of different sizes.

She slowly pulled to a stop between two cars. "I'll be right back." She twisted the keys and turned the engine off. "I have to go in and see if I can reserve a room."

Arthur glanced at Merlin, mystified.

"It is a type of inn, I think. Tavern?" Merlin explained, looking at Elanor to confirm.

"Yes." She nodded. "This is a hotel. Hopefully, I can get us a room. We need some respite from this *blasted* rain. I don't think we would enjoy sleeping squeezed in this little car like sardines all night. And it's getting late." She pointed through the windshield at the darkening sky. Lifting her bag that sat at Merlin's feet, she rifled through it and pulled out a rectangular object. "I will be needing this."

"What is that?" Arthur inquired, befuddled.

Elanor grinned. "Money." She hurried out of the car and disappeared toward the building, leaving them to wait.

The heat inside the car dissipated quickly as rain drained down the windows, blurring the view.

"This is a strange place," Arthur mused.

Merlin lifted his head in agreement. "Elanor showed me a place like this in a vision when she first came to Prydain. I thought everything to be magic, and the people, very bizarre. All of them so different in a range of noises and lights. It is still beyond me how anyone is to have a moment of solid thinking amid all the chaos."

"It is assaulting. To think… this is what comes of the world we fought for."

"It may be that the people of this time do not feel as abhorred as we do. There are freedoms I have observed here that could never be experienced in our time. The *science* has helped make some parts of their lives easier and more comfortable."

"The science?"

"All the things you see that seem like magic."

Elanor's figure came running to the car, waving a little white object in her hands. She opened the door. "I've got it. We have a room for the night. Come on, let's go in. We can get freshened up." She couldn't hide her excitement. "It will feel so amazing to take a hot shower."

Merlin did hope that a shower might wash away the past few days, and maybe even the dark circles from under Elanor's eyes.

"There is a restaurant in the hotel, so we can get some food while we're here. Come on," she coaxed, pulling impatiently on Merlin's good arm. "It's raining. Let's go! I'm tired of being soggy and wet."

"Come on, Arthur," Merlin hollered on his way out, urging Arthur along as he stared, distracted by the strange sites. "No time to figure it out right now."

Quickly, they splashed through the car park before reaching the building. As they entered, the lobby was offensively bright. A rotund, blonde woman watched from behind a counter, blinking her giant black eyelashes at them.

Elanor waved awkwardly as they passed by. The woman only stared back in shocked fixation at Arthur's unusual clothes. And she was probably taken aback by all their bumps and bruises. Merlin reached up to his cheek, remembering his bleeding gash, along with his slinged arm.

As they made their way to their room, Arthur brushed the walls with his fingers and observed the bizarre, oddly shaped furnishings. He stopped, perplexed at the strange red patterned fabric beneath his feet. Amazed, he pointed at the large photographs of real people and places that hung on the walls.

Merlin grinned. "Is that what I looked like when I was seeing it all for the first time?"

"Maybe a little." Elanor smiled. "Though I suppose you had more of a warmup. I am sure I had plenty of awe in my eyes when you took me through the Palisade that first day. I remember how amazed I was at the tiles on the floor and the large tapestries on the walls."

"Hah." Merlin's mood sparkled at the memory. "I do remember. I had to drag you along, as you stopped at every turn."

"The tiles depicting an enormous bear with warriors encircling him—that was my favorite."

Arthur's chest lifted; an air of sovereignty danced across his brow. "That is my seat amongst men. I *am* the Great Bear."

Bemused, Elanor turned her inquisitive eyes to Merlin. "Truly?"

"It is true," Merlin confirmed.

"Why have you never told me?"

Merlin tried to recollect why he hadn't told her. "I guess… the grief was still too heavy for me." He nodded to Arthur. "The floor was specifically designed to reflect a prophecy given just before Arthur's birth of a 'Great Bear.' The prophecy, sung by the druids, said that a new king would rise like a *Great Bear*, and *he* would become king above all the lords of Prydain. Most extraordinarily, a bear ran across the stones of Uther's fortress the night Ygraine—Arthur's mother—went into labor."

Arthur's countenance shifted sadly.

"The warriors detailed within the surrounding circles represent Arthur's mighty men and all their feats of bravery over evil men and devils."

Arthur sighed. "It is within the circle where I meet my men as equals. Kings also join this circle in times of great council. These are the ones that have my ear when I seek wisdom."

"Does Merlin have a circle?"

"No." Arthur grinned, placing his hand on Merlin's back as they wandered forward. "He joins the circle but does not have a circle of his own. He stands at my side, upon the back of the bear, so that all understand his place. He is my most trusted counsel and, in many ways, carries the heart of Prydain more than the rest."

Elanor gasped with revelation as they approached the end of the hall. "Wow. So, there is a round table?"

Merlin and Arthur glanced at each other, puzzled.

Elanor chuckled at their confusion. "Now, prepare yourselves." She moved to press a round fixture on the wall that lit when she pushed it. Merlin and Arthur's mouths gaped as silver doors magically slid open before them.

Elanor giggled at their expressions. "This way." She gestured for them to enter. "It's just an elevator. It will take us up."

Merlin and Arthur reluctantly scooted into the lift, their eyes erratic with mistrust. The doors glided shut, and instantly, they set their feet as if preparing to escape.

The elevator jolted, and Arthur almost dropped to the floor with fright.

Elanor doubled over, cracking up. She grabbed their arms with reassurance. "It's alright. We're safe. Don't worry, we are almost there."

As they continued their ascent, Elanor's face grayed with dizziness, stopping her laughter. Her brows lifted, and her mouth turned down.

Merlin noticed the drop in Elanor countenance and clung to her. Arthur was too occupied with the oddity of this new world's *science* to notice her sudden discomfort.

When the doors on the lift opened at last, Arthur darted out as if worried the elevator would swallow them if they didn't exit quickly.

Elanor pulled herself from the lift, forcing a smile. "M-maybe I should have taken you up the stairs."

"There were stairs?" Arthur blurted, annoyed.

Elanor grinned feebly, her knees wobbling. She stumbled into the wall, capturing herself before she fell. "Just dizzy," she said quickly to ease Merlin. "Too much excitement, I suppose."

"I almost forgot that you are still unwell," Merlin said, rushing to stabilize her.

Arthur also leaned forward to help. "Let me support you the rest of the way."

Her ashen eyes snapped up at him angrily. "My father is dead."

Arthur stepped back, offense tightening his brow as he turned to Merlin.

Let it go, he communicated with his eyes.

"I'm suh…sorry." Elanor glanced down wearily at Arthur's boots. "I did not mean to… I just need rest. I'm so tired."

"Come on," Merlin urged, "let's find the room."

Elanor nodded, leaning up from the wall. Steadying herself, she grabbed the crook of Merlin's arm as he led on. Turning the corner, they found a door marked 317.

"This is it." Elanor slid the strange white card into the door.

Click.

The door opened.

Jack blazed down the road as the night descended. Rain pelted the windshield of his car, blurring the lights in front of him. His angry trance intensified. He had gone to find his father at the university, but he was not there. The other staff confirmed that he had been gone since the week started, confirming Jack's suspicions. His emotions boiled over, fueling his determination to find his father.

Was he with her? Had he gone to Cumbria with them?

Jack fumed as he glared down the road. He had no idea how he might find them. His only clues were the red circles on the map around Carlisle.

"Nothing is going to stop me from finding them," he grumbled through his clenched jaw. The itch within him was growing. He would find them, somehow. He picked up his mobile to call Elanor for the millionth time.

Beep, beep… Beep, beep. Nothing.

"Damn it!" Jack threw his mobile down on the seat next to him. "How will I find them when neither of them will pick up their *rubbish* phones?" A knot formed in his stomach as he considered why his father wasn't answering the phone.

Jack gripped the steering wheel, white knuckled, and a scowl etched onto his face. He gritted his teeth. "Why has he gone with her?"

He sighed deeply, shaking his head as he attempted to calm his rage. His mind cleared, and he lifted his foot from the gas pedal to slow down. "What am I doing?" He sobered for a moment, wondering at his own anger.

"She doesn't deserve him—that's why," he answered himself. "Dad shouldn't be out here with her. He should be at the university or at home. Cumbria is too far away. What reason could he have—could any of them have—to have gone so far?"

He cocked his jaw, considering whether to turn around. "I could wait until he comes home. Talk to him then. Set him straight. Elanor, she…" Jack lost his grasp on his clarity as darkness settled over him again at the thought of her—and her wretched boyfriend. His thoughts flared with venom. "Merlin. That… th-that prat."

Jack hated Merlin—convinced he was trouble. "He is messing things up, making Elanor believe things she shouldn't." He smacked the wheel with his palm. "Aah—damn! What am I doing?" He veered over to pull off the motorway.

"Don't stop."

Jack jumped. He glanced at the passenger seat. The words sounded close to his ear, like someone had whispered them. His skin prickled, and his heart pounded. His eyes darted about the car, confirming that he was, indeed, alone. Jack rubbed his eyes. "Now *I am* losing my head." He continued toward the nearest exit.

"Keep going," the voice persisted.

Jack jerked the wheel and swerved. "Shit!" he yelled. He struggled to aright the car—his tires screeching as he pumped the brake. He sucked in a breath just as the car jostled to a halt.

"Who is that?" he demanded. "Who are you?" He looked around again, fear rising in his chest. "I'm-I'm just hearin' things. Yeah," he reasoned, "that's it. I need to go back home. Get some rest."

"He is your father. Not hers. You must find him."

Jack swallowed a sticky lump in his throat. "Who… who is that?"

"Jack… you must listen." The voice was breathy and aggressive. *"I can help you find them. Get them."*

"Wha—"

"Elanor… she is not trustworthy. She has taken your father."

"Y-y-you could help me find them?"

"Jack, they must pay. They must. It is all Merlin's fault. All of it. Make them pay."

"Make them pay?" Jack glanced down at his lap, surmising. "What right did they have to convince my father to go on whatever daft trip they are on?"

"They have hurt him. Merlin hurt him."

"What?" Jack trembled, an enraged, bitter tear dropping from his eye. "W-what has he done to my dad?"

"Elanor stood by and let it happen. She let Merlin hurt him, and now there is another one—another one that is with them."

A grayish apparition appeared in the seat beside him.

Jack gasped, pressing his back against his car door to distance himself from the figure. His lips quivered. "Who are you? Why should I believe you?"

"She never belonged, Jack. You know this. She ruined your family. All that could have been

the Evans' she destroyed. Her brightness stole him away like a moth to a flame. That is why you are angry. That is why you want to find them."

"She… she did do that." Jack nodded, rolling his hands over his knees. "Though I never really blamed her like my mother and sister did. She seemed alright. Never got in the way too much… She left after school and started working in the city. Everything went back to the way it should've been. But then, she came back with that bloke, and his eyes… his eyes…" Jack bristled, wiping his perspiring lips.

"I will help you find them. I know where they are."

"Then what would I do… once I find them?"

"Deal with them. Deal with them all."

Jack eyed the back of the car knowingly.

"That's right. You already know what you want to do."

Jack clenched his jaw and guiltily glanced back down at his lap.

"Went to your father's back shed to get it before you left, didn't you?"

"How'd you know that?"

"I am with you, Jack. You know me—I'm that voice in your head."

"Y-you're my conscience or somethin'?"

"More like a friend. We have had more conversations than this. Remember?"

Jack scrunched his brows together, trying to gather when he'd ever had a conversation like this before.

"You and Alister? With that boy in the back alley?"

Jack's mouth dropped. "I was drunk. Pissed right out of my mind. I didn't mean to. Alister… we… we haven't brought it up again."

"He was asking for it."

"Y-yeah—the little git. Thought he was a big man on the town. Wouldn't stop mouthin' off. We taught him. Still…" he murmured, grimacing, "…didn't mean to hurt him that badly." His eyes snapped with distrust, staring at the writhing shadow. "You are not my friend. Not if it was you that convinced me to do tha'."

An evil cackle filled Jack's head. *"Don't be an idiot. You decided to do that on your own."*

"Then what did you do?"

"I helped you. Told where to hide and helped you sneak away. Remember? When they took that boy to the hospital, did they ever come looking for you?"

"No… got away with it somehow." Jack squeezed his hand into a fist, remembering the blood on his knuckles. His fist quivered.

"You did that yourself. But you are strong, Jack, and sometimes you must take matters into your own hands. Set things right. Sometimes setting things right requires action. Who else is going to deal with Merlin? Teach him a lesson."

Jack felt strengthened. He was strong. He really did need to teach them a lesson. The more he allowed the dark shadow to speak, the more he felt his anger and resolve rise. The voice made sense. It connected to his hatred and loss. If something terrible had happened to his father, they would have to pay.

"Where are they?"

"They are in Cumbria—by the lake. I will lead you."

Jack pulled the car back into gear. "I *will* go then. That little *imp* and her boyfriend better not have hurt my dad."

Elanor slunk away to shower. When she returned, Merlin was encouraged to see her cheeks had reddened against her pallid skin. Her eyes, however, remained sullen and empty. Without a word, she crept onto one of the beds and melted back upon the comforter. Her eyes shut, and she quickly faded. Her face dropped to the side, and her death-like motion disturbed Merlin.

"Elanor?" Merlin prodded gently. He approached the bedside and stroked her cold cheek. There was no movement.

Arthur rose, a deep frown etched onto his mouth. "Is she alright?"

Merlin frowned. He lightly shook her shoulders. Elanor's head rocked, unresponsive, to the side.

"You must do something," Arthur pressed. "She has been unwell for far too long."

Merlin snapped, "I do not know what to do!" He dropped his head to his hands. "I have tried to free her. She is plagued by a darkness that I cannot seem to get my grip on." He lifted his head. "If only you could see her brightness. She is resilient, light, and free."

"We cannot be idle. This must be dealt with."

"Then *you* do something!" Merlin yelled, rising to his feet. He bitterly sucked in his lips, as he dropped his head. "I've done *everything* I know to do, and NOTHING. This all happened because of—" Merlin stopped, red faced, before he blurted something he would regret. "I need to clear my head." He strode to the door, slamming it behind him.

Merlin stormed through the hotel and out into the dark, rainy night. He let the precipitation wet his hair and clothes. The fresh air gradually cooled his temper. He felt freer away from Arthur's insistent gaze, even in the cold, damp rain.

What am I to do?

He had learned well enough that his power was more effective if he depended less on his druidic sight of his past. Answers evaded him that way. Perhaps reaching out to the *One* who had aided him before might provide a solution.

"Great God," he beseeched, gazing up at the silver rain falling from the black sky, "what do I do? Please help me. You must revive my bride and break this darkness. *Please!*" He paced restlessly. "What is it you have given me that could help her…I-I have found nothing."

In silence, he waited as the rain resounded, splashing in the puddles near his feet. Strange, electric lampstands lined the street ahead of him, and the windows glowed from the hotel behind him. He stared up at the particularly tall light above him. It beamed down, lighting the spot where he stood.

The light's dull buzzing drew his attention as it flickered. Whatever source sustained it was becoming weaker. He watched as the light went out, buzzed, and fluttered back on. The tinkling hum radiated, then the lampstand turned off completely. Now underneath it in darkness, the other lights on the lane appeared lonely in the quietness.

Merlin was staring up at the lampstand above him when its light suddenly blazed back to life—shining brighter than before.

Flinging his arm over his eyes, he shuffled backward. He pressed his hand against his brow as revelation unlocked. He squinted up at the light as it beckoned his attention.

"The source of light," Merlin whispered. "The light goes out when the source has been stopped or runs out."

Maybe Elanor hadn't been cursed. Perhaps she was only left vulnerable because the light had gone out.

"The light has gone out," he murmured as icy drops dripped from his hair down his face. Transfixed, he stared at the light as if it was the Great God himself speaking to him.

"But how do I restore that light?" Merlin yelled up to it. "What is the source?"

He thought about the enaid that Elanor called a unicorn and how it restored her to health, giving her the blue magic. He remembered the song.

Merlin smacked his forehead. "The song!" He spun on his heel, running back into the hotel doors to his beloved.

24

THE TRUTH SHALL SET YOU FREE

Elanor fell immediately into a dream. The smell of earth wafted into her nose. She was laying on her back in damp grass. She rolled to her side. *Where am I?* The sky above her was black, her surroundings lit dimly by the pale moon and stars, and crickets chirped.

She'd had dreams like this before. The kind that felt real and tangible. With the nightmares of her past, she learned how to recognize them, even when she was asleep.

A wraeth-like whistle pierced the air, and a chill wind blew past Elanor's face. She squinted to focus. She was surrounded by several gray pillars.

"Stones," she said, rising to her feet, "these are stones." She counted them. There were seven long standing stones surrounding her, and one directly behind. She turned to face it.

"Burial stones," she whispered. *The ones atop the Hero's Mound. The seven of Arthur's mighty men, and this eighth one.* She pondered who this stone represented. All the men accounted for one king and six warriors, including Bedwyr and Peredur. But this eighth one—could it be for her father?

Her hand rested on the cold stone as the wind steadily rose, whipping her hair and clothing. The trees on the hill jostled, creaking and groaning as though they might break.

Elanor shivered as the stormy gale grew violent. She was not safe here. She pressed her body against the stone, wrapping her arms around it tightly.

"Father, keep me safe," she yelled to the stone, but the wind swallowed her voice.

The howling changed. Resounding clearly over the wind came a shrieking wail, harmonizing above the fury. The eerie tremble drew nearer, like the voice of a weeping mother over her dead child.

Elanor froze. "No, no, no!"

She turned, pressing her back against the stone, her eyes searching for the source of the wail.

A steady, gray light from the eastern sky neared. Whatever it was appeared to be shrouded in a glowing mist. Its flowing form was revealed as it came closer—a long, mournful body hanging in the air like a ghost.

"Who are you?" Elanor demanded, forcing herself to square up against the demon.

Its mouth hung open like a deep, black hole. Its hollow eyes threatened her. Its face was ashen-gray, like the cyhyraeth of Arthur's tomb.

Elanor trembled, and terror rose in her chest as the wraeth floated closer, its long, icy fingers extended.

"You shall not have me!" she shrieked, but her words were powerless as the shadow persisted nearer.

Is this what has been haunting my mind?

Elanor pushed back against the rock, hoping its strength might somehow defend her. But it could not stop the wraeth's frigid fingers from rolling across her cheek.

"No… n-no!" She clenched her teeth, turning her head as far away as she could. She squeezed her eyes shut as it touched her.

In that moment, there was a flash like silent lightning, and the wind ceased. Elanor opened her eyes, and before her floated a gray, misty apparition.

"You are worthless."

That voice she'd been hearing for days. Helen's voice, baiting her into despair with its condemning words.

"It's your fault! You killed him. You took my husband away," it wailed. *"You ruin everything you touch."* The apparition wept, and the rending depths of its pain echoed in Elanor's ears. The ghost's wavering tone heaped guilt upon her, wave after wave, making her disparage her very existence. Shame cursed her, and she was sure she deserved it.

She closed her eyes, resisting the crying wraeth's claims. "Y-you do not know me. You know nothing." Trembling, she pulled herself up and faced the shadow.

The voice laughed at her, and a searing pain throbbed through Elanor's cheek, down through her neck and into her chest. She fell back onto the ground, folding her legs into her chest.

The voices of Jack and Nancy tumbled out of the shadow.

"You don't belong."

"You never have."

"Our father made a mistake bringing you home."

"You ruined our family."

Then, as if his lips were next to her ear, Jack seethed, *"I hate you. I… HATE you! You are not my sister. I will never forgive you for what you have done."*

Elanor screamed as tears flowed down her cheeks. "S-stop! Stop!"

"Dad was wrong to love you. You deceived him."

As she lay there, struggling against the shadow's words, a silver line of hope spoke, *Darkness is a liar. Do not listen… This is only a dream.*

Chapter Twenty-four

The pain coursed through her, but this new voice allowed her to muster the strength to push herself up onto her knees. She breathed, working to ease her own panic.

Within an instant, the evil hooded villain pouring poison down her throat raced through her mind. Elanor recoiled at the memory—at her powerlessness. Fear and panic enveloped her, and the air became hot and stifled. She couldn't breathe.

"N-n-n-no…" She pushed back as anger surged through her. Breathlessly, she muttered, "Grwyrthrhodd."

Still the pain surged, and as Elanor lifted her head, she saw that the shadow had grown. It encompassed everything around her. She swallowed. "Grwyrthrhodd," she said more forcefully. Her strength was kindled, like a lit candle in a dark room. She curled her fingers into fists at her sides, peeled herself from the ground, and forced herself to stand.

The authority of Arthur's eyes flooded her mind with an unexpected wish to wield a sword. The thought of Arthur gave her strength. A sweet whisper blew through her ears. *"You have your father's eyes."*

Elanor remembered the moment she and Merlin called Arthur out from his slumber. She saw herself extending her hand to him. She was going to sing. She remembered now. Before everything went wrong.

Why didn't I sing?

Through the darkness, from somewhere far away, she heard a song on the wind.

Teyrnas yr haul… Teyrnas yr haul… the lilting song whispered.

Mae'r haul wedi eiwneud ddydd…

The voice was sweet, lifting her above the darkness. She remembered something she had forgotten. She was not of *this* time, nor of *this* people, and this demon could not have its say.

She closed her eyes and listened to the song as it permeated her spirit:

> *Sweet… are the healing days, when pain will find no way.*
> *The earth will sing, for the Sun has made it day.*
> *The Kingdom of the Sun will reign.*

Elanor stared into the growing shadow, and her eyes glowed blue. "You do not know me!" she shouted, the declaration echoing in the darkness. "I am the daughter of kings, and I have power you know not of. I have the power to heal and dispel darkness."

The wind increased its gale, whipping up around her as her hands raised to the sky. She lifted her chin and opened her mouth, and out came a call louder than the wind, louder than the accusing voices and wailing of the cyhyraeth. Her magic flowed out as swirls of blue that pushed against the gray.

As if she had been in a trance, her eyes snapped open, and the cold creature's fingers still touched her cheek, leaching all hope from her. Elanor lifted her voice even higher, and fiercely, she gripped the wraeth's wrist and pulled its twisted fingers from her face. Her power radiated down the creature's bony arm.

As the wraeth's grip broke, warmth flooded Elanor's body. Energy pulsed inside her, like a dead battery being recharged. Life filled every part of her.

Her voice echoed with authority as she stared into the withered creature's hunched frame. "YOU HAVE NO MORE POWER OVER ME!"

The cyhyraeth straightened, giving one last attempt to overcome her. It wailed as it transformed into the humble image of Helen.

Elanor dropped her arms, and her magic dampened. The wind went still as she stared into Helen's face, which silently condemned her. She faltered; the sight pressed into the mournful depths of her heart. "I have always needed you"—she shook her head— "wanted you to love me. But the truth is…" Elanor stepped closer. "I no longer need you. I have been given back all that you deprived me from."

She began to walk away but turned back to face Helen's shadow. "I… I forgive you."

At the release of her words, Helen faded away. All that remained was a clear, silent, starry sky. Elanor let out a slow, somber sigh. She felt free from the shame and oppression that the Evans family had placed upon her presence all those years. She became aware of the stones surrounding her, as if each of the warriors represented stood there with her. The shadow of each hero faintly appeared before each stone. She was now more connected to them and their world—no longer an orphan from a world that didn't want her.

Elanor turned—half laughing, half crying—to embrace the stone memorializing her father. "I am not ready to let you go," she cried, tears flooding the bottom rim of her eyes. He was the only one that held any importance to her in this world.

As if in response to her cry, the warrior in white appeared before her. The antlers on top of his helm sparkled in the starlight.

"I knew it was you," she cried, diving into his chest, and wrapping her arms around him. His comforting breath echoed from underneath his helm. His chest moved up and down on her cheek, and she let his breathing soothe her.

He stepped back, placing his gloved hand on her cheek.

"I'm sorry," Elanor said. "I didn't mean for you to die." She waited, hoping to hear his voice, but nothing came.

"I told you not to come," she choked out, staring up at him as a tear trailed from her eye. Understanding dawned on her, and she nodded her head. "I have to let you go now, don't I?"

Elanor reached up and squeezed the hand that rested on her cheek. She savored the warmth she felt through the glove and wished she could take off his helm and see his face. She set her jaw. "I…" she sobbed. "I forgive you too."

A sad smile lined her lips as she somberly admired the guardian knight's appearance. "I am so proud of you, Daddy." A piece of anger that had so solidly gripped her heart was relinquished.

The white warrior vanished, leaving her hand empty.

"Hwyl," Elanor uttered softly in the Cymry tongue. "Nos da, thad."

She smiled, her eyes still full of tears as the world of her dream faded. The stones began to blur, but a loud swishing captured her attention. Cool air brushed her face with a pulsing thrum. It was familiar.

What is that?

Elanor strained to keep her eyes open within the dream, for she knew it was leaving her. The rushing *whoosh* increased, and sudden glints of green and gold overwhelmed her vision. She heard the hollow resonance of air filling the lungs of a gigantic creature.

Her eyes were closing inside the dream. "No," Elanor cried, "I must focus." She needed to know who this was—but it hadn't come to her yet.

A wing stretched out before her. "Gwenddydd… I am here. You will find me here. You must come quickly."

Arthur stood, thrusting his fists to his sides, and clenching his teeth. He'd tried so hard to acclimate to this new world, but it was too much. Maybe he had never truly woken from his slumber, and this was all some kind of strange, hellish dream. One where he was powerless to do anything. He wanted to go back to the dream where he charged into battle with his Cymbrogi. At least there he had the ability to do something… anything. Even if it meant dying, it was better than being a useless king, stuck in a world where everything appeared backwards.

He fumed, pacing back and forth. He tried not to catch a glimpse of the woman lying lifeless on the bed, but he couldn't suppress his concern. It was as though Gwynevere lay suffering beside him, and he was left paralyzed. The gray of her face disturbed him.

Unable to ignore her, Arthur stopped at Elanor's bedside, standing above her. Her brows were stressed, and her pale lips bent downward. He knelt, picking up her delicate hand in his. Her long fingers were so familiar to him.

He grunted. "If… If Merlin cannot find a way to you, then… perhaps his strength is not what leads you out. You must be the one. You must find the strength. You must curse this demon that haunts you." A lump of emotion grew in his throat. He shook his head, rattled by the effect she had on him. "Is this what it feels like to have a… daughter?" He pulled her hand to his bearded lips and kissed it.

"If it is true that you are my daughter, and this isn't a dream—you must fight. Pendragons are not cornered. A Pendragon sees where others cannot. We brave the battles when cowards say it is wisdom to flee. This is your birthright. Your… your mother would not suffer a demon without a dagger in her hand."

BAM! BAM! BAM!

Arthur shot up, releasing Elanor's hand.

"Arthur," came the muffled voice behind the door. "Let me in."

He rushed over to open the door. Merlin stood dripping wet but wasted no time pushing Arthur aside, marching into the room. "I think I've got it. I have been such a fool. It seems so obvious, yet it has evaded me this whole time."

"What have you found?"

"The song."

"What?" Arthur scrunched his face. "What would a song do?"

"Not *a* song, *the* song." Merlin smiled, hope alight in his eyes as he scrambled to Elanor's side. "Now, I must concentrate." He sighed, closed his eyes, and placed his palms over Elanor's chest.

In silence, Arthur waited. Merlin hovered motionlessly above Elanor, as though he were listening or waiting for something to happen.

Finally, Merlin beckoned, "Cyfod Elanor… mae'n bryd sinf." He tilted his head back. As he opened his mouth, his bright yellow eyes sparked, and a song emerged.

25

THE LADY OF THE LAKE

"Teyrnas yr haul… Teyrnas yr haul…" Merlin sang. Arthur clutched his heart and fell to his knees. He had forgotten it. It was *the* song. The one he had heard all his life.

Sweet… are the healing days, when pain will find no way.
The earth will sing, for the Sun has made it day.
Sweet… as it will be proclaimed the new days of the Sun.
Its rays will rise high, setting thrones upon kings' holds,
The New Way coming and the land set in gold.

Merlin had sung this song to Arthur throughout his childhood. It was Merlin's father who first sang the song, and then his mother, Adhan, after him. This was also the song the maiden of the fair folk sang to Arthur so many years ago. The day the Fisher King rowed to them through the mists on the shore of the lake.

Oh, Kingdom of the Sun, renew our land with grace.

The maiden sang…

Oh, Kingdom of the Sun, the warmth of its bounty upon our face.
Blood will stop dripping, as the oil of gladness is tipping.

Her eyes blazed into his soul as she prophesied his future…

The sword no longer killing, but its emblems triumphing.
A new day rising, with the old moons setting.
Sweet… days of the Sun are coming.

Arthur's heart pained to remember that day. His sword had been shattered in battle, and his spirit broken. He'd had no business becoming king without the sword he pulled from the stone—his father's sword. Now it laid in pieces—only a shard attached to a hilt set within the scabbard at his hip. A sad reminder of his foolishness.

That day, Merlin had quietly watered the horses while Arthur leaned against the trunk of a tree, despondent. The tranquil splash of the horses sipping water trickled in his ears. Out of the silence, he heard her voice. The haunting call echoing out from amongst the trees, reminding him of what he had once believed to be true. A new kingdom coming, where there would be no more sorrow or pain. Arthur yearned with every fiber of his being to be the one to establish that promise—to see a land renewed.

Merlin had always told him it was his destiny. The Great God had called them both to establish this New Way—a way never before seen in Prydain. After all the days of battle and death, Arthur doubted its truth. It sailed away from him upon a torrential sea.

All at once, the Fisher King appeared upon the lake, nearing them through the mists inside a gray, wooden boat. The bow was pointed high, carved in the shape of a curling silver fish. Arthur stood at the sight of him, his mouth agape.

Merlin stood still as the king rowed closer. Steadily, he approached, the rippling water lapping against his oars. He scooted onto the shore as the voice of the maiden flowed out through the trees.

Merlin bowed as the king rose, ethereal and tall, moving like a weightless warrior. The Fisher King had not been seen for many years. It was said he was lord of *all* fair folk, but time stole his kingdom, and it faded. His people scattered. The remnants were few but could sometimes still be seen in faces like Merlin and Adhan.

His hair, a solid white, brushed his tall shoulders. His eyes appeared ancient, but his skin and stature were ageless. Though he towered with strength, the Fisher King had sustained wounds that had never fully healed in a battle long ago. And so, evidence of the rumored stories was true as he approached, limping painstakingly on one side.

He gestured his broad arm across the expanse of the water. "This is my lake." His voice was deep and resonant. "This is all that is left of my kingdom. Which is well, for all I truly need are the fish and the lapping waters of the shore." He gazed over his shoulder, listening to the song.

Arthur and Merlin saw her shape moving through the trees.

"I also enjoy the sweet hum of my daughter's voice as she sings to me—I, the Fisher King, and she, the Lady of the Lake."

"I… I know this song," said Arthur.

The Fisher King leaned forward, smiling with his full silver eyes. "As you should." He turned to Merlin. "It was the foresight of Emrys to sing you the song, as it was his destiny to be born with it beating within his heart."

"We are sojourners after a long season of battle," Merlin said humbly.

"Mmm." The king nodded. He walked nearer to Merlin, staring deeply into his eyes. "I see the gold," he groaned with a hopeful sadness. "It is good to see the echo of our kin within your eyes. We have been waiting long for you… the one who has the eyes to see. They assure us, we will not fade without leaving a legacy behind."

Merlin's eyes went glassy as he gazed back at the king.

With a father's tenderness, the king said to Merlin, "Please, will you set us a fire? I desire to sit, and Arthur's sadness must be turned to strength."

"Please…" Merlin turned his knowing eyes to Arthur, now understanding the purpose of the encounter. "I already have the wood set. Come and rest." He held his hand out for the king, and gratefully the king took it, leaning into the nook of Merlin's elbow as he supported him to a stump beside the firewood. Merlin blew into the kindling, and a fire sparked and flamed. The king beamed at the magic and settled onto his seat.

Arthur's stomach fluttered as he followed and sat on the other side of the growing fire, across from the king. He glanced up and found the king's eyes already on him. He felt strange as if the mystical king knew more about him than he knew himself.

"Would you eat?" Merlin asked.

"Only some water," the king said, pressing his lips together. "I am thirsty."

Merlin shuffled away to collect a skin of water.

"Young king…" the Fisher King began.

Arthur interrupted bitterly, "I am not a king." He glanced at the ground dejectedly. "The lesser kings fight over my father's crown. Merlin deigned me as the High Battle Chieftain and believed that as I conquered the invaders destroying our lands, I would gain their favor. All I ever had to claim my birthright as king was Aurelius's sword. If it is even true, he was my father…"

"Romans fight after the birthright of kingship. Never have the Cymry."

"What do you mean?"

"Druids never appointed kingship just because they were the sons of kings. Those deemed worthy by the druidic order became kings. It was the druids who were the kingmakers." The Fisher King grasped the water from Merlin's hand and drank it down. "Thank you, Emrys." With a crisp gasp, he wiped his mouth.

"The druidic order is not what it was," Arthur said morosely. "The kings will *not* honor them. They want their own ways. Even though Aurelius's heir alone could pull the sword from the stone, they still would rather see themselves exalted. They have no respect for magic or the Great God who governs all."

"Ah. Now *that* is the point. For it is the Great God who is sovereign. It is in his hands that all the kings and lands of Prydain reside. Not in the lesser kings, nor in the druids. But"—the king's eyes lit on Merlin— "there are the ones the Great God does appoint. And it is they who will do all that has been laid out before the foundations of the earth. There is little anyone can do to stop it. Especially if the appointed ones are properly aligned." Still holding the waterskin in his hands, he lifted it high. "Understand, young king, that I came to you thirsty, and you quenched my thirst. But I will be thirsty once again. There is a vessel, a *cup*, that runs over with water and gives life. It will forever satisfy and bring healing. It was given to me by a man I met long ago. He was called Joseph the Arimathean. He showed me this cup, and now I will never truly know thirst again."

Arthur's chest burned with wonder. He wanted to know more. If he could but find such a cup, his lands could be healed. A flame of promise burst into his eyes.

"There it is," the king said, discerning Arthur's hunger. "Yes, this is why you are an appointed one. Let me see the sword."

Reluctantly, Arthur pulled the broken sword from his belt, staring at the reminder of his failure. He approached the king and placed it into his hands.

"Arthur," the king said, fixing his consoling eyes on Arthur's, "I am sorry your father's sword has been broken. For he truly was your father if you ever had any doubt. Though this…" He lifted the sword in his hands. "This sword is *not* what made you king. This was but a sign for others to see. They may resist the truth, but they all saw you lift the sword out of the stone when they could not." The king narrowed his eyes. "This sword was never properly weighted for you."

The king handed the sword to Merlin. "This is your appointed kingmaker. He is Emrys. Men may think they no longer have to honor druids, but the Great God has set that they will honor this one. This, the *One Druid* of the New Way. That is why Merlin gave you that song. The song my daughter sings to you now."

The king stood achingly from his seat and turned to the wood. "Daughter," he called.

With his gentle beckon, the lady appeared from the trees. She walked like the wind blowing through a willow tree, her hair golden radiant, as she came singing, *"The earth will sing, for the Sun has made it day."* Her dress was white with blue, appearing as flowing water waves that surrounded her as she moved.

Arthur whispered, "It is the Lady of the Lake."

She stood beside her father. Her eyes sparkled like the light green of the lake. "I must tell you a story," she said softly, her voice a soft hum on the breeze, "so that you will understand." She stared up at the sky. "A long time ago, these lands were ruled by a race of giants. That was when the fair folk came sailing in from their kingdom far away. Their lands had died, swallowed by the sea—their way of life had come to its end."

"Even once arriving on this shore, their race thrived for a time, but… they were never meant to continue on," she said, forlorn. "All have now faded like their brothers who were left behind under the water." She paused. "It was said that the fair folk had come from the otherworld, and maybe so, but not as some choose to believe."

"Once ashore, they hoped to start a new life, but the giants refused to share the land. The giants had great sight and power over all the land's creatures. They were clever and thought to frighten the newcomers with their wild creatures, but the fair people had magic of their own. They tamed the beasts with their harps' songs, and the creatures became gentle and brought them food. This angered the giants, so they derived another plan to steal the harps from the fair ones—believing this would rob them of their power.

"One night as the fair people slept, the giants came with their mighty hammers and smashed the harps into pieces. None were left unbroken, save one. The largest and most beautiful of the harps, its strings gold and handle lined with jewels. The lord of the giants was enamored by it and stole it. He whisked it away to his home within the mountains.

"The fair ones woke, discovering their harps destroyed, and the wails of their grief rose like a song, reverberating through the air, far into the mountains. Their grief-song roused the stolen harp. Its strings vibrated, and it lifted high into the air above the heads of the giants. The harp played a melody so enchanting that every giant wept for hearing it. It played and played, and the giants' tears poured relentlessly. In anguish, they cried for the harp's song to stop, but it did not cease.

"After many days the tune changed, and the giants began to laugh. Their sides split from laughing, but they could not stop. They rolled and pounded the ground, shaking the earth. The fair ones heard their harp's song through the quaking ground. They echoed in return so the harp would continue to play and follow its sound. They found the harp hovering above the giants inside their mountain.

"The giants' laughter fractured the mountain, so with haste, lest they be crushed under the rock, the fair ones took their golden harp. But before they left, they caused the harp to play a final song; loud and sweet. It was a song so pure and light that it lulled the giants into a deep slumber.

"Deep rumbles came out of the earth, and the walls of the mountain crumbled. The fair ones ran, carrying their harp with them. However, the giants kept sleeping while the mountain buried them. Now free, the fair ones made the new land their home."

The lady approached Arthur. Hidden within the folds of her dress, she pulled a long, silver sword with runes etched into the length of the blade. The hilt was golden, embossed with silver details—red leather wrapped the pommel. She lifted it up above her head, and the sword hummed.

Arthur was struck with emotion. His face reddened, and he crumbled to his knees before her.

The Fisher King placed his hand upon Arthur's shoulder. "This sword is all that is left of my people. Within it is the same magic that was born in Merlin—forged from the very harp that made Prydain our home. Its name is Caledfwlch, but Prydain will know its name as Excalibur." The king knelt before Arthur, whose eyes were now wrought with tears. The presence of magic tangible, he lifted Arthur's chin. "My young king, you cannot carry a sword that was not meant for you. It will be too heavy, and it will break. This sword was forged for the one who was destined to carry the heart of Prydain. Uther thought he was Pendragon, but you, Arthur... you are the Great Pendragon. You have been found worthy by the druid Emrys, and you will be appointed king by your people. You will dispel your foes and make friends of your enemies. Your heart will be for the cup that will never run dry."

The maid sang once again over Arthur, the Song of the Kingdom of the Sun. They all lifted their tearful voices together, and as they sang, the vision of a land green and blessed grew inside Arthur's belly. His heart felt knit back together, healed by the Great God he was sure hovered beside them. He would see a land flourishing and bright, and a kingdom restored.

Arthur would never forget that day. That was the day he became king within his own heart, and he was never the same again. He went from a young, broken orphan to a man with the authority to break the enemy's back.

And now, as Merlin sang that same song over Elanor, its power swept back over him. With tears running down his neck, he sang with Merlin, and the same, weighty presence from that day encompassed the room.

A blue light radiated and pulsed through Elanor's body. Merlin stepped back with a hopeful smile and gripped Arthur's shoulder.

Shivers ran through Arthur's body and excitement swelled in his chest.

The light dissipated, leaving the room quiet and dim. Elanor now slept peacefully, her skin healthy and bright and her lips red. The gray look of death had vanished.

Merlin rushed to her and whispered, "Elanor?"

As she sucked a deep breath in through her nose, her eyes fluttered open. Her eyes were radiant and blue once again. Merlin leaned forward with anticipation.

Elanor turned to look at Arthur, then back at Merlin. "I let him go. I let them all go," she whispered.

Merlin pulled her into his arms and pressed his lips to her head. "What was it that plagued you?"

She leaned up, rubbing her face with the flat of her palms. "I didn't sing," she said, furrowing her forehead. "W-when we were waking Arthur. I was going to sing, but then I didn't. And a dark shadow haunted my mind."

"What dark shadow?" Merlin pressed.

"It appeared the very same as the cyhyraeth, but… when the song came, the creature no longer had authority." Elanor turned sullenly to Merlin. "Do you think if I had remembered the song within the tomb—that we could have saved my dad?"

Merlin squeezed her back into his arms. "We cannot hope to erase what has happened. It will not heal you to think that way."

"The song I heard—the one I sang—was the song of the Kingdom of the Sun." Her eyes brightened as she spoke. "Merlin, it was your father's song. It did something within me. Changed me."

Arthur nodded, his face brightening. "It has a way of doing that."

"The Kingdom of the Sun," Merlin said proudly, "is where the song comes from. The good magic. The same magic that was in the Crystal Cave. It is a voice that cannot be conjured but comes when a heart is ready to hear it."

Elanor lifted one corner of her mouth, digesting the moment. "I think… I think I am well. And," she gripped Merlin's hand, "I think I know how to get home. I saw her… I saw Gwyliwr."

"The dragon?"

Elanor nodded. "She is waiting for us, or at least, I think *time* is waiting for us, at the Hill of the Kings—on the Hero's Mound."

26

NO MORE TIME FOR THE PAST

They woke early the next morning, eating a full meal before leaving for the trek back through the hills. Merlin never even questioned whether what Elanor had seen was true. Instead, he felt true hope for the first time since arriving in this strange future version of his world.

They drove back to the lake and parked behind the rail—same as before. Merlin's heart lightened with the prospect of knowing where they were headed—the dragon's magic hadn't led them astray. He leapt from the car, feeling refreshed. His wife sparkled with health. There were no more demons at their door. They were going home with Arthur by their side. *Nothing* would hold them back. Nothing.

The resonate song from the night before had reignited a purpose in them all. Merlin recognized that even Arthur's stature seemed taller as he strode across the road. This strange twist of time was about to be over.

He was happy to see the no trespassing sign. He climbed over the chains that held it and then up over the ramp leading to the field. He held out his hand to help Elanor over the cold metal and pulled her along with his light-footed traipse.

Once on solid ground, Elanor released his hand.

Merlin stopped. He turned around and saw Elanor peering back.

"Elanor?"

"Yes." She nodded. "I just… I am really leaving it all behind this time." She peered across the lake. "There is nothing here for me anymore. No one who will miss me. The only one who loved me is gone." She turned to Merlin and said more quietly, "This isn't my home anymore. Never really was." She hesitated, then pulled her mobile from her pocket, tapping away on the screen with an odd look in her eye.

Merlin leaned to look. "What are you doing?"

"Keeping my promise," Elanor murmured as she typed. "There." She exhaled, lifting her eyes. "I do have one friend who will miss me." Her stare became distant for a moment, but her face lifted.

"I have said my goodbyes to Jess, and," she chuffed, "let her know where to find her car. She is going to be a bit angry that her car has been abandoned in Cumbria."

"You do not have to look back anymore," Merlin said. He offered her his hand.

Elanor stuck her mobile back into her pocket and took his hand. "I already said goodbye to the rest of them, anyway." An odd glance of loss passed across her face as she raised her chin.

"Come. Let's hope the dragon's magic will meet us and we will be off; back to our home."

Elanor lifted her chest and sighed. With purpose, she turned back toward the field alongside Merlin.

He knew that closure had come for her. She hadn't yet told him everything that had happened within her dream, but he saw her strength had returned—and there was something more. A resolve. Almost as though she had glimpsed her own destiny. Her eyes had the flames of Prydain within them, a look he had only seen before in Arthur. In letting her past go, she had become Pendragon—and he saw, sitting in the corner of her eye, a warrior who had emerged from the ashes.

Even as he thought this, Elanor's fingers gripped the blue pendant at her chest. She touched the torc around her neck. It brought back to his memory what he had placed within the pendant. She would never know that the very song she had heard within her dream was living within the blue light of the sapphire stone. He put it there on purpose, for he aimed that she would never again be lost where he could not find her. Its light connected to his own, like his heart was connected to hers.

She smiled up at him, as though she guessed his thoughts, and let go of him to skip ahead toward the trees.

"Eager to get somewhere?" Arthur shouted after her jovially.

"Yes," Elanor chimed. "My heart aches for my child who has been too long without her mother, and I desire to see the look on Gwynevere's face when she sees you again."

Arthur smiled broadly, and his blue eyes gleamed with hope at the mention of his wife. "How is it," he said, "that I sleep for an age and wake to meet a daughter that is yet to be born, who has grown and been married to the one I know best—and now she reminds me I am a grandfather? I think I have gone mad." He chuckled, shaking his head down into his chest.

Elanor snatched Arthur's hand into her own, and her pair of radiant blue eyes halted him. His eyes grew large and he gasped.

Catching up to them, Merlin watched, awestruck, as Elanor's bright eyes leapt with an eagerness that had been gone for so long. His heart swelled as her connection with Arthur strengthened.

Then, just as quickly, Elanor turned to walk on.

"What did she show you?" Merlin asked, thrilled to see Elanor acting like herself again.

Arthur licked his trembling lips. "Sh-she showed me… Gwynevere holding your little one. My wife… she is so beautiful. And the child…" He cleared his throat, suddenly choked. He worked his chin, suppressing his emotion. He visibly swallowed and walked on.

Merlin beamed. After all they had been through, he could finally revel in the fact that Arthur was truly alive. The kingdom would once again be bright with the Great Pendragon back within Caer Lial. The prophecy of the three—the two stars and the Once and Future King returned. The original dream he had dreamt on Avalon so many years ago floated through his mind. How little he understood where it would all lead as he thought of Arthur upon his warhorse, ready for battle. Osian had failed to stop them. Now if they could only find the villain, he would be defeated.

"Stop here."

Jack had followed the shadow's instructions throughout the night—leading him to a lake. Within the deeper parts of his conscience, a pinging emergency bell rang. He knew that this voice was no good, and he wondered whether he hadn't just gone crazy. But he kept listening.

Why? Because every time his anger flared and jealousy pricked, the voice justified him. The shadow's malice made him want to listen. It validated his envy of Elanor.

He didn't want to listen to the smaller, weaker voice that told him to walk away. Elanor was stealing all his father's attention. She didn't deserve it. This was not justice. No. It was much easier to follow the path that restored his control. Besides, what if the shadow was right? What if his father had been harmed? He could not walk away with that matter unsettled.

Pulling the car over behind a shrubby grassy knoll, Jack discovered Elanor's friend's car parked on the other side. "Huh?" he mumbled, slowing to a stop and pulling his brake into place. "Can't believe it." He'd been almost certain he'd lost his grip on his sanity, but the sight of Elanor's vehicle reignited his determination.

Setting his jaw, Jack stepped from his car and walked over to the abandoned yellow Vauxhall with suspicion, glancing in through the windows. He pulled on the driver side door and found it unlocked. The inside of the car was still warm; it hadn't been sitting long. Jack glanced down—the keys still hung, left behind in the ignition.

He pulled his head out of the car and walked down to the lake. He scanned both sides of the shore but did not see them.

The shadowy voice whispered, *"They're not at the lake."*

"Then where are they?" Jack grunted.

"They are behind you—across the field—heading toward the hills."

"What? Why?" Jack snapped.

"You must hurry if you are to catch them."

Jack stormed back to his car and unlatched the trunk. He stared down at what he had brought. He didn't really have any intention of using it—he just wanted to make sure that if Elanor or Merlin gave him any trouble, they understood he meant business. He grabbed some shotgun shells from the box he had collected from his father's shed and shoved them deep into his jacket pocket. Then he unwrapped the shotgun from under the red blanket.

He had been shooting with his father before, so he knew how to use it. Still, his stomach knotted with sickness as he gripped it. He gulped, questioning what he was doing even as he closed the trunk and moved toward the road.

"Shut up!" Jack said out loud to himself. "Too late to get a conscience now. This is what needs to be done. Dad may not like it, but he will see my reason."

He stared down the road to make sure no one would spot his firearm, then he dashed across. The field went far; he had to squint to spot them. But there, against the trees, like three specs, he saw them entering the forest. They wouldn't see him, so he climbed over the chain and rail and started off at a run. He had to be quick—he didn't want to lose them.

Jack hoped whoever owned the field would not discover him as he passed the gray sheep with coiled horns bleating at him. Their jarring cries felt like they were alarming someone of his presence. He glared, curling his lips as he charged past. The long green and yellow grass brushed his jeans, and the earth thudded beneath his feet. His eyes were set on the trees.

Breathlessly, he reached the forest and launched himself behind a tree, carefully glimpsing past the prickly green pines. He couldn't see them. They were too far ahead. However, there was a clear trail between the hills.

Jack glanced up at the sun. "Plenty of daylight, I should think."

Certain he would find them on the trail, he raced forward but stayed close to the tree line for cover. After what seemed like an hour, he stopped, panting and huffing, ready to give up.

"How far have they gone?" Jack whined. "What in the world could they be doing this deep in?"

The wetness from the sweat on his clothes chilled him, and he shivered as he hid behind foliage. He wheezed as he pressed forward, but the further he went without seeing them, the more he considered turning back. He pulled his mobile from his back pocket to check the time with a dejected sigh. "It is well after noon." He wiped his forehead with his sleeve and grimaced.

"You're nearly to them."

Jack turned and looked behind him, then glanced back at what seemed like an endless trail between the pines. He knew the further he went, he would have that much further to return. It all began to feel like a wild goose chase. "How could they have gotten so far ahead of me?"

"You're almost on them. You can't let them get away from you now."

"Right." He nodded, reconnecting to his purpose. "Can't stop now." He plodded forward, attentively listening for any sign of them.

The twitter of a woman's laughter lit up the forest, echoing down the lane.

Jack dove into the trees, sneaking closer to the voices. He climbed up over a hill and arrived at a ledge where he saw Elanor, Merlin, and another man resting on the trail. They spoke lightheartedly, with happy, irritating smiles on their faces. Jack gritted his teeth.

Where's my father? What have they done with him?

The shadowy voice hissed, *"I told you they had hurt him."*

"Who is this third bloke?" Jack whispered, his eyes narrowing with suspicion. He laid down on his stomach, leaning on his elbows and edging closer to hear them. The third man wore strange clothes and spoke in a dialect Jack couldn't understand. It almost sounded like Welsh, but it was different. The words relayed were scrambled and strange. Oddly, Elanor and Merlin responded as though they understood him. Deep in the pit of Jack's stomach a rage festered. He already mistrusted Elanor and Merlin, but now he suspected they had done something villainous.

If they have done something to Dad, I'll kill them. Here, Jack thought he was coming to teach them a lesson, but now the hatred boiled.

He imagined taking the pommel of his gun and ramming it into Merlin's jawbone—then aiming the barrel into Elanor's chest. He trembled furiously. *How could she be part of this? I thought she loved him.*

Jack had never really thought much of Elanor, but he never imagined her capable of hurting anyone. "All she ever does is hide in her stupid flat," he muttered, "and feel sorry for herself. It has to be Merlin that has done it. Elanor is so daft; she has let him pull her along into his crimes. Probably so lonely, she'd do anythin' for his attention."

He lifted the gun from his side and cautiously pulled a shell from his pocket. He slid it into the chamber. He bit his lip and clicked it shut, then aimed it down through the trees at Merlin. Squinting one eye and pressing his teeth with his tongue, he stared down the barrel. He fumed as he tickled the trigger with his finger—willing himself to do it.

Should I? Jack's panting grew heavier, and hot, itchy perspiration gathered on his brow and chest. He tensely stared down at Merlin's prat-ish face.

"Shit!" he cursed, pulling the gun back into himself, away from the target.

SNAP!

Jack's foot rolled over a branch.

The three at the bottom of the hill sprang to their feet, gazing up the ridge into the trees where Jack lay hidden.

"Damn it," Jack snapped silently.

"Could it have been an animal? Deer?" Elanor asked.

Arthur mumbled with warning, "Animals scurry and halt once detected. Humans clumsily falter and conceal. The two do *not* sound the same."

Merlin stared up the hill suspiciously. "Who would be following us?"

Elanor whispered, "I don't know anyone who would even know we are here."

Arthur took a cautious step toward the hill, but Merlin flung his hand up to stop him. Placing his finger over his lips, he warned them both to stay silent. "Just wait," he whispered. "We will draw him out. We will pretend to be ignorant of him."

Arthur narrowed his eyes and screwed his mouth. "That is risky."

"We may already be in danger," Merlin cautioned. "Trust me."

"Why are we in danger? Couldn't it be some person hiking the forest just like we are?" Elanor whispered.

Merlin turned to face them, then nodded up at the hill. "Whoever is up there does not want to be seen. He is hiding."

Elanor eyed Merlin with uncertainty. "Surely, not everyone is out to get us."

"The demons of the otherworld still know we are here. Remember the crazy man we met on the street? We must be wary."

Merlin lifted his pack and threw it over his shoulder. "See!" he shouted. "No one is there. I told you. It is time for us to be moving on anyway."

The other two followed suit and gathered their things. They walked on, prickled and alert. Though he maintained a nonchalant façade, Merlin remained vigilant. He wanted to believe that the hider was no one of importance, but he knew better. The real question was, who was following them, and why.

Elanor caught up to him. "Could it not just be the owner of the property we trespassed through?"

"We have gone a long way from there. I cannot imagine he would have followed us this far, but… it is possible." Merlin took Elanor's hand. "Listen, it is possible that it is no one to be concerned about. But we must be wise."

Arthur clenched his fist. "This feels like trouble. A good warrior never closes his eyes to the possibility of death. They keep vigilant and do not enter into false safety." He looked over his shoulder. "They drink from the stream with eyes open, even when their most trusted friend is at their back."

"Shouldn't we draw him out then? Like you suggested?" Elanor asked.

"That is just what we are doing," Merlin said warily.

"We are leading them to open ground." Arthur pointed. "Out of the cover of the trees." Then, to Merlin, he said, "We are not far from the open plain."

"No, not far." Merlin confirmed. His fingers tapped his thighs, his stance tense and ready. "We will be there soon."

Steadfast, they crept, until Arthur cupped his hand over his mouth and released a quick, chirping whistle. Merlin scanned the field knowingly; Arthur had spotted their spy through the trees.

Merlin sped up his pace and reached out with his magic to discern a demonic presence. *Nothing.* Likely some human on their trail. With great relief, he saw the trees opening into the field—the Hill of the Kings at its center.

They pushed forward into the open before whipping around to see what lay behind them. Merlin huffed to catch his breath, his eyes darting across the plain. At any moment, their watcher could appear. He squinted between the shadowed trunks.

Arthur whispered, "Do you see anyone?"

Merlin sifted through the tree line. Whoever they were, they risked far more than they knew if they planned to harm them.

Soon, the sun would be setting. Merlin could not wait long for the villain to reveal himself. They needed the light of day. So, kindling his magic, he shouted, "COME OUT!" The force of his words shook the trees, sending birds to flight.

Arthur readied his stance, and Elanor positioned herself between them.

Through the trees emerged a figure, tall, thin, and trembling.

Elanor squinted at the figure as he approached. Her eyes widened with recognition. "Jack?" she called incredulously.

What would he be doing here? Merlin asked himself, perplexed.

Elanor impulsively moved closer; Arthur cautiously followed. "What are you doing out here?" She slowed, watching him with a peculiar stare. "How did you find us?"

As Jack neared, Merlin got a better look at his twisted and pale expression. Alarm radiated through him. "Stop, Elanor," he commanded, steadily lifting his hands.

"You—shut up!" Jack shouted at him.

In that moment, Merlin caught sight of the long, black baton hanging from Jack's hand. His fingers gripped it dangerously. His eyes had changed. They looked crazed and angry.

Merlin carefully asked, "How *did* you know to find us here, Jack?"

"There… there was a voice." Jack's face turned sad and lost for a moment but then shifted bitterly. His lips pursed against his teeth. He snapped the strange, long object up and threateningly aimed it at Merlin.

"Jack—what are you doing?" Elanor cried, freezing to her spot.

Jack's lips quivered as he shouted, "How—how did you make the trees shake like that, Merlin? Y-you some kind of… wizard?" His eyes darkened. "And… who is that with you?" His eyes shifted over to Arthur.

"There is a lot that can be explained, if"—Merlin nervously glanced sideways at Elanor— "if you will just set your weapon down."

Panicked, Elanor yelled, "Don't shoot! Jack…" She warily tried to shift Jack's focus to herself. "W-why do you have a gun?"

Gun, Merlin thought as Elanor named it. What kind of weapon was this?

Elanor timidly stepped toward Jack.

"God-damn-it, Elanor… Don't move," Jack threatened, flinging the barrel to point at her.

Elanor gasped, throwing her hands up.

Merlin's fear prickled, sending lightning through his veins. His mind scrambled to figure out his next move. If only he knew what sort of danger this *gun* posed.

"You…" Jack bristled, nudging the gun at Elanor. "Where is my dad? Wh-what has *he* done to him?"

"P-Please, Jack," she pleaded.

Merlin edged closer to Jack. "You don't understand. Please, let us explain."

"What? What don't I understand, eh?" Jack's jaw clenched. "You've gone filling

El's head with things you shouldn't've. You stupid… stupid girl." Flames burst within his eyes as he roared, "WHERE'S. MY. DAD?"

Elanor whimpered, steadily retreating. "D-D-Don't shoot, Jack. It can all be explained."

Angry tears welled in Jack's eyes. "Why… Why did he go with you? Why do you always get to have him…" He pumped the forearm of the gun.

CLICK.

"I h-hate you."

"Jack… NO!" Elanor shouted as a deafening *BANG* rattled their ears.

27

THE HERO'S MOUND

A crushing weight pushed Elanor aside, ramming her hard like a battering-ram. The loud *BANG* crashed into her ears. She slammed into the ground, the sound of pellets thudding mutely around her.

Merlin shouted thunderously, releasing a burst of his power that threw Jack into the air, flinging the gun from his hands.

"Ooff!" Jack crashed to the earth, the force knocking him unconscious.

Elanor lay there, stunned. Had she been shot? She couldn't tell. She waited in shock for some part of her body to radiate with pain. Slowly, she rubbed her hand across her chest and over her arm—there was nothing. But as she sat up, dazed, she saw blood. There was splatter on her shirt, but she couldn't see a wound.

"Are you alright?" Merlin hollered over at her, his face tense. His voice was muffled in her stricken ears.

Bewildered, she said, "I'm... I-I think I'm fine."

"Get her out of here," Merlin commanded Arthur, who remained above Elanor.

Elanor shook off the daze. "Wait... what? What about Jack?"

Arthur's strong arms lifted her to her feet, steering her away.

"Wait?" she snapped, yanking her arms free. She stormed over to Merlin. "We can't just leave him here."

"Don't worry, I will deal with him."

"Don't hurt him."

"Hurt him?"

Elanor's distress jerked Merlin out of his haste. "Of course, I will not hurt him. I am going to make *sure* he leaves this place and does not come back." He paused and turned to her tenderly. "Trust me."

Still rattled and unsure, she reluctantly nodded.

"Now go. Please. I must deal with this quickly."

Before she knew it, Arthur grabbed her by the arm and pulled her away. She was torn. Jack had tried to shoot her, yet she felt a responsibility to stay with him. Hurt was bubbling to the surface, and her knees buckled.

Arthur captured her before she collapsed. His arm gathered around her shoulders, and he pressed her into his side.

Elanor stiffened at his unexpected embrace. She wrapped her arms around her torso, but his sturdy warmth remained unmoved and secure. Finally, she melted into him, but not before glancing over her shoulder at Jack, who lay lifeless on the ground.

Arthur pointed. "Let's gather ourselves over by the stones."

"Uh-hm," was all she could say, her mind reeling. She swallowed, wrestling with the sadness lodged in her chest.

They marched soberly away from Merlin and closer to the hill. The stones were a welcome sight. Arthur crumpled to his knees and inhaled with a wince. He reached up to his shoulder, squeezing it gingerly with his fingertips.

Elanor gasped as she saw the dark red stain. She glanced back down at her shirt, now realizing where the blood had come from. "You're hurt."

"A little—" Arthur grunted painfully. "Who was that? He spoke in a strange dialect—I could not understand his insanity."

"Y-you saved me," she began, realizing it was Arthur who had pushed her out of the way of Jack's bullet.

Arthur's eyes softened. "I did not know what kind of death he held in his hands, but I could not let it harm you." He ripped his gaze away.

"Thank you." Elanor's face flushed. A small but powerful affinity stirred in her heart for him. "Let me help you," she offered before carefully pulling his tunic down from his shoulder. She sucked through her teeth, delicately inspecting the two wounds on his shoulder. One pellet had gone clear through to the back—the other lodged inside. "We'll need to stop the bleeding." She quickly recalled what she learned from Cilaen about caring for wounds. "I think there is still a bullet in this wound—it will need to come out."

"Aah…" Arthur groaned as she pressed. "Bullet?"

She pulled a t-shirt from her pack and pressed it against the bleeding gash, then leaned back on her knees and peered at Arthur sadly. "That was my brother…or at least"—she twisted her mouth while digging through her supplies— "he was David's son. I grew up with him." She dipped her chin into her shoulder and tsked. "I have no idea how he found us or why he would have even come."

Jack's words rolled through Elanor's mind. *I hate you.* She had heard him say it inside her head, but to hear it from his mouth stung even worse. The look in his eye was so wild and vengeful as he stared down the barrel at her.

She cringed, then glanced back at Arthur. "Anyway…" She swallowed. "That weapon is called a gun. It fires bullets of iron, and that is what you have lodged in your shoulder." She poured some water onto the cloth and started cleaning the wound.

Arthur placed his hand over hers, stopping her. He caressed her fingers. "It could not have been easy having your brother want to hurt you."

Elanor's chin quivered, and she sniffed, "No…" She dropped her head. "But, I let them go. All of them."

Arthur lifted her chin. She could feel the tears wanting to fall at his compassion. She wanted to suck them all back in—hide her weakness. That was all she had shown since she had met him. Weakness. That was her worst fear.

Helen had thought her weak. She had thought her husband weak for loving Elanor. Helen even taught her children to think Elanor was weak. This whole future world had already known that. But the moment she had stepped into Prydain, she had wanted to be stronger. She'd feared becoming valueless in Merlin's eyes if he discovered she was nothing. Her wounds slowly tore back open.

What would a king and high druid of legend want with a weak, witless woman?

With Arthur's eyes staying upon her, he said, "That boy was afraid. I have known ones like him before. I could see it in his eyes. You threatened him. People are only threatened when they know someone with more power has come. And so, they try to smash that life to keep it from growing. My uncle, Uther, wished that I had never been born." He stopped, his brows curving sadly. "Elanor, there is nothing any of them could have *ever* done to stop you from becoming Pendragon."

A tear fell from Elanor's eye. His words washed over her like a healing balm, and as she looked at him, she saw a bit of home. She took a restorative sigh, wiping her face with her sleeve. "I wonder what Merlin will do with him."

Arthur glanced across the field. "He will show that boy more kindness than he deserves—I am sure."

Elanor directed her attention back to Arthur's wounds. "I do not have a knife. I need to get that bullet out—I can't even tell how deep it is. I am not sure how we are going to get it out. I wish Cilaen were here." She sighed. "He once dug a splinter out of my hand, and I hardly felt a thing. This will not be so easily dealt with." She glanced over her shoulder. "I think there may be a knife in Merlin's pack."

"You have power. You could heal him," whispered a voice from within her.

She lifted her eyes. Maybe she could find the magic. Maybe she could heal him. It seemed when the time was right, the power was there. Maybe this was the right moment. With a spark of determination returning to her, Elanor spread her hand over his wound and closed her eyes.

Fear swept through her as she remembered trying to heal Merlin of the snake bite. Nothing happened. But then… there was the healing power of the Crystal Cave. Merlin had been healed after all. *Maybe… the power to heal is always there—it just needs to be fought for sometimes.*

She pressed in. Arthur glanced down at her, bewildered.

"It's there. It has always been there," the voice encouraged in unison with her own hope.

The healing reminder of forgiveness floated through her mind, and she sighed out a long breath. Pulsing inside her chest, the magic surged with blue light. She was Gwenddydd. She was healer. It wasn't something she hoped to be—it was who she'd always been.

Arthur's jaw dropped in awe as the holes in his shoulder shrank. Elanor tried not to be distracted by Arthur's pain. He gritted his teeth, his hands clenching his knees while she pressed even deeper into the magic. Gradually, a gray, round pellet pushed its way out from the bloody gouge. It fell, rolling down his sleeve and onto the ground.

"You healed me," Arthur said, mystified, as he rubbed his fingers over the smooth skin underneath the dried blood. He even reached to the back of his shoulder and found no wound there either. "How is it you have this kind of magic?"

Elanor smiled. "I am not sure. It was a gift from Grwyrthrhodd. Though somehow, it is a magic that has always been with me. Sometimes, I am aware of the healing magic, and it works through me. But other times, the magic evades me—I am relieved it has worked this time."

"Who is Grwyrthrhodd?" Arthur asked with a stunned chuckle.

Merlin stared at Jack's unconscious body. He had seen the madness in his eye the moment he had met him that night at the Evans' house. Merlin watched his jealousy manifest—rousing Jack's need to dominate and crush. He sought attention and became angry when he was rejected. Merlin's song at the dinner table lit a fire in all of them. Jack's jealousy now raged out of control.

Merlin didn't intend for Jack's thoughts to fall prey to darkness. Though there was something more stirring. Something more that Merlin had no control over. It was up to Jack to set himself right again since he had allowed a demonic presence to sway his heart.

He knelt beside him. Jack moaned, and his head lolled to the side. Merlin needed to act swiftly before Jack became conscious. He kindled his spirit and allowed the magic of the shade to come upon him.

Jack's eyes rolled open to the blurry vision of someone kneeling over him. He lifted his hand to his head and rubbed his eyes. He remembered he had been angry about something. Then… *FLASH*… the memory of him firing the gun at Elanor. Agonized, he twisted to the side, squeezing the regret into his stomach. The same regret he'd felt when he hurt that boy in the alley.

Why had he done that? Why couldn't he ever seem to control himself?

"Jack…" a soft, familiar voice said, "are you alright?"

"I—" he said woefully, "I think I shot her." He pulled his hands over his face. "I… I did not mean to." He began to sob. "I was just… so… angry."

"Elanor has not been harmed."

Jack exhaled, rolling onto his back as a tear dripped from his eye. He squinted at the one speaking to him. "I didn't shoot her?"

"You tried… but, no, you did not."

"O-o-h my God—" he groaned, rubbing his eyes to clear them. "Dad? Is that you?" The blurry figure above him said nothing. "I-I thought they had done something to you."

"They did not harm me, Jack. I made my own choices."

"Why?" he said with moist eyes, the wrinkles on his forehead creased. "Why did you go with them? Why, Dad? Why do you always choose her?"

The figure reached down and gripped Jack's arms.

"Sometimes I wish you'd never found her. I wanted you to be *my* dad."

"I am sorry, Jack. I know it will be hard for you to understand, but more than just my choice brought Elanor into our lives. I am sorry you were never able to see it. But…" he whispered dolefully, "I should have been there for you and your sister."

"Dad. Why can't I see you clearly?"

"You hit your head very hard."

"Am I dreaming?"

"You will remember this like it was a dream."

"I don't understand."

"Jack…" his voice almost echoed, "my time for making things right with you has come too late. Please know… I loved you."

"Loved me? You're speaking like you are dead." Jack's eyes squinted to focus, his chin quivering. "Please, Dad… please tell me you're not dead."

"I have been very sick, Jack. I hadn't told anyone—not even your mother." He hesitated. "I just… wanted to go on an adventure. That's why I went, Jack. One last adventure." With fervor, he said, "I wanted my life to mean something."

"Dad… no." Jack sighed, struggling through tears.

"I wanted to be a knight… and I was." The voice wavered. "If only for a moment." There was silence, then he said, "Jack, it is time for you to go home."

"No, Dad. I don't want to go. I don't want to leave you. I… I love you, Dad."

"Tell your mother and sister… I love them." He sighed. "Jack?"

He sniffed. "Yes, Dad?"

"I see you…" The voice echoed and faded away.

The figure that knelt beside him had gone. Jack searched for his father—his sight quickly fading as sleep began to take him. "No…" Jack struggled. "No… Dad… Don't leave me." But before he fell asleep, he saw a tall, white, glowing shape reach down and wrap his arms around him. Jack's eyes cleared for a moment to see a white helm glowing with antlers. Then, his eyes closed.

When Jack woke again, he was within the treed forest, leaning against the trunk of a pine. He snapped up and glanced around, reorienting himself. He began to tremble. Salty, tearful cracks had dried on his cheeks, and he reached up to touch them. As he did, something fell from his chest into the pine needles on the ground. He reached down to collect it. Rolling it through his fingers, he discovered a small, wooden knight. He clenched it into the palm of his hand and pressed his lips sorrowfully. Stunned, he staggered to his feet and pushed the knight into his pocket. Despondent, he ambled away into the failing light and back through the forest.

28

GWYLIWR AURES

Merlin rejoined Elanor and Arthur near the stones. Elanor sat in front of a gaping Arthur, holding his shoulder.

Elanor shot to her feet. "What happened?"

Merlin took her hand and folded his fingers between hers. "Your brother is on his way home. I had to use the shade magic to convince him to go." He cupped Elanor's cheek. "He is no longer angry with you or afraid, and if it is of any consolation—know he was in turmoil having thought he had shot you."

"Shot her?" Arthur blurted. "He shot me!"

"What?" Merlin's eyes widened as they settled on the blood covering Arthur's shoulder and the spatter on Elanor. "Oh, Great God—How bad is it?"

"I am healed," Arthur declared, still astonished, motioning to Elanor.

Merlin turned to her. "You healed him?"

"I am Gwenddydd," she replied with surety. Her eyes gleamed, and the corners of her mouth lifted with placid confidence.

"Ha-ha!" Merlin's emotions soared as he hugged Elanor. "That you are…" He beamed with pride. "That you are."

"What shade?" she implored up at him, her bright eyes brimming with hope.

Merlin's face dropped with remorse, and he sighed. "I showed him your father."

"Oh." Elanor lifted her chin and bit her lip, as though holding in the sudden swell of grief. "That… that was…" She stopped, her eyes misting.

"He will remember it as a dream, but my hope…" Merlin faltered morosely. "My hope is that it will help to bring him closure."

Elanor whispered, "Does he know his father is dead?" Tears streamed a crystalline path down her cheeks.

Merlin nodded sadly. "Jack will have understood that something dire has happened and that it was his father's choice—not of our doing."

Elanor pressed her forehead into Merlin's chest and wept. He squeezed her tightly as his tears fell too. This cry—this grief—felt good. The loss and the trauma of David's death had been heavy on them both. And this finally felt like an acknowledgement of that truth—washing away the dross of the past few days.

Sighing, Merlin lifted Elanor's hand to his lips, kissing her fingers. "The light is fading." He faced the hill, peering up through the trees. "Let's get to the Hero's Mound before anything else tries to hinder us."

"Right," said Arthur solidly, lifting his pack. "There is life awaiting us back in Prydain. Let us not wait another minute and hope that we find our doorway home."

The darkening sky made navigating the caved hill difficult, but they found their way over the hill to the Hero's Mound. Night fell, and the stones glowed white in the moonlight.

Merlin dropped his pack and stared at the surrounding stones.

"I know this stone," Elanor said, brushing past him. "In my dream, my father was here."

"Ah." Merlin smiled at the revelation. "It is David's stone—the mystery of the eighth stone revealed."

Arthur nodded, patting the stone with his hand, drawing his eye up its height. "It was in my mind that one should be erected."

"I wish I knew what was written on it," Elanor said. "Time has erased most of the lines."

"You will know," Arthur told her, searching her eyes in earnest.

Merlin beamed at them, and a sudden awareness passed through him like a shadow fading at the end of the day. Crickets played in his ears the quiet rhythm of serenity. His spirit rose even higher as the wind shifted at their presence. He smiled. "The magic is here."

Elanor lifted her arms into the wind. "I can feel it."

"Call to the dragon."

She lifted her chin and called into the silver silence, "Gwyliwr!" The stars twinkled, illuminating their faces as they silently waited. "Gwyliwr..." she called again.

Nothing but the gentle chirps of the night responded.

Elanor walked to the center of the circle, lifted her hands, and closed her eyes. Out of the stillness, she sang, "It's time... Gwyliwr deffro a chodi." She paused to listen, then continued, "Mae'r amser wedi dod i'n hanfon adref. The time has come to send us home."

Merlin's heart ignited. Elanor had always carried a powerful magic, but now she followed after it, moving as he had learned to do. She now understood that the magic was an extension of her, and not just something that happened. Merlin felt her call to the dragon excite his magic, like they were in unison. They were one chord, vibrating together at the Master's strum.

All at once, a rush of wind blew across the mound. The kind of gale that only came at the swish of a dragon's wings. They stared up at the sky with expectancy, but no dragon appeared. The wind rushed and swirled, forcing the three of them to huddle together. At one final gust, the ground rattled beneath them.

"Gwyliwr?" Elanor bade, staring ahead.

"I am here…" came a strange, whispering voice that floated through the breeze.

Merlin called out, "Why can we not see you?" He squinted his eyes, engaging his magic to see beyond the natural. Finally, there appeared a faint, iridescent line. It sparkled with a spectral silhouette, almost invisible. "There you are, my friend."

The whisper came again. "I am old, Emrys. I have waited many years for this day."

Elanor stretched out her hand, searching blindly, to brush the dragon's nose. The giant, twinkling shadow pressed against her tiny palm with affection.

"I have been sleeping here for many long years. I would wake, here and there, to a traveler as they walked through. Most could not see me, and almost never did they need me. Some I have helped with my whispers—while others, I wished to crunch their bones between my teeth. But I have ever watched these hills, invisible to the world, waiting and longing for the day I would see you again. And now, at long last… I can diminish."

Elanor dropped her hand, her countenance somber.

"Yes, dear Gwenddydd. Now my time has surely come. Now I may join my ancestors who lay within the earth—forever becoming part of this ground, unrecognizable. But the Master sees me. He sees me. I will be free from this world to fly in His kingdom. And… this is well." Her breath blew the three of them back. "For I have fulfilled my duty as a guardian by sending the Pendragon home."

As she spoke, a spark of time sprang in Merlin. A tingling edge of magic raced from his chest down through his arms, sparking the white fire to emanate from his hands. He glanced over, and Elanor's had also come alight.

The dragon continued, "You and Gwenddydd already have the magic. But you can only return *yourselves* back to the world of Prydain. Only one can pass through a singular stream of time. You and Gwenddydd each have a stream because you have already been to all the places you will ever go in time. That is what the magic does and why most cannot hold it. But Arthur does not have the magic, nor could he wield it. So, I have waited to send him upon *my* last stream of time."

As the magic deepened, a memory formed in Merlin's mind. He glanced up at the dragon in amazement as her silhouette gave way, revealing her full form—though still shadowed.

"I remember," Elanor exclaimed. "The hill and the cottage."

Merlin's excitement forced the magic to grow. "Yes, I remember as well."

"My last breath will now be spent on the Pendragon."

Elanor's eyes turned forlorn at the dragon as the flames licked and crackled around her.

"Do not be sad for me, child. I will be free, and all will be set as it should be. You will see me again, though this is the last time I shall see you." The dragon's eyes gleamed. "It has done my heart a kindness to see your faces once again. Even if it has only been for a short moment." She turned to Merlin. "Know this, Emrys," she said, her voice growing louder, "Arthur cannot hold this magic. Only those who have the magic can travel with no ill effect. Arthur will be greatly affected and will need you to care for him. He is strong, and he will survive. Elanor survived with the aid of your magic when she did not have time—I believe Arthur will have nothing to fear either. But it *will* be extremely painful for him."

Merlin frowned at Arthur, remembering Elanor's deep sickness when she arrived in Prydain.

"Arthur Pendragon," the dragon declared as her green and gold scales emerged through the darkness. Her voice boomed, "Are you ready?"

Arthur stepped forward, tall like the valiant king he was, and declared, "I am ready!" With a bold fierceness in his eyes, he opened his arms to be sent through time.

Merlin was enveloped in the white flame as it flared. Through the flames, he still saw Arthur as the dragon opened her mouth, breathing on him the fires of time. Elanor had become consumed by the white flame and was no longer on the hill.

Arthur's screams rang through Merlin's ears as the white flames engulfed him. The raging, whipping of the fire surged, and at once, all went silent.

Within moments, the world transformed, becoming dark blue. The sky illuminated again with bright white stars. A breeze howled across an open plain, and Merlin stood upon a hill overlooking it all. He felt Elanor's gentle fingers twist between his. The smells of home drifted into his nostrils, and with exceeding relief, he pulled Elanor into his side. "We're home."

"Yes…" Elanor smiled, dazed. "But where are we?"

"This is not the Hero's Mound." Merlin glanced around. "Where is Arthur?"

A burst of wind rushed across the hill, and they shielded their faces. Merlin peeked between his upheld arms and saw a vibrant, golden-green Gwyliwr descending near them. She was quick and fierce. "Stand ready," she trumpeted. "I will do what I can." Her yellow chest pumped, and her throat trembled with a growling hum. She beamed at Elanor, and a rumbling purr emanated down toward her. "I am happy you have returned."

Before either of them could respond, a loud clash vibrated the air, and white fire burst between them and the dragon. As it dissipated, a quaking Arthur was there seizing on the ground. His teeth were clenched and his back arched. The intensity of his spasms sent his heels digging into the ground. His hands ripped handfuls of grass without finding a hold.

The dragon breathed, and a billowing cloud of electric yellow vapor surrounded Arthur. As it dissolved, Arthur's seizure calmed, but now he lay groaning with pain, his face wet with perspiration.

"I have removed the trauma of time. Now you must heal the pain," the dragon hastened to Merlin.

Merlin jumped into action. He remembered how he and Cilaen had rushed to help Elanor all those years ago. He leaned over Arthur, covering his chest with his palms, and sent pulses of power as he mumbled healing words with great effort.

Elanor placed her hands over Merlin's. Her magic enhanced his—releasing more power.

The dragon stared down with her massive nose hovering above them—watching the small king with fiery eyes. And at last… Arthur released a healing sigh. Calm settled over his face.

At this, the dragon declared happily, "He will be well!" She stretched her long neck high and released a guttural repeating pulse. "We have nothing to fear. You have completed your time in the future, and now the king has returned." Gleefully, she almost danced, shaking the ground with her leaps.

"How long have we been gone—where are we?" Merlin asked breathlessly.

"Time could not allow you to be gone long, as you are needed here. I know Osian has been silently busy. The moon has turned its circle only once since you left for the future."

Merlin's tense shoulders fell, relieved.

"And you are but a small distance into a deep wood, east of Caer Lial. Here you will be safe while Arthur recovers. He must be strong before he returns. There is an empty cottage at the bottom of this hill. I have killed a stag and left it there for you."

Surprised, Merlin chuffed, "You killed us a stag?"

"I wanted to eat it but knew you would need it."

Merlin turned to face Arthur. Concerned, he placed his hand on Arthur's head. "He still has a fever."

"He has the sickness," the dragon said. "It will pass, but it will take a little time."

Elanor said, "I know some herbs that will help with his fever."

Merlin nodded. "Yes, there should be some in this forest. I know the kind." He glanced up at the dragon and twisted his lips. "I sought you, dragon—tried to find you so that I could know if my wife lived. Why did you not come to me? Why did you not help me?"

The dragon stilled at his questions. She lowered her giant head and stared Merlin in the eye. "Emrys…" she rumbled, blowing back his hair with hot breath, "you must learn to not fear time. It was a magic you had to find as the time became right for you to know it. I could not have been more of help to you. Time's journey happens as it moves forward, and the hasty drive themselves to fear as they wait for it."

"That sounds like wisdom, dragon." Merlin laughed, gazing into her round, golden eyes, her pupils black slits almost man-sized. "I have heard this from another before and now am finally beginning to understand."

"Yes," she grumbled, pleased, "you would have."

She turned to warble up at the sky, then padded the ground with her front legs, her talons piercing the turf. Great chunks of earth tossed into the air as she burst high into the sky, releasing her wings at the highest point. She turned and soared away into the night—dwindling to a speck against the moon. Merlin and Elanor's mouths hung in wonder as they watched her disappear.

Merlin leaned down closer to Arthur, observing him intensely. "The *once and future king* has returned," he whispered. "They are waiting for you, Arthur. Prydain will have its high king again."

29

HOME AGAIN

Merlin and Elanor carefully carried Arthur down from the Hill. At the bottom, they found the small stone cottage nestled amid shadowy trees blackened by the night. The dragon's promised deer lay in front of the cottage's old rotten door, which barely hung from one rusty hinge at the top.

"I shall need to do something with that, or the meat will be wasted," Merlin huffed. "Over here." He shifted his head over to a lump of hay resting against the side of the cottage. "Let's place him there while we look inside this dilapidated shelter."

They dragged Arthur over and settled him safely against the hay. Elanor pulled a flashlight from her pack. She grinned with a wink. "Still have a bit of that future magic."

Merlin chuckled. "Cannot take those to the Caer. I am afraid most will not be ready for that sort of magic. We will bury them somewhere tomorrow. Right now, it is useful."

Together, they leerily approached the dark, dusky door frame. Elanor shined the beam of light into the void and stepped over the threshold. Bursting out from above her, a bird escaped, rattling its wings. Elanor threw her hands up, covering her head.

Merlin leapt back. "Blasted bird!"

Elanor giggled, placing her hand on her chest. "Shall we go in?"

"Come on," Merlin grumbled, pulling his jumper with a testy jerk.

Elanor moved on through the door, shining the light on all that remained within the cottage. Leaves lay scattered on the dirt floor, and several birds' nests overhung the wooden beams above. At the center, a round iron hearth sat, begging for a fire.

"Excellent," Merlin said, "I think I saw some scattered bits of wood just outside." He left to gather some before returning with a few logs folded in his arms. He set them inside the hearth and blew upon them. Flames rose immediately, lighting the rest of the cottage with a wavering orange glow.

"Look over here," Elanor said, pointing. "This will be a good place for Arthur."

A long platform sat against a side wall, covered by old, gnawed-upon, woolen blankets. Elanor grabbed up a few. "These will need to be cleaned." She took them outside to shake them out.

There wasn't much to the rest of the cottage. Old, dried herbs hung on a broken shelf, covered in webs. There were two wooden chairs: one intact, but likely not trustworthy—the other on its side with a leg nibbled off.

Merlin folded his arms. "Could be worse," he murmured over his shoulder as Elanor entered back in.

"Well, it doesn't appear the thatch is caving in, though I am worried about the amount of vermin that likely live in it," Elanor said with a look of disgust. She laid some hay onto the platform's frame and folded the freshly fluffed blankets on top to give Arthur some layers. "Hardly fit for a king."

Merlin firmed his lips as he nodded. "It would almost be better to sleep outside, except for the fire warming the walls."

Elanor sighed, and her shoulders relaxed. "We did it."

Merlin grinned. "Yes, we did."

"I can't believe it. Now that we are here"—she glanced around curiously— "it doesn't seem real."

Merlin gazed at her from the other side of the growing fire. Dirt marked her cheeks, and her hair was frazzled from the long day. She was beautiful. His heart panged at the reality of all they had been through. She had been dead. Dead. And Arthur had been dead too. Now they both breathed, alive, and in Prydain.

Elanor was right—it didn't seem real. None of it. From the moment he had stepped into that future world to finding Elanor and Arthur, it had all felt surreal. Merlin exhaled heavily. He dropped his head and lifted his hand, rubbing his eyes as his stress melted away.

When he glanced back up, he found Elanor's fond eyes staring at him, the rose of her lips drawing on him like a flower to the sun. He crossed the room towards her; her eyes sparkled with the yellow reflections of the fire. Pulling her close, he lightly kissed her lips. The warmth of her mouth against his left a satisfying burn upon his lips, and his heart ached for more. He deepened the kiss, breathing in the allure of her presence. He savored the feel of her in his arms and sank his chin into her disheveled hair. "It doesn't seem real, but… I am so glad it is."

The hollow clunk of one of the logs toppling in the fire snapped him out of the moment. "Blasted…" He let go of Elanor, grimacing. "That dragon has left me with work to do."

Elanor laughed, returning to fluff out another blanket. "I think this is all ready for Arthur. Shall we go get him?"

Merlin smirked and mumbled, "I will get more wood for the fire and get that deer gutted and hung."

"Right. I'll settle Arthur and go foraging for what I can find for his fever."

"Is our work never done?" Merlin said, taking her by the hand and pulling her in at the waist. He could not let her go again without pressing his lips to hers. Longing for her, he ardently kissed her, letting go of all the long days of roving through a world set against them. But for this short moment, he felt relief. Her warmth and his, igniting the connection between them. Resting his cheek on hers, he whispered, "One day… we can have this, and just this. No more evil set on destroying us."

"Do you really think that day will *ever* come?"

"I don't know…" Merlin mused, lifting his head. "But once, a long time ago, there was a young woman who told me there was hope."

Arthur now safely rested on the blankets beside the warming fire. Merlin had begrudgingly completed his tasks—having processed the animal that now hung in the back of the cottage. Elanor brought in more hay, shaking it free and settling it into a nice heap for herself and Merlin.

On the ground beside Arthur sat a chipped bowl Elanor had recovered from the cottage. She'd filled it with water and freshly crushed herbs. Arthur slept with a cold, wet cloth resting on his forehead while the fire popped. The frigid night air blew in through the door cracks, and Merlin, exhausted from the long day, lay sleeping in the hay.

Elanor tossed and turned, unable to sleep. She was both disturbed and excited. She worried for Arthur as he moaned and struggled on his bed. She empathized, remembering what it was like to have this sickness. It was strange and disorienting. The crashing symbols of electric pain that bombarded the head. It was like nothing she had ever felt before.

She also couldn't stop thinking about arriving back in the Caer once again. The sight of her daughter's tender fingers and toes. Her mind raced, imagining the jubilant reception at Arthur's return.

As she daydreamed, she pulled uncomfortably on her sweater and t-shirt. She glanced down at the dirty, off-white tweed, wishing she had something else to wear. It felt bizarre now to be in clothes that didn't belong in this world. Her jeans pinched and restricted her skin—reminders of where she had been. Helen, Jack… they were all gone now. And her dad… She groaned as she remembered him. Her heart stung with grief.

Unsettled, Elanor sat up and puffed through her lips. She stared at the door as it creaked in the wind, then turned to where Merlin slept soundly. It was no use trying to sleep, so she checked on Arthur. She lifted the cloth from his head and soaked it again. His forehead was hot, but the radiating heat had dissipated.

She stroked his forehead. Something about his face. She remembered the stone image of him at the top of the Palisade. Strangely, the cold stone had always brought her comfort. Her brows laced together, and she whispered, "Doesn't look anything like you."

Restless, she got up and crept over to the door. Lifting it so it would not drag across the grass and weeds, she quietly pushed it open. She walked out into the crisp night air as the gentle wind blew her hair from her face.

The hill sat on her left, and tall trees surrounded the area. Everything felt so different compared to her time in the future. The moon shone brighter and the wind smelled sweeter. Even the trees felt more alive than the tranquil pines of the forest they had just come from. Consoled to be home, she stared up at the stars, taking it all in.

"Could not sleep either?" Merlin beckoned, walking out from the cottage.

Elanor smiled. "I worried we would never see this place again, and now that we are here, my mind is too full of expectation to sleep."

"Gwendolen told me I would bring you home—though I doubted."

She turned to face Merlin as he approached. Even in the darkness, she could see the shining gold of his eyes. She pinched at the fabric of his shirt. "I will be glad to see you with your colors wrapped around your shoulders again. These modern clothes are not right for you." She reached up and combed her fingers through his hair. His curly tendrils easily rolled through her fingers. She cupped his cheek and whispered, "You are not an ordinary man. You should not wear such ordinary things."

Merlin drew her body closer to his. "And what is to be said of you then?"

"I am not ordinary—" Elanor's eyes sparked with blue.

"I am so glad." He leaned closer, his lips nearing hers. "You are finally seeing what I saw the moment I met you."

She kissed him, muttering, "I left the orphan in the future."

Merlin smiled. His eyes flashed with light, and he lifted her into an impassioned embrace. He kissed her mouth with an arousing sense of oneness. His passion enlivened her, and her heart beat faster. She pulsed closer, keen to have him, and the earth and the fragrance of the grass enveloped them.

The sun rose, and the birds lightened the air, tweeting and chirping in the cold frosty morning. Elanor and Arthur slept inside the cottage while it warmed with fresh logs on the fire. Merlin paced outside, pondering their next step. The cold season was coming. Though unfamiliar with this section of the forest, he had a clear idea what direction the Caer lay in.

He needed to get help. They could not just camp and wait for Arthur to be well. He wouldn't be ready to travel on foot for a while. He remembered how weak Elanor had remained from the sickness. Arthur needed a horse.

With the meat left for them by the dragon, Elanor could take care of Arthur on her own. They were well protected within this grove of trees.

Returning inside the cottage, he knelt over Elanor, brushing the hair off her sleeping eyes. He enjoyed how her hair messily wrapped her face in the morning. He whispered, "Elanor."

Chapter Twenty-nine

She opened her eyes, stretching herself awake. "Is the sun already up?" She yawned and sat up to kiss him. Her loving gaze searched his eyes.

Merlin sat down beside her. "I have been thinking."

"Uh oh," Elanor said with a smirk. "I know what it means when you've been thinking."

"I need to go to the Caer and leave you here with Arthur. You have learned enough from Cilaen to care for him. I have seen you."

She nodded. "I agree. We should be safe here." She rose with a serious stare as she checked on Arthur. "His face looks brighter. He is stronger than I was."

"Arthur is never down for long." Merlin chuckled.

"I hate not being able to go with you."

"I know. But I must get help quickly. Arthur is recovering fast but not fast enough to trek through the forest when the time calls for it. And… I do not know how far we are from the Palisade until I get on the other side of this forest. I need to get my bearings. If we are in the north already, Caer Lial cannot be too far." He picked up his container of water and swished it in the bottle. "Almost empty. There is a stream, not far, on the other side of the cottage. I explored around a bit this morning. There is also more wood just outside." He pointed. "Some of it is wet and will need to be brought in to dry. But there should be enough in here for you to use for a few days."

Elanor nodded again, then dropped her head. Merlin could tell she was mulling it over. Always, it seemed, she chose to be brave when she had to be. He knew she didn't like the idea of him leaving but wouldn't let him know that it bothered her.

Merlin touched her cheek. "You will be safe, or else I would not leave you. There is something magical about this place. Keeps it hidden. I can feel it. That is likely why we are here." He paused, letting his hand fall, then stood. He pulled a knife from the wall where he had stuck it the night before and handed it to Elanor. "You know what to do with the meat?"

She nodded with a sigh but grinned up at him. "Don't worry. I am not out of my element anymore now that we are in Prydain." She rose, gripping the knife in her palm. "They're going to think you strange when they see you in those clothes."

"Hah. Well, what choice do I have?"

Elanor rushed to him, wrapping her arms around him and burying her face into his chest. "Please come back soon."

He kissed the top of her head. "It will be my full aim to return as quickly as I can."

"And it will be mine," mumbled Arthur's weak voice, "that she would not be alone."

Gasping, Elanor ran to his side. Arthur's face twisted and sweat beaded his forehead.

"Not so fast, my friend," Merlin said, encouraged to see him awake.

"Ah… this pains my head."

"I know." Elanor dabbed his brow with a cloth. "You must keep resting."

Arthur rolled to his side and reached out for Merlin. "Are we home?"

"Yes, brother, we are home, but not yet to the Palisade. We are in a forest cottage while you recover."

Arthur breathed out in relief. "I do not *ever* want to do that again. I thought I would die from the pain ripping at my flesh. I am amazed I sit here whole."

"Sleep," Merlin said. "You are still sick. Elanor will be here to care for you. Take the medicines she has made for you, and do not try to be more helpful than you ought to be."

Arthur groaned, shutting his eyes without resistance.

"This is hopeful." Merlin squeezed Elanor's arm. He glanced over his shoulder at the door. "I must leave while it is still early."

Elanor gave him a delicate kiss. Then he grabbed his satchel and pack and reluctantly marched for the door. Elanor rushed to the door to watch him depart, but Merlin kept his eyes forward, pressing into the trees—eager to bring the help that would get them all back to Caer Lial.

30

MARKS OF DEATH

It did not take long before Merlin emerged from the forest, seeing the surrounding mountains and plains. Immediately, he recognized the land. He was only a little south of Haldin's village—the hateful place where he had destroyed the cursed plague less than a year prior.

He peered West, pondering whether to walk straight to Caer Lial which would take him a few days or claim a horse from the small village and get there much faster. He loathed the idea of going back to the plagued village. So many angry and grievous emotions floated to the surface as he remembered the trauma. The end result of his last sojourn there was the trap where Elanor had been shot through the chest. It almost seemed worth the extra time it would take to trek to Caer Lial on his own rather than return there.

He gritted his teeth, shifting his cold, reddened hands over the straps of his pack. He knew what the wise choice would be. He mumbled defiantly, "I have no choice. I promised Elanor I would return swiftly." He looked back over his shoulder. "I must not delay even for Arthur's sake. Haldin's village is my best option. Maybe the Great God has blessed me to find myself here—not far from people who can help. Likely, Haldin would jump at the chance to make up for his treachery…Choice made," he said decisively.

He moved toward the village, but the closer he got, the more he resented his choice. At each step, he had to force himself to continue. After a few hours, he knew he was near. He braced himself, anticipating his anger at the sight of Haldin. "Especially," Merlin stewed, "if he tries to threaten my pride with groveling to gain my favor."

The round huts and cottages came into view, but Merlin slowed his approach as the sight of empty fields unsettled him. He stopped as the hollow wind blew. The village sat strangely quiet. It was midday, and almost harvest. There should have been a buzz of activity about the fields.

Merlin's pride and anger fell away as his concern deepened. Cautiously, he pressed closer to the settlement, hoping for a good sign. *If something has happened to these lands, what of Caer Lial?*

Worry rose in his chest. As he neared the village, he heard the tinkling of a sheep's bell and hoped that the bell remained around the neck of a living creature. He quickened his pace and entered the center square. The yards and lanes were also eerily deserted. Cottage doors sat open, yawning black and mute.

Gulping, he yelled, "Hello!"

A bleating sheep dashed from one of the doorways, startling Merlin as it pushed past him and scampered down the path between the homes. He inhaled sharply. "Accursed sheep!" Breathing back out, he guardedly considered the house closest to him. Shaking his head, he bit his lip, then crossed the threshold—gazing around for evidence of people.

"Hello?" he beckoned again, hoping for someone to respond. No one returned his call.

There appeared no signs of attack. A table laid with food was left behind. The meat had molded, and the stale bread had been nibbled on by vermin. Chairs sat empty, and the hearth was loaded with old, black ash. The house sat prepared for the people who lived there but lingered cold and void. "Did they just leave? Where would they have all gone?"

Merlin heard a clip-clopping sound coming from outside. With haste, he ran to find a brown, thin horse standing outside the door. "Whoa," Merlin calmingly hummed. "Whoa." He reached his hand to its eager nose, and it pressed back with a grateful whinny—nibbling his fingers.

"Where has everyone gone to, eh?" he asked the horse. "Left you here all alone, did they?" The horse had no saddle or reins. "Well, at least you are a welcome sight. Let us see if we can get you a saddle." He scanned the village to locate the stables. "I guess we will go down this way, shall we?" He patted the horse's cheek, shaking his head despairingly. "This is not good. What foul thing has happened here, eh?"

The horse willingly followed beside Merlin as he moved down the lane, looking in at each house he passed. The people could not have been gone long, as lone goat, sheep, and cows ambled around the lonely village.

He located the stable, but as he neared, his new companion halted, and resisted going any further. Appearing spooked, the horse puffed and neighed lightly.

"What's wrong, boy?" Merlin asked, staring suspiciously at the structure before he continued his approach. Now closer, he heard more animals restlessly crying from inside. His heart beat faster as he reached for the large door, hoping to only find animals inside.

The sight hit him in the stomach even before he smelt the foul odor. He had found the villagers. Their bodies hung down from the rafters that held them aloft, and the ground lay covered in the stinking dried blood of the innocent. He looked up and instantly regretted it. The rotting, gray skin on their dead faces carved a jagged trail straight to his heart.

Merlin yelled out, horrified, and the horse bounded back away from the stable doors. The animals—some living, some dead—trapped in the pens, called out at the sight of him, begging to be set free.

Throwing his arm over his nose and mouth, he scrambled around the edges to the pens, avoiding going underneath the dangling feet. Unlatching the first pen, the gate swung open and the animals bounded out, rushing into the fresh air. The same with the second and the third pen. As the last animal ran free, he turned, and on the largest post at the center, he saw the markings.

"Osian," he spat. Those same, awful, fallen runes—the sign of Osian's evil— were scratched upon the wood.

Is this what we have come home to?

Urgency surged through him to get to Caer Lial as soon as possible. He quickly located a harness and saddle, ripped them from their hooks, and rushed from the stable. As soon as he hit the fresh air, he drew in large gasps. He bent forward, putting his hands on his knees. The revelation of what he had just seen widened his eyes with horror and made his mouth drop. He turned to stare back at the stable. "Great God, help us." Guilt crawled inside his guts at how vehemently he had resisted coming to this little village. Now only remorse captured him for the people—even Haldin.

Was he in there amongst them? Merlin was not willing to go in and search the faces of the dead. *Maybe this was retribution from the enemy after I broke the curse.* Merlin didn't know. His mind searched for answers. What *reason* could there *ever* be for Osian's atrocities?

Pools formed in Merlin's eyes. It grieved him, knowing there was no one left to mourn them.

"Come on," he said to the horse, whipping the ground with the reins. As the horse approached, he pressed his forehead to its muzzle for a moment of comfort. He went on to prepare the horse, but as he tightened the saddle strap, he stopped.

Merlin turned back to the stable. He couldn't leave it that way. The barbarity of the enemy could not be allowed to remain, and the Cymry people left dishonored.

He approached the accursed stable, rested his hand on the outside wall, and prayed. "Great God, yn eich dwylo chi yr wyf yn codi'r eneudiau hyn. Into your hands, I lift these souls." His eyes lit golden, and a circle of red sparks shot out from his hand, sprawling up the walls and igniting the beams on fire. "Gorffwys nawr," he said. "Rest now."

He stepped back from the hot flames blazing up to the thatch. Merlin knelt on his knees and took a moment as it smoldered. That all too familiar rage of battle beat in his breast as the red flames burned in his eyes. Arthur had returned but hopefully not to a devastated Prydain. Between his teeth, Merlin seethed, "Osian shall not be allowed to ruin these lands."

He got up from the ground and flung himself onto the horse's back. "YAH!" he yelled, burning with rage as he kicked the horse's flanks. They burst into a run, and Merlin hoped the weakened animal could carry him the distance. The horse willingly ran, happy it seemed to be free from the village.

Osian has burned, raped, and murdered long enough. His hand steadily becoming a worse plague than the Saecsans.

Merlin could think of nothing else as trees blurred past and hills disappeared. "Yah, yah!" he demanded, pushing the animal forward.

He was making good time. The sun was setting, but at this pace, he would reach Caer Lial before dark. When he heard the thudding hoof beats of pursuers behind him, he sped up, glancing over his shoulders and seeing them still a long way off. The forest was before him—the same tree line the assassin who pierced Elanor with an arrow had emerged from. This… the last forest between him and the lands of Caer Lial.

But his horse panted with exhaustion, its sprint laboring. The horse grunted as it wildly ambled, its legs beginning to give out.

"Come on!" Merlin urged aggressively, hoping the horse wouldn't falter. He turned again to look behind. The riders were closing in on him, but now, Merlin caught sight of the colors wrapping the shoulders of the pursuers. Red and gold. His horse, screaming a whinny, collapsed, sending Merlin sailing over its head. He and the horse careened into the ground and skidded across the grassy turf.

Merlin slowly became conscious. The moaning of a suffering horse assaulted his ears—the metal rings of its harness rattling as it struggled.

"Ah!" Merlin hollered. Pain pinged his sides, and he tasted salty blood on his lips. The hoofbeats of those chasing him had ceased, as they now surrounded him. He tried to sit up, but stabbing pain kept him on the ground.

"Merlin?" came a familiar voice. The leather saddle creaked as one of the riders dismounted.

"Yes…" Merlin groaned. "I am Merlin."

Merlin fully opened his eyes, registering the six riders circling him. Atop their horses sat Cymbrogi, wearing the colors of Caer Lial, and kneeling beside him was Bedwyr.

"Oh, Great God," Bedwyr shouted. "What are you doing here? When did you come back?" Shock played over his face as he reached for Merlin. "You are hurt, my friend."

Merlin nodded. "My horse was weak. Why were you chasing me?"

"I am sorry, brother. You know the queen has us wary of all who come onto our lands. I did not recognize you from afar. How badly are you hurt?" Bedwyr assessed Merlin but halted at his strange attire. "What are you wearing? You look ridiculous."

Merlin chuffed, grabbing at his side in pain, and groaned, "Glad to be home, my brother. Damn." He buckled over. "Help me sit up, will you?"

Bedwyr reached his hand beneath Merlin's back.

"Carefully," Merlin said through his teeth as he leaned forward.

"Being thrown from a horse at that speed—you're lucky you are not more hurt."

Merlin glanced at the panting horse struggling and foaming with sweat on the ground. "I am so sorry, my friend," he said to the horse with rising sorrow. He scooted over and laid his hand on its nose. "He was half-starved when I found him.

I should not have pushed him so hard. "I…" He winced. "I was eager to get to the Palisade."

One of the Cymbrogi observing the horse shouted over, "I am afraid his leg appears broken."

Merlin nodded, forlorn. The horse's strained huffs were weakening. It rested its head on the ground, grumbling while Merlin stroked it. Blood rolled out from its nose. Merlin leaned in. "Be at peace, my friend. I… I thank you for your help."

Bedwyr bowed his head and drew his blade. "It is not only the leg, but his heart will also soon fail. I am afraid this was his last charge."

Merlin closed his eyes.

The sword came down swiftly, silencing the horse's cries. Bedwyr knelt beside Merlin and placed his hand in blessing upon the animal's neck. They silently honored the horse's passing. Merlin's lip lifted bitterly; his gut wrenching for allowing the horse to come to such a sad fate.

Bedwyr looked at Merlin from the corner of his eye and prodded, "Did you find her?" Hope and sorrow emanated from Bedwyr's eyes. "Is she alive as we all hoped?"

Merlin lifted his hand and placed it on Bedwyr's arm. The sting of his injured shoulder was once again inflamed. He sucked in the ache. "It is better than we had hoped."

"Elanor is alive? Where is she?" Bedwyr's eyes darted around as if to find her.

Merlin sighed, a smile tugging at his lips. "I missed you. I thought I may never see any of you again. You are a welcome sight, my friend. Even if you did almost kill me."

"Merlin," Bedwyr demanded. "Is she alive?"

"Yes… yes," he huffed. "She is indeed."

Bedwyr gasped, lifting one hand to his forehead. His chin trembled.

"She is alive… and there is more. Though I hope we have come home to a world not destroyed by Osian."

Bedwyr snapped his head up. "What do you mean? It is the same as you left. We have heard nothing from the forsaken bastard."

"Well," Merlin said, twinging through the aches, "the village… Haldin's village… that I have just come from, would tell another story. That is where I recovered this poor horse that served me without question." He stared back at the horse with regret.

Bedwyr leaned in fiercely. "Tell me."

"Osian… he has killed them all."

31

ALIVE & WELL

It had been a full day since Merlin left. On the second morning, Elanor wandered through the trees outside the cottage, foraging for herbs that would help mend Arthur. She mainly searched for fenyw root, which had been readily available when they arrived but now became increasingly difficult to find.

"Less and less grows as the days become colder," she grumbled to herself.

She loved the skills she gained all those days helping Cilaen but now felt helpless without him to tell her what to do. Arthur's fever had lessened, but she wanted to have supplies on hand in case he needed more.

"Drat," Elanor said, throwing down what roots she had gathered. "None of this will be of any use." She stared off into the thicket, then back at the cottage where Arthur lay asleep. She let out an exasperated sigh, folding her arms. She just wanted to go home. All the way home. To be so close, yet stuck waiting, killed her.

She leaned her shoulder against a nearby tree, and a smile spread across her face as she thought of Gwynevere and Adhan. Letting go of Helen made her long for them even more. She kicked her feet across the wet leaves, pushing a long branch out from underneath the brush. Picking it up, she turned it in her hand to inspect it. "Just the right size."

For the past few days, she had been engrossed with the idea of swinging a sword again. Taking a focused breath, she lunged, pointing the tip of her imagined sword just as Merlin had taught her. Over the years in the Palisade, she continued to learn swordcraft. Even Bedwyr had taken the time to instruct her. But always she practiced for Merlin's sake—never because she desired to.

Slice.

She whipped the branch through the air, arching it above her head, then swung it down as if clashing her sword against an imaginary foe's blade. With controlled speed, she pivoted, spinning to avoid the defender, then thrust her sword forward. Now she had captured the feel of it—she lost herself in the flow. Strength increased in her arm as her eyes snapped toward her enemy.

"I can see Merlin's technique in your footing."

Like a child caught, Elanor swiftly dropped the stick and threw her arms behind her back. Her cheeks flushed as she turned to see Arthur leaning against the side of the cottage. She gave him a disconcerted grin.

"He has been teaching you. I can tell."

Elanor dusted her hands on her clothes and scrunched her nose. "You are up. You must be feeling better."

Arthur chortled, as if amused by Elanor's flustered demeanor. "Yes. A little better. Mostly just weak. A bit… fuzzy in the head."

"Well, you still had a fever last time I checked." She approached him and placed her hand on his forehead. "Still do," she said, grimacing. "Do you feel like you could eat? That might help."

"I could definitely eat."

They walked back inside together, and Elanor grabbed some of the skewers she had whittled the day before. She retrieved the knife Merlin had left for her and began hacking away at the deer carcass.

"No. Not like that," Arthur said, jerking the knife from her hand.

Elanor's eyes flared at his brash condescension.

"Look." He waved the knife at her. "If you saw back and forth, you tear up the meat." Placing the knife against the deer, he pulled the blade through. "See? Right up against the sinew. Like this."

Elanor gave him a sideways smirk. "Well, I am glad the sickness hasn't hurt your charm."

With a smug look, Arthur slapped a chunk of meat into her palm.

She rolled her eyes and, with a level of purposeful sass, skewered the venison.

Arthur chuckled, sighing back into a restful incline, and closed his eyes.

It wasn't long before the meat finished cooking and they were happily eating their morning meal.

Elanor pointed her skewer at Arthur and said between chews, "I never liked learning the sword."

Arthur leaned forward with interest.

"It felt pretentious to hold a weapon in my hand. I am not a warrior or… or daring." She furrowed her brow. "Though, I never really imagined I would have magic… or be a part of this world… or even be a significant part of anything. But now," she said, lifting her eyes to meet his, "I am part of this world."

Arthur lifted his chin in agreement. "There was a day I never imagined I would be a king."

"Didn't you always know you would be one day?"

He shook his head and threw what was left of his meat into the fire and rolled onto his back. "No," he said with a sigh, "I spent most of my life an orphan." He turned to face her. "I did not know who my parents were. Raised by other men I came to know as father." He lifted his eyes to the holey thatch. "Merlin was my one constant. He was like a big brother all my life. I remember feeling so angry at him."

Arthur clenched his fists above his face. "Angry that he had always known who my father was and never told me. He knew I would be king someday but allowed me to believe I was going to grow and be like all the other young boys."

"But you never were."

"Never was what?"

"Like all the others."

Arthur tsked. "No… I was never like the others. Somehow, I always knew, deep down. I knew I had a destiny. Just like you." He gave her a knowing glance. "You knew, too. Did you not? Though you grew up far from all you were meant to know… you knew you were different. Destined for more."

"I guess, deep down, I always hoped it was true, but… I was afraid to believe it. I am still afraid."

"You must begin to believe. Don't cast away your identity as easily as you did that stick. Let them see you." Arthur fixed her with a serious gaze. "If you do not believe it, then the enemy won't either."

Snap.

Twigs breaking underfoot broke their conversation.

Elanor stood. "Someone has come?"

Arthur had specks before his eyes and a tingle in his head from all the talk. He was not keen on jumping to the ready. He rubbed his head. "Hopefully, it is only Merlin returned. I am not up for any trouble."

"It should be safe." Elanor leerily walked closer to the door. "Merlin said he felt this place protected—possibly enchanted in some way." She peered around the door, surveying the trees. "I don't see anyone… wait—" She pushed the door open carefully and wandered out.

Arthur leaned forward, ready to charge the door.

Elanor's muffled voice called from outside the cottage, "It is Merlin!"

Arthur sighed with relief. "Thank the Great God for that." Then he heard another voice that was not Merlin's. Arthur jumped up, recognizing the voice, but tumbled. He grabbed the wall to steady himself as a dizzy spell spun the room. At last, he gained his balance, and his head cleared.

This blasted sickness, he thought, gritting his teeth.

Now more cautiously, he moved outside. There, spinning Elanor in an embrace, was Bedwyr.

Arthur's heart leapt. His friend and brother. The one who he had been raised with until they were separated—sent to kingdoms a great distance apart. As men, it was Bedwyr and Cai who were his right and left hand.

Hobbling out the door, he almost called out to his friend but stopped short. One glimpse of Bedwyr's countenance as he peered at Elanor revealed a story. Arthur stepped back. The exuding emotions and tears in Bedwyr's eyes captured his curiosity. He saw how much Elanor meant to him. A whole history existed here while he had been absent, and Bedwyr's love for Elanor was a part of it.

Arthur glanced at Merlin inquisitively, but the bard seemed unthreatened by the intimate moment shared between Bedwyr and Elanor.

The display reminded Arthur of one of his greatest lost warriors, Llenllaewg. He had a love for Gwynevere that had always been difficult for Arthur to understand. He had come with Gwynevere from Eire—always her loyal guard. Oh, the sting of jealousy Llenllaewg created within Arthur, but in time, he understood that Llenllaewg's loyalty and love for Gwynevere would forever prevent his heart from yearning for her. He chose to become her champion in the entirety of the call, surrendering everything else—including his heart. And so, Llenllaewg gave all his strength to Prydain. He was a trustworthy warrior, living for Arthur and, eventually, dying for them all.

Merlin lifted his chin. "Bedwyr." He motioned with his eyes for Bedwyr to look beyond Elanor.

Bedwyr's gaze flicked away from Elanor and landed on Arthur. His eyes widened as though the impossible stood before him. His knees buckled, taking him to the ground. As he sucked in breath, tears filled his eyes. With one languishing breath, he yelled, "MY BROTHER!"

Arthur's heart wrenched. He stumbled to his friend, meeting him in a solid embrace.

"You live," Bedwyr cried, pounding his fists into Arthur's back. "Merlin told me you had returned, but I still scarcely dared to believe it. How… How can this be? With all my hope I wished… Is it really you?"

Merlin's eyes were tearful as he grinned ear to ear. "Your eyes do not deceive you, my friend. Arthur lives."

Bedwyr smacked Arthur's cheeks. "Ai…" He beamed. "I could never ask for one thing more."

"When I last saw you—standing beside Gwynevere—I was sailing away to my death. I believed I would never see you again. I… I remember dying." Arthur stumbled weakly. "And then when I woke, so many strange things happened." He faced Elanor. "Sh-she the most mysterious of them all. I thought I would eventually discover it all to be a dream." Exhausted, he tumbled to the ground, resting his head in the moist grass. "I still think it may all be a dream."

Elanor rushed to kneel beside him. "You should be inside resting."

Alarmed, Bedwyr asked, "What is wrong with him?"

"Nothing to be worried about, my friend," Merlin encouraged. "The journey through time has made him sick. Much like Elanor was when she found us."

Elanor pressed her hand to Arthur's head. "Yes, and Arthur refuses to properly rest."

"Well," Arthur said, looking at Merlin sideways, "the girl was ruining the meat."

"*The girl?*" Elanor protested, miffed.

Chapter Thirty-one

Bedwyr laughed, wiping his face free of tears. "Apparently," he said to Merlin, "we have missed something."

"No doubt," Merlin replied. "If we are to have you well again, Arthur, we need to get you back in by the fire. This cold will not help you recover faster."

"Ai… We must get you well. Caer Lial cries out for its king." Bedwyr held out his hand and pulled Arthur to his feet. "Whoa—whoa—whoa! Not so fast." He placed his hand on Arthur's chest to steady him as another dizzy spell hit.

"I cannot believe you are here," Arthur said to Bedwyr.

"I cannot wait to see Gwynevere's face when she sees you riding up over that hill. Peredur might even crack a smile."

"Do they know I am returning?"

"Myself and five other riders found Merlin on the road toward Caer Lial. We sent the riders on to the Caer; a few without their horses. They will bring word to the queen. Likely, you will be met with a celebration beyond celebrations—for the king has returned." Bedwyr beamed with jovial praise, patting Arthur's chest.

Arthur muttered, "It's never right when the two of us are separated."

Bedwyr gladly nodded. "No. You need a brother willing to wrestle your arse to the ground now and again. And this time, your feet will stay solidly held in Prydain. No more mystical cups calling you away."

Regret hit Arthur between the eyes. *None of this would have happened if I had never gone across the sea.* More of his men would still be alive to greet him.

"No use leaning on the past," Merlin consoled, as if seeing the heaviness in Arthur's eyes. "You are the once, and *now* future, king. The once has past, and the future has come."

"Heh," Arthur puffed, his head pounding. "There you are—I have missed Merlin the druid. I wondered when I would hear his riddled wisdom once again."

Merlin stepped forward, grunting as he limped.

"Merlin! What has happened to you?" Elanor's eyes panned his frame, noticing his injuries for the first time since his return.

He touched the wound on the corner of his mouth and chuckled—his effort making him twinge. "Bedwyr and his men tried to kill me."

"What?" she asked.

Arthur sputtered through his lips as Bedwyr moved him back to the cottage. "That sounds like Bedwyr."

"It was a misunderstanding," Bedwyr chimed, giving an impish smile. "Besides, seeing a strange man darting across the open lands in those strange clothes causes alarm. Really, what *are* you all wearing?" He gibed as he helped Arthur down onto his bed.

Merlin gingerly sat down onto the hay, hissing and groaning with the aches. "I think I may have damaged my ribs. Nothing too serious though, I hope."

Elanor shook her head. "Well, we are a miserable lot."

Bedwyr nodded. "How are we going to get you all back to the Caer?"

"Well," Merlin replied, "Arthur should be much more improved tomorrow, and

I shall just have to grit my teeth. Unless the healing powers of my love can deliver me."

"Of course." Elanor hastened beside him. "It's worth a try at least. Which side is it?"

Merlin lifted his left arm, painfully exposing his ribs, and Elanor placed her careful hand on his side.

Bedwyr leaned forward in eager anticipation. Then, they all waited and…

She huffed, exasperated, "Nothing. Why can't I find the magic?"

"You're exhausted," Merlin said. "And sometimes, the magic isn't necessary."

Elanor grumbled, "Seems to me it should always be necessary to heal when there is pain."

Merlin smiled, peering at her from underneath his arm, which rested over his head. "That is true."

"Damn," Bedwyr cursed. "I was really looking forward to seeing the miracle… No bother. Sorry, Merlin, guess you will be in for a painful journey."

Arthur's eyes grew heavy from the exertion, and he started to close them.

Bedwyr chuckled. "I will tell you what will be painful. As soon as Arthur falls asleep our ears will be assaulted with his snores."

Arthur shot his eyes open with a smirk. "I do not snore."

"Brother" —Bedwyr pointed at him— "I have known you the whole of my life. If I say you snore, you snore."

Arthur rolled his eyes, choosing to ignore Bedwyr's ribbing.

Bedwyr leaned on his elbow, shooting Arthur a cheeky grin. "Right, then, before you shake the thatch loose—I'll go set us a fire outside."

32

ARTHUR'S RETURN

Merlin waited another day before he felt Arthur had recovered enough for their short journey to Caer Lial—which also gave him more time to recover from his wounds. They loaded the horses in the darkness of the morning before the sun had even risen.

Merlin bemoaned his afflicted side and how it would trouble him on the road home. But with the high anticipation building amongst them, he knew they could no longer delay. The thought of seeing the brightness of Caer Lial and the shining Palisade atop the hill lifted his heart beyond the ache. He savored the thought of the crisp scent of the apples that would fill the air.

He closed his eyes, satisfied to know the ones they loved would be there to greet them. He inhaled sharply, reaching for his saddle, and pushed off from the ground. A stinging twinge of pain shot through him. He grimaced but hoisted himself atop his horse, and then they were off.

Pain stabbed Merlin's side and stole his breath at every trotting step. He tensed his muscles to control the jostle, but the action worsened his aches. His injuries forced them to travel at an unfortunately slow pace, but he bore the pain with determination.

As the morning sun rose, the warming air lessened Merlin's ache. A waft of air brushed through the trees, bringing with it the familiar smells of home. They would see the citadel soon. The edge of the forest neared, and butterflies of hope danced in Merlin's stomach.

Hoofbeats stamped the ground, echoing through the forest, warning them of approaching riders. The horses whinnied and heaved, coming to a halt before them. Twelve Cymbrogi arrived upon their horses, fully armored with their proud colors wrapping their shoulders and shining helms atop their heads.

The riders scanned the four of them, seeing Bedwyr, their commander, first. Their eyes rounded in astonishment as they caught sight of Merlin and Elanor. Their awe intensified when they discovered Arthur—their king—sitting tall upon his horse behind them.

One of them gasped, "It's true."

Another whispered, "He's alive."

The horses clopped in place as hope gripped the warriors' countenances. The Cymbrogi pounded their fists to their chests, dropping their heads with honor. The sigh of tearful moans leaked out underneath their helms.

The leader bowed his head. "My… m-my king."

Silently, they waited. The brevity of the moment captivated them in reverence. Merlin glanced behind to look at Arthur, whose eyes had reddened at the sight of his men. He clutched his reins closer to his heart as he stared wordlessly, like a king that was still a ghost.

Bedwyr broke the moment with an excited command. "Quickly, men. Go! The people must know… They must know their king lives."

Sniffing back his tears, the leader lifted his head. "Yes… yes, my lord. We heard you were coming. We scouted the land so we could herald your arrival. The citadel stands ready to receive you." He quickly sobered, then commanded his riders, "To the Caer!" He kicked his horse's flanks. "Ya'!"

His steed reared and whinnied, and they were off, headed toward Caer Lial.

Arthur tightened his lips, and emotion flooded his face as he watched his Cymbrogi gallop to the citadel. Bedwyr pulled beside him and slapped his back. "Your men are ready to receive you home."

Arthur nodded somberly. He clicked his tongue and jerked his reins to press on.

A tingly anticipation heightened within the four of them. They lifted their chins with a flutter in their hearts. *This*, Merlin thought, *must be what a reception would be like, entering the realms of the ever hoped for celestial promise.*

Elanor cupped her hand behind her ear. "Can you hear it?"

Merlin stopped to listen. The sound resonated through the air. The roar of voices, the booming of drums, and the deep, reverberating horns intensified the closer they came.

Bedwyr laughed exuberantly, glancing over his shoulder at them. He looked like a child on the morning of Beltain as he flipped back around and excitedly dashed ahead.

Coming into sight, the great outer wall appeared, and Arthur stopped.

Merlin rounded to him and saw Arthur's countenance appeared sanguine, yet reluctant.

"What is it?" Merlin asked.

Arthur stoically observed the citadel walls. "I am not sure. I long to be there… with my people… yet…" He dropped his head. "I am not sure I still deserve the right."

"Mmmm." Merlin nodded. "If we are true, we know that not one of us deserves that right. You never did… I never did."

Arthur glanced at him, baffled.

Chapter Thirty-two

"But being deserving is not what is important. We place ourselves under the humility of the call—as servants unto it. That is what remains of greatest importance."

Arthur clenched his reins and lifted his chin toward the Caer. "Am I still called?"

"I did not feel called, nor deserving, when I returned after abandoning them—all of them," Merlin said with regret. "But…" He peered at Elanor. "The Great God forced me home. Over time, I did remember the call." He reflected for a moment. "You are Pendragon. All of Prydain remembers you, has cried out for you, and still has need of you. They are already calling you home. Can you not hear them?"

Arthur strengthened his stare. "Then I will return the call."

Merlin nodded, smiling. "As you should."

Bedwyr came galloping back to them. "Why do you linger? Let us go!" His eager horse, Hwyddan, stomped the ground.

Merlin gripped Arthur's shoulder with a sober glint in his eye.

Arthur did the same, holding Merlin's shoulder with a determined grasp. He nodded. "Let us go."

Merlin knew this familiar feeling. The feeling of hope and desire, mingled with the need to escape and run from the emotions forming in the pit of his stomach. The closer they came, the more tense he and Arthur became.

Elanor and Bedwyr beamed, their eyes glistening from the sunlight reflecting on their faces. As they approached, Cymbrogi could be seen perched high upon the ramparts, while two lines of Cymbrogi riders aligned the front of the open gates.

Merlin remembered returning with despair in his heart not long ago, hoping—wishing—to see Arthur on those very same ramparts, though he believed he never would. And now, by some abundant miracle, he returned with a living, breathing Arthur. His chin trembled, seeing his friend riding at his side. Arthur's chest pumped with swelling emotion.

The Cymbrogi waved their capes of red and gold above their heads, and their shouts reverberated, swallowed up by the booming instruments that pounded the air.

The lines of riders before the gate also unclipped their colors to wave them as Merlin and Arthur approached. Then, removing their helms, the warriors bowed. Their eyes brimmed with glee and unbelievable hope. It was almost too much to look at them; so much turmoil and grief now melted away at the sight of their king.

Merlin beamed up at the men above, hanging over the stone ramparts, as they rode underneath the wall and through the gates. The revelation hit him—that he never thought he would have back what he had lost. The grief of losing Arthur drove him to remain on the Isle of Avalon, longing to never return. What if he had stayed? What if he had chosen to ignore the dreams and wallow in his pain? This moment may never have come.

As if the clouds parted, the sun beamed down, lighting them as they entered into the citadel. The glorious thunder of cheers and the beautiful faces of the towns-people was a radiant display of utter fulfillment.

A shadow overhead caught Merlin's attention as they rode in. He lifted his eyes and saw the black silhouette of a great bird, its large, expansive wings hovering above them. Focusing his eyes, he identified the bird as a brown falcon. Its head stared down at them.

Seeing a bird like this in Caer Lial was not uncommon, but still, its ominous presence unsettled Merlin. As it hovered closer, its eyes keenly searching the four of them, he observed that it seemed unusually large. Then, as though the bird realized Merlin had seen it, it cried a long, mournful song and soared away. Merlin's brows curved in curiosity as it dwindled into the distance.

"What is it?" Elanor asked, no doubt seeing his troubled expression.

Merlin stared off in the direction the falcon had flown. "N-nothing. Nothing." He turned a reassuring smile to her, then, with a suspicious glare, ruminated back over his shoulder as they trotted forward.

33

THE KING & HIS MEN

The celebration roared from the fields, all the way through the town, as the people threw ribbons and waved green branches. Some remained still in amazement, as if their eyes betrayed them. Many embraced in tears, while many others leapt and spun, lifting their children high. For not only had Merlin and their lady of hope returned, but unbelievably, so had the Great Pendragon.

As Arthur went through the second gate and into the warriors' fields, a battalion of Cymbrogi stood, stoic and silent, in lines on both sides of the lane. Over the roar of the town, this hush was deafening.

Arthur halted, riveted by their strength. They faced him with their chests lifted, their long hair blowing gently over their shoulders. Their eyes glinted with courage and steel. Pride swelled within Arthur's chest as he gazed at the spectacle. His mind now brimmed with the memories of leading these worthy ones into battle.

His heart soared even higher as Peredur emerged from the ranks, raising his spear above his head. He turned toward Arthur and took a hard stance, staring with the solidarity of a battle chieftain. He sucked in deeply, then whooped a warrior cry, leading the Cymbrogi to echo a fierce chant; their voices intimidating the very fibers of the air.

With tears wetting Peredur's cheeks, he threw down his spear. Unsheathing his sword, he also cast it to the ground. The warriors took the signal from their chieftain and began throwing their weapons down. The loud, hollow clinking and clashing thundered as they showed fealty to their king.

Peredur unclipped his colors and lifted his cape above his head, roaring a brazen battle cry. The Cymbrogi lit the field with their voices, waving their colors. Passionate tears flowed as they beat their chests, mirroring the cadence of their beating hearts.

At the sight, Arthur felt the unbearable weight of his emotions pressing down upon him. As king, he wanted to respond to those who so ardently honored him. With a loud cry, Arthur ripped his shirt, having no colors of his own to honor them back.

215

"My king!" Peredur shouted, running to meet him. He placed his hands upon Arthur's knee and peered up sorrowfully. His cheeks shone from his tears. "My king." He caught his breath. "M-my friend. You live."

Arthur reached out his hand to grip Peredur's palm. Tears welled in his eyes as Arthur slid down from his horse and threw his arms around Peredur.

"Do not rip your shirt. The grief has ended," Peredur said, lifting his head from Arthur's neck. "Have mine." He took the colored cape locked within his fist and wrapped it around Arthur's shoulders.

Arthur sighed through his tears and grabbed his friend solidly by the shoulder. "It is good to see you, brother."

Peredur nodded as a smile lifted his cheeks. He stepped aside, allowing Arthur to mount his horse. He rose up in his stirrups, then boldly lifted the colors—his fist thrusting the red and gold high above his head. The Cymbrogi thundered in response. Triumphant, Arthur led his procession to the hill, swinging the colors for all to see.

Peredur pulled his horse from the sidelines to ride alongside Bedwyr.

Amid the celebrations, Arthur glanced up the hill, and there, standing upon the edge of the stone steps of the Great Hall, he saw her dress billowing in the wind. The hill—too long of a distance between them. His eyes remained fixed upon her as he climbed. He could see how she peered down at him in disbelief.

The nearer he drew, the more of her he could see. Her raven hair brushing her face, the lines of silver tears upon her cheeks. Her tense fingers clenched and unclenched at her sides. The whole world faded away as he stared up at her. She was Prydain; the completion of all he had longed for.

At last, Arthur crested the top of the hill through the overhanging apple branches on his right.

Gwynevere lifted her hands, covering her mouth, as now she could clearly see his face. She gasped as Arthur dismounted and moved toward her with his hand clutching his heart.

She took one slow step, observing him, then another.

Arthur heard each step as her feet brushed the stone of each stair. Her green eyes were like the sea as they mournfully explored his face.

"Is it truly you? Have you"—she sighed through her tears— "returned to me?"

His heart stuttered, and he could form no words—too choked at the sight of her. He forced himself to stammer, "I… I have… come home."

Gwynevere inhaled. "It is you." Throwing her arms out, she ran for him, and he for her. She leapt into his arms, and they collided like two ocean waves melding together. Arthur squeezed her in, sobbing audibly as he pulled her tighter. He would never let her go.

She lifted her head to look at him, her hands cupping his face. There he finally saw the face of the one he had seen echoed in the expressions and movements of Elanor—strengthening his wish, moment by moment, for his queen.

Quickly, he pressed his lips to hers, leaning in hard. All of the grief and longing throughout the long years that separated them—the forlorn loss in his heart as he sailed away to die—he pressed into the warmth of her lips.

Elanor was instantly caught up in Cilaen and Adhan's arms. The cries of their happiness and love filled her ears like warm oil. It happened so fast. She saw them running toward her. Gwendolen, wrapped in Adhan's arms, wiggled free with excitement at the sight of Elanor.

Elanor's heart burst. She felt she couldn't get her feet to the ground quick enough. She thought she must have blacked out, for she couldn't remember how she had gotten from her horse into their arms. But it didn't matter. Her daughter's soft little arms wrapped her neck, and Adhan and Cilaen's quickly followed. It became a heartfelt tumble of love as Elanor repeatedly kissed Gwendolen's face.

"Mommy… Mommy," Gwendolen's little voice said as she nuzzled into Elanor's neck.

Elanor felt Adhan's kisses on the top of her head and the warmth of Cilaen's cheek against her own.

"I thought you were dead," he whispered through tears. "I-I saw you die." The trauma of grief poured out of his mouth, melded with the happiness of knowing he had been wrong.

"Look." Elanor indicated where the arrow had been, still squeezing her daughter tightly. "No wound remains."

"But how?"

"I don't know." Elanor beamed through happy tears. "The dragon's magic, it—"

"I don't care," Cilaen said, rushing back in. "I don't care. I am so relieved you are alive."

"Me too." Elanor sighed, glancing up into Adhan's twinkling eyes.

Cilaen saw Merlin approaching and shouted, "You did it!" He dove to clutch Merlin in his arms next.

"Whoa, whoa, whoa!" Merlin threw his arms up, halting Cilaen with an unstable grin.

"What's wrong?"

"Gently." Merlin extended his arms and carefully pulled his friend close.

"Ah." Cilaen clicked his tongue, seeing Merlin wince. "You are hurt."

Merlin clenched his jaw and bent forward slightly—exhausted by the persistent pain. "I will be alright. Injured my ribs falling from a horse. And then, there is my shoulder."

"It seems bringing the Pendragon home was no easy task."

"It is a long story. One I will tell while you are patching me up. I am going to need some of your pain-relieving medicines."

"The sooner, the better, it appears."

Adhan tenderly reached for Merlin—kissing his cheek and caressing his face.

"What a triumphant day to see my son return, along with my daughter and the lost son of Prydain."

As Elanor sat on the ground with Gwendolen securely in her arms, she felt the brush of fingers through her hair. She turned her head. Gwynevere's happy, wet cheeks smiled down at her. She set Gwendolen down and hugged her mother. "I missed you so much," she whimpered.

Gwynevere squeezed Elanor a little tighter. "I should have never let you go to that terrible village."

"Don't you see?" Elanor said, glancing up as Arthur neared. "It was meant to be, or else we would have never found him."

Gwynevere turned to Merlin, her chin quivering. "How is it possible you found him? How…?"

Cilaen carefully lifted Merlin's arm to support him, and Merlin grunted painfully.

"Here, lean into me," Cilaen encouraged.

Merlin nodded to Gwynevere. "It was not without difficulty. As you can see. And, there is more." Merlin cringed, sucking in a sharp breath as Cilaen moved him forward.

Gwynevere's eyes widened. "You need medicines." Turning to Elanor, she asked, "Are you hurt as well?"

"I am not hurt—" Elanor halted, sadly remembering her father, David. "Gwynevere, I…"

"Stop that," Gwynevere interrupted, facing her solemnly with her eyes full of tears.

Elanor's brows lifted sorrowfully in a quandary.

"Please… Please…" Gwynevere gently rebuked. "We knew from the start that the prophecy was true, and now there is no doubt. By some miracle, I am your mother, and I will have you call me by that name."

Elanor's eyes welled with tears. "Yes," she murmured, blowing the emotion through her lips, "you are my mother."

34

OSIAN'S CURSE

The falcon flew outside the walls of the citadel and landed in a tall tree on the edge of the forest. It leaned its head forward and stared menacingly toward the Caer. It screeched at the echoing music and cheers that emanated through the air. Disturbed, it ruffled its feathered chest and stretched its wings in and out. Its talons dug into the branch, crunching it until it broke. As the branch fell, the falcon flew high into the sky and opened its wings, catching the air, then—with a snap—vanished.

A form materialized inside a dark chamber. Moisture dripped from the ceiling, the lonely droplets echoing throughout the dankness. The wet stone of the cave shimmered in the dull light of large candles whose flames had magically fluttered to life.

The falcon's ominous shadow stretched across the walls as it grew. The hunched figure snapped his neck to the side as his beak morphed into a nose. The feathers slowly shifted into hair, and a dark cloak appeared around his shoulders.

He glared; his features now fully returned. A young, sharply rigid, and bearded face glowed pale in the dim light. Dark, long hair like the falcon's feathers sat tied behind his neck with a leather strap.

Now in human form, he clenched his hands, then threw his head back, shouting with rage. At his scream, the lights of the candles flickered. He shot his black eyes across the room and lurched over to a long, thin table set against the stone. He grabbed various elements, tossing them into a bowl.

"Ash of acorn and rowan," he growled, dropping the cindered black elements into the concave stone. Hastily, he ground them into a powder and snatched a dagger from his belt. He sliced the knife through his palm and sucked through his teeth as blood dripped down his wrist. Hovering his hand above the bowl, he squeezed his blood into the mixture. His eyes rolled back into his head as he chanted, "Agor fy llygad." Louder, he repeated, "Agor fy llygad!"

The blood and ash swirled as he spoke, then lit with violet flame. He lifted the bowl to his lips and sucked down the contents. Blood rolled down the corner of his mouth and neck. He dropped the bowl, and it shattered with a loud crack. His head dizzied, so he leaned his hands upon the table and sighed, waiting silently.

He whispered, "I must hear your voice. I need to hear you speak to me."

Doubling forward onto his knees, he retched, groaning as the insidious potion surged in his stomach. "Please… my lady…" He cringed with pain. "Come and speak… to me." As sweat formed on his brow, he groaned through clenched teeth, grinding the remaining ash. His consciousness left him, and he fell all the way to the floor.

The world swirled with gray until finally, he became conscious of a new realm. The dark awen had taken hold. He stared into the blackness, daring the veil of the otherworld to open. He saw a faint, gentle pulse of light. He threw up his hands and yelled, "Dangoswch eich hun!" His voice rang out into the gray, echoing as it disappeared. He waited for a reply. Hearing nothing, he shouted, "Show yourself!"

At his command, wisps of violet smoke steadily grew.

"I need to see you… please," he pressed "Show me your face."

The smoke illuminated brighter and moved in fierce billows. Its swirls sparked, growing taller until it infiltrated the blackness and hovered above him.

Out of the purple haze, a face formed within the raging smoke. The beautiful face of a woman whose eyes begged to entice. Her face appeared, then disappeared—continually reforming all around him.

Her beguiling voice called to him, ringing like vibrating metal. "Why are you here, Osian? What has you calling to me in the otherworld?"

"Y-You have helped me to awaken the deep, slumbering magic of old, and I have faithfully strived to decimate all who have risen against the old religion. But…"

"Yes?" she said.

Tendrils of smoke curled around Osian's pointed chin. Her beautiful voice distracted him as she pulled him closer. He hungered for her. He gaped at the lines of smoke shaping her form. Everything she stood for, he wanted; attracted to her power and sensuality.

She lilted seductively, "What is it you need, my sorcerer?"

Osian lifted his shoulders, squinted his eyes, then said bitterly, "Haven't you seen? Has the otherworld not already told you the tale?"

"Mmmm," she replied with cackles that reverberated around him. "Why do you fear?"

"Fear?" he fumed. "That… th-th-that damned witch. We killed her. I did as you said. We set a twofold trap, and we won. An arrow ran straight through her chest. All of Prydain mourned her. But… some kind of impossible magic"—he spit hatefully as his rage amped— "has given her life. And…"

"And what, my druid?" she soothed.

Osian pursed his lips. "Arthur has awakened… He's awake!" he spat angrily. "All that we have done to prevent this—we cannot seem to crush them."

"We knew that the prophecy would come…"

Chapter Thirty-four

"No… no…" Osian protested. "We took hold of the prophecy to stop it from happening."

"NO!" her voice boomed. Streaks of lightning sparked through her smoke. "You misunderstand." Her voice grew deep and intimidating. "Hear me, Osian. The prophecy was to help us know how to weaken them." The vapor curled into a fist of flashing lighting and hit the ground with thunder.

Osian stepped back, lifting his hands to cover his face. As it dissipated, he persisted, "H-How have we weakened them? They seem to be gaining."

"Ssshh!" The swirling smoke diminished back into an alluring form that brushed his lips.

"We must take the citadel. We have waited too long to attack."

"No, Osian. Do not allow your haste to make you foolish. You know we do not have the numbers to attack them. Your best move is to remain hidden, but"—the face of the apparition hovered nearer— "they will not long remain unconquered."

Again, the smoke jolted back and illuminated, and the billows built as if angry. "They freed the cyhyraeth. Breaking him free from our control. How *dare* they!" The smoke pulsed. "Though, we have not lost *all* ground. Blood will still be spilt. You know the plan." Her voice now echoed all around him. "We move in quietly. Like a plague, we spread. We take hold of the weak-minded and twist them. We shed blood to make them fear. And before long, the *Chalice of Life* will be poured upon the living, creating the *undead*. And then… then, there will be nothing they can do to stop us. We will not need to take the citadel."

A scream rose, reverberating from far away, drawing closer until the voice boomed, "Arthur will *never* have his kingdom, and Merlin"—a crawling, cringing growl pitted from her throat— "will *never* bring the Kingdom of the Sun." The smoke turned red, and blood rained down, covering Osian in crimson. "You will rule as my king of the old religion. WE WILL NEVER RELINQUISH CONTROL. NEVER WILL THE BLOOD CEASE. NEVER. NEVER. I can taste the blood." She groaned, sending a creeping fear up Osian's spine. He yearned to escape the vision.

The blood rain ceased. The red that covered Osian drained from him—running down his face and dripping off his fingers—pouring onto the floor. Suddenly, she stood beside him, not a vapor, but alive. The breath in her chest moved Osian's eyes over her breasts and down the curves of her figure. He gulped as he glanced up to see her full lips and shining eyes moving closer. Sweat formed on his brow as she ran her palms over his chest and around his neck. Her lips drew toward his.

"Do you want this? Don't you desire for us to be together?"

Fear mingled with desire in Osian's stomach. He couldn't move, or even reply. He had never seen her so real and vivid. Stunned, he managed to say, "Y-Y-Y-Yes!"

"Good." She smiled darkly, then snapped hold of his wounded hand. She pressed hard, sinking her nails into his cut. Unbelievable pain shot through his hand. It burned as though he had stuck his hand into a bed of fiery coals. She turned back into a violet smoke, and the vapor poured into his wound.

Osian screamed, taking hold of his arm—his fingers splayed in agony. The blood that pooled on the ground sprang up and rushed into his palm. The entire dark eminence of the otherworld sprang into him, and the pain invaded his entire body.

All at once, he returned to consciousness, heaving and cringing from the awen. He snapped up his hand and held it before his face. His eyes widened as he flipped his hand back and forth. His palm was completely healed. No remnants of the wound could be seen—not even a scar.

Perspiration fell from his forehead as he perceived something. He felt strengthened from within—empowered. He stood, lifting his hand above his head and clenched it into a fist. Inside his mind, he heard whispers. Her voice now dwelt inside him. He lifted his strong chest and sucked in a powerful breath. His wicked eyes darkened, and he laughed. The power was now in his hands.

"They will have no power to stop me," Osian said, a venomous grin dancing on his lips. "They will be like ants before me."

The white stone talisman set within the bronze moon started to glow at his chest. Osian gripped it, and his eyes flared with evil purpose. "Merlin will be no match for me now."

35

THE TWELVE HEADS OF WAR

Three days passed, and the cool morning breeze blew in from the window. The sun's rays touched Arthur's eyes, waking him. He breathed a fulfilling sigh. This was the day when he would address his people for the first time since returning from the dead. He rolled from the loving embrace of his wife. Her lips remained sweet in his mind. He still could not believe he had her back within his arms.

He stretched, flung his legs over the side of his bed, and stared across the room at the long-forgotten trunk that held his things. He stood, approaching it with an air of diffidence, and knelt to open it. A stale smell filled his nose as his eyes scanned the belongings that represented his sovereignty.

His golden torc remained wrapped around his neck, but now he pulled the brightly colored red and gold cape out from amongst the folded clothes and effects. He glanced at it, remembering the last time he had worn it. The last time was an age ago, before he journeyed to the east in search of the cup.

He tucked his tunic into his brown breeches, then wrapped his boots tightly at the knee. He unshackled a freshly oiled leather breastplate, the other left behind in the future world. The leather had been pressed with whorls and entangling knots that detailed a red dragon, painted by hand. Newly polished gold Cymry dots gleamed where they lined the edges. Without stopping to linger on the emotions rising in his throat, he silently buckled the breastplate over his shoulders and sides—the bronze chinking as he fastened it.

"It will do the people well to see you in the regnant garments of our people," Gwynevere said, lifting herself up onto her elbow.

He glanced over his shoulder at her while lifting his golden brooch from the table. The ruby gem gleamed as he rotated it in his fingertips.

"What is it?" his wife asked, as if sensing his hesitancy.

"I feel like I did as a child, when I pulled that sword out of the rock. I was awestruck that the sword had moved at my hand, and immediately, I felt weighed down and unworthy." He pulled the colors across his hands, feeling the fibers, and whispered, *"Oh, Kingdom of the Sun, renew our land with grace. Oh, Kingdom of the Sun, the warmth of its bounty upon our face."*

"You have always wielded your authority with grace. Your people will not struggle handing you back their fealty." She slid from the bed and approached him, taking his cape of colors from his hands. She wrapped it around his shoulders, cuffing it lovingly around his neck. Gwynevere held out her hand.

Arthur lifted the brooch and set it into her expectant palm. "Perhaps the people prefer the High Queen who cared for them over a king who abandoned them… then died," he said with an insecure lilt.

Gwynevere dismissed him with a wave of her hand, not even willing to engage with his statement. "There." She clasped it all together. She rested her hands on his chest and gazed at him. Her eyes sparkled with a hopeful joy. "I am seeing you return to me more and more. Selfishly," she said, staring affectionately at him, "I am not ready to let them have you."

Her stare captured the longing in his heart, and he basked in her emerald eyes. But conceding, his thoughts drew back to his people. "Where is my sword?"

"Of course." She turned and pulled a long wooden box from underneath the bed. "I kept all your things, in hopes that at least another man of honor would rise to wield them. Your shield Bedwyr has saved." She sighed, unlocking the lid and lifting it up. The light glimmered off the blade as she opened it.

Arthur whispered, "Caledfwlch."

Gwynevere smiled as she first withdrew the belt and sheath, then steadily lifted the sword aloft. It rang as if in response to the timbre in his heart. Gwynevere grandly laid the sword in Arthur's palms. His chest rose. She then tightened the belt and sheath around his waist.

Arthur stared at the sword. It had always been more than a sword. It vibrated with life. It had power that arose from the ancient song, and he had always been sobered by the fact that the sword had chosen him—not he the sword. In the midst of battle, there were times when he felt his strength diminishing, and the sword empowered him.

His emotions swelled, peering into Gwynevere's proud eyes. "I am home."

"And just in time. The kings will unite under the Great Pendragon, and I fear we need them now more than ever."

"The devastation Merlin reported of that village…" Arthur growled, baring his teeth.

"Osian has kept himself well hidden. His evil plots continue to evade us. Always we find the damage long after it has already been done. His schemes are sporadic and unpredictable. Thul alone has caught the enemy in the midst of an onslaught."

"No longer," Arthur said with assurance, lifting his chin. He moved to the window and noticed the fields that already bustled with his people.

"What will you say to them?"

Arthur pointed the tip of his sword to the ceiling, pausing before sheathing it at his side. "I will remind them of the song."

The procession sat ready outside the Great Hall. Arthur beamed with pride as he passed through the doors and gazed down at the expectant people upon the field. Merlin and Elanor already stood by their horses, waiting to follow behind him. He smiled at them to approach, but halted. He observed a furrowed and distressed expression on Elanor's face. She leaned against her speckled horse, and Merlin worriedly scanned the sky, his druidic rowan staff gripped within his fist.

Arthur quickened his pace to Merlin, and Bedwyr and Peredur came alongside.

Bedwyr shouted, "I see the druid has his staff."

Merlin lifted his staff. "The true king has returned, and the druid," he said, opening his arms and presenting himself, "must be prepared to do his duty."

"Ai... it is like old times."

Arthur noticed tension persisting on Merlin's face and asked, "What is it? What has you gazing up at the sky so disturbed?"

Merlin pressed his lips, and his eyes turned tense. "Nothing to raise alarm, but... I think it would be wise to be attentive today. Something is amiss."

Bedwyr glanced knowingly at Elanor, then back at the men. "What is making you leery?"

"Last night, Elanor had a distressing dream. There was a falcon with the face of a man and the voice of a woman. She said that the falcon's wing grew large and long—its shadow covering all of Prydain. Small men tried to kill it, but it would not die." A dark consideration passed over his face. "Elanor's dreams always speak true, and... there is more... When we arrived back at Caer Lial, I, too, saw a falcon as we marched. It soared with foreboding above my head."

Bedwyr chimed, "It is not unusual to see falcons in the sky."

"I sensed it was not as it appeared. It flew away when its eyes noticed my stare."

Peredur glared. "This is all important but what does it mean?"

Merlin leaned in with a grim stare. "It means that Osian is aware that the king has returned, and we should not be ignorant of our enemy."

"Bah!" Peredur spat. "This... this enemy..." He clenched his gloved hand into a fist. The leather crunched as he squeezed. "I already have men stationed at their posts both inside and outside the citadel. Should I send more riders?"

"We cannot be too careful. Though these omens may not afflict us this day." Arthur lifted his eyes to the sky. "Our awareness will be everything."

"Fear," Merlin said suddenly.

Arthur turned, puzzled. "What?"

"Fear," he warned a second time. "It is the weapon of the fallen ones. The way of the old religion to control and manipulate." Merlin eyed the three of them intensely. "We cannot allow these omens to inflict us with fear. Elanor's dreams have always brimmed with warning, but rarely have they played out exactly as we surmised. In many ways, her dreams give us the upper hand. We now know the faces of our enemy and his plot to destroy. We must be emboldened, as Osian may raise his hideous head, intimidated by the king's return and his foiled plot."

Arthur gripped the hilt of Caledfwlch, ruminating. "On this day, we will lift the hearts of the Cymry. We must remind them, and ourselves, that we are a mighty force that Osian is daring to reckon with. If he is amongst us on this day, then he shall hear it. Now…" He lifted his eyes to the fifty Cymbrogi who were saddled and prepared to follow the procession. Their eyes brimmed with hope. "Let us lead them down to the people and show them their courageous hearts have a purpose."

They all nodded in solidarity and climbed upon their horses, ready to descend where the people cheered in expectation. All the way down the hill, Arthur remained markedly determined. Cymbrogi marched alongside as they crossed the field.

These are no mere men. No. These are formidable warriors.

At the hill, he dismounted, and the party followed him as he ascended the hill with Gwynevere at his side. The crowd silenced, and he took his place above them.

He stared at the shining faces below. He felt choked but pressed himself to speak.

"I know it seems… a miracle that I stand before you now. The miracle is the second chance I am being given. I begin by…" Arthur stopped, his lips quivering. "I must begin by asking your forgiveness, for leaving you for so long. I regret that I am responsible for the grief you have endured."

Tears glistened on the faces of the people below; their grief released at his words.

"Although I have been away, the Great God gave you strength through the High Queen Gwynevere and my men. Merlin returned to you first, and then the gift of the lady Elanor was sent to you. I assure you: the Great God has never forsaken you and has held these lands more solidly than a king *ever* could."

He turned and bowed his head toward his loyal friends. The crowd erupted with praise at Arthur's honor. He lifted his hands as he spoke. "While I have been gone, there has been a great necromancer who, like a coward, hides himself as he kills and destroys. We know his name, and we know his face. I ask that you would not fear him but recognize that his acts of devilry and murder are because *we* are a threat. *We* frighten him. *We* remain the greatest strength in these lands.

"I have been reminded recently… of a promise. It was the very promise that took seed in my heart when I became your king. And it is the promise that you must remember as these days threaten what we have built. And it is this…"

Arthur nodded to Merlin. "You must sing the song." He unsheathed his sword and knelt, raising it flat across his palms.

Merlin stepped forward, lifting his rowan staff. His eyes blazed yellow as he sang:

Sweet… Are the healing days, when pain will find no way.
The earth will sing, for the Sun has made it day.

Sweet… As it will be proclaimed the new days of the Sun.
Its rays will rise high, setting thrones upon kings' holds,
The New Way coming, and the land set in gold.
Oh, Kingdom of the Sun, renew our land with grace.
Oh, Kingdom of the Sun, the warmth of its bounty upon our face.
Blood will stop dripping, as the oil of gladness is tipping.
The sword no longer killing, but its emblems triumphing.
A new day rising, with the old moons setting.
Sweet… days of the Sun are coming.

Silence fell over them all as the druid finished his song. It was as though they all heard the Great God Himself speak the promise directly to them. One at a time, voices rose in response, singing. Ever louder, the song amplified in an ever rising crescendo. It resounded throughout the citadel, catching the hearts of even those that waited far down the lanes and into the town, like dry trees caught by fire on a windy day.

Every person was enraptured as the sword in Arthur's hand shimmered at their sound. The promise was more than just words. It had power, and the more the people sang, the more it became truth. The song rededicated a land lost to grief with hope. It restored the hearts that had stumbled through the years of loss. It shook off the dross that kept them from knowing who they were. The sun beamed down upon them, seeming brighter and warmer as they lifted their voices.

And then… breaking through the praise, five horsemen from the gate came riding through the crowds, disrupting the awe. The crowd gasped as they boldly pressed through to the mound.

The Cymbrogi quickly dismounted and waited, pale faced, at the bottom of the hill. Peredur hastened to them. They bowed before him, and Peredur nodded for them to speak. In hushed voices, they reported the news that couldn't wait. Peredur's face dropped. He turned, looking up at Arthur on the mound.

The crowd gaped as Peredur rushed back up the hill, gathering Bedwyr and Merlin to Arthur's side. The people waited with bated breath.

"Tell me," Arthur demanded.

Peredur hesitated, catching his breath, forcing his hand to his chest. "There is something you must see outside the main gate. There has been an attack."

Arthur snapped, "What kind of attack?"

Merlin turned, staring ominously at the great wall that surrounded them.

Peredur sucked in tightly. "Twelve Cymbrogi… killed."

Arthur narrowed his eyes, setting his jaw. The time had already come. There would be no safety as he settled back into his kingdom. He held up his hands, still deciding what he would tell the people he had just empowered to hope.

"Do not forget the words of the song, though forces come to push the truth from your heart. We have all become accustomed to crises, but… we will be the ones to define our strength, not the evil that would make you feel weak." He paused, then reluctantly said, "Be at peace, and return to your homes."

Confused, the crowd slowly dispersed.

Arthur, and those with him, saddled their horses and rode to the gate. As they neared, they saw the low hanging heads of the Cymbrogi guarding the door of the gate. They hardly lifted their eyes to their approaching king.

Arthur leapt down from his horse. "Show me," he commanded.

The guards hesitantly shifted as they banded together, pulling on the large metal handle to open the wooden door. The gate yawned open, growling at its hinges. The green grass before them, their eyes drew across the landscape before settling on the horrific scene.

Arthur stepped, then doubled forward as though he had been punched in the gut. Twelve severed heads rested atop pikes. The mouths of the murdered Cymbrogi hung open like ghosts heralding their own deaths.

Arthur couldn't speak. He slowly stumbled to the pikes. The buzzing of flies grew louder the closer he came.

Merlin stepped in close. "These are the riders that were sent to scout the forests?"

Peredur's eyes flared as he nodded.

Arthur turned to one of the guards. "Were these men just discovered? Did no one hear the enemy set the pikes outside the gate?"

The guard's finger trembled as he pointed at the ramparts. Timorously, he reported, "I saw them from there. The hooded men appeared so quickly. Out of the air they appeared with the heads and pikes already in their hands. Th-The men's blood was spattered upon their yellow cloaks. I was about to raise alarm as they stabbed the pikes into the ground, but… they disappeared. G-gone."

Arthur's face trembled with rage. "This…" he spat, "an enemy that is not even honorable enough to engage us face-to-face." He turned to Merlin and, through gritted teeth, said, "They hide."

Merlin spewed bitterly, "They will not come out into the light, for they know I would crush them."

Arthur stared at the ground in stunned silence. The eager Cymbrogi waited on his command. "Take these men down," he spewed like spitting poison from his mouth. "Have men sent out to recover their bodies, if they can be found. They will be buried and honored."

Fire blazed in his eyes as he called to Bedwyr. "Have your riders summon the five kings of Prydain." Arthur clenched his jaw, firm like iron, then said, "The Britons are at war."

TEASER FROM BOOK 3

Arthur quickly discovers that the threats to the lands of Prydain are more than he could have dared to imagine. Through Elanor's seeing power, she discovers someone even more insidious behind the rising darkness than just Osian. Minds of the youth are stolen by Osian's nefarious talisman, weakening Merlin and Elanor's magic. All the while, old demons from Arthur's past rear their heads, forcing Prydain's armies to leave Caer Lial to reclaim the southlands. When the *Chalice of Life* is uncovered, giving the enemy power to raise an army of the undead, only the mysterious *Man in Blue* and his *golden dragon* may have the answers if they hope to save Prydain and their own lives. The battle begins, as Arthur's past and future collide in this final, enthralling conclusion of THE ONCE & FUTURE CHRONICLES.

ARTHUR
& THE
GOLDEN DRAGON

THE ONCE & FUTURE CHRONICLES, BOOK 3 COMING SOON!

ABOUT THE AUTHOR

ANGELA R. HUGHES

is a historical fantasy author based in Waco, Texas. Her ambition is to write stories that grip and inspire readers, alluring them into her fascinating world of myth and legend.

Angela believes in the power of dynamic, inspired storytelling. She has always been intrigued by folklore and legend, and desired to create her own. Particularly drawn to Arthurian legend and its ancient roots in the history of the Cymraeg (Welsh) people, she has extensively studied Arthurian legend and Celtic mythology.

Much of her fascination with the Celtic world began during her time living in Ireland, where she fell in love with the history and landscapes of Ireland, Wales, Scotland, and England.

In addition to writing, Angela spends her time researching ancient histories and languages—which led her to learn to speak the Welsh language. She also enjoys painting, inspiring others, being with her family, chatting with fellow fantasy nerds over coffee, baking, visiting wineries, and traveling.

The Once and Future Chronicles, Book One: Elanor and the Song of the Bard is her first published novel. She is currently working on sequels including *Book Two: Merlin and the Magic of Time,* and *Book Three: Arthur and the Golden Dragon.*

Learn more about *Elanor and the Song of the Bard* by visiting www.angelarhughes.com. You are also invited to follow Angela's author journey on Facebook, Instagram, and Amazon.

LET'S BE LEGENDARY!

Instagram/TikTok: @angela.r.hughes
Facebook: Angela R. Hughes @onceandfuturechronicles
Twitter: @ARHughesAuthor

PRAISE FOR THE SHADOW GUARDIANS BOOK 1

FOUR-TIME AWARD-WINNING AUTHOR

"CB Samet is a master at weaving a story full of suspense, supernatural, and characters that make you swoon! [*Raine Down*] will knock your socks off!"

— AUTHOR H.M. GOODEN

"Omg wow *Raine Down* the first book of the The Shadow Guardians Series was such a great read. Be prepared to finish it all at once. It's the right mix between supernatural, mythology and don't forget romance."

— BOOKBUB REVIEWER (FIVE STARS)

"Sleep is over rated right?? At least that's what I am telling myself after basically staying up pretty much all night, well until 4.30am, reading this incredible book because I just couldn't put it down."

— BOOKBUB REVIEWER (FIVE STARS)

"[*Raine Down*] was a fabulous beginning to a fast paced, action packed, paranormal/supernatural series.."

— GOODREADS REVIEWER (FIVE STARS)